BODYGUARD
AMBUSH

CHRIS
BRADFORD

PUFFIN

Warning: Do not attempt any of the techniques described within the book without the supervision of a qualified martial arts instructor. These can be highly dangerous moves and result in fatal injuries. The author and publisher take no responsibility for any injuries resulting from attempting these techniques.

PUFFIN BOOKS

UK | USA | Canada | Ireland | Australia
India | New Zealand | South Africa

Puffin Books is part of the Penguin Random House group of companies whose addresses can be found at global.penguinrandomhouse.com.

puffinbooks.com

Penguin
Random House
UK

First published 2015
006

Text copyright © Chris Bradford, 2015

The moral right of the author has been asserted

Set in Sabon by Palimpsest Book Production Limited, Falkirk, Stirlingshire
Printed in Great Britain by Clays Ltd, St Ives plc

A CIP catalogue record for this book is available from the British Library

ISBN: 978-0-141-34007-4

www.greenpenguin.co.uk

In honour of the HGC –
you know who you are!

'The best bodyguard is the one nobody notices.'

With the rise of teen stars, the intense media focus on celebrity families and a new wave of millionaires and billionaires, adults are no longer the only target for hostage-taking, blackmail and assassination – kids are too.

That's why they need specialized protection . . .

BUDDYGUARD

BUDDYGUARD is a secret close-protection organization that differs from all other security outfits by training and supplying only young bodyguards.

Known as 'buddyguards', these highly skilled teenagers are more effective than the typical adult bodyguard, who can easily draw unwanted attention. Operating invisibly as a child's constant companion, a buddyguard provides the greatest possible protection for any high-profile or vulnerable young person.

In a life-threatening situation, a buddyguard is the **final** ring of defence.

No Mercy shifted the AK47 assault rifle in his grip. His hands were slick with sweat, the weapon heavy and cumbersome. The jungle around him pulsed with danger, each and every murky shadow hiding a potential enemy. The sun beat down from the African sky above, but its scorching rays struggled to penetrate the dense canopy running wild along Burundi's northern border. Instead the day's heat was slowly yet steadily absorbed, like a pressure cooker, turning the jungle into a living hell.

Clouds of mosquitoes buzzed in the humid air and monkeys chattered fearfully in the treetops as No Mercy advanced through the bush alongside his brothers-in-arms. No Mercy was dying for a drink. But he wouldn't stop – *couldn't* stop – not until the general gave the order. So he was forced to lick the sweat from his upper lip in a vain attempt to ease his thirst.

As he trekked towards the rendezvous point, ever watchful for booby traps and old civil-war mines, No Mercy became aware that the monkeys in the trees had gone quiet.

In fact the whole jungle had fallen silent. Only the faint inescapable drone of insects remained.

The general held up a closed fist and the troop halted. Scanning the dense vegetation for the threat, No Mercy saw nothing besides towering tree trunks, green vines and thick palm fronds. Then out from behind a tree stepped a white man.

No Mercy thrust his AK47 at him, his finger primed on the trigger.

The white man, his skin more ivory grey than flesh white, didn't move a muscle. With unblinking eyes, he surveyed the band of rebel soldiers in mismatching uniforms and aid-distributed T-shirts, along with their ageing and rusted weapons. Finally his unflinching glare fell upon No Mercy pointing the AK47 at his chest.

To No Mercy, the white man was something almost alien, totally out of place in the heart of the jungle. Dressed in a spotless olive-green shirt, cargo trousers and black combat boots, he didn't seem affected by the stifling heat at all. He wasn't out of breath, let alone sweating. Even the mosquitoes appeared to be giving him a wide berth. The stranger was like a lizard, cold-blooded and inhuman.

No Mercy kept the barrel of his assault rifle targeted on the man's chest. His finger itched to pull the trigger. Just one word, even the slightest nod, from the general and he would blast the man away in a hailstorm of bullets. That's how he'd earned his warrior name, 'No Mercy', for killing without remorse or pity.

General Pascal stepped forward from among his band of

soldiers. As intimidating and large as a silverback gorilla, the Burundian general was a head taller than the white man. He wore army fatigues and a beret as red as fresh blood. His dark pockmarked face sent shudders of fear through the local villagers who knew him, and his fists bore the calloused scars of countless beatings that he'd personally inflicted upon those same villagers.

'Dr Livingstone, I presume?' said the general, his pencil-thin moustache curling up into an unexpected and disarming smile.

'You have a sense of humour, General,' the white man replied without any trace of having one himself. 'Now tell your boy soldier to lower his gun before he gets himself killed.'

No Mercy bristled at the insult. He may have been fifteen, but age meant nothing when you had the authority of a firearm.

The general waved at him to stand down. Reluctantly No Mercy did as he was ordered, pouting his lower lip in a sulk. The AK47 hung limp from its strap, looking like an oversized yet deadly toy against the young boy's side.

'Do you have the stone?' the stranger asked.

General Pascal snorted. 'You white men! Always straight down to business.' He looked the man up and down. 'On that point, where are my guns?'

'Stone first.'

'Don't you trust me, Mr Grey?'

The white man didn't respond. This unsettled No Mercy even more. The fact that the stranger showed no fear in the presence of the general made him either unbelievably brave or unbelievably stupid. General Pascal had hacked the hands off people for lesser crimes than failing to answer a direct question. Then No Mercy was struck by a terrible and chilling thought. This Mr Grey was somehow *more* dangerous than the general himself.

General Pascal nodded to No Mercy. 'Show him the stone.'

No Mercy pulled out a grimy cloth bag from the pocket of his oversized camo-jacket. He passed it to Mr Grey, careful not to touch the man's ashen skin. Mr Grey emptied the contents of the bag into his hand. A large rock with a pale pink hue fell into his open palm. Taking out an eyeglass, he inspected the rather unassuming stone. After some consideration, he declared, 'This is of poor quality.'

The general let out a booming laugh that shattered the silence of the jungle. 'Don't take me for a fool, Mr Grey. You and I both know this is a very valuable *pink* diamond.'

Mr Grey made the pretence of re-evaluating the stone, the power play between the two men all part of the negotiation process. He sighed with some reluctance. 'It'll cover your first shipment of weapons,' he agreed, then casually added, 'Are there more where this came from?'

The general graced him with another of his disarming smiles. 'More than you could dream of.'

'Have you secured the area the diamonds are in?'

'Not as yet,' admitted the general. 'But with your guns we will.'

Mr Grey pocketed the stone. 'Equilibrium will supply

the weapons you need on condition that once you've seized power they're granted sole mining rights. Agreed?'

'Agreed,' said General Pascal, offering his meaty slab of a hand.

Seemingly loath to take it, Mr Grey nonetheless extended his own hand.

No Mercy watched the two men shake on the deal. Then his heart leapt in surprise as the jungle erupted with the roar of engines. Two immense military trucks bulldozed their way along an overgrown dirt track. Their rear trailers contained an armoury of brand-new AK47s, Browning heavy machine guns, rocket-propelled grenades, mortars and box upon box of ammunition.

'Double-cross us,' warned Mr Grey over the thunder of engine noise, 'and your civil war will be nothing compared to what we'll do to you and your men.'

Still smiling, the general replied, 'Same goes for you, my friend, same for you and yours.'

'Then we are in business,' replied Mr Grey, melting back into the jungle.

Connor was violently woken by a bag being thrust over his head. As he gasped for breath, the thick black fabric smothering all light, strong hands pinned his arms and legs behind his back. He fought to free himself. But plastic zipties were quickly fastened round his wrists and ankles, binding him tight.

'Let me go!' he cried, thrashing wildly in a desperate bid to escape. Wrenched from a deep sleep, his mind was a whirl of confusion and blind panic. Lashing out, his heel struck one of his captors and he heard a grunt of pain.

More hands seized Connor, yanking him upright. As he was hauled from the room, his trainers dragging across the carpet, he screamed, 'HELP! SOMEONE HELP ME!'

But no one answered his call, his cries muffled by the bag.

All of a sudden Connor was hit by a blast of ice-cold air as his captors bundled him outside. Heart pounding and body trembling from the shock of the attack, Connor knew that if he was to survive this ordeal he had to get a grip on himself. During his bodyguard training in hostage survival, he'd learnt that the first thirty minutes of any abduction were the most dangerous. The kidnappers were on edge and highly volatile.

Although it goes against every human instinct, his instructor Jody had explained, *this is the time to stay calm and stay sharp. Be aware of anything that could provide a clue to your whereabouts or your kidnappers' identity.*

Feet crunched on gravel. *Three sets,* Connor noted, trying in some small way to take control of the situation. He heard the boot of a car being opened. A moment later he was dumped in the back and it was slammed shut with an ominous *thunk.*

No, it isn't a car, Connor corrected himself. He'd been *lifted* not dropped into the luggage compartment. The deep throaty rumble of a powerful diesel engine confirmed his suspicions. *It's a 4x4.*

Wheels spun on gravel as the vehicle roared away. His body flung around, Connor's head struck the rear panel with a crunch. Stars burst before his eyes and pain flared in his skull. Any last vestiges of grogginess were wiped out in an instant.

Someone must have seen me being taken, thought Connor, his mind now sharp. *Someone will raise the alert.*

The wheels hit tarmac. The vehicle banked left, before accelerating away fast. With the bag still over his head, Connor attempted to visualize the route his abductors were taking. He carefully counted off the seconds before the next turn.

Sixty-seven . . . sixty-eight . . . sixty-nine . . . The 4x4 took a hard right. Connor began counting again, building up a crude map in his head. He felt the vehicle rise and fall as they passed over a small bridge. He continued his count . . . *twenty-four* . . . *twenty-five* . . . *twenty-six* . . .

Connor was totally baffled by his abduction. Usually it was the Principal, the person he was assigned to protect, who was the target for a kidnapping. Surely his captors had made a mistake? Got the wrong person? Besides, he wasn't even on an official mission. Then an uncomfortable truth struck Connor: perhaps his kidnappers had indeed snatched the *right* person.

Crumpled in a heap against the rear panel, Connor shifted position to create a space for his hands. The ties round his wrists and ankles were digging painfully into his flesh, cutting off the circulation. He tried to pull a hand free, but the zip-ties were heavy-duty and the plastic just cut deeper into his skin. However hard he strained, they simply wouldn't break.

At a count of forty-seven, the vehicle swung right. Then barely ten seconds later bore left. And soon after that left again. By the sixth turn, Connor's mental map had become a confused mess. It seemed like the 4x4 was going in circles, as if his captors were purposefully trying to disorientate him. Connor now tried to listen above the noise of the road for any conversation in the vehicle. He hoped to gain some insight into his abductors' identity: *accent, language, gender, even a name.* But they all stayed disturbingly silent. From this Connor deduced they were professionals. They had to be in order to break into Buddyguard HQ undetected.

Maybe my kidnapping's connected with a previous mission?

The best he could hope for was that his captors intended to ransom him. That way he'd be worth more to them alive than dead. But if they wanted to interrogate him, or use him as a pawn in some political or religious protest, then he'd likely be killed. In that case he would risk an escape attempt.

Whatever his abductors' intentions, he needed to find out as soon as possible – his life could depend upon it.

The 4x4 ground to a halt and the engine was switched off. The back door opened and he was manhandled out. A gusting wind sent a chill through his body, his T-shirt offering little protection against the winter freeze. Gripped tightly on either side by his captors, Connor detected the faintest trace of perfume through the bag. Was one of the abductors a woman?

'Where are you taking me?' asked Connor, his voice now steady and calm, hoping that the woman would respond.

But his kidnappers remained tight-lipped as they escorted him away from the 4x4. They moved briskly, not allowing Connor to find his feet. He heard the soft swish of a door sliding open, a welcoming warmth embraced him, and the ground changed from tarmac to cushioned carpet. As he was borne deeper into the building, Connor caught the aroma of frying onions and the distant clatter of pots and pans. Heading away from what he presumed was a kitchen, he was dragged several more paces before being shoved into a chair. Its hard wooden slats dug painfully against his bound hands, but at least he could plant his feet on the floor. Connor tried to sit up straight to maintain some dignity before his anonymous enemies, at the same time readying himself to spring into action at the first opportunity.

The place he'd been brought to was oddly quiet, indicating that other people were there with him.

When nobody spoke, Connor demanded, 'Who are you? What do you want with me?'

'It's not about what we want,' a man's voice replied. 'It's about what *you* want.'

CHAPTER 2

The bag was whipped off Connor's head. Squinting from the glare of an overhead spotlight, Connor discovered that he was sitting at a long glass table laid for dinner. Disorientated by the unexpected surroundings, it took him a moment to register the people with him.

'*Surprise! Happy birthday!*' chorused Alpha team.

Connor stared open-mouthed at his fellow buddyguards. Charley, Amir, Ling, Jason, Marc and Richie were seated either side of the table. At the opposite end were Colonel Black and his close-protection instructors, Jody, Steve and Bugsy.

'What the . . . ?' Connor exclaimed. He didn't know whether to feel relieved, overjoyed or downright furious.

Colonel Black's craggy face broke into a rare grin. 'Glad you could join us.'

Connor was now lost for words. He'd honestly believed he was doomed to some terrorist prison cell or, worse, a torturous death. Not a fancy restaurant on the borders of the Brecon Beacons in Wales.

Beaming a smile at him, Charley passed across a menu. 'So what do you want?' she asked.

Connor barely glanced at the menu, still reeling from the shock of their deception.

'You almost wet yourself with fright!' laughed Ling.

This remark snapped Connor out of his daze. 'No, I didn't! I was still in control.'

'Yeah, about as in control as a turkey at Christmas,' sniggered Jason.

'Well, I knew I'd been taken in a 4x4 and driven no more than fifteen minutes from HQ. I also worked out there were at least three kidnappers and one of them was a woman.' He glanced over at Jody, who was dressed in a black leather jacket, her dark brown hair tied back in a ponytail.

'Really?' said Jody, unfazed. 'How so?'

'Your perfume gave you away.'

She raised an eyebrow in admiration. 'Then it appears you *were* keeping a cool head. A good thing for a bodyguard.'

'You're definitely one slippery fish, Connor,' admitted Bugsy, the bald-headed surveillance instructor, rubbing his stubbled jaw where Connor's heel had connected. 'I'm just glad we managed to restrain you first, otherwise we'd never have got you in the back of the Range Rover.'

Connor felt some dignity return, knowing that he'd at least proven himself in the situation, even if he hadn't been able to save himself. And now, with the shock fading, he began to see the funny side.

'Well, it's one birthday surprise I won't forget in a hurry! And your little prank has certainly taught me not to fall asleep in the common room again after a night shift,' he announced with a laugh. Standing, he turned and presented his bound hands. 'Now will someone please get me out of these zip-ties?'

Amir rose to help, but the colonel shook his head and waved for him to sit back down.

Connor's brow furrowed. 'But how am I going to open my birthday gifts?' he asked in a mock plea.

'With difficulty,' stated Colonel Black flatly. '*Unless* you can free yourself.'

Connor eyed the colonel, incredulous at the suggestion. 'You're kidding me, right? I can't break these zip-ties. Believe me, I've already tried.' He parted his hands to show the red weals on his wrists as proof of his efforts.

'Then it's time you learnt how,' said the colonel. He directed a nod towards Steve, Alpha team's unarmed combat instructor. At six foot two and built like a tank, the ex-British Special Forces soldier towered over everyone as he got up from his chair. Holding out his sledgehammer hands to Jody, the muscles in his forearms rippling like black waves, he waited while she produced a heavy-duty zip-tie and fastened his wrists together.

'The best way to defeat any type of restraint is to analyse how it works,' Steve explained. 'Zip-ties consist of a grooved nylon strip and a ratchet with tiny teeth housed in a small open casing. The weak point, therefore, is the ratchet. So that's where you have to direct any force.'

Taking the zip-tie in his teeth, Steve adjusted the locking mechanism so that it was positioned midway between his wrists. Then in one fluid motion he raised his hands above his head and came down hard in an arc on to his torso, chicken-winging his arms at the same time. The zip-tie pinged off like a rubber band. 'There you go. It's that easy.'

'*C'est facile pour vous*,' said Marc, then switching from French to English, added, 'You're built like the Terminator.'

'Yeah, and Connor's arms are behind his back,' Amir pointed out.

Steve shrugged. 'Same principle applies. Just bend over and bring your hands down against your hips at the same time as pulling your arms apart. Besides, it's about technique and speed, not strength.'

Adjusting the zip-tie's position, then bending over, Connor followed his instructor's technique. A second later his hands were free. Until that point he'd been pulling and yanking at his restraint when all it needed was a single strike at the right angle. He shook the blood back into his hands. 'That's impressive. But what about my ankles?'

Steve nodded to the dining table. 'You've got a steak knife. What more do you need?'

'But what if you don't happen to be in a restaurant?' asked Jason as Connor cut himself loose.

'Then, if you've replaced your shoelaces with paracord as I've recommended, you can use your laces as a friction saw.'

Ling jumped up and presented her hands. 'That looks like fun. Let me have a go.'

'A sucker for punishment?' Steve grinned, taking a spare zip-tie from Jody and wrapping it round Ling's wrists.

'Oww! Not *that* tight,' Ling squealed as the instructor yanked on the strip.

'The tighter it is, the easier to defeat the locking mechanism,' Steve replied with zero pity.

'Good luck, skinny!' called out Jason.

Ling narrowed her half-moon eyes at him, then raised her hands above her head. Despite her slender physique, she broke apart the zip-tie on her first attempt.

'Who needs muscles, eh?' she remarked with a ceremonial bow towards Jason.

'My turn now,' said Amir, springing to his feet.

This time Steve tied Amir's hands behind his back. 'Go for it.'

Bending over, Amir slammed his arms against his backside. But the zip-tie failed to break. Amir tried again. Still it held.

'Is this the same as the other zip-ties?' asked Amir.

Steve nodded.

'Have another go,' urged Connor. 'You just need to get the right angle.'

Amir kept thumping away, but the zip-tie refused to snap. Becoming more and more frustrated with each attempt, Amir waddled round the restaurant's private dining room, grunting, his arms flapping wildly.

'He's like a chicken doing a breakdance!' cracked Richie.

Everyone at the table collapsed into fits of laughter as Amir stumbled into a chair and fell over.

Steve glanced across at Colonel Black, unable to suppress a grin. 'We should make this a regular party game!'

CHAPTER 3

'So whose idea was it to kidnap me?' asked Connor, eventually cutting Amir's zip-tie for him.

'Mine,' said Jason, raising his glass of Coke in salute.

Connor should have guessed. It was typical of his Aussie rival's sense of humour. 'Couldn't you have just ordered me a taxi?'

Jason responded with an arch grin. 'Wouldn't have been half as much fun.'

Amir plonked himself down at the table beside Connor. Studying the menu intently to hide his embarrassment, he whispered, 'It's harder than it looks.'

Connor nodded in sympathy. 'Let's just hope you're not kidnapped with zip-ties on the mission, eh?'

'Yeah, your Principal might actually die from laughter before being rescued!' chortled Richie.

Amir sank back in his chair as if his plug had been pulled. His fringe of slick black hair flopped forward, covering his dark brown eyes but not hiding his dismay. Connor glared at Richie, whose caustic Irish wit had fallen far from the mark this time. Richie shrugged an apology, but it was a little late for that.

Connor patted his friend on the shoulder. 'Don't worry. You'll be fine.'

'That's all right for you to say,' muttered Amir. 'You've earned your gold wings.' He indicated the gleaming badge pinned on Connor's T-shirt: a winged shield with the silhouette of a bodyguard at its centre. 'I'm still unproven.'

Ever since joining Buddyguard the previous year, Connor knew his friend had been desperate for the colonel to select him to lead a mission. Now Amir was just three weeks from his first solo assignment and his nerves were starting to show.

'Don't you remember how nervous I was before my first assignment?' said Connor. 'I barely slept for a week. And I'd only just completed basic training. You've the benefit of almost a year of instruction, as well as learning from *all* my mistakes!'

Amir managed a strained smile. 'Doesn't make it any easier.'

'From my experience, it isn't ever easy.'

'But what if I fail? Like I just did with the zip-ties. Or I freeze at the moment of an attack?'

'You won't,' reassured Connor. 'Trust me, every bodyguard worries about such things. But, I promise you, your training *will* kick in. You will react. Besides, I'll be back at HQ providing you support, instead of the other way round.'

Amir swallowed hard and nodded. 'Thanks. It's good to know you'll be there for me.'

'OK, birthday boy,' interrupted Charley, 'what would you like?'

Connor turned to Charley, who was sitting next to him. She looked stunning in a glittering silver top, her long blonde hair braided into a golden plait and a touch of make-up highlighting her sky-blue eyes. It took a few seconds for Connor to become aware of the waitress standing behind her, patiently waiting for his order.

'I can come back to you if you need more time,' said the waitress, smiling.

'No, it's all right,' replied Connor, hurriedly scanning the menu and hoping Charley hadn't noticed him staring at her. He asked for a large steak with extra fries. The adrenalin rush of the fake kidnapping had given him a serious appetite.

'So, are you heading home to see your family?' Charley asked after placing her own order.

Connor nodded. 'The colonel's given me leave at the end of the month.'

Charley studied his face, surprised to see a frown. 'Aren't you excited to be going?'

He sighed quietly and, lowering his voice, confessed, 'Yes, it's just . . . I'm worried how my mum will be. Last time she was so weak.'

Charley's hand touched his arm. 'Look, if it would help, I can come with you.'

Connor hesitated. 'Thanks, but I don't want to put you out.'

'It's not a problem,' she insisted. 'Besides, I could do with a change of scene. I'm getting cabin fever at HQ. Californian girls aren't suited to long winters stuck in Wales.'

Connor smiled. He had to admit it would be good to have her company on the long train journey. And at least he could satisfy his mother's curiosity about his friends at his 'private boarding school'.

'OK, that would be great –' A large box was thrust between him and Charley.

'Present time!' Ling announced excitedly.

Connor dutifully unwrapped the gift and laughed at what was inside.

'To replace the one I broke,' said Ling with a grin as Connor lifted out the padded headguard. Earlier that month he'd been sparring with Ling and she'd executed a devastating jumping axe-kick on him. The blow had split his old headguard in two, as well as losing him the match.

'I'm just glad you didn't crack my skull open,' said Connor, admiring the new full-face guard with shock-suppression gel for maximum protection. 'That would've been a lot harder to replace.'

'Oh, I don't know,' said Ling. 'I saw some footballs about your size. Give me something else to kick!'

'That's if you're still standing,' Connor shot back. With the score even at four bouts each, they both knew their next sparring match would be hard fought. He'd even heard rumours that the instructors were laying down bets on who would win.

Jason tossed Connor a poorly wrapped gift. 'Hope it fits.'

The packaging split open on landing to reveal a garish yellow T-shirt with the picture of a koala with sharpened teeth and the warning BEWARE DROP BEARS! The design was a painful reminder of the time he'd fallen for Jason's hoax about killer koalas. Holding the T-shirt against himself for size, Connor couldn't help but smile.

'Is it bulletproof?' he asked.

'Nah,' said Jason in his Aussie twang. 'But it's guaranteed to repel drop bears!'

'Like the aftershave you wear to repel girls then?' quipped Richie, causing the others to laugh.

Jason snarled. 'Hey, my aftershave works just fine,' he said, putting an arm round Ling.

Ling smiled sweetly before elbowing him hard in the ribs.

Jason doubled over in pain. '*Oof!* Talk about tough love,' he wheezed.

While Jason recovered from Ling's 'affectionate' elbow strike, Connor unwrapped his other gifts. Marc had bought him a designer shirt from Paris. Richie had given him the latest *Assassin's Creed* game, and last but not least was a joint gift from Amir and Charley.

'I hope you like it,' said Charley, biting her lower lip anxiously as she handed him a small presentation box. 'Amir helped choose it.'

Connor pulled off the lid. Inside was a G-Shock Rangeman watch.

Amir leant over, eager to show him the watch's features. 'It's solar powered with multi-band 6 atomic timekeeping, auto-LED super illuminator, a triple sensor and digital compass. But, most important for you, it's waterproof and shock resistant. Engineered to stand up to the most gruelling conditions imaginable. Basically, this is one gadget you *won't* be able to break.'

'Thanks, guys . . . it's awesome,' said Connor, slipping the watch on and holding up his wrist for the others to admire it.

'An ideal gift for a bodyguard,' remarked Colonel Black with a nod of approval. 'An accurate timepiece is essential on missions. But there's one final present to go.'

He slid a set of car keys down the glass table to Connor. Everyone's jaws dropped open in shock.

'You're giving him a *car*!' exclaimed Jason.

'Driving lessons, to be exact,' replied Jody. 'The car is for all Alpha team to use.'

Connor picked up the keys, staring at them in astonishment. 'But I'm too young to drive.'

Colonel Black shook his head. 'In a dangerous situation, no bodyguard's too young.'

CHAPTER 4

'The heart of Africa will *beat* again!' exclaimed Michel Feruzi. The Burundian Minister for Trade and Tourism thumped the well-worn wooden conference table with a fleshy fist, the glasses of iced water tinkling from his over-zealous blow.

'I agree,' chimed Uzair Mossi, the eyes of the Finance Minister sparkling like the very diamonds they were talking about. 'Too long has Burundi been the poor man of this rich continent. If the rumours are true, then this is a turning point for our nation, a –'

President Bagaza held up his hand for silence and waited for his ministers to curb their premature celebrations. He did not share their enthusiasm at the news.

'Angola. Sierra Leone. Liberia. The Congo,' he stated in his low solemn tone. 'Do their tragic histories not mean anything to you?' He let the ghosts of each country's brutal civil war, fuelled by blood diamonds, settle in the minds of his ministers before continuing. 'The reported discovery of a diamond field is a reason to both rejoice and despair. After a generation of tribal conflict, our country's peace is fragile at best. We cannot, *must not*, let ourselves be dragged back into civil war.'

The ministers exchanged uneasy looks. Although the bloodshed was over a decade ago, scars still ran deep and the tensions between rival Hutu and Tutsi factions bubbled just beneath the surface, even within the government itself.

'The president is right,' declared Minister Feruzi, his chair creaking as he settled his ample bulk into the seat. 'We've only recently relocated all the Batwa tribes from the expanded Ruvubu National Park. If they learn that there's a diamond field, they'll make a claim over their ancestral lands. We cannot allow one minority tribal group to solely benefit. The whole country must prosper from this discovery.'

'That's *if* there are diamonds in the first place,' commented the Minister for Energy and Mines. Adrien Rawasa, a thin man with a shaved head, hollow cheeks and rounded spectacles, stood and tapped a faded out-of-date geological map of Burundi on the whitewashed wall.

'As you're well aware, Mr President, our mining sector is still in its infancy. We have substantial deposits of nickel, cobalt and copper that can only be exploited with the help of foreign investors. We even have some seams of gold and uranium. But we're not blessed – or cursed as you may see it – with the same bounty of natural resources as our neighbours. The land within the national park isn't typical of the geology in which diamonds are found. The rumour might well have started from stones illegally smuggled across the border from the Congo or Rwanda.'

'But is it conceivable there *could* be diamonds in the park?' questioned President Bagaza.

Minister Rawasa sucked at his lower lip as he studied the map. 'Well . . . let's just say it's not impossible.'

'Then we must tread very carefully. Minister Feruzi, close off the national park and order the rangers to begin a sector-by-sector search. I want confirmation that the diamond field is real before we start raising hopes and making plans. Tell the rangers they're looking for poachers but to report anything else unusual. The last thing we need is a false diamond rush.'

'Should I delay the French ambassador's visit?' asked Minister Feruzi.

President Bagaza repeatedly clicked the top of his ballpoint pen out of habit, considering the proposal for a moment. 'No. Not after the millions France has invested in the conservation programme. If we don't show them progress, they'll cut off all our international aid. And we can't afford to lose such funding.' He gave everyone at the table a meaningful look. 'In the meantime, this news isn't to go any further than this room. Understood?'

His ministers nodded obediently. But President Bagaza knew it was a futile request. He trusted no one on his Cabinet to keep a secret. And if his government ministers had heard about the diamonds, then he was in no doubt that other more dangerous individuals would know too. Diamonds lured corrupt men like wasps to a jam jar.

'ATTACK FRONT!' shouted Jody as a car sped out of a side street and screeched to a halt in the middle of the road.

Connor slammed on the brakes. Jody braced herself in the passenger seat, while Charley and Marc were flung forward, only saved by their seat belts in the back. Crunching gears, Connor battled to find reverse. He'd been driving only three weeks and the pressure of an attack was seriously testing his new skills.

'*Come on,*' he muttered in frustration, rattling the gear stick furiously. Finally he managed to engage reverse, looked over his shoulder and accelerated away hard. The engine whined in protest as the rev counter maxed out.

Gripping the steering wheel tightly, Connor fought to maintain a straight line and keep on the road. Driving at speed in reverse was judged extremely dangerous – one tiny misjudgement and he could send the car into a fatal spinout.

By now their attackers had jumped from their vehicle and begun firing at them. Connor's car was going flat out, but reverse gear wasn't anywhere near fast enough to escape an ambush. To do so, he had to change direction. Adrenalin pumping, he took his foot off the accelerator, wrenched the steering wheel hard to the right and applied the handbrake, all at the same time. His car went into a tyre-screeching 180-degree pivot and came to a tight stop. Releasing the handbrake, he floored the accelerator pedal and they shot off again, speeding away from the kill zone.

Behind him, Connor heard Marc whistle in relief and Charley whisper, 'That's one hell of a roller-coaster ride!'

'Well done, Connor. Aside from the poor gear change, that was a textbook J-turn,' Jody commended, ticking off another box on her clipboard.

Connor eased off the accelerator, pleased to have passed the first stage. As he continued down the road, he routinely checked his rear-view mirror in case the ambushers decided to pursue them. After three weeks of intensive lessons, he and the rest of Alpha team had completed their basic driving test and were on to advanced evasive driving skills. They'd been taught how to execute a bootlegger's turn, drive safely at high speed, control a skid, push an immobilized vehicle out of the kill zone, and even force another car off the road in a pursuit. Now it was time to put their newly acquired skills to the test.

Jody had explained that car travel was inherently dangerous. Compared to the security in place at a VIP's home or a school, a vehicle was a mobile target. At these times, the Principal was at their most vulnerable to attack or kidnap attempts. This was why each member of Alpha team had to be able to drive with confidence and at high speeds. One never knew when they might have to take charge of a vehicle in an emergency.

'Watch out!' cried Marc, just as Connor turned a corner.

Up ahead two cars were parked nose-to-nose across the street. There wasn't enough distance to execute a hand-brake turn. So, this time, Connor didn't stop. He drove straight at the roadblock. He knew his aim would be critical. It had to be the front wheels of the blockading cars, otherwise it would be impossible to ram them out of the way. The cars' front-wheel arches were solid and would give him the resistance he needed, as well as the angle of force to pivot the vehicles aside.

When he was twenty metres away Connor purposefully slowed down, dropped into first gear, then accelerated hard. He had to hit the roadblock at just the right speed. Too slow and he'd get stuck. Too fast and he'd damage his own car.

'Brace yourselves!' he warned.

There was a gut-wrenching crunch as they struck the blockade. The impact was jarring, but not devastating enough to disable his own vehicle. In preparation for the training exercise, the car's airbags had been disarmed so the collision didn't trigger their inflation and cut the engine.

As he pushed on through the blockade, Connor heard another horrible *scrunching* sound and went to brake.

'Don't stop,' urged Charley.

Connor kept his foot firmly on the accelerator, but the

scraping between the cars was like fingernails being clawed down a chalkboard. Then, with a final *screech*, they were beyond the roadblock.

Charley looked back out of the rear windscreen. 'Don't worry, it was just your front bumper,' she said, keeping her voice light and breezy.

Grimacing, Connor prayed Jody wouldn't penalize him for such an error. He'd been warned about the danger of getting tangled up with another vehicle. Driving on, he tried to sneak a glance at Jody's test sheet just as a masked man leapt into the road. On instinct, Connor braked, stopping a couple of metres short of hitting him. Unfazed, the attacker raised his gun and fired. A red paint-ball exploded on the windshield, directly in line with Connor's head.

'Test over,' declared Jody.

The gunman walked up to the driver's side and tapped on the glass. Connor wound down the window. Bending down, the gunman removed his mask.

'Better luck next time,' said Bugsy as Jody put a cross through the last box on her clipboard. 'Consider us even for kicking me in the jaw!'

With a sinking heart, Connor flicked on the windscreen wipers and washed off the splodge of dripping paint. Turning the car round, he headed back to the starting point – the forecourt of the abandoned business park commandeered for the exercise. He stopped beside Amir, Ling, Jason and Richie, huddled in a group, all wrapped up in thick puffer jackets against the winter chill.

Stepping out of the car, Connor noticed Marc clasping his right side as if in pain. 'Are you all right?' he asked.

'Fine,' replied Marc, waving him away. 'The seat belt must have caught me when you did the emergency stop. Don't worry about it.'

'How did the test go?' asked Amir, his breath puffing out in small white clouds in the cold air.

Connor responded with a half-hearted smile.

'Not good by the looks of it,' remarked Richie, examining the crumpled wing. 'He's trashed our car!'

'Sorry,' Connor mumbled. 'I must have got caught up.'

Jody inspected the damage herself. 'It's mostly cosmetic. The good thing was you didn't stop and the car wasn't disabled.' She stood and addressed all of Alpha team. 'The number-one rule in an ambush situation is to *always keep moving*.' Making another mark on her clipboard, she glanced over at Connor. 'Shame you didn't do that on the final stage of the exercise.'

'But I'd have run Bugsy over,' protested Connor.

'It was *only* Bugsy,' she replied, the corner of her mouth curling up in a wry smile. 'Seriously, in such a situation you shouldn't hesitate to use your vehicle as a weapon to attack a threat head on.'

'But you could kill someone!' said Amir.

'That's their decision. If there's an armed attacker in front of your car, you either drive into, around or over that attacker. No hesitation. And, when you drive directly at the enemy, their self-preservation instincts kick in. This affects their ability to shoot straight, as well as shifting their focus from killing you to not getting hit themselves. Either way, the threat is neutralized or escape achieved.'

'So I've failed the test then?' said Connor, glumly looking at the smear of red paint still visible on the windscreen.

'You're technically dead,' Jody admitted. Then she gave him an encouraging wink. 'However, your overall score was seventy-eight per cent. A solid pass.'

Ling punched Connor on the arm. 'Slick driving, hotshot! Almost as good as Mad Max here.' She nodded at Jason. 'In his test, he nearly mowed Bugsy down.'

'At least I didn't get shot,' stated Jason defensively.

'But you almost lost control of the car,' cautioned Jody. 'That's why a vehicle is probably the deadliest weapon you'll have at your disposal. And, like any other weapon, if handled incorrectly you can kill yourself, and your friends, with it. But handled correctly you can save lives.'

'Connor, you're home!' his mum called out brightly as he and Charley were dropped off by the taxi. She came down the path to greet them. But, as she approached the rickety gate of their East London terraced house, she suddenly lost her footing. Her walking stick went from under her and she toppled over. Only Connor's fast reactions saved his mum from a nasty fall. He leapt forward, catching her in his arms.

'Whoops,' said his mum with an embarrassed glance up at him. 'Must have slipped on some ice.'

Connor nodded, accepting her excuse without argument. However, as cold as the winter weather was, he couldn't see any ice. As he helped her to stand, he noticed a distinct tremor in his mum's body. While it might have been the shock of the fall, he suspected it was another symptom of her multiple sclerosis. His mum looked more fragile than ever, as if the slightest breeze might blow her away like a leaf. Her cheeks were more sunken and the constant pain she suffered seemed to have etched permanent wrinkles at the corners of her eyes. Connor felt tears welling up in his own and fought against them. It was tragically apparent to him that the disease had strengthened its grip on his mum and was slowly yet surely squeezing the mobility from her frail body.

But his mum's smile remained defiant and her embrace was powerful with love. As he returned her hug, glad for the chance to blink away his tears, she seemed to take strength from his presence; when he pulled away, her face had visibly brightened as if a shadow had been lifted.

'It's so good to see you,' she said, kissing his cheek. Then she looked past him to Charley, only a flicker of surprise passing across her face before she offered a heartfelt greeting. 'You must be Charley. Welcome! Sorry about the dramatic reception.'

'Don't worry, Mrs Reeves,' replied Charley, entering the front yard. 'I'm just pleased to meet you. Connor's talked about you a lot.'

'Really?' said his mum, taking her walking stick from her son but declining his offer of support. 'Well, I hope it was all good. Now, you both must be tired from your journey. Come in before we all freeze to death.'

They followed her through the front door, where Connor noticed a newly installed ramp and a folded-up wheelchair in the hallway. His mum's deteriorating condition was worse than he'd feared.

In the living room his gran was waiting by the fireside. The coals in the grate glowed red, giving off a steady warmth and flickering light that Connor always associated with being home.

'How's my big man?' asked his gran, rising slowly from her armchair, as old and worn as she was.

'Fine, Gran. And you?'

'As fit as a fiddle and . . .'

'. . . as right as rain,' Connor finished for her.

'Hey, you cheeky scamp! That's my line.' She laughed, pulling him into a hug. 'Now, who's the beauty behind you?'

Stepping aside, Connor introduced Charley, who handed his gran a gift box of fine teas.

'Connor told me you like Earl Grey,' she explained.

'Why, that's very thoughtful of you,' his gran replied, admiring the fancy label on the box. Connor could tell his gran instantly warmed to Charley by the way she gently patted her hand in thanks. 'Make yourself at home, Charley, while me and Connor get some tea and biscuits.'

Connor dutifully followed his gran into the kitchen, leaving Charley with his mum. He briefly looked back to check that Charley was all right but they were already chatting happily.

'Where's Sally?' Connor asked, referring to the live-in carer that the Buddyguard organization provided in return for his services as a teenage bodyguard.

'Oh, we've given her the afternoon off since you're here,' explained his gran, flicking on the kettle and taking out her best china from a cupboard.

'Is that wise?' asked Connor, his eyes drawn to the wheelchair in the hall. 'Mum seems rather . . . weak.'

His gran paused in making the tea. With a heavy sigh,

she answered, 'Your mum's having a relapse. She won't admit how much she's suffering. That's why she insisted on greeting you at the door, despite my protests. She wanted to prove to you she's doing well. Didn't want you worrying at school.'

Connor glanced into the living room, where his mum now sat by the fire, the tremor in her hands still visible. Despite everything he was doing to provide their live-in care, he still felt powerless to help her where it mattered most. He wished he could somehow *protect* his mum from the disease, rather than merely help ease her suffering.

His gran saw the anguish in his face. 'Don't worry, my love. Your mum's keeping up her spirits. And Sally's a godsend. I honestly don't know how we'd cope without her help. Anyway, your Charley seems a lovely girl,' his gran remarked, changing topics as she popped three Earl Grey teabags into the pot and poured in hot water. 'So what's the story with you two?'

'We're just friends,' replied Connor, realizing where this was leading.

Gran gave him a look.

'No, really,' insisted Connor.

'I believe you,' she said with a knowing smile as she arranged some biscuits on a plate. 'But I hope you don't mind me saying, she seems an unusual choice of student to be in a "school" like yours.'

Unlike his mum, Connor's gran knew the truth about the 'private boarding school' he attended. Although Colonel Black had sworn him to secrecy as the Buddyguard organization relied on its covert status to function effectively, Connor had realized his gran was too sharp-witted to be fooled. She'd have seen straight through any lies. So, trusting his gran implicitly, he'd told her about the deal – the scholarship programme set up by Buddyguard to fund their care and his education in exchange for becoming a bodyguard. She hadn't liked the proposal one bit, yet was a realist when it came to their family's desperate situation. She'd also recognized his late father's steely determination in him – a determination that had made his father the best of the best: a soldier in the SAS. So, while not giving her full blessing, she'd accepted his decision to join.

From the living room, Connor heard Charley laugh at something his mum said and just hoped his mum wasn't telling any embarrassing stories of him as a boy.

'So what happened to Charley?' pressed his gran, picking up the tea tray. She directed her gaze to the wheelchair Charley sat in.

Connor barely noticed it any more. Charley had made clear, both in words and action, that her chair did not define her. 'I don't know exactly,' he replied. 'She's never told me. It happened before I joined, on an assignment.'

His gran almost dropped the tray, the cups clattering and the pot splashing steaming tea on to the lino floor. '*On an assignment!*'

Unable to meet his gran's hard stare, Connor grabbed a cloth from the sink to wipe up the mess.

Putting the tray down on the worktop, his gran looked thoughtfully out of the kitchen window. 'It doesn't seem right that this colonel of yours is allowed to recruit young people for such a dangerous job. Sacrificing their futures to protect others.' She shook her head in sad disbelief. 'What is the world coming to when an organization like this is even *needed*?'

Connor's gran turned back to him, her expression set. 'I'm no longer comfortable with this Buddyguard arrangement. Not any more.'

'But, Gran, I can assure you, the risks are minimal,' insisted Connor. 'We're very well trained and plan for all eventualities.'

'Obviously not *all* eventualities,' retorted his gran, directing her gaze to Charley in the living room. 'I want you to quit. Before something terrible happens to you.'

'But I can't,' argued Connor. 'It pays for all the care you and mum need.'

'I know . . . I know,' said his gran, taking a step towards him and cupping his face between her palms, just like she used to when he was a little lad. She studied it with a pained expression of love and deep concern. 'There's so much of your father in you. And of course I realize this organization pays for our care. But at *what* cost exactly?'

'You two took your time,' remarked his mum, breaking away from her conversation with Charley as Connor and his gran came back into the living room. 'We thought you must have been scoffing all the biscuits!'

'No, dear, I just spilt some tea on the floor,' Gran explained, settling into her armchair.

'But it's all cleared up now, isn't it, Gran?' said Connor as he placed the tray on a side table.

In return, she offered him a tight-lipped smile. After much persuasion, he'd managed to convince her that he should continue being a bodyguard, at least for the time being. He'd assured her that he wasn't assigned to the next mission so would be safe back at HQ. His gran had relented, albeit reluctantly, but only on the proviso they'd discuss the issue again at the Easter break. She was adamant that he shouldn't be risking his own life to pay for their care. Connor, however, felt differently. With his father dead, he had a responsibility to provide for his family, especially when their needs were so great – even if there were risks.

Connor certainly wasn't blind to the dangers. He'd faced deadly situations on both his missions so far. But his training, and admittedly some luck, had helped him to survive. Besides, he didn't *want* to leave Buddyguard. The intensity of the training and the pressure of being on a mission had forged an invisible bond between the members of Alpha team. They were now his closest and most trusted friends. He didn't want to break that bond, especially with Charley.

'I like your hairstyle in this photo,' said Charley, holding up a picture of him at five years old. He was wearing just a pair of shorts and held an ice lolly in one hand. His green-blue eyes were bright with delight and his dark brown hair was shaped into a humiliating bowl cut, a far cry from the spiky modern style he now sported.

Connor squirmed with embarrassment when he realized his mum had pulled out the family album. 'Mum! That's *not* cool.'

'But it's a mother's prerogative to embarrass her teenage son,' she said, sharing a mischievous wink with Charley. 'In fact, I was thinking of telling Charley about the time you put your underpants on your head and –'

'No!' cut in Connor, mortified.

Charley suppressed a giggle and pointed to another photo of him dressed as Superman. 'You were so cute as a little boy. What happened to you?' she teased.

'I decided to keep my alter ego hidden,' replied Connor, retrieving the family album from her and returning it to its rightful place on the shelf. He gave Charley an imploring look. 'Please don't tell anyone back at school.'

'Too late.' She held up her smartphone. 'I've shared it online.'

Connor's jaw dropped in dismay. 'You're not serious, are you?'

Charley and his mum burst into laughter.

'Would I do something like that?' Charley replied with an impish curl of her lips. 'Although I might save a copy, just in case I need to keep you in line!'

Hoping to move swiftly on from the cringeworthy photos, Connor poured out the tea and handed everyone a cup.

'Shall we give Connor his birthday present now?' his gran suggested as he sat down beside his mum on the sofa.

Nodding, his mum produced a parcel from behind a cushion.

Connor unwrapped the gift to reveal a black knitted jumper.

'Thanks . . . it's lovely,' he said, trying to sound enthusiastic.

'To keep you warm in the Brecons,' explained his gran. 'I resisted the urge to knit a snowman on the front. I thought that wouldn't be very hip for school.'

'Quite right,' agreed Connor.

'Why not try it on?' encouraged his mum.

Connor unfolded the jumper and that's when he discovered the other gifts: a medal embossed with an American eagle and a survival knife.

'These were my dad's!' he exclaimed breathlessly. Connor swallowed hard as he found himself overcome with emotion. Following his father's death, his mum had kept such things in a memory box, along with photos and other personal items that defined his father.

'Well, they're yours now,' declared his mum with a bitter-sweet smile. 'I've checked with your school and there's no problem taking the knife back with you. In fact, your head teacher, Mr Black, positively encouraged it.' She raised an eyebrow to express her surprise. 'I don't know if I ever told you, but that medal was awarded posthumously to your father for saving a US ambassador's life.'

Connor nodded. 'Yeah, he's now the president of the United States,' he said without thinking.

'How do *you* know that?' exclaimed his mum. 'I don't think I was even told the ambassador's name.'

Connor immediately tried to backtrack. He only knew this fact because, on his first assignment to protect the US president's daughter, he'd met the man himself, who had told him about his father's heroic sacrifice. 'I . . . must have read it in a newspaper.'

'Would you like some more tea, Mrs Reeves?' asked Charley, intervening before his mum could interrogate him further. Connor realized that if she discovered about his secret life as a bodyguard it would bring an end to everything, however much she was in need of proper care. And although he didn't like deceiving his mum, in this case, the ends justified the lie.

'Erm . . . yes please,' replied his mum, holding out her cup with a tremulous hand.

While the others drank their tea and Charley led the

conversation away from US presidents, Connor, avoiding his mum's quizzical gaze, examined his father's survival knife. The handle was made of rosewood, well oiled and smooth to the touch. When he slid the blade out of its leather sheath, he could see that it was razor sharp and in perfect condition. Holding the knife in one hand and the medal in the other, memories of his father came flooding back, in particular those of their camping trips together – *cutting down branches and making a bivouac shelter, using a flint-and-steel to start a campfire, skinning a rabbit and cooking it over the open flames, lying beneath the night sky and learning how to navigate by the stars . . .*

'Would you help me clear away, Charley?' said his gran quietly.

'Sure,' replied Charley, moving the tea tray on to her lap.

When the two of them had left the living room, Connor's mum edged closer on the sofa and put her arm round him. Connor let himself be drawn into her comfort, allowing the grief for his dead father to flow out.

Eventually, wiping his eyes with the back of his hand, Connor looked up. 'Thanks, Mum,' he said, hugging her. 'This is the best present possible.'

'I'm glad you like them,' she said, kissing him on the forehead. Then lowering her voice and glancing towards the kitchen, she asked, 'So is this the girl who's been distracting you from your school work?'

Connor felt his cheeks flush. 'She's just a friend,' he insisted.

'Well, she's lovely.' His mum tousled his hair

affectionately. 'And you're such a good boy. Always look-ing out for others.' Her expression became solemn again. 'Now please don't get me wrong when I say this, but do you really need to burden yourself further?'

'I'm not sure I understand,' said Connor.

His mum sighed softly and her gaze drifted to the kitchen and Charley in her wheelchair. 'You've got enough on your plate with me and Gran. Should you really be taking on Charley's needs as well?'

In the kitchen, Connor saw his gran fumble with a teacup and Charley catch it in mid-air, her reflexes as sharp as ever.

Connor smiled to himself. 'Charley doesn't need *me* to look after her,' he assured his mum. 'She can more than handle herself, in any situation.'

'Well, *that* I can believe,' said his mum, giving him a final inquisitive look but taking it no further. 'I was only think-ing of you. Forget I ever mentioned it. If the truth be told, I should take my inspiration from Charley's attitude to life's daily challenges . . .'

Connor became aware that his mum's tremors were get-ting worse. But it wasn't her MS this time. He could see she was on the verge of tears. At that very moment Charley and his gran re-entered the living room with a large choco-late birthday cake decorated with fifteen candles. His mum immediately rallied and joined in singing 'Happy Birthday' as the cake was placed before him on the table.

'Don't forget to make a wish,' urged Charley when he leant forward to blow out the candles.

Closing his eyes, Connor had only one wish in the world.

CHAPTER 8

'Is this where you found the diamond?' demanded General Pascal, surveying the hidden valley. Thick vegetation cloaked the steep sides and a primeval mist hung ghost-like in the dawn air, seemingly undisturbed for millennia. A wide shallow river snaked its way over rocks and through gullies, twisting downhill towards a waterfall that joined the Ruvubu River in the distance. To the west was a craggy peak atop which stood a single acacia tree.

No Mercy recognized the peak from his former life, a life erased since his abduction and forced conscription into the ANL, Armée Nationale de la Liberté. The peak was called Dead Man's Hill. An ancient sacrificial site. No one from the villages ventured near for fear of evil spirits and man-eating leopards. It was little wonder this valley had lain undisturbed for so long – until now. No Mercy kicked at the mud and stones with his bare feet. Who would have imagined there were diamonds here? They all looked like worthless rocks to him.

General Pascal turned impatiently to a thin gaunt-faced man at his side. Tongue-tied, the prisoner stared up at him with round fearful eyes.

'Answer the general!' ordered Blaze, striking the man so hard across the jaw that the prisoner dropped to his knees, spitting blood.

A tooth fell from the poor man's mouth and he reached with a trembling hand to pick it back up. Blaze stepped on the man's fingers, crushing them against the rocks.

'Another for my collection,' Blaze remarked, taking the tooth for himself. The general's right-hand man had a reputation for cruelty. Never seen without his mirrored aviator sunglasses or the fearsome machete that hung from his hip, he wore an army-green T-shirt, black combat trousers and matching boots. He kept his head shaved and round his neck hung a beaded necklace, which on closer inspection was comprised of human teeth.

Beaten into submission, the prisoner pointed to a sandy bank on the bend of the river. 'Right here,' he spluttered through a mouthful of blood. 'I found the diamond right here.'

General Pascal pulled a brand-new Glock 17 from his hip holster and pressed the barrel against the man's temple. 'You wouldn't lie to me, would you?'

The man shook his head, his whole body trembling in terror. 'No, General! I swear!'

'Good,' said General Pascal, smiling at him as he squeezed the trigger.

The gunshot echoed round the valley, startling birds from treetops and sending monkeys into a shrieking panic. The man flopped lifeless into the river, his blood mixing with the water and turning it pale pink. Pink as a rare diamond.

A child soldier, wearing combat fatigues and a black bandana with DREDD emblazoned across the brow, prodded the bleeding corpse with a toe.

'Why you kill him?' he questioned the general, more bemused than shocked.

General Pascal sneered at the boy as if the answer was obvious. 'He tried to steal *my* diamonds. This land belongs to me now.' He planted a foot on the dead man's back and declared, 'We'll start digging here.'

No Mercy jerked the barrel of his gleaming AK47 at the group of prisoners they'd rounded up from a distant village. Without needing to be told twice, the men picked up their shovels and sieves and set to work panning for diamonds. No Mercy smirked at their dog-like obedience.

'I don't want anyone else knowing where this diamond field is,' announced the general. He pointed to a number of potential access points around the secluded valley. 'Blaze, set up guards there, there and there. Kill anyone who attempts to enter or leave this valley.'

Connor stifled a yawn as he tapped away on the keyboard in the operations room at Buddyguard HQ. Equipped with state-of-the-art computers, satellite phones and HD flatscreen displays streaming live news feeds and the latest world security updates, the operations room was the hub of Alpha team's activities. Every piece of intelligence, every threat assessment and every mission profile was stored here. All security decisions and operational orders were issued from this room.

Connor was at the end of his shift and completing the daily occurrence log. Dull but essential work. Each shift leader had to record everything that occurred during an assignment, whether routine or out of the ordinary. That meant every phone call, every communication, every incident, every change in plan. *Any* occurrence no matter how seemingly insignificant – from the driver's name of a delivery company, to the scheduled maintenance of an air-conditioning unit, to the details of a vehicle parked outside a Principal's house. Such mundane information, as Bugsy their surveillance tutor had repeatedly stressed, could become crucial later in an operation – when the driver of the delivery company became a suspect, or a bugging device was detected in a vent, or the same vehicle was spotted in another location.

But, as important as his work was, Connor simply couldn't get excited about it. After a week stationed at HQ supporting Amir on his first mission, Connor was yearning for the challenge of an assignment himself. Nothing compared to the 'buzz' and heightened perception that came from protecting a Principal in the field. Colours seemed brighter, sounds sharper and sensations stronger. He could now understand what his father meant when he'd referred to the 'combat high' that soldiers experienced during battle. Connor experienced a similar 'protection high'.

Finishing the log entry, Connor leant back in his chair and stretched his limbs. He felt his father's knife pressing against his hip, as if spurring him to go on another mission. He'd originally become a bodyguard not just to provide care for his family but to follow in his father's footsteps and discover more about the man he'd barely known – an SAS operative in the Special Projects Team, responsible for counter-terrorism and VIP close protection, a man who'd not only saved a future president's life but also that of Colonel Black. And now, after two successful missions, Connor felt as if he was walking side-by-side with his father. He'd come to appreciate why his father had dedicated himself to protecting others – that sense of pride and purpose in keeping someone safe. But it was only on an assignment that he felt so close to him. Back at HQ, his father seemed to withdraw into the picture Connor kept of him on his key fob.

Yet, despite the lack of thrills that came with being stuck at HQ, Connor couldn't deny there were some benefits. He got the chance to hang out with Charley and the rest of Alpha team. He could keep up his kickboxing training, critical for his forthcoming match with Ling. He even had the time to read and watch some TV. That said, he and the others wouldn't be getting any free time over the coming week or so. Alpha team had been tasked with running two assignments simultaneously – Operation Hawk-Eye, which Amir was already on, and Operation Lionheart, which Marc was due to commence in just under twenty-four hours.

Connor glanced over to the briefing room where Marc, Jason, Ling and Charley were finalizing the op-orders. Marc had been assigned to protect a French ambassador's family on safari in Africa. It sounded like a dream assignment to Connor. Yet Marc didn't appear too thrilled at the prospect. A sheen of sweat glistened on his forehead and his complexion was rather pale. Suddenly Marc made a retching sound, clamped a hand to his mouth and ran from the room.

Jason looked round at the others in bewilderment. 'I know Marc gets the jitters before a mission, but I've never seen him *that* bad.'

Connor rose from his seat, intending to see if Marc was all right, but at that moment his computer monitor flashed and an alert sounded, notifying him of an incoming video call. Connor clicked Accept and Amir's face popped up on the screen.

'You're not due to report in for another hour,' said Connor. 'Everything OK?'

But he could tell from Amir's expression that things were far from right.

'Is anyone else with you?' Amir asked.

Connor looked across to the briefing room, then shook his head. 'They're all dealing with Marc at the moment. Seems like he's having a panic attack.'

'He's not the only one,' replied Amir, his voice strained.

Connor leant closer to the screen, his concern growing. 'What's happened?'

Amir took a deep breath. 'I'm not like you, Connor . . . I'm no kickboxing champion. I don't have a fighter's natural reflexes.'

Connor could see his friend was trembling. 'Just tell me what's going on.'

'We were in a crowd . . . there was a man. I thought he had a grenade . . . I froze. I didn't do anything to protect my Principal, not even shout a warning . . .' Amir lapsed into silence, an expression of deep shame on his face.

'Is the Principal OK?' asked Connor.

Amir nodded, but still didn't raise his eyes to the camera. 'Yes, fine. The grenade turned out to be an egg!' He shrugged with embarrassment. 'But what if it hadn't been –'

'Amir, calm down,' interrupted Connor. 'It sounds to me like first-operation nerves. You're bound not to react instantaneously, especially when it's the first *real* threat you've encountered. The main thing is your Principal is alive and unharmed.'

'Sort of,' admitted Amir. 'The egg ruined his clothes.' He sighed heavily and stared glumly down at his lap. 'I don't think I'm cut out for this buddyguard work. I'm just a slum boy who got lucky. I'm a fake!'

'Don't you dare say that,' replied Connor. 'Listen, Amir, if you can survive a slum upbringing, get yourself out and provide for your family back in India, then you're more than capable of protecting someone.'

Amir had once confided in him about his past. He was the sixth son of a migrant worker from a slum on the out-skirts of Delhi. He'd been working as a rag picker, earning a few rupees a month to help stave off his family's hunger, when Colonel Black had discovered him through an unusual 'hole-in-the-wall' experiment. An Indian IT com-pany had installed a computer in a concrete wall facing the slum. Without any training or help, Amir and some other slum children had taught themselves how to use the computer. Within a day, Amir was accessing the internet and creating folders. After a week he was downloading apps, music files and games. By the second month he was writing his own simple programs. With no formal educa-tion, Amir had proven himself a natural with computers. He came to Colonel Black's attention when one day he hacked into the IT company's server – a server that was under the colonel's security remit at the time. Recognizing his natural talent for problem-solving, Colonel Black sponsored Amir through school and recruited him as a potential buddyguard.

'Remember what the colonel said, the mind is the best weapon a bodyguard can possess,' continued Connor. 'And you've got a phenomenal mind. So stay focused and in Code Yellow,' he advised, referring to the default alert status for a bodyguard. 'Next time you'll spot the threat earlier and be able to avoid turning your Principal into an omelette!'

Amir managed a half-hearted laugh. 'Thanks, Connor . . . I'm glad I've got you for back-up.'

'You'll be fine,' reassured Connor.

Charley came up behind him as Amir signed off. 'Any problems?'

Connor turned round and shook his head. 'No, Amir's doing great.'

'Good,' replied Charley, 'because Colonel Black needs to see you urgently.'

CHAPTER 10

'Change of plan, Connor,' said Colonel Black, seated in his antique red leather chair behind the mahogany desk in his office. On the wall, a widescreen monitor displayed the news of a terrorist attack in China; another was showing the continued riots in Thailand. 'You're to be BG on Operation Lionheart.'

'What about Marc?' said Connor, confused by the sudden reassignment.

'He has acute appendicitis,' explained Charley, rolling up beside him. 'He believed it was just stomach ache and had been trying to tough it out. Jody's rushed him to hospital before his appendix bursts.'

Connor recalled how his friend had been clutching his side after the advanced driving test the week before. 'Will he be all right?'

'He'll be fine,' stated the colonel. 'But you're to stand in for him. You leave tomorrow.'

'But . . .' Connor's feelings were conflicted. He was obviously thrilled at the prospect; yet at the forefront of his mind were Amir and his agreement with his gran. 'I'm supposed to be Amir's support.'

Colonel Black waved away his concerns. 'Charley will cover for you. Besides, it's only for ten days.'

'What about Jason? Or Richie?'

The colonel shook his head. 'They don't have the necessary vaccinations for travel in Africa. Yellow fever and Hepatitis A need to be administered at least two weeks in advance. Thankfully, after your last assignment you're already immunized.'

Connor appreciated the decision was out of his hands. Thinking about it, he supposed a short mission was acceptable. His gran wouldn't even know he was gone and he'd be back in time for the second phase of Amir's assignment. With his conscience almost clear, Connor began to feel the familiar pre-mission rush of anticipation.

'Charley, brief him on the assignment,' Colonel Black instructed.

She spun towards the wall monitors and clicked a remote. The news feeds disappeared and were replaced by a picture of a smiling family of four. 'As you already know, Operation Lionheart is tasked with protecting this French ambassador's family on safari in Africa.'

'You do realize I don't speak French?' Connor asked.

'Not to worry,' Charley replied. 'The Barbier family all speak English as a second language. And Bugsy will supply you with a new smartphone with a real-time translation app. He has requested, though, that you try to keep *this* phone intact on this mission.'

Connor shrugged. 'I'll do my best.' On his last assignment, his phone had been destroyed by a bullet, though it had saved his life.

'The two Principals you'll be buddyguard for are Amber and Henri,' continued Charley.

A close-up of a flame-haired girl with green eyes appeared on-screen. Next to her, on the other monitor, was an image of a red-headed boy in a blue-and-white football top.

'Amber is sixteen years old, a keen climber and with a passion for photography. Her brother, Henri, is nine. As you can see from the photo, he's into soccer – a supporter of Paris Saint Germain – but he suffers badly from asthma so he can't play the game himself.'

'Does Amber have any medical conditions?' Connor asked, making mental notes as Charley ran through the brief.

Charley shook her head. 'She once broke her foot after a climbing accident, but there weren't any long-term issues according to her medical files.'

With another click of the remote, detailed profiles of both parents were displayed. On the first screen appeared a man in his fifties with cropped grey hair and glasses; on the second, a glamorous middle-aged woman with high cheekbones and auburn hair.

'Laurent, the father, is a long-serving French diplomat with responsibility for managing aid programmes in Central Africa. As would be expected of an ambassador, he is well-mannered, well-connected and sociable. He's also astute and intelligent, with a master's in politics and economics. From what we can gather, he has no known enemies. His only shortcoming was keeping a mistress, although that appears to be in the past.'

Charley indicated the mother. 'Cerise is a former fashion editor and now a cultural attaché for the French foreign office. A caring mother and apparently forgiving wife, she now accompanies her husband on all diplomatic and foreign trips. By all accounts, she has good relations with family, friends and business colleagues. Nothing unusual – beyond a love of jewellery and an expensive taste in clothing – has been flagged during our profiling of her.'

'So, if the Barbiers don't have any obvious enemies, what's the threat?' asked Connor.

Colonel Black leant forward on his desk, steepling his fingers. 'No *specific* threats have been identified for the family. Hence, it's a Category Three operation and the reason why only one buddyguard has been assigned to two Principals in this instance. Primarily it's the location that raises security issues.'

He nodded to Charley, who brought up a map of Central Africa on-screen.

'Laurent Barbier and his family are visiting Burundi by invitation of President Bagaza,' Charley explained, pointing to a small heart-shaped country landlocked between the Democratic Republic of Congo, Rwanda and Tanzania. 'The purpose of their trip is to experience the country's soon-to-be-opened national park, one that France has heavily invested in.'

She enlarged the map to focus on an expanse of un-inhabited land in the nation's north-east. Hemmed in by high mountains on either side and split down the centre by a silver seam of a river, the area was identified as Ruvubu National Park.

'You see, Burundi is currently the fourth poorest country in the world,' she continued. 'After years of civil war crippling their economy, the government is largely dependent on foreign aid. But, with peace finally descending some years back, this country is attempting to rebuild itself. Besides exploiting its natural resources, tourism is seen as a potential major source of income. Yet, while the security situation has improved in recent years, the country remains subject to political instability and the threat of violence. It's a young, somewhat fragile peace.'

The colonel took over. 'There's a delicate power-sharing arrangement in place between Burundi's majority Hutu and minority Tutsi communities. The two sides are still struggling to reconcile after decades of conflict. President Bagaza has been sworn in for a second term, which is positive. But he does have his enemies: mainly leaders of former resistance groups, including the FPB – the Front Patriotique Burundais – and the UCL – the Union des Combattants de la Liberté. So, though unlikely, there's always a chance that things could kick off again. That's why the ambassador himself made the request for our services, to ensure his family are one hundred per cent safe.'

Charley handed Connor a mini USB flash drive. 'The op-order has more detail and background on Burundi's civil war, along with an overview of the current state of the country. Don't get your hopes up. It makes for grim reading. The infrastructure is virtually non-existent. There's little electricity and the roads are primarily dirt tracks. For what it's worth, I've included the official number for the police under emergency contacts, although it's unlikely anyone will answer your call. So you'll have to rely on your smartphone to contact us if there are any problems – and your only emergency evacuation option will be a private plane.'

Pocketing the mini drive, Connor remarked, 'Doesn't sound like much of a holiday destination.'

Charley smiled. 'Don't worry – I've seen pictures of the safari lodge. Luxury is an understatement. Just as an example, the bedroom suites are glass-fronted with their own sun decks and plunge pools! It looks like *millions* have been spent on this tourist project. And, with the president's own security forces on hand, this assignment should be a walk in the park for you.'

'Still, don't drop your guard, Connor,' said Colonel Black. Reaching into his desk drawer, he pulled out a battered pocketbook. 'Here, something for you to read on the plane.'

He tossed it to Connor. The green-and-orange cover sported the title: *SAS Survival Handbook*.

'Expecting problems?' asked Connor, glancing up at the colonel.

Colonel Black shook his head. 'No, but it's always best to be prepared for the worst. Especially in Africa.'

CHAPTER 11

A crude bamboo barrier forced the ageing Land Rover to a sudden halt, its tyres kicking up plumes of dust from the single-track road that cut through the bush. Two men in threadbare army fatigues, any official insignia long since faded or else purposefully removed, stood guard behind the barricade, their assault rifles trained on the vehicle's sole occupant.

The tallest of the men, a gangly Rwandan with deep-set eyes, approached the driver's side. He made a sign to wind down the window. Whether a legitimate border guard or not, the driver complied with the instruction.

'A little off the tourist trail, aren't you?' said the guard, leaning in and eyeing the interior of the 4x4 with greedy interest.

'The main road was blocked,' replied the driver.

The guard snorted sceptically. 'Passport,' he demanded, thrusting out a hand.

The driver reached into his rucksack and produced a navy-blue passport. The guard snatched it from his grasp and flicked it open to the ID page. A photo of a lean-faced man with a pale complexion, ice-grey eyes and a dour expression stared back at him. There were no distinguishing features but the photo more or less matched the driver's appearance. 'Stan Taylor. Canadian?'

Mr Grey nodded, the fake passport just one of his many false identities.

Leafing through the pages, the guard discovered a crisp ten-dollar bill tucked into the back. He glanced up. 'Bribing an official is a crime in our country.'

'What bribe?' replied Mr Grey evenly. 'I just gave you my passport as asked for.'

The guard closed the document, palming the ten dollars into his own pocket but not returning the passport. 'Come with me,' he ordered.

Mr Grey knew the routine. Ten dollars was hardly enough for the two or more guards stationed at this remote border crossing. They would try to squeeze him for more money. Accepted practice. Which was why he hadn't offered anything larger.

Taking his rucksack and car keys, Mr Grey followed the guard into a small wooden building with a corrugated tin roof. Inside it stank of stale sweat and cigarette smoke. After the glare of the African sun, his eyes took a moment to adjust to the dim interior – the only sources of light were the open doorway and a square hole for a window in the back wall. There was a bucket in one corner, a rusted machete leaning against the near wall and an unlit kerosene lamp hanging from a rotting beam. The only pieces of furniture in the room were a battered wooden desk and a chair in which reclined a pot-bellied official, his feet propped up and a cigarette lolling from his pudgy lips.

The border guard dropped Mr Grey's passport on to the desk. The official barely glanced at it.

'The purpose of your visit to Rwanda is?' he asked, the cigarette bobbing up and down, discarding ash on to the dirt floor.

'Business,' replied Mr Grey.

'And what business might that be?'

'Wildlife photographer.'

The officer's eyes narrowed. 'Where's your camera?'

'In my bag.'

'Search him,' he mumbled, jutting his chin in a command to the guard.

Mr Grey allowed the man to frisk him. His pockets were turned out and his car keys and a slim black wallet deposited on the desk. The official leant forward and inspected the wallet as the guard rummaged through the rucksack.

'For the record, I note you have one hundred dollars in here,' he said.

'Two hundred,' Mr Grey corrected.

'No, one hundred,' stated the official, extracting five twenty-dollar bills and slipping them into his shirt pocket.

'I must have been mistaken,' said Mr Grey with a thin smile.

The border guard pulled out an SLR digital camera with telephoto lens and held it up for the official to see.

'As I said, wildlife photographer,' repeated Mr Grey.

At that moment the guard from outside entered the

shack. Looking directly at the official, he shook his head once. 'Nothing in the vehicle.'

Not even attempting to hide his disappointment, the official reluctantly opened a drawer and produced a rubber stamp and ink pad. After a protracted and unnecessary examination of the passport, he inked the stamp and was about to authorize entry when the taller guard fumbled and dropped the camera. It hit the floor, the telephoto lens snapping off and rolling to a stop at the foot of the desk. Concealed within the casing was a large pinkish rock.

Mr Grey silently cursed the guard's clumsiness. It would likely cost the man his life.

Tutting his disapproval, the official set aside his rubber stamp.

'I can explain,' said Mr Grey, his eyes hardening.

'No need,' replied the official, bending down to pick up the precious rock and examining it with avaricious delight. 'Arrest him.'

The tall guard seized Mr Grey's arms. But a trained assassin isn't easy to restrain. A single reverse headbutt to the face fractured the guard's nose. A spinning elbow strike to the temple rendered him unconscious. And, as he crumpled, a sharp violent twist to the head snapped his neck.

The other guard went for his gun. Grasping the barrel, Mr Grey wrenched the weapon up and round, spinning it so fast that the man's finger broke in the trigger guard. A single knife-hand strike to the throat crushed the windpipe, cutting off any cry of pain and suffocating the guard even as he writhed on the floor.

In a wild panic, the official snatched up his machete and swung the fearsome blade at Mr Grey's head. With lightning reflexes, Mr Grey ducked and simultaneously pulled at the metal buckle of his belt. It came loose to reveal a hidden blade. Before the official could swing again, the assassin leapt across the desk and drove the sharpened point into the man's throat. The official's eyes bulged in agonized shock. The machete clattered to the ground, the cigarette tumbling from the man's quivering lips. As he bled like a stuck pig, his carotid artery severed, Mr Grey let the official slump into the dirt at his feet.

In less than ten seconds, the three men were dead.

With disconcerting calmness, Mr Grey retrieved the diamond, his passport, rucksack, camera, car keys, wallet and money the official had stolen, including the ten-dollar bribe in the border guard's pocket. That done, he took the kerosene lamp from the beam and smashed it on the floor. Oil splattered across the corpses, upon which flies were already settling. Then retrieving the still-smouldering cigarette, Mr Grey tossed it on to the kerosene and the bodies went up in flames. When anyone eventually reported the men's deaths, it would be assumed a rogue band of militia had attacked the border post.

As the stench of scorched flesh filled the room, Mr Grey made to leave. Almost as an afterthought, he stopped, opened the small ink-pad on the desk and stamped his passport before strolling out of the burning building.

'Are you *really* a bodyguard?'

Connor nodded as he washed down the bitter aftertaste of his malaria tablets with a swig of bottled water.

Henri's eyes widened in awe and he rocked back in his airline seat. '*C'est trop cool!*'

The small yet luxurious eight-seated Cessna plane banked left as they flew over dense jungle towards Ruvubu National Park. The African sun gleamed golden off the aircraft's wings and the sky was as blue as pure sapphire. Below, the steamy green tangle of trees pulsated with heat and life. Connor could scarcely believe that twenty-four hours earlier he'd been stationed in cold, grey snowy Wales. But after an eleven-hour flight from Heathrow via Brussels he'd landed in the surprisingly sedate and swelteringly hot airport of Bujumbura, Burundi's capital city. There, he'd joined the Barbier family for their connecting flight to the safari lodge.

Henri leant forward. 'Do you have a gun?' he whispered, keeping his voice low so that his parents in the front-row seats wouldn't hear.

Connor laughed out loud, thinking of the trouble he'd have had getting one through airport security at Heathrow, even if he had been allowed to carry a gun. 'No,' he replied.

Henri frowned in evident disappointment. 'So how will you protect us?'

'By staying alert for danger, then avoiding it.'

'*Mais que ferais-tu si tu ne peux pas l'éviter?*' asked Amber, who was reclined in one of the Cessna's cream leather seats.

Connor looked across the narrow aisle at her. Far prettier than her photo had given her credit for, Amber was also more frosty than her flame-red hair suggested. She had either forgotten that he couldn't speak her language, or was being deliberately awkward for some reason.

Having exhausted the extent of his French in the brief and mumbled intro he'd learnt by rote for their first meeting, Connor wished he had Bugsy's translation app to hand, but his smartphone was switched off for the flight. With an apologetic smile, he replied, 'I'm . . . sorry. What did you say?'

'I said, but what if you can't avoid the danger?' repeated Amber in English graced with a soft French accent.

'Then we'll A-C-E it out of there.'

She raised a slender eyebrow in puzzlement. '*A-C-E?*'

Connor was so familiar with the jargon that Alpha team used on a daily basis that he forgot others didn't know the terms. 'It's the course of action I'll take to keep you safe. I'll first *assess* the threat, whatever it may be: a shout, a gunshot, or something that raises my suspicions. Then I'll *counter* the danger – either by shielding you or eliminating the threat itself – before we *escape* the kill zone.'

'So, as our bodyguard, if someone tried to shoot my sister –' a playful grin sneaked across Henri's face as he formed a gun with his fingers and took aim at Amber – 'would you dive in front of the bullet to save her?'

Connor felt a dull ghost-like throb of pain along the scar on his thigh where he'd been shot protecting the daughter of the president of the USA. 'If I have to, yes. But with the right security measures in place it won't come to that.'

Henri looked suitably impressed as he fired off several imaginary shots.

Amber pushed aside her brother's finger gun in annoyance. 'Papa says Africa is dangerous and that's why we need a bodyguard. But we're not to tell anyone who you really are. Why is that? Surely it would be better if people *knew* we were being protected.'

Connor shook his head. 'Buddyguard works on the principle that the best bodyguard is the one nobody notices.'

'So, are you the *best*?' asked Amber.

Her piercing green eyes seemed to challenge him, and Connor, still unsure why she was giving him a hard time, was careful how he answered. 'Well, I'll certainly do my best to –'

'This is your captain speaking,' a voice crackled on the intercom, interrupting their conversation. 'We're now flying over the national park. If you look to your right you'll see the Ruvubu River, after which this park is named. And to your left, our destination and your residence for the next week, Ruvubu Lodge. We'll be landing in a few minutes. The runway is a little bumpy, so please fasten your seat belts.'

As everyone strapped themselves in, Connor peered out of the window. Below, the jungle had thinned out into grassy savannah bounded by hills and craggy peaks. He couldn't see the lodge from his side, but the river was clearly visible, a wide meandering stretch of ruddy waterway that divided the park in two.

'*Regardez! Regardez!*' Henri cried, pointing excitedly at the ground. '*Des éléphants!*'

Connor followed his line of sight and spotted a parade of elephants, with two babies in tow, ambling towards the river. A herd of impala – too numerous to count – grazed in the golden afternoon sun, and zebra and giraffe dotted the landscape. There was no sign of human habitation as far as the eye could see. No towns. No villages. No roads, aside from a few dirt tracks that threaded through the bush like dried-out veins.

Taking all this in, Connor realized that they truly were landing in the heart of Africa.

As Connor disembarked from the plane on to the make-shift runway – no more than a dusty strip of cleared land – he felt as if he'd stepped into a blazing furnace. The sudden temperature rise from the air-conditioned cocoon of the Cessna to the intense heat of Africa was almost overwhelming. The sun was so dazzling in the burnished sky that he was forced to squint, and the earth was such a deep red it looked sunburnt. Breathing in the oven-hot air, Connor was hit by the heavy scent of dried grass and wild animals, a rich earthy smell that was distinctly African.

Shading his eyes, Connor scanned the surrounding area for potential threats. Any nearby wildlife had been frightened off by the noise of the plane. It was just open savannah with a scattering of large flat-top trees. A mile to the north the land rose into a ridge, upon which was Ruvubu Lodge, commanding panoramic views of the entire plain.

Two brand-new 4x4 Land Rovers were waiting to escort the ambassador's family and their luggage up the hillside to the lodge. Climbing aboard the rear vehicle with Amber and Henri, Connor was glad of the breeze as they sped along the dirt track. So too it seemed was Amber, who paused in fanning herself with her sunhat.

'*Est-ce qu'il fait toujours aussi chaud?*' she asked the driver.

Connor hurriedly switched on his smartphone, launched Bugsy's translation app and secretly fitted his wireless earpiece. French was Burundi's second official language after Kirundi, the country's native tongue. And, if he was going to effectively protect Amber and Henri, he needed to understand what was being said at all times.

'*Excusez-moi, madame?*' replied the driver as they bumped and lurched their way up the potholed track.

Amber repeated her question. After a couple of seconds' delay, Connor heard through his earpiece: 'Is it always this hot?'

'Only during the daytime,' the driver replied with a broad grin.

'Well, that's a relief!' Amber laughed, amused by the man's answer.

A few minutes later, their Land Rover pulled up in front of the lodge's grand timber-framed entrance. Several porters rushed to take their bags as they clambered out.

'*Bienvenue, Ambassadeur Barbier. Quel plaisir de vous revoir. Comment s'est passé votre voyage?*'

After a pause, Connor heard in his ear: 'Welcome, Ambassador Barbier. It is so good to see you again. How was your journey?'

Connor was taken aback at the smartphone's almost instantaneous translation. Although the programmed voice was a little robotic, with a bit of concentration he could follow the conversation virtually in real time. It was as if he held a *Star Trek* Universal Translator in his hand.

'Very good, thank you,' replied Laurent in French, shaking President Bagaza's hand as they entered the welcome shade of the stylish reception area, all dark wood and leather armchairs. On the wall behind the reception desk hung the stuffed head of an immense African buffalo, its curved horns polished to a bright sheen, its glass-bead eyes blindly tracking the arrival of the new guests.

A line of smiling men and women, dressed in colourful robes, stood waiting as a welcoming committee.

'It's a pleasure to return to your beautiful country,' continued Laurent. 'Please allow me to introduce my wife, Cerise.'

'*Enchanté*,' said the president, kissing the back of her hand.

'Likewise,' Cerise replied with a graceful nod.

Connor had formally met both the parents in the airport and chatted with them before boarding the internal flight. They had been extremely pleasant as well as understanding of the last-minute change in buddyguard, much to Connor's relief. Laurent had reiterated that he wasn't expecting any problems; he just wanted to guarantee his family's safety during the formal visit. Cerise had seemed a little perplexed at the need for such unorthodox security measures but was reassured to know that her children would have 'level-headed' company while the two of them were engaged in their diplomatic duties.

'And these are my children, Amber and Henri,' said Laurent.

The president beamed a sunshine of a smile. 'Wonderful. I do hope you'll enjoy your stay, children,' he said, his voice deep and smooth as molasses. 'Ask for anything you want from the staff. You'll be pleased to know that this safari lodge has its own swimming pool –'

'Will we see lions?' interrupted Henri, barely able to contain his excitement.

'Why, of course! The lion is the symbol of our nation,' replied the president proudly. His gaze fell upon Connor. 'And who might this fine gentleman be?'

'Connor Reeves,' replied the ambassador. 'A friend of my daughter.'

The president shook Connor's hand. He was a big man with a domed head and trimmed moustache. His smile was infectious and his handshake firm and heartfelt. Connor instantly warmed to him.

'You're most welcome to my country, Connor.' The president's eyes flicked between him and Amber before he turned to Laurent and quietly remarked, '*Ah, être jeune et amoureux!*'

Connor noticed Amber's brow wrinkle and Henri giggle. A moment later the translation came through on his earpiece. 'Ah, to be young and in love!'

Connor decided to play it cool and not correct him. It was to his advantage that the president had got the wrong impression, for it would allow him to remain close to Amber without arousing any suspicion as to his true role.

One by one, they were introduced to the welcoming party.

First of all there was Michel Feruzi, the Minister for Trade and Tourism, whose ample bulk rivalled a hippo in size. Despite being born and bred in Burundi, the heat appeared to affect him too, for he continually mopped his moist brow with a handkerchief. His wife was also on the large side, but she carried herself with remarkable grace and style, her vibrant purple robes only seeming to enhance her imposing presence.

Next was Uzair Mossi, the Finance Minister, an older man whose tight-knit hair was peppered grey but whose eyes still sparkled with youth. His surprisingly young wife, a tall willowy woman with eyes as black as onyx and long braids down her back, stood in stark contrast to Mrs Feruzi.

Finally they were introduced to Adrien Rawasa and his wife. The Minister for Energy and Mines was a softly spoken man with a light handshake and an expensive taste in cologne, a fine French musk perfuming the air around him. His wife, Constance, was more forthcoming, embracing the children and presenting Cerise with a gift of a hand-woven basket and a beaded necklace.

'Now, Ambassador Barbier, please allow me to give you and your family a tour of the lodge,' said President Bagaza. 'I want to show you how magnificent this project is. You're our first guests here!'

President Bagaza led the way into a lavishly appointed lounge and bar area. Timber-framed and thatch-roofed, the expansive room was furnished with plush sofas, leather-backed armchairs and a red velvet chaise longue beside a stone fireplace. Floor-to-ceiling glass doors opened out on to a sun deck. In one corner was a wooden tribal mask and in another a handcrafted ivory chessboard. Stretching the entire length of the rear wall was a polished mahogany bar, behind which stood a smartly attired barman putting the final touches to a round of welcoming drinks. And laid out in the centre of the parquet floor was a zebra-skin rug, which Connor noticed Amber sidestep while everyone else strode across with barely a second thought.

'This is a *five-star* luxury lodge,' stated President Bagaza with a proud sweep of his arm at the furnishings. 'But I can't lay claim to its construction. That was overseen by Minister Feruzi here.'

The president indicated for the Minister for Trade and Tourism to take over.

The minister coughed into his fleshy fist before beginning

his spiel. 'The lodge features eight glass-fronted, air-conditioned suites, each with private plunge pool and spectacular views over the Ruvubu Valley. In addition to this lounge, there's a library, a gymnasium and a smoking room, for those less inclined to exercise.'

He patted his ample stomach and a ripple of laughter spread among the gathered party. A second later, once the translation app had caught up, Connor joined in. As the minister continued with his speech, two waiters handed out glasses of iced mint lemonade.

'Along with this cocktail bar, the lodge is blessed with a fully stocked wine cellar and the dining room offers the finest in cordon bleu cooking from a world-class chef. Trust me on this – I've sampled it myself.'

There was another ripple of polite laughter.

'And, rest assured, the service for guests will be uninterrupted throughout your stay. The lodge has its own electricity generator and I can guarantee no problems with your phones since a mobile mast has been installed. The lodge even has wireless internet access!'

'We might just move in here permanently,' commented Minister Mossi in a half-whisper to his young wife.

'Guests will be spoilt by the highest standards of comfort,' went on Minister Feruzi, 'and combined with superb game-viewing opportunities, overseen by only the most experienced rangers, this resort promises to deliver the safari experience of a lifetime!'

Minister Feruzi gave an affected bow to indicate his speech was over and was rewarded with gracious applause.

'I must say it's very impressive,' remarked Laurent, eyeing the sumptuous luxury surrounding them. 'Has *all* of France's aid gone into developing this lodge?'

The minister gave a hearty laugh, his jowls wobbling slightly. 'No, I can assure you it hasn't, we –'

'Wow, are these *real*?' exclaimed Henri, drifting away from the main group as he tired of the speech. He was pointing to a wall display of a leopard-skin shield and two crossed spears with broad-bladed iron tips.

'Not only real,' answered Minister Mossi, joining him by the display, 'but once used by the local chief of a Hutu tribe to kill a lion.'

Henri stared in wonder at the fearsome weapons.

'Do you want to hold one?' asked the minister.

The ambassador's son nodded eagerly.

'Do you kill everything here?' asked Amber, looking up in dismay at the stuffed head of an antelope on the opposite wall.

Her father shot her a warning look. But Minister Mossi just smiled as Henri brandished the spear. 'This is Africa. In the past, killing a lion was a symbol of manhood. But now –' he shrugged, taking the spear back from Henri – 'attitudes have changed.'

'They most certainly have, Amber. And for the better,' assured President Bagaza. 'This project is all about conservation. The park has been revitalized, thanks to France's aid. We've reintroduced lion, elephant, rhino and many other species – all of which you'll spot on the game drives we have planned for you. But why not see for yourself now?'

The president ushered Amber and the rest of the party through a set of bay doors on to the open-air veranda. There they were greeted by a spectacular view across the Ruvubu Valley. The African bush was spread out like a gilded blanket in the mid-afternoon sun. A natural waterhole nestled at the base of the slope in which a hippo wallowed. At the water's edge, several long-horned oryx drank their fill beside a group of fawn-coloured gazelles. A kingfisher flitted among them, catching insects and dragonflies. Approaching the waterhole from the south was an elephant and her calf, and beyond was an abundance of zebra, wildebeest and buffalo. The scene was like a privileged peek into the Garden of Eden.

Amber was left speechless.

'This is no longer a "paper park", Ambassador,' declared the president. 'The land has been returned to the wild. No human habitation at all.'

'And, with your country's continued support, we intend to establish this as a prime tourist destination,' asserted Minister Feruzi, 'as well as deliver the discussed conservation and development objectives, of course.'

'This is truly magnificent,' agreed the ambassador, shaking hands with the president and all the ministers. 'The French government will be most pleased with the progress that's been made. Burundi will certainly take its place on the map for this.'

The breathtaking beauty of the location had made Connor almost forget why he was there in the first place. Rather than admiring the view, he should have been assessing it from a security perspective. In such a remote and unfamiliar location he needed to be vigilant for all danger, whether from man or beast.

'Can't the animals just wander in?' Connor enquired, unable to spot any obvious protective measures in place.

Minister Feruzi shook his bowling ball of a head. In fluent English he replied, 'The lodge is surrounded by an unobtrusive electric fence. It does not spoil the view, but it is effective enough to keep any dangerous animals at bay.' He switched back to French. 'So you won't be needing that spear, Henri,' he said with a wink at the boy.

Trying to make out the fence line, Connor spied movement in a clump of bushes. A soldier in combat fatigues appeared, an assault rifle over his shoulder.

'Who's that over there?' asked Connor, his alert level shooting up as he instinctively moved closer to Amber and Henri.

'One of the presidential guard,' replied Minister Mossi. 'No need to be alarmed. They'll be patrolling the area around the lodge, day and night. You'll barely notice them.'

President Bagaza offered his guests a reassuring smile. 'I'm so used to their presence that I no longer even see them! Now please take your time to unpack and freshen up. This evening we're celebrating your esteemed arrival with a Boma dinner.'

CHAPTER 15

Connor laid out the contents of his Go-bag on the king-size bed of his suite. In the rush to prepare for his mission, he hadn't had the chance to double-check his gear. On the flight over, he'd read in the *SAS Survival Handbook* that one's kit could make the difference between success and failure – even life and death.

Usually Amir would set him up with all the necessary equipment he might need for a particular operation. But Connor hadn't even had the opportunity to contact his friend, let alone inform him he would no longer be providing support. He just hoped that Amir had overcome his initial bout of nerves. Charley was acting as base contact for both of them now. Nevertheless, Connor couldn't help feeling he was letting his friend down by not being there for him.

It had fallen to Bugsy to supply Connor with his gear and, by the looks of it, his surveillance instructor had done a thorough job. He was equipped with a comprehensive first-aid kit, including emergency antibiotics, syringes and sterile needles – vital in a country with almost non-existent medical facilities. There were spare malaria tablets, sun lotion and DEET insect repellent. He had his sunglasses from his previous assignment – essential for daytime, but equally useful at night due to the layer of nano-photonic film that converted infra-red light to visible, enabling him to see in the dark. He also had a Maglite with spare batteries, a portable solar charger for his smartphone and a pair of high-powered compact binoculars. Among his clothes, Bugsy had supplied a stab-proof short-sleeved shirt, cargo trousers and a baseball cap with integrated neck shade. But the standard-issue bulletproof jacket would simply be too hot to wear in this climate. He'd have to rely on the Go-bag's internal body-armour panel for protection against any gun attack.

The most intriguing item of kit was a slim blue tube with a drinking nozzle at one end. A 'Lifestraw' Bugsy had called it. The device instantly turned muddy puddles into clean drinking water simply by sucking through the tube. With a distinct lack of sanitation in Burundi, the last thing Connor needed as a bodyguard was to come down with diarrhoea. Small enough to fit in his pocket, the Lifestraw, Bugsy had assured him, removed 99.9 per cent of water-borne bacteria and could filter a thousand litres, enough for one person for an entire year.

'Unusual kit for a holiday,' said a gravelly accented voice in English.

Connor spun to see a stocky man in a khaki shirt and knee-length shorts standing at his open doorway. He wore desert boots and a wide-brimmed safari hat. His suntanned face was rugged, furnished with a goatee beard, and deeply lined from a life spent outdoors.

'I'm Joseph Gunner,' said the man, entering the room and extending his hand in greeting. 'But you can just call me Gunner. I'm your park ranger.'

'Hi, I'm Connor.'

'You're British!' he remarked, somewhat surprised and, judging by the extra squeeze in his handshake, pleased at the discovery.

Connor nodded. 'Where are you from? You don't sound or look like you're from Burundi.'

'South Africa, born and bred,' he replied with a hint of pride. 'Used to work in Kruger National Park until I was offered this opportunity.' He cast his eye over the gear spread across the bed. 'You're more prepared than most tourists. What are you, a boy scout?'

'Sort of,' admitted Connor, beginning to repack.

The ranger pointed to the knife. 'Do you mind?' he asked, picking it up.

Connor shook his head. 'It was my father's.'

Gunner examined it. 'Well, he's a man who knows his knives. Solid wooden handle. Full tang.' Eyeing the blade, he carefully ran a finger along its edge before grunting in satisfaction. 'There's a saying in bushcraft: *You're only as sharp as your knife.* Glad to see you've kept this one well honed.'

Resheathing the blade, he handed it back to Connor, who felt oddly gratified that his father's heirloom was held in such high regard.

'Always important to carry a good knife in the bush,' Gunner explained, tapping an impressively large hunter's knife on his hip. The ranger picked up the SAS handbook lying on the bed and leafed through the pages. 'You interested in survival skills then?'

Connor nodded. 'More than you might believe.'

Gunner smiled. 'Well, you've certainly come to the right place to test them out.'

CHAPTER 16

No Mercy stood guard on an outcrop of rock overlooking the hidden valley. Below, men worked like ants, digging at the earth with shovels and their bare hands. Like layers of peeling skin, the green vegetation was stripped back to expose rocks and mud and hopefully diamonds. Other press-ganged workers panned the sediment of the dammed river for the precious stones. They toiled in grim silence, their clothes mud-stained and drenched in sweat.

Keeping a watchful eye over their labours, General Pascal's army of child soldiers stood with their guns lazily trained on the men who were all old enough to be their fathers. Not that any of them thought they needed fathers now they were warriors of the ANL. No Mercy dimly recalled he'd once had a father, but the general had shown him the weakness of such men. His father had failed to protect his family – slaughtered at the hands of a rival rebel group. And now they were all gone No Mercy only had himself to fend for and he wouldn't be as feeble as his father. The general had taught him the power of the gun. And led him on to the righteous path of glory.

No Mercy heard a whoop and saw one man stand up, his arm raised high.

General Pascal, reclining in a plastic deckchair beneath the shade of a palm tree and sipping from a water bottle, beckoned the worker over. The man handed the general his find. Closing one eye, General Pascal held the rock up to the sparkling sunlight and inspected the stone. Even from where No Mercy stood, he could see the reflected gleam and the grin spread across the general's pockmarked face.

Another diamond had been found.

General Pascal waved the worker away, no longer interested, and the man trudged to the makeshift workers' camp, little more than some pieces of tarpaulin strung between the trees. For his valuable find, he'd been rewarded with an hour's extra rest and a double ration of food.

No Mercy, impelled by the call of nature, left his lookout point and found a suitable clump of bushes. Resting his AK47 against a tree, he pulled down his trousers and squatted. As he wiped himself with a leaf, he heard a rustle in the bushes. No Mercy stayed very quiet. This was leopard country, after all.

Silently pulling up his trousers, he listened to the noise drawing ever closer. Then he spied movement and the olive-green uniform of a park ranger materialized out of the bush. The ranger, shouldering a backpack and carrying a rifle, approached the outcrop. The sight of the open-cast mine in the valley below stopped him in his tracks.

Cautiously the ranger backed away from the edge. From his hip he pulled out a two-way radio. Only as he went to switch it on did he spot No Mercy crouching in the bush. For a moment, they both stared at one another, neither knowing who was hunter and who was prey.

The ranger offered a tentative smile and put a finger to his lips. No Mercy nodded in obedience.

Reassured, the ranger whispered into the radio's mic, '*Echo 1 to Echo 2, over.*'

The radio crackled. No Mercy stood, revealing his combat fatigues and the AK47 in his grip. The ranger's expression went from shock to horror as No Mercy depressed the trigger. Bullets ripped into the ranger's body and he fell to the ground, dead.

The radio, still clasped in the ranger's hand, burst into life. '*Echo 2 to Echo 1. I hear gunfire. Are you OK? Over.*'

No Mercy stood beside the twitching body of the ranger, watching the blood flow over the edge of the outcrop. He felt no emotion having killed the man. No guilt. No thrill. Nothing. Just an enveloping numbness. Above the dull ringing in his ears, caused by the thunderous roar of the AK47, he heard something crashing through the undergrowth. He spun to see another ranger appear. Without a second's thought, he shot this man too.

The ranger collapsed in a heap. But he wasn't dead – not yet. He made wet choking sounds as he gasped for breath. No Mercy approached, gun in hand, barrel still emitting a wisp of smoke.

'P-please . . . have m-mercy,' begged the ranger, holding up a trembling hand in surrender, his eyes full of fear.

'That's not how I got my name,' No Mercy replied, planting the barrel on the man's forehead.

'Hold your fire!' ordered General Pascal, appearing with a unit of soldiers.

The boy backed down, not caring whether the man lived or died. He'd done his duty and kept the valley guarded.

General Pascal knelt beside the dying man. 'I'm sorry, my friend. My soldier is trigger-happy. There has been a grave misunderstanding.'

The ranger nodded, his fingers slick with blood where they clasped at his chest wound.

The general unclipped the man's radio from his hip. 'Tell me, where are the other rangers so I can contact them for medical help?'

The ranger shook his head feebly. 'No more in this . . . sector,' he wheezed.

'No! Then what are you doing here?'

'Looking for . . . poachers.'

'There are no poachers here,' assured General Pascal, then his expression hardened. 'What are you *really* looking for?'

The ranger's glassy eyes squinted in puzzlement before widening in sheer agony as the general drove the radio's aerial into the open wound. He let out a tortured scream.

'Who sent you?' demanded the general, twisting the radio.

'The president . . .' gasped the ranger, 'at the safari lodge.'

'Really?' said the general, brightening at the news.

Discarding the blood-smeared radio, he rose to his feet and clamped a hand on No Mercy's shoulder. 'Excellent work, my young warrior.' He took off his red beret and fitted it on the boy's head. 'Consider yourself promoted to captain.'

No Mercy felt a burst of pride.

'Now take this ranger to the river.'

No Mercy's brow furrowed in confusion. 'You want me to let him go?'

'In a manner of speaking. Yes. The crocodiles are hungry!'

CHAPTER 17

'See anything?' asked Henri eagerly.

Connor lowered his binoculars. After prepping his Go-bag for the safari drive the next day and sending a message to Charley to confirm their safe arrival, he'd set off on a security sweep of the lodge. He needed to know the building's layout and where his Principals and the other guests resided. He also had to familiarize himself with the surrounding grounds. Pinpoint where the entrance and exit points were. What access roads the park had. Establish routes out in case they needed to make a quick escape. Identify any areas vulnerable to attack or infiltration. And determine what security measures, if any, were in place.

Henri had joined him on this task, thinking Connor was looking for lions and other big game. Amber had still been unpacking and said she'd join them later at the swimming pool.

'Not yet,' replied Connor, passing Henri the binoculars to have a look for himself.

So far what Connor had seen hadn't given him any reassurance. The lodge was the perfect setting for a holiday but a nightmare in terms of close protection. While their location on the ridge offered unbroken views of the valley and its wildlife, it also meant they were open and exposed. A potential enemy could approach from any direction. And the advantage gained from being able to spot someone a mile off was lost due to the cover provided by the long grasses and clumps of bush carpeting the landscape.

The lodge itself possessed no perimeter alarm system. Nor did it have CCTV. The bedrooms weren't even equipped with fire alarms. And the luxury of the glass-fronted suites was a major liability when it came to providing a safe barrier for his Principals in their rooms – a single gunshot would shatter the entire wall. Connor had inspected the door locks on his own suite and discovered they were flimsy. One hard kick and an intruder could break in with little problem.

The only fixed security measure Connor could identify was the electric fence – a substandard three-wire barrier that encircled the lodge – or at least partly did. He'd already spotted two sections that had fallen flat, stretching the wires to breaking point. He would have to inform Gunner of this and hope they were fixed quickly.

There were park rangers around, monitoring for intrusion by wild animals. But his key concern was the presidential guard. This should have been their primary ring of defence. Yet the unit of soldiers patrolling the grounds appeared relaxed to the point of negligence. Some were chatting and smoking in small groups, others strolled wearily from one patch of shade to the next, while at least two guards were fast asleep at their posts. Maybe it was the heat, or the lack of obvious threat in such a remote location, but the presidential guard didn't appear to be guarding anything or anyone.

'They're barely in Code White,' Connor muttered to himself.

'Code what?' asked Henri, still scanning the bush for game.

'Code White. It refers to a person's level of awareness.' He indicated a soldier near the electric fence, picking his teeth with a twig. 'See him? He's totally switched off. If someone attacked now, he'd go into shock before being able to react.'

Lowering the binoculars, Henri stared at Connor with a mixture of alarm and delight. 'Are we going to be attacked?'

'No, very unlikely,' replied Connor. 'But, as a bodyguard, you can't allow yourself to walk around like a zombie. You have to be alert at all times – Code Yellow, we call it. When a possible threat is spotted you enter Code Orange – a focused state of mind for making crucial decisions, such as wait, run or fight. And if the threat becomes real, then you hit Code Red – basically "action stations". But the main thing is you're in control at all times.'

Nodding earnestly, Henri began to scan the horizon with renewed intent. 'So if I see something I should tell you.'

'Yes, but I think you can relax,' said Connor, taking back his binoculars. 'The likelihood of an armed assault is low. The main threats are going to be from an accidental injury or wild animals.'

'Like those monkeys?' suggested Henri, pointing behind Connor to a cluster of giant boulders that marked the top of the ridge.

Turning, Connor saw a troop of large dog-faced monkeys atop a huge rock. 'I think they're baboons,' he said, before spotting Amber clinging on to a boulder a few metres below the animals. 'What's your sister up to?'

The outcrop of rocks was clearly beyond the safety of the electric fence's perimeter and he immediately set off towards her. Protecting two Principals at once was always going to be a challenge. But his task wouldn't be made any easier if one of them was a wayward thrill-seeker. Crawling under the wire, Connor hurried over, Henri following behind.

'What are you doing beyond the fence?' Connor demanded as Amber effortlessly traversed the rock face. Her hair, red as the African soil, swung free in a long ponytail as she leant back to assess her route.

'Bouldering,' she replied, nimbly switching from one handhold to another.

'Next time, can you tell me if you're going to wander off?'

'Why?'

'It could be dangerous.' Connor glanced up at the baboons. They were now making cough-like barks while the younger ones scampered from rock to rock excitedly.

'They're only baboons,' she said, hanging from a pocket in the rock by the tips of her fingers.

For such a slender girl, Connor was stunned at her strength. He didn't reckon even the super-tough Ling could manage such a feat.

'You look like a monkey!' cried Henri, jumping up and down, scratching his armpits and whooping.

'And you're just as annoying as one,' she muttered. 'Can't you go lion hunting or something?'

As Amber worked her way across to the next boulder, one of the male baboons grunted and bared his large yellow teeth.

'I don't think that one's too happy about where you're climbing,' Connor remarked.

'Why should I worry?' replied Amber. 'I've got you to look out for me.'

'That's what I'm *trying* to do.'

'Connor's right. You need to be careful, Amber.' Gunner had suddenly appeared behind them. Despite his anti-surveillance training, Connor hadn't even heard the ranger's footsteps. This was the second time Gunner had crept up without Connor being aware of his presence.

'Baboons can be highly aggressive if their territory is threatened,' explained the ranger.

Glancing over her shoulder, Amber smiled an apology. 'I just needed some exercise after the long flight.'

'Understandable . . . but I wouldn't go for that hand-hold, if I were you,' advised Gunner.

Amber frowned. 'Why not? Are you a climber?'

'No,' said Gunner, picking up a long stick and prodding the crack next to Amber's right hand.

A brown scorpion scuttled out. Amber yelped and dropped to the ground.

'Tempting as it is to go exploring, always bear in mind this is Africa,' said Gunner, leading them away from the baboons. 'Wild country with wild animals. Just a few steps from the cosy confines of your suite, there's a whole host of hidden dangers.'

He lifted up a nearby rock with his boot. A snake slithered out, hissing loudly. Connor swore out loud in shock and leapt aside as the snake disappeared into the long grass.

Amber barely suppressed a smirk. 'Hey, you're white as a sheet. And I thought you were supposed to be a tough guy!'

'I don't like snakes, that's all,' Connor replied, his mouth dry with fear. He'd had a phobia ever since an adder had crawled into his sleeping bag on a camping trip with his father and bitten him. He still had nightmares about it.

'Don't fret, Connor. It's just a hissing sand snake. Not poisonous,' Gunner explained.

Connor nervously eyed the grass around his feet. 'Looked pretty deadly to me.'

Gunner shook his head. 'Nah, the ones you really have to watch out for are black mambas. Easy to identify by their coffin-shaped head and black mouth. Not only the fastest snake in the world but also one of the most aggressive and poisonous. A black mamba is capable of killing an adult human in as little as twenty minutes. That's why its bite has been called the kiss of death.'

'Boys have said that about my sister too!' sniggered Henri.

Amber scowled at him.

'Joking aside, little man, the black mamba is the most dangerous snake in Africa,' Gunner cautioned. 'Believe me, you do *not* want to meet one of those in the bush.'

Enclosed within a ring of dry reed walls, the Boma possessed a magical, almost timeless air. Bleached skulls of
antelope and wildebeest marked the entrance. The hard-
packed red earth appeared flattened by the tread of
generation upon generation of Africans. And at the heart
of the enclosure was a blazing bonfire that crackled and
spat orange sparks like fireflies into the glittering starlit
night.

Spellbound by the scene, Amber, Henri and Connor sat
at one of the simple wooden tables that had been arranged
in a semi-circle round the ceremonial fire. The only sound
in the night, aside from the pop and crack of burning logs,
was the ceaseless drone of cicadas. As the insects sang on,
waiters appeared with a variety of local delicacies from
red-bean stew to sweet potatoes to *ugali*, a traditional dish
made out of maize. These proved to be merely side dishes
to a feast of impala, kudu and other exotic bush meats.
President Bagaza invited everyone to begin and, as the
drinks flowed among the adults, so did the conversation.

'Are you following any of this?' asked Amber in English.

'Some of it,' Connor replied. He pointed to his smartphone on the table. 'Translation app.'

'And I thought you were being spared the pain!' She laughed and peered at the device, impressed. Leaning closer to him, she lowered her voice. 'I can't wait to go on safari tomorrow and get away from the adults and all this dull diplomatic talk. But let's see if we can – how do you say in English? – set the cat among the pigeons!'

With an impish curl to the corner of her lips, Amber had turned to the Minister for Trade and Tourism, who was discussing the expansion plans for the park with her father. 'Tell me, what happened to the people who lived in the park before?' she interrupted in French.

Her father stiffened at the brazen question. Minister Feruzi smiled graciously, although his eyes turned flinty in the flickering firelight. 'They've been given lovely new homes on the park's border, with a school and freshwater wells. Much aid has been invested in the local communities, who will of course benefit directly from the tourism this lodge will attract – *this is typical food, Cerise – besides pottery, basket-weaving is a very popular craft among Burundian artisans –* '

Connor tapped at his earpiece. The translation app seemed to be struggling with the multiple conversations happening around the Boma. The microphone kept honing in on different people. He fiddled with the settings on the app, switching the mic's sensitivity from omnidirectional to 'shotgun', enabling him to isolate a single conversation. As he adjusted his smartphone's position on the table to listen to Amber's increasingly heated debate with Minister Feruzi, Connor caught a line of untranslated language through his earpiece. His phone flashed a message and the app automatically switched from French to Kurundi.

'. . . do you believe Black Mamba's back?'

Connor glanced up and saw Minister Rawasa whispering to the grey-haired Minister Mossi on the opposite side of the Boma.

'Of course not,' snorted Minister Mossi. 'I have it on good authority he died in the Congo.'

'But what if he didn't? He's the devil incarnate. More poisonous to our countrymen than a real black mamba! His return could trigger another civil war –'

'I tell you, he is dead.'

'I've heard it said, no one can kill the Black Mamba –'

Out of the darkness a thunderous beat of drums burst forth, drowning out any further conversation. A line of men clad in white, red and green robes marched into the Boma, balancing large drums on their heads. Chanting, they set their instruments down in a semi-circle round one central player. Then, to the heavy tribal rhythm, the lead drummer came forward and leapt impossibly high into the air. Whooping and waving his sticks, the man danced as if possessed.

The earth-shuddering beat of multiple drums thrummed in Connor's gut. He'd never experienced such a wall of sound. Another drummer entered the arena and took over the dance. He backflipped into the air, landing with perfect precision and timing. The performance was utterly awe-inspiring as each drummer took their turn in the centre. Then, lifting their drums back on to their heads, the procession disappeared into the night, the pounding of drums fading like a receding thunderstorm.

President Bagaza stood and clapped the performers, everyone else following his lead. When the applause had faded, he said, 'Those were the Royal Drummers of Burundi. What distinguishes their music from other African music is that the movement of the dancers dictates the rhythm of the drummers, rather than the other way round. This is another example, Ambassador Barbier, of what makes Burundi unique among African nations. And we *will* beat to a different drum.' He raised his glass in a toast: 'May Burundi prosper!'

'May Burundi prosper!' repeated everyone, raising their glasses.

With the performance over, the conversations returned to the previous topics.

'So can we go and see this new village you built?' Amber asked Minister Feruzi.

The minister frowned as if irritated, then smiled. 'Of course,' he replied, 'but it'll have to be on another visit.'

'Why?'

'I think you've interrogated the minister enough, Amber,' her father interrupted, laying a pacifying hand over hers as he noticed Minister Feruzi's frown return.

Amber pulled her hand away. 'But I want to meet the people that this park displaced.'

'Amber, I realize you're idealistic,' said her father under

his breath. 'But you can't conserve nature without a certain amount of sacrifice.'

'But –'

'Enough,' warned her father. 'I think it's time you went back to your room.'

Amber's jaw tightened but she held her tongue. Rising from her seat, she strode out of the Boma.

'Can I stay a bit longer?' asked Henri.

'Of course,' replied his mother with a smile as Connor got to his feet.

'I'll just make sure Amber gets back to her room safely,' he explained.

Leaving Henri with his parents, Connor stepped from the flickering orange glow of the Boma into the almost pitch-black of the night. Only a trail of candles lit the path back to the lodge.

Halfway along, he caught up with Amber. She stopped and stared at him. 'Why are you following me?'

'I'm escorting you back to your room,' replied Connor.

Amber fixed him with a look that said otherwise. 'I realize you're here to protect us, but I can look after myself, thank you. And *I'm* not scared of snakes.'

Connor felt that remark bite. 'Listen, I've trained for over a year in unarmed combat, defensive driving, anti-surveillance, body cover drills –'

'Body cover?'

'Yes, using my body to shield you in an attack.'

'Is that your intention with me?' she said, crossing her arms and tilting her head slightly.

'Yes . . . no!' protested Connor, flushing slightly as he realized her double meaning. 'Look, I'm just trying to do my job.'

'So, tell me, how many have you protected before us?'

Connor replied, 'This is my third assignment.'

Amber pouted in disappointment. 'Not many then.'

'Well, they're all still alive!' retorted Connor. He took a breath to calm himself. 'Listen, I think we've got off on the wrong foot. I'm not here to stop you doing things. I'm here to keep you safe.'

'From what?' Amber asked, indicating the tranquil night. 'Mosquitoes? It's a mystery to me why my father even employed you. I simply don't need a boy looking after me. If you want to be useful, protect my brother and keep him away from me. Now, goodnight.'

He watched her stride off into the darkness.

'Women, eh?' snorted Gunner, coming up from behind and shrugging in sympathy. 'As wild and unpredictable as Africa –' he winked at Connor – 'and just as captivating.'

'Those drummers were awesome!' exclaimed Henri, beating at the night air with his fists as Connor led him up the path, the boy's parents having joined President Bagaza and his ministers for a nightcap on the lodge's main veranda.

'I mean, how high could they leap!' Henri jumped into the darkness.

Connor grabbed him before he stumbled into a thorn bush. 'Careful, Henri, remember what Gunner said. Stick to the path, there might be snakes.'

'O . . . K,' he wheezed.

'Are you all right?' Connor asked, hearing the slight whistle to the boy's breath.

'*Fine*,' replied Henri, pulling an inhaler from his pocket and taking a puff. After ten seconds he breathed out, his lungs already sounding clearer. 'Just a bit of asthma.'

Connor slowed his pace up the hill. From where he was, he could see the light on in Amber's suite. She'd drawn the curtains and her shadow flittered across them.

Connor turned to Henri. 'Is your sister always so . . .'

He tried to think of the most diplomatic word. 'Head-strong?'

Henri nodded, sighing in recognition. 'And grouchy. Even more so since her boyfriend dumped her last week, for her best friend . . . by text message!'

'That sounds harsh,' Connor remarked.

Henri shrugged. 'Yeah, well, Maurice was an idiot. I think she's most upset about her friend betraying her, though. She cried a lot about that.'

'That's understandable,' said Connor. He walked Henri to his room. 'See you at dawn for the safari.'

Yawning, Henri nodded. 'I hope we spot lions tomorrow,' he murmured before disappearing inside.

Heading back to his own room, Connor opened the glass door to the private deck and sat in a lounger. He gazed up at the blanket of stars overhead. Never had he seen so many in his life. The night was so clear they truly sparkled like diamonds in the sky.

He glanced over at Amber's suite. The lights were still on, but there was no movement. At least her recent heartbreak explained her frostiness, thought Connor. She'd probably had enough of boys for the time being. And if she knew of her father's past affair, she likely had a trust issue too – especially following the betrayal of her best friend. Connor decided to cut Amber a bit of slack. He'd give her some space. As long as he knew where she was and she didn't wander beyond the lodge's grounds, he could legitimately protect her.

Pulling out his phone, Connor dialled Buddyguard HQ

to check in for the night. Charley answered within two rings.

After going through formal call-in protocol, she asked, 'How are the Cubs settling in?'

Prior to any mission, call signs and code words were agreed, since it was always assumed that radio communications could be easily intercepted and no network was a hundred per cent secure. So Amber and Henri had been assigned the call signs Cub One and Cub Two.

'As well as can be expected,' Connor replied. 'The youngest has accepted its new brother; the older one is a little more resistant.'

'What about the Nest?' enquired Charley.

Connor delivered his assessment of the lodge's lax security situation, being careful not to reveal anything too specific that might identify the location.

'Not ideal,' she agreed. 'But there aren't any storms on the horizon so you should be OK. Have you anything else to report?'

'I've heard talk about the Black Mamba coming back. Any idea who this might be?'

'Not off the top of my head, sorry. I'll look into it and get back to you.'

'Thanks,' said Connor. 'It might be nothing, but a couple of the ministers here seemed concerned. How's the bird-watching going, by the way?' he asked, subtly referring to Amir and Operation Hawk-Eye.

Charley lowered her voice as if she didn't want anyone else at HQ to hear. 'It's having its ups and downs, but don't worry – our friend hasn't had his wings clipped yet. Tell me, how's your luxury suite?'

'Pretty shabby,' Connor replied, reclining further back in his padded lounger. 'There are only two showers, and the private plunge pool isn't that big.'

'Sounds *horrible*.'

'Yeah, but I'll survive.'

'We're counting on it,' said Charley warmly. 'Listen, I have to go. Stay safe.'

She signed off. Connor sighed contentedly and returned to gazing at the stars. He always felt better after talking with Charley. More grounded. Talking through the mission helped him put it in perspective. While the security arrangements were less than perfect, the remote location reduced the risk of direct threats. He thought that he might even be able to relax enough to enjoy the safari tomorrow morning. Connor pocketed the phone and closed his eyes . . . A second later they flew open as a piercing scream shattered the peace of the night.

CHAPTER 20

Connor catapulted himself off the lounger and leapt from the decking. Pushing through the privacy barrier of bushes, he scrambled on to the neighbouring deck. The scream had come from within Amber's suite. It sounded as if she was being attacked, but the curtains obscured whatever was going on inside.

He yanked at the glass door. Locked. He heard another desperate cry. Connor sprinted round to the front. The main door was also bolted. Taking a step back, he front-kicked it with all his might. The lock gave way and he burst into the room. Amber wasn't anywhere to be seen. Connor's first thought was that she'd been kidnapped. Then another scream erupted from the bathroom.

Throwing open the door, Connor found Amber standing in the middle of the tiled floor, wrapped in a towel, shaking her head furiously.

'Get it off me! Get it off me!'

'What?' said Connor, looking round the room for the threat.

'The spider!'

Connor felt a surge of relief. He'd thought it was something deadly serious.

'Hold still,' he instructed, grabbing her by the shoulders and searching her damp locks of hair for the intruder. When he saw it, he jerked away. No wonder Amber was screaming – the spider's body was the size of a golf ball. Dark brown with spindly hairy legs and two prominent fangs, it was fearsome enough to give anyone a heart attack.

Connor grabbed Amber's hairbrush from the shelf and batted the spider off before it could sink its fangs into her. The creature scuttled across the tiles at a horrific speed. Amber yelped again and leapt into the bath for safety.

Gunner ran in. 'What's going on?' demanded the ranger, looking between Connor and Amber, still dripping wet from her shower.

'Spider,' explained Connor, pointing to the creature now scurrying up the wall.

Gunner eyed it, whipped off his hat and plonked it over the offending arachnid.

'Just a rain spider. Nothing to worry about,' he said, picking up a magazine and trapping it inside his hat. 'Relatively harmless. They hunt at night and sleep during the day. They can bite, but their venom's no more dangerous than a bee sting . . .' He glanced at Amber, trembling in the bathtub. 'Granted, though, they look bloody terrifying.'

Amber nodded mutely, her eyes not leaving Gunner's hat for a second.

'It's the small black-button spiders with red underbellies you need to avoid like the plague,' warned the ranger, checking the bathroom for any other creepy-crawlies. 'They have one of the most toxic venoms produced in nature, fifteen times stronger than a rattlesnake's. You'll probably know them as black widow spiders –' He was interrupted by two soldiers from the presidential guard appearing at the door.

Better late than never, thought Connor.

'False alarm,' said Gunner to the soldiers, and they wandered back outside, muttering to themselves.

Gunner held up his hat cheerily. 'Well, Amber, that's your official welcome to Africa. All clear now.'

He headed for the main door and spotted the damaged lock. 'I'll have someone fix that tomorrow. Oh, and remember to shake out your boots before putting them on in the morning. You don't want any other nasty shocks.'

He disappeared into the night to release the eight-legged intruder.

Connor turned to Amber. 'Will you be all right?'

Quickly recovering her composure now the spider was gone, she pulled her towel closer around her and shooed him out of the bathroom. 'Yes, absolutely.'

There was a flush to her cheeks and she wouldn't quite meet his eye. But, as she closed the door on him, she smiled shyly. 'At least you're tough enough to fight off spiders.'

CHAPTER 21

Dawn had barely broken and the sun, low on the horizon, cast a golden sheen across the wakening savannah. A few zebra glanced up from their early-morning grazing as the convoy of Land Rovers bumped their way along the dirt track, sending up clouds of dust into the warm, still air.

In the lead vehicle Connor sat next to Henri, who was fidgeting with excitement, his head darting left and right like a meerkat's as he searched for animals. Stifling a yawn from the impossibly early start, Amber steadied herself in the front seat beside Gunner, who was at the wheel. Although there was ample space, Laurent and Cerise had elected to go in the second vehicle to give their children the freedom to enjoy the safari alone. The other four Land Rovers transported the president, his ministers, their wives and a detachment of the presidential guard.

Perched on the bonnet seat of Connor's vehicle was their tracker, Buju, a quiet man with soulful eyes and a shy smile. Upon introduction, Gunner had spoken for him, explaining that Buju had grown up in the Ruvubu Valley, lived off the land by hunting and gathering, and that he knew every gully, waterway and crevice of the national park like the back of his hand. Buju would be their eyes and ears on the safari.

From the man's watchful gaze and calm, almost still, presence, Buju appeared very attuned to his environment and Connor realized it would be hard for any predator to sneak up on them without their tracker noticing. Yet, despite this assurance, Connor didn't allow himself to lower his own guard. Although it was good to have another pair of eyes on the lookout for danger, his Principals' safety ultimately lay with him.

Buju held up his hand and the safari convoy came to a halt. Gunner killed the engine. Behind, the other five drivers did the same and the rumbling of motors ceased, to be replaced by a chorus of birdsong, buzzing insects and the occasional braying of zebra. The soundtrack of Africa. Then in the distance they heard a haunting *whoop-whoop*.

'Hyenas,' Gunner explained under his breath. 'A long way off, probably in those hills.' He indicated a far ridge, crowned by the rising sun.

'So why have we stopped?' asked Henri.

Gunner put a finger to his lips to silence him as Buju pointed to a clump of thorn bushes some twenty metres ahead. Amber craned her neck to see what the tracker had spotted, her camera at the ready.

'What is it?' whispered Henri, kneeling up in his seat.

Amber shook her head and shrugged. Then out from behind the thicket emerged a creature as grey as slate with an immense barrel body and stumpy legs, its sloping neck and low-slung head finishing in a large, pointed double horn. Like a creature straight out of *Jurassic Park*, the rhino appeared truly prehistoric. It tramped into the middle of the dirt track and stopped, suddenly sensing them.

Connor, Amber and Henri stared in awestruck silence.

Gunner kept his voice to barely above a whisper. 'You're very fortunate to see a black rhino in the wild. Their species have been driven to the point of extinction. Less than five thousand left in the whole of Africa.'

The rhino stood stock-still, only its ears twitching, then it swung its head towards them, snorting at the air.

'Rhinos have poor eyesight but an excellent sense of smell and hearing,' continued Gunner as Amber began shooting away with her camera. He pointed to a small red-billed bird on the animal's back. 'That's an oxpecker. It was thought they removed ticks and insects for the benefit of the rhino, as well as providing an early warning system by hissing and screaming if a predator approached. But more recent research suggests these are actually bloodthirsty bodyguards.'

Amber looked back at Connor and raised an eyebrow.

'Rather than eat the ticks, the oxpeckers have been seen removing scabs and opening fresh wounds to feed on the rhino's blood,' explained Gunner. 'So, while in part a mutually beneficial relationship, the oxpecker is also a parasite.'

Connor hoped Amber didn't consider him a parasite. He'd been careful to keep his distance and focus on Henri when they'd been prepping for the dawn safari. And, since the spider episode the previous night, he'd noticed she had become more open towards him.

They watched as the little bird pecked with its red beak at the rhino's rump. The rhino twitched and turned slowly, until its back was to them. Then it excreted several huge dollops of dung that plopped on to the ground in a steaming heap.

'Gross!' exclaimed Henri.

'Well, that's certainly put me off my breakfast,' agreed Connor.

Gunner grinned. 'An adult rhino can produce as much as *fifty* pounds of dung in a day. Did you know each rhino's stool smell is unique and identifies its owner? They often use communal dung deposits, known as middens, to serve as local message boards. Each individual dung tells other rhinos who's passed through, how old they are and whether a female is on heat or not. Think of it like a post on one of your social networks.'

'That's a pleasant image!' said Amber, laughing.

Having done its business, the rhino trotted off and disappeared into the thicket.

'What a spectacular start to the safari!' declared Gunner, switching on the Land Rover's engine. 'Your first close encounter with one of the Big Five and it's only six a.m.'

'What are the other four?' asked Amber.

'Elephant, lion, buffalo and leopard. Can't guarantee we'll spot a leopard, though. They're pretty elusive.'

Henri frowned. 'Why isn't a hippo one of the Big Five? Surely it's larger than a leopard?'

Gunner shook his head. 'It isn't about size. The "Big Five" was the term used by white hunters for the five species considered the most dangerous to hunt. Although you're technically right, a hippo should be on that list. Hippos kill more people than any other animal in Africa.'

'Really? What about mosquitoes?' said Amber.

'Yeah, I'll give you that. They're responsible for millions of deaths through the spread of malaria. But mosquitoes aren't directly attacking you, unlike hippos who are fiercely territorial. I can assure you, you *don't* want to get between a hippo and water. But if you really want to be picky, then there's one beast in Africa that's killed more than all the mosquitoes, hippos, elephants, crocs and lions combined.'

'Which one?' asked Connor, intrigued.

'The most deadly species on Earth,' said Gunner, fixing him with a grave look. 'Man.'

A single fan whirred like an oversized mosquito in the corner of the makeshift office, no more than a lopsided whitewashed brick hut with a corrugated tin roof, situated on the edge of a Rwandan border town. The fan's feeble breeze was barely enough to stir the stifling air as the diamond merchant, a thin-faced man with half-moon spectacles and a shirt two sizes too big, removed the stone from its bag. He deposited it under the microscope with the infinite care of a parent holding a baby for the first time. Then, setting aside his glasses, he peered through the eyepiece.

'A pink, very rare . . . and desirable,' he said, adjusting the focus and magnification. 'Clarity is almost flawless, at least internally.'

The merchant pulled back and blinked, as if he couldn't believe his eyes at the quality. Retrieving his spectacles, he glanced up at the client sitting opposite him. The white man hadn't moved a muscle since taking his seat. Yet his posture suggested he was ready to strike like a panther at the slightest provocation.

'Where did you get this?' asked the merchant breathlessly.

'I'm not paying you to question,' said Mr Grey. 'I'm paying you to appraise.'

'Of course,' replied the merchant, immediately returning to his work. No stranger to violence, the merchant recognized the implied threat in the man's tone and had no intention of antagonizing him further. With due diligence, he transferred the stone from the microscope on to a set of digital scales. The merchant tried not to show any surprise at the reading, but it was impossible to hide the shocked dilation of his pupils.

'A little over thirty carats, in its rough state,' announced the merchant, somehow managing to keep his voice even.

'Estimated value?'

The merchant licked his lips as he considered the rare diamond before him. 'Twenty million dollars, if not more.'

Mr Grey nodded, picked up the stone and laid out ten hundred-dollar bills on the table. 'For your appraisal. Plus another ten for keeping your tongue.' He added more notes to the pile. 'Or else I'll return to *take* your tongue.'

'Discretion is my religion,' assured the diamond merchant, pocketing the money. As his client reached the doorway, he cleared his throat. 'You'll have trouble getting that stone out of Africa without the correct certificates. I could h–'

'That's my concern, not yours,' said Mr Grey, stepping out into the hot midday sun.

He crossed the potholed road to his battered Land

Rover. Once aboard, he pulled a phone from his pocket and dialled. A voice answered, slightly distorted by the encrypted line. 'Status?'

'The stone is legit. Twenty million, minimum.'

'A satisfactory investment then,' said the voice. But Mr Grey couldn't tell whether the person on the end of the line was pleased or disappointed by the figure. 'Have you secured means of export?'

'Yes, I'm meeting the contact in six days for transport to Switzerland where it will be KP-certified.'

'Fine work, Mr Grey. Everything else on schedule?'

'Ahead, by all accounts. The coup appears imminent. The general's hungry for war. He's contacted me for more weapons.'

'That's easily enough arranged. But can we trust him to stand by our agreement?'

'He knows the score if he doesn't,' stated Mr Grey. 'But the general is a loose cannon, no ethics and no boundaries.'

'Sounds the ideal candidate to ignite chaos,' replied the voice. 'What's the status of the opposition?'

'Unprepared, according to my source. But its army is well-enough equipped. I would anticipate heavy losses on both sides.'

When the voice replied, the pleasure was unmistakable this time. 'A fight between grasshoppers is always a joy to the crow.'

CHAPTER 23

'*Safari* is Swahili for *journey*,' explained Gunner, grabbing a small backpack from the rear of the Land Rover. 'And the only way to truly experience Africa is on foot.'

It was now afternoon and the ranger had offered to take them on a walking safari. Enticed at the prospect of such a unique opportunity, Laurent and Cerise had decided to join them, the president and his entourage having returned to the lodge.

Connor shouldered his Go-bag, containing his water bottle, insect repellent, the first-aid kit and other critical supplies. In the side pockets of his cargo trousers, he stowed his smartphone and Lifestraw and, on his hip, his father's knife. Although they were being guided by an experienced ranger and tracker, Connor was taking no chances. In the SAS survival manual, he'd read *always to expect the unexpected* – a motto equally relevant to a bodyguard's philosophy. And, without the back-up of the presidential guard, he wanted to be prepared for any eventuality.

Henri was protesting loudly as his mother smothered him in factor-fifty sunscreen. Amber, in shorts and a T-shirt, her hair tied back by a bandana, rolled her eyes at her younger brother's whinging. After applying some lip balm, she picked up her camera and water bottle, keen to get moving. Connor was just putting on his sunglasses and baseball cap when the ambassador approached.

'How's the trip so far?' he asked.

'All going very smoothly,' replied Connor. 'Nothing out of the ordinary to report.'

'It seems my fears may have been unfounded,' admitted Laurent, admiring the glorious expanse of open savannah. 'Still, it's good for Amber to have someone around her own age. She's been a little down recently. Perhaps you can cheer her up? Keep her occupied while I'm involved in diplomatic discussions.'

He gave Connor a pointed look and Connor recalled the awkward conversation between Amber and Minister Feruzi at the Boma dinner.

'I'll do my best,' said Connor, sensing the ambassador wasn't aware of his daughter's recent break-up.

Once everyone was ready, Gunner drew the group together. 'A few basic rules for this safari. Follow my instructions at all times, without delay or debate. Stick together and walk in single file. No talking, unless we're gathered to discuss something of interest. And if we do happen to confront any dangerous game, whatever you do, *don't* run. You'll trigger the hunting instinct and become prey. Remember, you're not in a zoo. This is Africa.'

'Are you sure we'll be safe?' asked Cerise, putting a protective arm round her son.

'Haven't lost anyone yet,' replied Gunner. 'Though you are our first guests!'

He smiled to show this was a joke, then thumbed in the direction of a young park ranger, a rifle slung over his shoulder. 'Don't worry, Mrs Barbier, Alfred's here to protect us.'

Gunner nodded at Buju to lead the way, and Laurent, Cerise, Amber and Henri followed in single file, with Connor and Alfred taking up the rear. They tramped through the long grass in silence. Although Connor's baseball cap shielded him from the blazing sun, the ground itself radiated heat like a mirror and, within minutes of the trek, he was drenched in sweat.

All around, the savannah buzzed with life. Insects flitted from bush to bush, guinea fowl squawked as they scurried for cover, and brightly coloured birds darted between the trees dotting the landscape. The air, no longer tainted by the Land Rover's exhaust fumes, was heavy with the scent of animal dung, dried grasses and the dust kicked up from the baked red earth.

The whole experience was totally different from riding within the safe confines of the Land Rover. Connor felt exposed and, for the first time, vulnerable. He was suddenly aware they were on an equal footing with all the other animals in the park. Were it not for Alfred's rifle, they'd be poorly equipped to defend themselves against lions and other predators with teeth and claws.

Yet, at the same time, he felt a thrill at being so immersed in the wild. His senses seemed sharpened and he was alert

to even the tiniest of details: a column of black ants march-
ing across their path, the scrunch of dried grass beneath
their boots, and a shiny beetle rolling a ball of dung three
times its size up a slope. This was Africa in its rawest form.

Buju came to a halt beside a clump of thorn bushes.
Gunner beckoned the group to join them. Peering over,
they spotted a bull elephant feeding on the leaves of an
acacia tree. Henri's eyes widened at the sheer size of the
animal no more than ten metres away from them.

'The largest land-living mammal in the world,' explained
Gunner under his breath as the elephant entwined its trunk
round a branch and ripped off the leaves, the twigs crack-
ling in its grip. 'They can spend up to sixteen hours a day
foraging for food. The trunk is remarkable. Made up of
over a hundred thousand muscles and no bones, it can tell
the size, shape and temperature of any object. And its sense
of smell is four times more sensitive than that of a blood-
hound. Thankfully, due to Buju's guiding skill, we're down-
wind of this one.'

'It's magnificent,' Cerise remarked as Amber focused her
camera and took a photo.

'What would happen if he noticed us?' asked Connor,
the thorn bush seeming an ineffective barrier against an
elephant charge.

'Most elephants are understandably wary of humans
and will move off,' Gunner replied. 'But if threatened it
would stomp the ground, fan out its ears and raise its head.
However, you know you're in real trouble when it pins
back its ears, curls its trunk and issues a loud trumpeting.

That means it's about to charge. And, for their bulk, elephants are extremely fast and surprisingly agile. If on foot, as we are, I'd advise making for the nearest tree or embankment. Elephants seldom negotiate those obstacles.'

'Are the elephants protected within this park?' asked Amber, taking another photo.

'They're as safe as in any other national park,' said Gunner. 'They have no natural predators, apart from man, of course. But they've developed an extraordinary ability to differentiate between humans. They can tell a man from a woman, an adult from a child – all from the sound of a human voice.'

'What about poaching?' asked Laurent.

'Armed rangers patrol the different sectors. However, with ivory fetching up to sixty-five thousand dollars per kilo – more than gold and platinum – I admit poaching is still a massive problem.' Gunner sighed heavily. 'The poachers of today are well-resourced and heavily armed. A few will be rich Europeans and Americans seeking the thrill of the hunt, but most are locals looking to make a quick buck. Organized crime gangs, rebel militia and even terrorist organizations are getting involved. But we're fighting back, thanks to the funding from countries like yours.' He nodded towards the elephant. 'And if this one, with tusks his size, can survive this long, we're doing a good job.'

Having had its fill of the acacia tree, the elephant lumbered off. Buju waited until the animal was a good distance away before continuing the safari. In single file, they crossed a dry riverbed and passed a herd of impala. The wind shifted slightly and the herd started as they caught the human scent. Buju paused beside an enormous tree that looked as if it had been planted upside down. The trunk was several metres in diameter and towered some twenty metres above them, where the leafless branches spread out like a profusion of roots in the sky. From these hung velvety pods the size of coconuts.

'This is a baobab tree,' said Gunner, patting the massive trunk. 'Otherwise known as the tree of life.'

'Why's that?' asked Cerise.

'For both wildlife and the local population, the baobab is a vital source of shelter, clothing, water and food. The bark is fire resistant and can be used for making cloth and rope. The fruit –' he pointed to the hanging pods – 'can be broken open and eaten raw. Its flesh, somewhat crumbly and dry, is packed with vitamin C. The seeds can be ground into coffee. And, if you're thirsty, just cut out little sections of the trunk's inner bark and suck them to get the moisture out. Mature trees are also often hollow, providing ideal shelter, and traditionally the children of Hadza tribe are born inside a baobab tree. So, with very good reason, it's called the tree of life.'

As they rounded the colossal trunk, they were met by a cloud of black flies. They buzzed round the remains of a carcass that lay festering in the sun. The stench of rotting meat was overpowering and made Connor and the others gag.

'What's that?' asked Laurent, holding his hand over his nose.

Gunner knelt down and inspected the ravaged remains. 'A gazelle.'

'Poor thing,' remarked Amber.

'In Africa only the strong survive,' stated Gunner. 'Every morning, a gazelle like this wakes up and knows it must run faster than the quickest lion or it will be killed. And every morning a lion wakes up knowing it must outrun the slowest gazelle or it will starve to death. So, it doesn't matter whether you're a lion or a gazelle in this life; when the sun comes up, you'd better be running.'

'Did a lion kill this gazelle?' asked Henri, fascinated by the fly-infested carcass.

'Most likely,' replied Gunner. Then Buju said something and pointed to a patch of sandy ground. 'Hang on, I might be wrong.'

They gathered round the tracker, who was crouched on his haunches.

'See track here?' said Buju softly. 'Four toes, no claw marks, rear pad with three lobes. That's the spoor of a big cat.'

Henri glanced up at Connor, his eyes wild with excitement.

'It's relatively small and circular in shape, so indicates leopard,' said Buju.

'A *leopard* killed the gazelle?' gasped Henri. 'I'd love to see a leopard.'

Buju pointed to another set of prints. 'Here are lion tracks.'

'How can you tell?' asked Connor, unable to spot any difference.

'More oval and larger, because of the animal's weight.'

The tracker's eyes scanned the ground as if reading the scene that had played out. He waved a hand east. 'Leopard made the kill on the plains. Dragged the gazelle here.' He indicated the wide scuff marks and broken grass. 'Tried to carry his kill up the tree, but three . . . no, four lions chase leopard off.' He drew everyone's attention to the cluster of paw marks by the base of the trunk. 'Then hyena come and drive away lions.'

'They look the same as leopard tracks to me,' remarked Laurent.

'No, see the claw marks,' said Buju, his finger tracing the tiny points by the toes. 'And only two lobes on the pad. Definitely hyena.'

'So which way did the leopard go?' asked Henri eagerly.

Buju cast his eyes around, then pointed north-east towards a craggy peak in the distance, atop which stood a single acacia tree. 'That way, towards Dead Man's Hill.'

'Sounds a pleasant place for a picnic,' remarked Amber as she took a close-up of a lion print.

'It's a known haunt for the leopard,' Gunner explained. 'Locals have always been fearful of the hill and its adjoining gorge. Superstition says those who venture there never return. But let's see if Buju can track these prints for a little while. We might get lucky enough to come across the leopard if it's settled in a tree, or otherwise the lions who stole its kill.'

At Gunner's suggestion they swapped places in line to give everyone a chance upfront and Connor found himself behind the ranger. They trekked in silence as Buju paused every so often to examine the ground before heading off again, sometimes in a different direction.

'Buju can read the bush better than anyone I know,' Gunner whispered over his shoulder to Connor as the tracker studied a clump of grass. 'By following tiny traces, he gains a sense of the animal's direction, then assesses the landscape as a whole to gauge where it may have gone next, before searching for another sign. It's much quicker than following each track slavishly.'

'What sort of things is he looking for?' asked Connor.

'Grass that's been trampled down. Vegetation that's been broken or bruised. Soil or rocks that have been disturbed. But where he really comes into his own is ageing the tracks. Buju can determine how long it's been since the animal passed by simply from how dried out a broken leaf or stem is, or by the moisture in the ground beneath a disturbed rock. A good tracker is like an expert crime-scene investigator.'

After half an hour of tracking with no sighting of a leopard or a lion, Henri declared, 'I'm hungry.'

'But we've only recently had lunch!' his mother sighed.

'Not to worry,' said Gunner, bringing the party to a halt. 'Out in the bush there's always food. You just need to know where to look.'

He led them over to a fallen acacia tree, put his ear to the trunk, listened, then pulled back the bark. The rotting wood was infested with white worm-like creatures.

'Rhino beetle larvae,' said Gunner in delight, picking out

a plump one between his fingers. 'Cooked, they're a bush delicacy, but you can eat them raw.'

'You've got to be joking,' said Amber, eyeing the creature with disgust.

Gunner shook his head. 'Pound for pound such insects contain more protein than beef or fish; they're the perfect survival food.'

He held the bulbous wriggling larva in front of Henri's nose. The boy grimaced. 'I think I'll pass.'

'Fair enough. But I'm sure you eat honey and that's been regurgitated by bees countless times. So this food's no more unsavoury.' Gunner popped the larva into his own mouth and began chewing. 'I have to admit, though, rhino beetle larvae do taste a bit like bogeys!'

Henri sniggered as the ranger washed down his live snack with a swig from his water bottle.

'If that doesn't appeal to you, then you could try termites,' Gunner suggested, heading over to a tall earthen mound. He plucked a long grass stem and fed it into one of the small holes in the structure. 'These are an excellent food source and if you chuck a piece of termite nest on to the embers of a fire it'll produce a fragrant smoke that keeps the mozzies away.'

He tugged the stem from the hole, which was now swarming with pale brown ant-like insects.

'Connor, perhaps you'd like a taste?' said Gunner, offering him the stem.

'I'm not *that* hungry,' Connor replied, wafting a hand at the persistent flies that buzzed round their heads.

'You can't be too choosy in the bush.'

'Go on,' urged Amber, her green eyes watching his reaction.

Not wishing to be thought of as a wimp, Connor took the stem and ate a mouthful of termites. He felt the little insects crawling all over his tongue. After a couple of quick chews, he swallowed, swearing he could feel them wriggle down his throat. 'They taste like . . . dirt,' he admitted.

'But they're fresh!' said Gunner with a grin. 'Fried, the termites have a lovely nutty flavour. Well, if that's not to your liking, we could always hunt for snake.'

'*Snake?*' exclaimed Connor, his stomach turning at the thought.

'Yeah, a snake is steak in the bush!' Gunner laughed. 'Sixty per cent protein and that means energy.'

'But aren't most of them poisonous?' questioned Laurent.

'Only the end with fangs. Chop off the head, sling the body on some hot coals, skin and all, and you've got yourself a hearty meal. The only problem is killing the snake in the first place without getting bitten!'

He turned back to Henri. 'So what will it be – larva, termite or snake?'

His face a little pale, Henri replied sheepishly, 'Umm . . . I was hoping for something along the lines of a chocolate bar . . .'

'They're not doing very much,' whispered Henri as he crouched with the others, peering through Connor's binoculars. The pride of four lions lay listless under the shade of a tree, their tails flicking every so often at the buzz of flies.

Amber looked sideways at her brother and tutted. 'You're never satisfied, are you? Buju's guided you to lions and all you can do is moan.'

'But on TV they're hunting or doing something exciting,' Henri muttered. 'Not just *sleeping*.'

'Well, why don't you go for a run and see if they'll chase you?' suggested Amber with a sardonic smile.

'I wouldn't if I were you,' cut in Gunner. 'Lions are mostly nocturnal hunters, resting up to twenty hours a day, but they'll still attack if they spot an opportunity. And you'd make a fine snack, Henri.'

'If lions hunt for themselves, why did they steal the leopard's kill?' questioned Laurent.

'Because out of every five attempts a lion will only make one kill. That's why scavenging is a vital food source for them.'

'I feel sorry for the leopard,' said Cerise. 'It did all the work and these lions reaped the benefit.'

'Don't be. Leopards are the great survivors,' said Gunner. 'They may be slower than a cheetah and weaker than a lion, but they'll beat them all in the end.' He pointed to the grassland surrounding them. 'At this very moment there could be a leopard only a few metres from us and we wouldn't even know.'

As if there'd been a sudden drop in temperature, the atmosphere within the group became tense as their eyes darted from bush to grass to shrub, wondering if there *really* was a leopard nearby.

'They're superbly camouflaged hunters. Also excellent swimmers and climbers and they can leap long distances,' Gunner went on. 'A male leopard can drag a carcass three times its own weight – including small giraffes – up a tree. No prey is safe from a leopard. Believe me, of all the cats, a leopard is the most cunning and dangerous. The perfect predator.'

'Would they ever attack humans?' asked Cerise anxiously.

'Absolutely,' replied Gunner. 'A leopard is easily capable of killing any one of us. It might drop out of a tree or pounce from behind a bush, then seize you by the throat and suffocate you between its jaws.' Connor could see that the ranger was enjoying the looks of horror on their faces. 'Leopards eat whatever form of animal protein is available, from termites to snakes to waterbuck. But, when there's a shortage of regular prey, a leopard may resort to hunting humans. A few are *true* man-eaters, having got their taste from scavenging on human corpses during the civil war. Such leopards are truly to be feared.'

Connor and the others were stunned into silence. The savannah no longer seemed a perfect paradise – rather a hunting ground where *they* were the prey.

Gunner checked his watch. 'Well, time to head back,' he announced cheerily. 'Dusk is only an hour off. And we don't want to become dinner for these lions.'

With uneasy looks at the surrounding trees and bushes, Connor and the others hastily followed him. Buju led the way, guiding them back along the banks of the Ruvubu River. The late afternoon sun had turned the waters golden, and hippos wallowed in the meandering current, snorting and making strange *muh-muh-muh* sounds. Every so often Connor would spot the snout and black slit-eyes of a crocodile as it broke the water's surface. A few basked on mudbanks, their saw-toothed jaws wide open.

'Those crocs are trying to cool off as they sweat through their mouths,' explained Gunner. 'They've the strongest bite of any animal in the world and one of the quickest too – able to snap their jaws shut round prey within fifty milliseconds!'

'It seems everything in this country is lethal,' remarked Connor.

Gunner laughed. 'Survival of the fittest, my friend. Oddly enough, though, the muscles that open a croc's jaws aren't so powerful. A reasonably strong person like yourself could hold a croc's mouth closed with just their bare hands. The problem is most victims never see the croc coming, since it uses surprise rather than speed in an attack. That's why you should never take water from the same spot twice on a river. Crocs watch you the first time, then get you the next –'

'Ow!' cried Amber.

Connor spun, fearing the worst. Then he saw her camera strap had become entangled in a thorn bush. Amber struggled to free herself but merely became more entwined within its branches.

'Careful, that stuff's like barbed wire,' said Gunner, heading back along the trail to help her. 'It'll rip your clothes to shreds, as well as your skin.'

With great care, the ranger began to work her free, unhooking the thorns one at a time. Connor tried to help too, but only succeeded in pricking his own thumb.

Amber gritted her teeth as the thorns scratched at her bare skin.

'Sorry,' said Gunner. 'This is why it's called a wait-a-while bush. The South African Special Forces used it to snare prisoners and stop them escaping.'

'I can believe that!' said Amber, inspecting the blood seeping from her cuts.

When she was finally free, Connor took out an antiseptic wipe from the first-aid kit and offered to clean up her scratches. She willingly let him hold her arm and wipe off the blood. Amber smiled at him – her first with genuine warmth. 'Thanks.'

'Any time,' replied Connor, putting his first-aid kit back in his Go-bag.

'Right, let's move on,' said Gunner.

'Wait, where's Henri?' asked Cerise.

Connor glanced around. The boy was nowhere to be seen. Connor had been so absorbed tending to Amber that he hadn't kept an eye on her brother. He cursed his lapse of concentration.

'*Henri!*' called his father. But he got no answer.

Connor retraced their steps back down the trail. But the tall grass and thick undergrowth meant anyone straying even a few feet from the path could easily disappear from view and become lost.

'Buju and Alfred, spread out,' instructed Gunner. 'Everyone else stay with me. We don't want to lose anyone else.'

Cerise started to sob. 'You don't think he's been taken by a –' she glanced at the bushes – 'a leopard?'

'Don't fret, Mrs Barbier,' said Gunner. 'He's probably just wandered off. My men will find him.'

But it was Connor who spotted Henri first, through a gap in the bushes. He was standing on a mudbank overlooking the river. A crocodile's head broke the surface.

'Henri! Stay back from the water!' shouted Connor, rushing over to him, the others close behind.

'I found another dead gazelle,' said Henri, oblivious to the panic he'd caused and the predator eyeing him.

Connor peered over the lip of the bank. A carcass was washed up at the water's edge. It wasn't much more than a bloodied ribcage with a few flaps of skin hanging off. Then

Connor realized the skin was actually khaki-coloured and made of cloth.

'I don't think that's a gazelle,' said Connor, drawing Henri away from the dismembered corpse.

CHAPTER 26

'A dead body isn't exactly good PR for the park,' said Minister Mossi sarcastically, turning his gaze on Minister Feruzi, slouched in the leather armchair of the lodge's smoking room. 'Come to Ruvubu, swim with man-eating crocodiles!'

'It wasn't a crocodile that killed the man,' stated Gunner, who stood beside the stone fireplace, his safari hat in his hands.

'What do you mean?' said President Bagaza, stiffening in his chair.

'He was shot first. *Before* the crocodiles ate him.'

Minister Feruzi stubbed out his cigarette in a silver ashtray. 'How did you come to that conclusion?'

'Buju found a bullet embedded in the ribcage.'

A haze of tobacco smoke hung in the air as the president and his ministers sat silent, contemplating this fact.

'So do we know who the victim is yet?' asked Minister Rawasa quietly. 'A local villager?'

'Impossible to tell for certain, considering what's left,' replied Gunner, his expression grim. 'But I am guessing it's either Julien or Gervais. The khaki cloth matches our park uniform and both rangers have failed to report back.'

'This is a disaster! The last thing we need on the ambassador's first visit.' The president got to his feet and gazed pensively out of the window across the valley. 'Who do you think did it?'

'Poachers, most probably.'

'What sector were the two rangers patrolling?' asked Minister Feruzi, lighting up another cigarette.

'Sector eight, north-east,' replied Gunner.

'Keep your men clear, Gunner.'

Gunner frowned. 'What about catching these murderers?'

'We will. But wait until we've the necessary reinforcements.'

'It'll likely only be a small group of poachers,' pressed Gunner. 'I can lead a unit of rangers; while their tracks are still fresh, Buju can follow them to their camp.'

'Let *us* decide on the best course of action,' said Minister Feruzi firmly.

Gunner's jaw tightened. The president came over and laid a reassuring hand on the ranger's shoulder. 'I promise you, Gunner, we will find these criminals. But your job is to ensure the French ambassador and his family have the best safari possible.' He led Gunner towards the door. 'When you do confirm the body's identity, pass on my condolences to any relatives and, if there's a wife, inform her that she'll be suitably recompensed for her loss.'

'Yes, Mr President.'

'Oh, and Gunner,' called Minister Feruzi, 'I'd advise

against saying anything to the ambassador and his family at the moment. Leave that to us. No need to worry them unnecessarily.'

'Understood,' said Gunner before leaving the room.

When the door closed, President Bagaza looked to his ministers. 'So, how should we handle this?'

Minister Feruzi coughed into his fist. 'Tragic as it is, a dead ranger might give us leverage in requesting more aid to combat poachers.'

'I don't think that's the point here,' responded the president. 'What if the rangers stumbled across the diamond field and paid for it with their lives?'

'We should send in a unit of soldiers to search sector eight,' suggested Minister Mossi.

'Isn't that a bit of overkill?' argued Minister Feruzi, flicking ash from his cigarette.

'I agree,' said Minister Rawasa. 'We don't want the ambassador spooked by an increased military presence.'

'I hear you all,' said the president, 'but the priority is to secure any diamond field within the park. If the rumoured return of Black Mamba is to be believed –' he glanced round at his ministers – 'we need to take steps *now* to protect our country's interests.'

CHAPTER 27

'They're insisting there's nothing to worry about,' Connor relayed to Charley back at HQ. 'A tragic accident, but one they say is all too familiar over here.'

'I suppose swimming in a river has its dangers, especially within a national park full of wild animals,' replied Charley, her image pixelating on the phone's screen as the internet connection slowed. 'Do they know who the victim is?'

Connor shook his head. 'They're guessing it's a local.'

'You don't look so convinced.'

Charley read him too well. 'I get the sense they're hiding something. Or at least not telling the whole truth,' he explained, keeping his voice low even though he was alone in the lodge's reception. He walked over to the entrance just to make sure. 'I didn't study the corpse for too long, but bits of clothing looked very much like the park rangers' uniform. Plus our ranger appeared more concerned than I'd expect him to be for someone he didn't even know.'

Charley pursed her lips thoughtfully. 'Maybe there is more to it, but remember this safari is meant to be a goodwill exercise for the Burundian government. They're probably wanting to gloss over the incident and move on. How are the Cubs taking it?'

Connor glanced back into the lodge's lounge area where Henri was playing a game on his phone and Amber was reading a book. 'Only the youngest got a good look. He's a little shocked but otherwise fine. Cub One kept her distance. I think the parents are more upset than them, the mother in particular. But Cub Two is already asking when the next outing will be.'

'And when is it?'

'Tomorrow: a sunset safari. The tourism minister suggested we spend the day enjoying the pool before heading out.'

'Well, let's hope this next trip's a little less eventful. By the way, I've pulled some information on the snake you mentioned.'

Connor felt his stomach tighten. And, by the grave look on Charley's face, he had every reason to be concerned.

'Black Mamba is the nickname for the notorious rebel fighter, General Pascal,' revealed Charley. 'Born in Burundi, he began his fighting days aged sixteen, alternating between being a rebel and a soldier both in his own country and the Democratic Republic of Congo. At the age of eighteen he joined the FDD – Forces pour la Défense de la Démocratie – but deserted them a few years later to wage war on behalf of the Union of Congolese Patriots. Eventually he founded his own rebel group, the ANL – Armée Nationale de la Liberté – who gained infamy almost overnight for killing three hundred refugees in a United

Nations camp on the Burundian border. Most of the victims were women, children and babies, beaten with sticks, shot dead or burnt alive in their shelters.'

Connor sat down heavily in one of the reception's leather armchairs. 'He sounds like a monster.'

'That's barely scraping the surface,' sighed Charley. 'His group attacked the capital Bujumbura, leaving three hundred dead and twenty thousand people displaced. He sparked a rebellion that led to several massacres amounting to genocide, and it set back the peace process by several years before the ANL were defeated and pushed back into the Congo. Responsible for countless atrocities, the Black Mamba has also been indicted by the International Criminal Court for recruiting child soldiers.'

'Children?' said Connor, almost unable to believe what he was hearing. 'Kids like us?'

Charley nodded solemnly. 'His tactic was to abduct them and force them to kill their own parents. Those who refused were beaten to death. Those who obeyed had sacrificed all ties to home and family. With nothing to go back to, their new family became the ANL.'

'But why children?'

'Because children are easier to condition and brainwash,' replied Charley. 'Also, child soldiers don't eat as much food as an adult, don't need paying and have an underdeveloped sense of danger, so are easier to send into the line of fire.'

Connor was struck by some of the parallels to their own situation. But *he* hadn't been forced to become a bodyguard. And he'd been trained to save lives, not kill and murder.

'That's why General Pascal was nicknamed the Black Mamba,' continued Charley, 'for being the most dangerous and poisonous "snake" in Africa. He is a ruthless and evil man. Or I should say, *was*. All reports indicate the general died in the Congo two years ago. However, there's no hard proof. That's why I'm recommending to Colonel Black, based on the concerns of the ministers you overheard, that we up the threat status of Operation Lionheart to Category Two.'

The significance was not lost on Connor. In operational terms, this meant the threat was considered real and could conceivably happen.

'Keep a close watch over the Cubs, Connor . . . and stay safe. You're in wild country.'

Connor slapped at a mosquito on his neck. 'Don't I know it,' he muttered, pulling his hand away to see a smear of his own blood.

The full moon, bright in the coal-black sky, silhouetted the skeletal acacia tree atop Dead Man's Hill, and cast a ghostly sheen on the valley below. Like discarded trash, clusters of men and boys were curled up beneath the scant shelter of ripped tarpaulins, each and every one of them too exhausted to care that their beds consisted of little more than rocks and dirt. In the darkness at the edge of the makeshift camp, a handful of rebel soldiers kept watch – not for danger but for any worker attempting to escape.

A little further upstream, General Pascal paced outside the entrance to his tent, sipping from a bottle of hard liquor, a satellite phone clamped to his ear. Blaze sat nearby, sharpening his machete while listening to gangsta rap on a pair of oversized headphones. Beneath the spluttering light of a kerosene lamp, No Mercy played cards with Dredd and two other boy soldiers, Hornet and Scarface, the rickety makeshift table threatening to collapse as the dog-eared cards were slammed down with gambling zeal.

'I win,' declared Hornet, reaching forward to claim the cash.

Dredd clamped a hand over the winnings. 'No, you cheated!'

'You want to argue with me?' said Hornet, standing up to his full height and flexing his formidable muscles.

With a scowl, Dredd pulled back his hand and began dealing afresh as Hornet sat down and counted his prize money.

'Let them come,' said General Pascal into his phone. There was a pause as he listened. 'Don't fret. We've the firepower, and more is on the way. Besides, it will be all over by tomorrow.'

Ending the call, the general turned to Blaze, who lifted one ear of his headphones away, music blasting out.

'A unit of government soldiers has been sent to search this area,' explained the general. 'So from dawn I want scouting patrols in all sectors. Understood?'

Blaze nodded and glanced over at No Mercy and the others. 'You hear that, boys?'

They all saluted in acknowledgement, then resumed their game. But they'd barely gone a round when a blood-curdling scream echoed through the valley, followed by shouts of panic.

General Pascal discarded his whisky bottle and grabbed his gun. Abandoning their card game, No Mercy and the others raced after the general and Blaze to the source of the cries. They found the enslaved workers huddled together, their eyes wide and fearful as they stared into the pitch-black interior of the jungle.

'What happened?' demanded General Pascal, sweeping the undergrowth with his Glock pistol.

'The idiots just started screaming,' replied one boy soldier with a shrug.

Blaze backhanded the boy. 'You were supposed to be keeping watch!'

As the boy nursed his split lip, a rake-thin worker stammered, 'It-it . . . took him.'

'Who?' demanded General Pascal.

'Jonas,' replied the worker.

'No, *not* the man,' spat the general in disgust. 'The attacker. Did you see who it was?'

The worker shook his head, but another proclaimed, 'It was an evil spirit. A skin walker!'

A spasm of fear rippled like a wave through both workers and soldiers alike.

'This valley is cursed,' wailed a voice.

Others started moaning softly to themselves as the panic began to spread.

'It was no evil spirit,' corrected an elderly man, his voice low and reverential. 'It was a leopard. The largest I've ever seen.'

He pointed a gnarled finger to some rocks and then a tree. Shimmering in the moonlight, a trail of slick blood was the only evidence of the prisoner's disappearance.

'A man-eater!' General Pascal breathed in awe.

All eyes went to the jungle, the supernatural fear of spirits hardening into an instinctive terror of the wild. A big cat with a taste for human flesh prowling their valley meant no one was safe.

'This is a bad omen,' muttered Dredd.

'No! This is a *good* omen,' corrected General Pascal with a smile as white as bleached bone. 'The leopard is by far the most cunning of killers.'

Crouching down, the general dipped his index finger into the blood of the leopard's victim, then daubed the sign of the cross in red on his forehead.

'Blood has been let. But not from one of our soldiers, for we are the chosen ones,' he declared, now painting upon the brows of No Mercy, Dredd, Hornet and his other foot soldiers. 'For we are the hunters, not the hunted.'

'Dusk is one of the best times to spot predators,' Gunner explained to Amber, Henri and Connor as he drove with the safari convoy towards a ridge in the distance.

Although sunset was still a couple of hours off, the late-afternoon light was already transforming the savannah into a bronzed mythical landscape. The red-rich earth seemed to glow with warmth and the Ruvubu River flowed like molten gold through the sweeping expanse of the national park. As the convoy bumped and weaved its way across the rolling landscape, Buju, strapped into his bonnet seat, drew his young passengers' attention to many of the wondrous sights surrounding them: a parade of elephants lumbering towards a watering-hole, their enormous ears flapping like great sails; impalas and antelopes leaping into the air as if dancing for joy; towers of giraffes striding regally between clumps of acacia trees; and a mighty herd of black buffalo, their hooves dredging up clouds of red dust as they thundered away from the approaching Land Rovers.

Although the mood at the start of the safari had been a

little more subdued than the previous occasions, the discovery of the dead body still on everyone's minds, the Eden-like wonders of the park soon pushed aside any sombre thoughts. In awe at the sheer diversity of wildlife, Amber eagerly snapped away with her camera while Henri searched the savannah for lions on the hunt, desperate to see a real kill in action. Even Connor had his smartphone out, filming some of the more impressive animals to show the rest of Alpha team, back in cold snowy Wales, what they were missing.

'Look! A cheetah!' said Gunner, slowing the Land Rover and bringing the convoy to a halt.

Buju was pointing into the near distance where a distinctive black-spotted form was slinking through the long grasses towards a herd of antelope. Totally oblivious to the predator stalking them, the antelopes continued to graze contentedly in the golden sunlight. Suddenly the cheetah burst from its hiding-place in an explosion of speed. The antelopes scattered in panic. Weaving and zigzagging, its tail whipping this way and that, the cheetah bore down on its chosen prey – a young buck. The antelope switched direction again and again, trying to shake off its pursuer, but despite its valiant efforts the cheetah was faster and more agile. It knocked down the buck with a swipe of its claws, then pounced on its throat. The antelope struggled in its vice-like grip, but was soon suffocated.

'That was awesome!' Henri exclaimed, grinning from ear to ear.

Amber glanced over her shoulder at her brother in the back seat beside Connor. 'Satisfied now?'

Henri nodded excitedly. 'That was about the *best* thing I've seen in my whole life. I can't wait for a lion kill.'

Amber sighed. 'Haven't you seen enough killing and dead bodies for one holiday?'

'Are you kidding?' replied Henri, using Connor's binoculars to watch the cat devour its kill.

She gave him a despairing look before returning to face the front.

'It's just part of the circle of life, Amber,' said Gunner. 'Life and death go hand in hand in Africa.' He paused, staring off into the distance, before continuing: 'More often than not, a cheetah will fail in its attack. It may be the fastest land animal in the world, but it tires quickly.'

'How fast can a cheetah run?' asked Connor.

'Up to seventy miles an hour in around three seconds. That's quicker than most sports cars.'

Connor was astonished. With the 'show' over, the convoy set off again.

Keeping one hand on the wheel, Gunner leant over to Amber. 'I think the sunset will be more to your liking. The viewpoint we're going to is a photographer's dream.'

Cresting a hill, he indicated the small plateau they were heading for. As the convoy dropped down into a dried-out riverbed as wide as a four-lane motorway, its treelined banks forming steep slopes on either side, Buju held up his hand for them to stop again. He dismounted from the bonnet seat and walked over to a patch of sandy ground. Crouching, he inspected the earth.

'What's Buju spotted now?' whispered Amber.

'I'm not sure,' replied Gunner, switching off the engine.

Behind, the other five Land Rovers – transporting Laurent and Cerise, the president and his guard, and the ministers and their wives – switched off their engines too and waited. After a minute or so, Buju beckoned Gunner to join him. Clambering out of the driver's seat, he went over and began studying the ground with the tracker.

The vehicle now stationary, the muggy heat of the late afternoon pressed in on Connor and the others. Batting away the ever-present flies, Connor looked up into the cloudless sky and saw a vulture hovering overhead. For a moment he imagined himself the prey and felt a chill run down his spine.

'What do you think they've found?' asked Amber.

'Lion tracks?' suggested Henri optimistically.

'Maybe leopard,' said Connor, scanning the surroundings as Henri's eyes widened at the thought.

The rest of the convoy was strung out along the broad riverbed, the rear vehicle a good distance back, still on the bank. Laurent and Cerise were listening intently to their ranger, who was pointing out a striking red-and-yellow bird in the branch of a tree. The driver in the president's vehicle was craning his neck, wondering what the hold-up was, while the Burundian ministers and their wives in the other 4x4s appeared hot and bored.

For some reason Connor's sixth sense began twitching. All around seemed unnaturally still. Maybe the presence of the vulture had spooked him. Or maybe it was because they were in the sweltering hollow of a riverbed. But he couldn't hear any birdsong; even the insects had stopped chirping. Connor knew from what Gunner had told him that when the bush went quiet, it was a sure sign that a predator was about.

He scanned the clumps of tall grasses, dense scrub and nearby trees for movement or anything unusual, but his eyes weren't trained to spot the telltale signs of hidden wildlife, a skill that would be second nature to Buju or Gunner. Then a glint of reflected light at the base of a bush caught his eye. Retrieving his binoculars from Henri, Connor focused the lens on the undergrowth and his breath stopped dead in his throat. A pair of eyes, cold and calculating, stared right back at him.

Connor saw intelligence in those eyes. And in that instant he knew they were all in grave danger.

CHAPTER 30

'What have you seen?' asked Henri excitedly.

All of a sudden a lone impala bolted from behind a clump of tall grasses. At the same time a short sharp *crack* punctured the still silence. Pivoting in his seat, Connor spotted the president's driver slumped over his wheel. For a moment Connor thought he was just resting, then he noticed the splatter of fresh blood on the Land Rover's windscreen. A second later the president's 4x4 rattled as if being pelted by hail.

'GET DOWN!' yelled Connor, shoving Henri into the footwell of their vehicle and throwing his Go-bag on top of him, its body-armour panel acting as a shield.

The ferocious roar of heavy gunfire filled the air and Amber screamed, frozen where she was like a startled deer. Realizing she had 'brain fade', Connor threw himself into the driver's seat and forcibly pushed Amber's head down just as their windscreen shattered under a strafing of bullets, glass raining down on them.

'*What's happening?*' cried Amber, her whole body trembling as Connor tried to shield her.

'It's an ambush,' said Connor.

He risked raising his head for a moment to take stock of the situation. From the banks on either side, the black barrels of a dozen AK47s protruded from the bushes, their muzzles flaring with gunfire. President Bagaza was cowering in his vehicle, his presidential guard all but decimated. His personal bodyguard lay across him, a bullet through the head, while two other guards hung limp out of the doors, their blood dripping into the sand. The unit of soldiers in the back-up vehicle were firing indiscriminately at their hidden adversary, pulling the trigger with panic rather than accuracy. Only their driver seemed to have his wits about him as he restarted his engine, floored the accelerator and raced to rescue the president.

As more bullets peppered their own vehicle, Connor recalled Jody's number one rule in an ambush situation: *always keep moving.*

Buju and Gunner were nowhere to be seen, so it was down to him to get them out of the kill zone. Twisting the keys in the ignition, Connor heard the engine turn over but fail to start. He tried again. It spluttered then died. Connor cursed but waited a moment, afraid of flooding the engine. Hearing a shrill *whoosh*, he braced himself as a rocket-propelled grenade screeched overhead. A second later, the finance minister's Land Rover exploded in a ball of flames. Their own vehicle rocked with the force of the blast.

'Mama! Papa!' screamed Amber, rising up from the footwell.

Connor pushed her back down. 'It wasn't *their* car,' he shouted, trying the ignition once more.

The stench of burning diesel now filled the air and a column of black smoke billowed into the sky. Third time lucky, the engine kicked into life.

'Stay down,' Connor instructed Amber and Henri as he sat up and grabbed the steering wheel. He went to put the Land Rover into gear and found the door handle instead. Only then did it dawn on him that the vehicle was a left-hand drive. In Britain it was the other way round. Battling the mental confusion of using his right hand on the gear stick, he crunched the Land Rover into first gear and floored the accelerator. The tyres kicked up dirt, then gained traction and shot forward. Laurent and Cerise's Land Rover was already ahead of them, the driver hunkered down low as he sought to escape the lethal ambush.

Connor followed close behind, forcing the Land Rover into second gear and keeping to the driver's tyre tracks. With the steep banks corralling them in, they had no choice but to head upstream. The worst of the firefight was still concentrated on the president's vehicle and his remaining guard. But, just as Connor dared hope they might make their escape, the front tyres of the Barbiers' Land Rover were shot out. The driver lost control, hitting the bank, and the vehicle flipped over. It crashed directly into their path. Connor wrenched the steering wheel hard left. They swerved, barely missing the upturned Land Rover and almost overturning themselves. In the back, Henri squealed as he was flung from one side of the footwell to the other.

'Do you *actually* know how to drive?' shouted Amber, clinging on for dear life, unable to see the chaos unfolding.

Connor nodded. 'Sure, passed my test last week.'

But that knowledge didn't seem to reassure her. He was about to slam on the brakes and return for her parents when a gunman in faded army fatigues rushed out from behind a tree, an AK47 targeted on their vehicle.

Connor realized it would be a death sentence if he stopped. Ducking behind the dashboard, he accelerated hard. The gunman stood his ground, emptying his magazine into the charging Land Rover. Over the roar of the engine, Connor could hear the impact of bullets pinging off the steel bullbar at the front. As the 4x4 picked up speed, the gap between them and the gunman rapidly closed and for one horrible moment Connor thought the man wasn't going to move. Then, with death almost upon him, he leapt aside. But too late. Connor heard a heavy *thunk* as the Land Rover's bullbar caught his trailing leg. In the side mirror, he saw the man writhing on the ground, alive but out of action. He also glimpsed the Barbiers' vehicle, smoke rising from the engine compartment. There was no sign of life from its occupants.

Connor kept his foot flat to the floor, telling himself that his priority was Amber and Henri. Not their parents. He hated having to make such a ruthless decision, but he knew if he turned back now they'd all be slaughtered.

Rounding a bend and leaving the carnage behind, Connor spotted a route up the bank and headed for it. He was concentrating so hard on driving that he failed to notice the deep trench running from one bank to the other. Only at the last second did he slam on the brakes and the Land Rover came skidding to a halt just short of the ditch.

His heart thudding in his chest, Connor desperately searched for another way out. But with its steep treelined banks the riverbed made the perfect choke-point for an ambush. Once the trap had been sprung, there was no escape.

Gunmen rushed out to surround the Land Rover. But Connor refused to surrender without a fight. With the engine revved to the max, he threw the gearstick into reverse – almost getting fifth by accident – and sped away from the trench. It was a desperate decision to head back into the kill zone. But it was his only option.

The gunmen opened fire and bullets thudded into the retreating Land Rover.

'You're going the wrong way!' yelled Amber, her face pale, blood trickling from a cut to her cheek.

'Just taking a little detour,' he explained. 'Hold on, you two!'

Taking his foot off the pedal, he spun the steering wheel hard right and yanked on the handbrake. The Land Rover went into a spin. But Connor's planned J-turn quickly turned into a disaster. Driving on dirt rather than tarmac, the 4x4's tyres weren't as slick and the vehicle only pivoted halfway before stopping abruptly. The Land Rover keeled over like a ship capsizing in a storm as Connor and his two Principals clung to anything they could grab. For one terrifying moment the vehicle threatened to flip on to its side. Then it lost momentum and righted itself, landing on all four wheels with a bone-jarring crunch.

Shaken but unhurt, Connor released the handbrake and spun the wheel the opposite way. As he fought to turn the Land Rover fully round in the unforgiving sand, the gunmen bore down on them. More rounds peppered the bodywork, shattering the wing mirror and shredding one of the headrests. As they drew closer, Connor got his first good look at their attackers and was shocked to see some were boys his age. One lad in a black bandana, hefting an oversized assault rifle, was firing with wild abandon into their vehicle as if he was playing a video game.

The glazed, deadened look in the boy's eyes was even more disturbing, spurring Connor to get the hell out of there. With a crunch of gears, they shot off along the riverbed and back round the bend. As they raced past the Barbiers' upturned Land Rover, Amber poked her head up and desperately searched for her parents. The vehicle was now on fire, tendrils of flame and smoke licking the undercarriage. The roof was half-crushed, blocking their view of the rear compartment. When Connor caught a glimpse of a bloodied lifeless arm hanging from the driver's window, he held out little hope for Laurent or Cerise. Their park ranger was sprawled a few metres from the wreckage. He'd survived the crash, but not the bullets through his chest.

Connor drove on and Amber slumped back into the footwell. Ahead he saw that President Bagaza had been evacuated to the back-up vehicle, the only functioning

Land Rover left apart from their own. But he and his guards were under heavy fire. And, with little cover to protect them, they were being slaughtered. Bodies lay everywhere, the dry riverbed now flowing freely with their blood.

Connor dared not stop. His only goal was the dirt road the convoy had come in on. Passing the blazing twisted shell of Minister Mossi's Land Rover, he tried not to look at the burning bodies inside. The other Burundian ministers, who'd been at the rear of the convoy, weren't anywhere to be seen and Connor prayed they'd somehow escaped this bloodbath. All of a sudden the ground in front of their Land Rover erupted as a rocket-propelled grenade shot past and detonated. Rocks and debris rained down, red dust obliterating all visibility. Driving blind, Connor instinctively swerved, narrowly avoiding the smoking crater before bursting out the other side. Then they were tearing up the bank and leaving the sound of gunfire behind.

However, just as Connor thought they were in the clear, two flat-bed jeeps appeared, blocking their escape.

'Brace yourselves!' Connor shouted to Amber and Henri, both now mute with terror.

Dropping into second gear, Connor accelerated hard up the slope. The gunmen in the jeeps began firing at them. Connor kept going. The Land Rover struck the roadblock, smashing into the front wings of both vehicles. The men on the backs of the jeeps were flung off. The Land Rover's bullbar crumpled but did its job of saving the engine from being crippled. Connor pushed on through, metal scraping on metal as the two jeeps were shoved aside. With a final roar of the engine, the Land Rover burst free and tore off down the road.

CHAPTER 32

'What happened back there? Who was shooting at us? *Why* were they shooting at us?' babbled Amber, propped up in the passenger seat, the wind whistling through the broken windscreen and whipping at her red hair.

'I don't know,' said Connor, focusing on the dirt road ahead. 'All I know is we have to put some distance between us and them. Are you hurt?'

Amber put a hand to her face. 'I don't think so . . . it's just a little cut.'

'Good. Henri, how about you?'

Her brother didn't answer.

'*Henri?*' Connor repeated louder. 'Speak to us.' He glanced into the rear-view mirror but couldn't see him. He prayed the boy hadn't been shot.

Amber clambered round in her seat and looked down into the footwell. 'Henri, are you all right?'

She turned to Connor. 'He's not responding.'

'Can you see any blood?'

Amber shook her head. 'No, he looks fine.'

'He's probably in shock,' explained Connor.

Amber reached through to her brother and gently shook him. 'Henri, are you OK?' She shook him again. 'He's nodding.'

Connor breathed a sigh of relief. It was a miracle all three of them had escaped without injury. Then he noticed a patch of blood staining the left-hand side of his T-shirt. He felt no pain, but the adrenalin was probably masking that.

'Our first priority is getting back to the lodge,' he announced, deciding not to examine his wound any further. Serious or not, they couldn't risk stopping so close to the ambush site. 'That'll be the most secure location. At least until Buddyguard can arrange a flight out of here.'

'But we can't just . . . leave,' stuttered Amber, her voice cracking with emotion. 'M-my parents . . .'

Connor kept his eyes on the road, unable to meet her pleading look. 'If they've escaped, that's where they'll go too,' he replied.

'*If?*'

'Pass me my phone,' he instructed, wanting to avoid the topic, at least until they were out of immediate danger. He indicated the back seat where he'd dropped it in the rush to protect her. Amber numbly reached behind and it was this action that saved her life. A bullet ripped through her headrest, missing her neck by a fraction. More lethal rounds zinged past.

'They're following us!' she yelled, sliding down low in her seat.

In the rear-view mirror, Connor saw a jeep hurtling

along the road, a dust cloud billowing up in its wake. Connor increased speed, urging the Land Rover to go faster. The whole chassis shook as the dirt road punished the 4x4's suspension. He wrestled with the steering wheel, his bones jarring as they hit pothole after pothole.

Another bullet ricocheted off the dashboard and a glance behind told him what he feared most. The gunmen were gaining on them. And they were still miles from the lodge. Realizing the odds of outrunning their pursuers were close to zero, Connor made the decision to head off-road.

'Where on earth are you going?' said Amber, baffled by his seemingly crazy actions.

'The jungle,' he replied, nodding towards the trees bordering the savannah. 'We'll try to lose them in there.'

Connor weaved between the bushes at high speed, taking advantage of their cover. As they bounced and rocked over the rugged terrain, he almost collided head-on with a boulder, then narrowly avoided a clump of trees. He simply ran straight over any small thorn bushes, their branches screeching and scraping at the undercarriage.

'Watch out!' cried Amber.

A herd of impala bolted in fright, leaping across their path. Connor swerved madly to avoid hitting them. Behind, the sound of gunfire drew ever closer but he didn't dare look back again for fear of crashing. Cresting a slope, the Land Rover cleared the ground and came down with an almighty thump. Part of the exhaust system fell off and the engine began roaring like a lion. Caught in a deadly game of hide-and-seek with his pursuers, Connor drove on for all he was worth towards the sanctuary of the jungle. The undergrowth thickened around them and for a moment he believed he'd shaken them off. Then a blast of bullets pulverized a nearby tree trunk, bark and splinters flying into their path.

Connor swung the Land Rover hard right, following what appeared to be animal trails deeper into the jungle. Sunlight flickered through the canopy overhead and the encroaching undergrowth slapped at the vehicle's sides. They quickly lost sight of their pursuers. Then without warning the ground dropped away and the Land Rover tipped forward. It hurtled out of control down a sheer slope, bouncing off rocks and careering through bushes. Connor, Amber and Henri were flung around the cabin, powerless to stop their breakneck descent. A massive tree loomed up in front of them and the Land Rover came to a violent shuddering halt, the bonnet crumpling like cardboard as they struck the trunk head-on.

Groaning in pain, Connor pressed the palm of his hand to where he'd hit his forehead on the steering wheel. Blood was seeping from a gash above his left eye. He was dazed but alive. Amber was slumped next to him, her head lolling on the door frame.

'Are you OK?' he asked, laying a hand on her shoulder.

Amber let out a soft moan. 'I think so,' she managed to reply. To add to the cut on her cheek, she now had a split lip, countless grazes and a dark bruise along her thigh.

'Anything broken?'

'Yes . . . my camera.' She held up the shattered remains. 'But I'll survive.'

Clambering out of the vehicle, Connor's legs gave way beneath him and he had to drag himself back to standing. He peered into the rear compartment. Henri was curled up in the foetal position at the bottom of the footwell.

'How about you, Henri?' Connor asked, gradually feeling his strength and senses returning.

Henri gave him a thumbs up. Connor smiled. From what he could see, his position in the footwell had protected him from the worst of the crash, although he was going to sport some pretty impressive bruises. Connor held out his hand and pulled Henri from the wreckage, before going round to help Amber out through her window.

Surveying the scene, Connor discovered that he'd driven into a hidden ravine. The Land Rover was a write-off, the crash having broken the front axle and torn off the nearside wheel. The only way they'd be getting to the lodge now was on foot.

Reaching inside the vehicle, Connor retrieved his Go-bag. He also found his binoculars jammed against the door. But, worryingly, there was no sign of his phone. He leant in further through the window to look under the seats when suddenly the jungle erupted with the sound of gunfire. Connor dived behind the nearest tree, dragging Amber and Henri with him. The gunmen were now at the top of the ravine, shooting blindly into the bushes. With no time to grab anything else, Connor propelled Amber and Henri forward and the three of them fled for their lives.

CHAPTER 33

'It's hard to dodge a spear that comes from behind!' growled President Bagaza.

He knelt in the bloodstained sand, his hands bound but his head held high. The unexpected appearance of Black Mamba, still alive, had shocked him and his surviving guards. But he was determined not to show any weakness in front of his lifelong adversary.

General Pascal sneered and prodded the president's belly with the tip of his boot. 'You've gone soft while in office, Bagaza.'

'You're still the coward you always were, Pascal. Killing innocent women and children. And when you can't kill them –' the president glanced over at No Mercy – 'you use them to fight your own battles.'

General Pascal laughed. 'As if *you* haven't committed enough of your own crimes! Your hands are as dirty as mine.'

'At least I've tried to wash them of my sins. I've brought this country back from the brink,' argued the president fiercely. 'Are you determined to plunge us back into civil war *just* to line your own pockets with diamonds?'

'Why not? You appear to have done well enough from the last war. Now it's my turn. I've decided to run for president.'

President Bagaza couldn't hide his astonishment. 'But . . . no one will vote for you! Not the Black Mamba.'

'Are you so certain?' The general turned to his rebel soldiers. 'Who thinks I should be president?'

Every one to a man and child raised their hands.

'How about my old friend here?' he said, patting President Bagaza amiably on the shoulder.

All the hands dropped.

General Pascal offered his opponent a conciliatory smile. 'Election over. You lose.'

He drew his Glock 17 pistol and shot President Bagaza straight through the eye. The president flopped backwards into the dirt. Holstering his gun, the general stepped over the lifeless body of his enemy, then strolled up the bank.

'What about the prisoners?' asked Blaze, waving the barrel of his AK47 at the row of terrified guards.

General Pascal considered them for a moment, then said, 'Give them a choice of long or short sleeves.'

The guards exchanged horrified looks as Blaze produced his machete. Two gunmen seized the first guard in line and the rebel fighter indicated the elbow or wrist as to where he'd hack the man's limb off. As the guard began begging for mercy, a jeep skidded to a stop at the top of the riverbank. A soldier jumped out and saluted the general. 'We caught up with the first vehicle but lost the children.'

'How could you *lose* three children in a Land Rover?' demanded General Pascal, his tone exasperated.

'They drove into a ravine,' explained the soldier.

General Pascal gave a snort of amusement. 'Are they dead?'

The soldier shook his head. 'They disappeared into the jungle.'

The smile evaporated from the general's face. 'My orders were explicit. No one must be allowed to escape. No one can raise the alarm.'

The general turned to Blaze.

'*Hunt them down!*'

'I think we've lost them,' said Connor, slowing their pace through the bushes.

'I think *we're* lost,' replied Amber with an uncertain glance at the encroaching jungle.

Scanning the disorientating tangle of thick vegetation, Connor was forced to agree. His only objective had been to escape the gunmen, so he'd paid little attention to the direction they'd run in. A potentially critical error of judgement. He *should* have been thinking like a bodyguard, assessing the situation at every point and noting their escape route. Now they were completely lost in unfamiliar and dangerous territory with no back-up.

Henri stumbled over a branch and Connor caught his arm to stop him falling. Wheezing heavily from their mad dash through the jungle, the boy's face was pale and sweaty and his lips had a worrying blue tinge.

'Where's your inhaler?' asked Amber as Connor guided her brother over to a fallen tree and helped him to sit down.

'*Poc . . . ket*,' he rasped.

Amber fished it out for him. Henri grabbed it as if he was drowning, immediately taking two puffs. A minute went by and he was still clawing for breath. Panic welling in his eyes, he inhaled another two doses.

'Calm down, Henri. Slow steady breaths,' soothed Amber, gently stroking his arm. 'We're safe now. You can relax.'

Gradually Henri's wheezing eased and his lips regained their colour. Closing his eyes, he leant forward, his head in his hands.

'Will he be all right?' asked Connor, aware that a severe asthma attack could be fatal.

Amber nodded. 'He just needs some time to recover.' Her gaze fell to Connor's chest and her pale green eyes widened in alarm. 'You're bleeding!'

Connor glanced down. The patch of blood on his T-shirt had blossomed. Gingerly lifting up his T-shirt, he peeled away the sodden cloth from his skin. A bullet had clipped his side, leaving a long gash. His T-shirt, while stab-proof, offered no protection from a 7.62mm high-velocity bullet, and blood seeped steadily from the wound. As soon as he examined the injury, his brain registered the damage and pain rushed in.

Grimacing, Connor put down his Go-bag and extracted the first-aid kit.

'Let me do that,' said Amber, taking the kit from him and insisting that he sit down.

Tired and hurting, Connor did as she instructed. Using an antiseptic wipe, Amber cleaned away the blood.

'Ouch, that stings!' he said, wincing.

'Don't be a baby,' she chastised, inspecting the wound. 'It's not as bad as it looks. I think the bullet only grazed you.'

She took out a gauze pad, placed it over the gash and applied pressure. 'Hold that there.'

Connor kept the pad in place as she found some dressing tape and a bandage. 'How come you know what to do?' he asked.

'I'm a junior rock-climbing instructor. First aid is part of the training.' She wrapped the tape round his midriff several times, securing the gauze pad and stemming the bleeding. 'That should do it.'

Connor found a spare shirt in his Go-bag and put it on. Amber then turned her attention to the cut above his left eye.

'So, what do you think happened back there? Why were they trying to kill us?'

'They were trying to kill President Bagaza,' replied Connor. 'We just happened to be in the way.'

'Who'd do such a thing? He seems like such a nice man.'

Connor shrugged. 'Any number of rebel groups in Burundi. My operational brief listed at least four active militia units who oppose him. But I'm guessing it's the ANL, led by a man known as Black Mamba.'

'Who?' said Amber, discarding a bloodstained wipe and covering his cut with a plaster.

'You really don't want to know. But he's notorious for

using child soldiers. And some of the attackers today were kids our age.'

Amber's mouth fell open in shock. '*Kids?*'

Connor gave a grim nod. 'My turn to fix you,' he said, finding another antiseptic wipe from the first-aid kit.

'I can't believe kids were shooting at us with machine guns! Do you think –' Her lower lip began to tremble and her eyes flicked briefly to Henri before she managed to whisper, 'Do you think they killed our parents?'

'Hold still,' said Connor, gently dabbing at the cut on her quivering lip.

As Amber sought a response from him, her eyes welled up and a tear rolled down her cheek, washing a thin line through the blood and dirt smearing her skin. Connor wiped it away. In truth, he thought it was highly unlikely that Laurent or Cerise had survived the ambush. Their Land Rover was a total wreck and if by some miracle they'd escaped the crash unhurt, then the gunmen would have shot them down, just like they had the ranger. But Connor also realized that, if Amber and Henri were to survive this ordeal, they needed to hold on to the hope that their parents were still alive.

'I didn't see their bodies. So there's a good chance they escaped like us.'

'Really?' said Amber, brightening. Connor could tell she was desperate to believe him.

'The crucial thing now is for us to get to the lodge and contact Buddyguard.'

'But won't this Black Mamba head to the lodge too?'

said Henri, who'd been listening the whole time, his breathing having finally returned to normal.

'That's a risk we'll have to take. The lodge is the only property for a hundred miles and has the only means of communication . . . unless either of you have a mobile phone?' he added hopefully.

Henri shook his head. 'Not allowed one.'

'Sorry,' said Amber with a regretful smile. 'Left mine in the bedroom.'

'Then we've no other option.'

Connor packed away the first-aid kit and shouldered his Go-bag.

'But how do we even know which direction to go in?' asked Amber, waving her hand round the shadowy jungle.

Connor pivoted on the spot, trying to get his bearings. There were no obvious paths, no visible landmarks, and the sun was obscured by the canopy above. And they couldn't retrace their steps for fear of encountering the gunmen. He glanced at his watch. Sunset was less than an hour off. It would be dark soon and then they'd have absolutely no chance of finding their way.

Conscious that both Amber and Henri were waiting for him to make a decision, *relying* on him to take command, he was about to make a wild guess when he looked again at the G-Shock Rangeman watch that Charley and Amir had given him for his birthday. It barely had a scratch on it. Amir was right; the watch was indestructible. He silently thanked them for their inspired gift as he rotated the bezel and switched to compass mode.

'From what I remember, the viewpoint lay north-east of the lodge and we've travelled more or less west,' he explained to Amber and Henri. 'So, all being well, we just follow the compass south and we'll find the lodge.'

'Are you sure we're going the right way?' asked Amber, panting from the exertion of their trek.

The jungle had thickened and progress had become painfully slow as they tramped through dense undergrowth and clambered over rotting tree trunks. Mosquitoes buzzed in their ears, a constant irritation despite having doused themselves with insect repellent. In the treetops, monkeys chattered unseen and leapt from branch to branch, sending leaves falling like rain on to the earth below.

Connor wiped the perspiration from his brow and checked his compass again. It was proving impossible to keep to a straight bearing as trees, ferns and vines choked the jungle floor, forcing them to constantly alter course.

'We need to head to higher ground,' he said. 'Work out where we are.'

Coming across an animal trail, he led them upslope. The light was fading fast and the jungle was being swallowed by shadows. Soon they wouldn't be able to see each other, let alone their pursuers. Henri, his eyes darting towards any strange sound or movement, was becoming more and more scared, and he didn't protest when his sister took his hand. The terrain beneath their feet grew rockier as they ascended towards a small ridge, the trees thinning as they climbed. Suddenly, as if emerging from a deep dive, the canopy parted to reveal an indigo-blue sky, the first stars of night blinking in the heavens.

Standing atop the rocky ridge, Connor was able to look out across part of the Ruvubu Valley. Using his binoculars, he tried to spot any familiar landmarks. The sun, a ball of fiery orange, was burning low on the horizon, giving him true west. To the south, the Ruvubu River wound lazily through the valley basin. And, off to the east, he could make out the craggy peak of Dead Man's Hill. The dried-out riverbed where the ambush had taken place was hidden from view by the trees, but Connor was able to work out the lodge's rough direction from a single dark line that cut across the savannah. With so few roads, the main dirt track stood out like a scar on the landscape.

'We're a little off course,' he admitted, directing their gaze to a midpoint in the distance. 'That's where the lodge is. Somewhere on the other side of that ridge.'

Amber squinted into the twilight. 'How far do you think?'

'At this pace, half a day's walk, I guess, maybe more.'

Amber glanced at her brother, who was wheezing again from the climb. 'We need to rest,' she said.

Connor looked at both Henri and Amber. They were all tired, hungry, hot and thirsty. They'd been running on adrenalin and shock for the past hour. Now that was beginning to fade, their bodies were crashing. He nodded in agreement. Finding a patch of clear ground, they sat down and Connor retrieved the water bottle from his Go-bag. Barely a couple of gulps remained. He offered the bottle to Amber, who let her brother drink first. Then, after taking a sip herself, she handed it back.

Despite his own thirst, Connor waved the bottle away. 'You have it.'

'No,' insisted Amber, forcing it into his hand. 'No heroics. You need it as much as we do.'

Connor drank the last dregs, the warm water wetting his mouth but doing little more. Only now did it hit him that they were in a survival situation.

Running from the gunmen was just the start of their problems. The main threat to their lives came from being in the wilds of Africa without food, water or weapons.

Colonel Black's departing words rang in his ears: *It's always best to be prepared for the worst, especially in Africa.* In light of their current situation, Connor thought that the colonel had never said a truer word and wished now he'd spent more time studying the SAS survival handbook he'd been given.

Recalling that the right equipment could make the difference between life and death, Connor emptied his Go-bag and took stock of their resources. He'd lost the most crucial item – his smartphone – back at the crash site, but he did have a small first-aid kit, empty water bottle, binoculars, malaria tablets, sun lotion, insect repellent, a Maglite, a single energy bar, sunglasses with night-vision capability and, still attached to his belt, his father's knife.

'What's that?' asked Henri, pointing to a blue tube in the bottom of the bag.

Connor fished it out and smiled, glad of Bugsy's foresight. 'A Lifestraw,' he explained. 'We just need to find water and we can all drink safely.'

With one key survival factor half-solved, Connor asked, 'What do you have in your pockets?'

Amber produced a cherry-flavoured lip balm, a packet of tissues and a hairband. Henri had a couple of sweets and his inhaler. Hiding his disappointment at such meagre offerings, Connor opened the energy bar and divided it up between the three of them. 'Not much of a dinner, I'm afraid, but it's better than nothing.'

The oat bar was gone in one bite, only serving to remind them of how hungry they actually were.

'Is this edible?' Connor asked, half-joking, as he picked up the lip balm.

'Tastes nice and keeps your lips soft,' replied Amber, 'but not an ideal dessert.'

Henri offered his two sweets to Connor and his sister.

'Save them,' said Connor, smiling at his generosity. 'We'll be needing them for breakfast.'

Dusk was falling fast. Even with his night-vision sunglasses and a small torch, Connor knew that it would be foolish to negotiate the jungle at night.

'We need to find a safe place to sleep,' he said, repacking everything into his Go-bag.

'We're not going back to the lodge?' Henri asked with an anxious glance at the gloomy jungle surrounding them.

Connor shook his head. 'Too dangerous. It's best we hole up somewhere until daw–'

A rustle in the bushes alerted Connor to something approaching. He put a finger to his lips, urging Amber and Henri to remain silent.

The rustling drew closer. To Connor's ears, it sounded like more than one person, all converging on the ridge. The gunmen had caught up with them fast! But no doubt they had trackers with them.

Looking for a place to hide, he hustled Amber and Henri into a crevice in the rocks. They lay flat, waiting for the gunmen's approach. Reaching for his belt, Connor unsheathed his father's knife. While it was no match for an assault rifle, he gained strength and courage from having it in his grasp.

The noise grew louder. Connor could hear Amber's panicked breathing in his ear and feel Henri's body trembling at his side. His grip on the knife tightened as a bush only a few metres from them began to shake. Then a snout with two large curved tusks appeared, followed by a large flattened head and a grey bristled body. Snorting, a warthog trotted over the ridge, followed by a litter of young piglets.

Connor relaxed his grip on the knife and slowly let out the breath he'd been holding. The warthog suddenly turned her head in their direction. Sniffing the air, she grunted furiously, flattened her mane of bristles and bolted away, her piglets squealing in terror as they too ran for cover.

Amber laughed, more in relief than anything. 'I'm glad there's something in this jungle more scared than us!' she said.

But, as they crawled out of the crevice, they discovered what the warthog and her piglets had really been running from.

A harsh hissing sound greeted them and Connor's blood turned to ice in his veins. Slithering over the rock towards them was a long, slender olive-brown snake. Three metres in length and with a body as thick as a man's wrist, it was the largest snake Connor had ever seen. As it reared up and challenged them with its dark malevolent eyes, Connor's chest suddenly tightened and he began to fight for breath. The sight of the snake turned his skin clammy and his fingers went numb, until he could barely grip his knife any more.

'I think we're in its lair,' whispered Amber.

The pounding of his heart was so loud in his ears that Connor heard her as if she was in another world. Her voice, distant and ghost-like, drifted through his fearful state. '*We need to move.*'

Hypnotized by the creature swaying before him, his limbs had turned heavy as lead. However much he willed himself, he was rooted to the spot by sheer terror.

Amber eased herself away. Henri went to do the same

but, as soon as he moved, the snake hissed sharply in warning. Rising a full metre off the ground, it opened its jaws to reveal a pair of razor-sharp fangs and a jet-black mouth.

Henri froze. 'A black mamba!' he gasped.

Connor now recognized the coffin-shaped head that Gunner had described. *Believe me, you don't want to meet one of those in the bush.*

Face-to-face with his darkest nightmare, Connor couldn't have agreed more. He knew from the ranger that the black mamba possessed the most potent snake venom in the world. Unpredictable and highly aggressive, in an attack it would strike multiple times, injecting lethal amounts of poison with every bite. Within minutes, the victim would experience dizziness, sweating, crippling headaches and severe abdominal pain. Their heartbeat would become erratic, leading to violent convulsions and collapse. The whole body would go into shock, inducing vomiting, fever and paralysis of the limbs. Finally, the victim would succumb to respiratory failure or else a heart attack.

A horrific and agonizing death, whichever way it ended.

All this knowledge only served to immobilize Connor further.

The black mamba, its tongue flicking and tasting the air, expanded its narrow hood and hissed aggressively. It made a mock charge and Henri jerked back in panic. The sudden move triggered the black mamba to strike for real.

Time seemed to slow as Connor battled his phobia, struggling to overcome his self-induced paralysis and protect Henri. But all he could do was watch as the snake's venomous fangs closed in on the boy.

Then a stick came crashing down on to the head of the snake, clubbing it senseless. The stick struck again and again until it snapped with the force of the blows, leaving the coffin-shaped head pulverized on the rock.

Amber stood over the dead and battered snake, her body trembling, her eyes fierce.

'I don't know about you two, but I've had enough ambushes for one day.'

CHAPTER 37

Connor knelt beside the teepee of sticks, his knife and a flint stone in hand. Feeling as if he was back camping with his father, he struck the edge of the blade against the flint, trying to create a spark and set the small pile of wood shavings alight. He'd had reservations about making a fire. There was a risk that the gunmen would spot the flames in the darkness. But he weighed this against the danger from wild animals and the need for warmth during the chilly night ahead.

They'd found the ideal place to set up camp, a shallow cave a little further down from the ridge, where a stream ran through a gully into a pool before flowing on through the jungle. Connor had made certain that the cave was empty first, throwing in a stone, then checking the entrance for any signs that an animal might be using it as a den. With no obvious remains of food or droppings, the cave appeared uninhabited.

Connor struck the flint harder. Still getting no spark, he persisted, becoming increasingly frustrated and worried he might damage the steel blade. His memory of lighting fires with his father seemed to be a simple matter of a quick strike followed by the whole pyramid of sticks bursting into glorious flame. But so far all he'd managed to do was graze his knuckles and blunt his knife.

After ten minutes of futile striking, he was on the verge of giving up, when a single flicker like a tiny falling star dropped on to the tinder. Connor blew softly, desperately trying to coax the spark into a flame. But the small glow died away rapidly. Tired and hungry, he tossed aside the flint in a fit of frustration.

'Would this be easier?' asked Henri.

Glancing over, Connor saw he was holding up a small book of matches.

'Where did you get *those*?' he cried.

Henri offered a sheepish grin. 'My back pocket.'

'Why on earth didn't you give them to me earlier?' Connor said, shaking his head in disbelief as he grabbed the book from him.

Henri shrugged an apology. 'I forgot I'd taken them from the lodge's bar. Besides, you looked like you knew what you were doing.'

'I don't have a clue what I'm doing!' shouted Connor.

Henri wore a wounded look. 'But you're our body-guard . . .'

Connor took a deep breath, trying to rein in his annoyance. 'Sorry, I didn't mean to snap at you. That snake freaked me out, that's all.'

He struck one of the matches and the tinder immediately caught alight. With a few gentle puffs, he coaxed the flames and the teepee of sticks began to crackle and burn. 'So much for my SAS survival skills,' he sighed, pocketing the matches and hoping his father wasn't looking down on him, shaking his head in despair.

At that moment Amber returned with another armful of sticks for the fire. Or at least Connor thought they were sticks at first. Instead she dumped the dead black mamba at his feet. Connor flinched and scrambled away.

'Dinner,' Amber explained.

'You've got to be kidding!' said Connor, eyeing the mamba warily, expecting it to come back to life and strike at any moment.

'Remember what Gunner said: snake is steak in the bush. And we need to eat.'

Connor felt the ache in his stomach and knew she was right. No wonder he was so short-tempered. Swallowing back his revulsion, he forced himself to crouch beside the black mamba. He reached out a hand to hold the snake's head in position, but shuddered at the thought of touching the smooth oily scales of the creature.

'Sorry, I simply can't do it,' he admitted, passing Amber his knife.

'If it was a spider, I wouldn't be able to either,' she replied.

Taking great care not to go anywhere near the fangs, Amber used the blade to cut the snake's head off. Then, once the fire had settled down, she laid the body on the hot embers. The skin sizzled loudly and soon after the cave filled with the aroma of cooking flesh. Despite his phobia of snakes, Connor's mouth began to water in anticipation.

Having each drunk from the pool using the Lifestraw, they sat round the fire and waited for their snake dinner to be ready. Night had truly fallen and their shadows played out against the cave wall. Insects whirred and chirped, bats fluttered overhead and unseen creatures leapt from the branches, screeching and hollering. The incessant noise of the jungle was unnerving and the three of them huddled closer to the fire. Somewhere in the darkness they heard a series of low threatening growls, like the sawing of wood.

Amber gazed nervously into the pitch-black. 'What do you think that is?' she whispered.

'Whatever it is,' Connor replied, 'it's a long way from us.' Or so he hoped.

After half an hour, Amber tested the snake with his knife. 'I think it's cooked.'

Pulling the body off the coals, she sliced it open and cut a portion of steaming meat for each of them.

Henri examined his unusual meal with trepidation. 'Do you think it's safe to eat?'

'The poison's in the head, according to Gunner, so it should be,' replied Amber, sniffing her piece cautiously.

Hunger overcoming his aversion to snake, Connor took a bite. 'Tastes like chicken!' he said in surprise.

The other two tucked in, devouring their meal quickly.

Once their bellies were full, exhaustion soon overtook them.

'I'll build up the fire,' said Connor as Amber settled her brother at the back of the cave.

As he piled on some larger logs, Connor could hear the two of them whispering, their voices echoing off the rock wall.

'Ow! The ground's all stony.'

Amber swept away the debris with her hand. 'You can rest your head on these leaves,' she said, gathering up some green branches.

Henri lay down. 'No animals will get us, will they?'

Amber shook her head. 'The fire will scare them off. Now go to sleep.'

She appeared to hesitate, then leant forward and kissed him on the forehead. Henri stared up at her, evidently surprised by her unexpected tenderness. Then he said, 'Mama and Papa are dead, aren't they?' His tone was matter-of-fact and all the more heart-rending for it.

Amber stroked his tousles of red hair gently from his face. 'They might have escaped, like us.'

'But how could they? They don't have a bodyguard like Connor to protect them.'

Amber glanced over her shoulder at Connor. Their eyes met and he tried to offer her a reassuring smile. She turned back to her brother. 'I'm sure they'll be waiting at the lodge for us,' she said. 'Now close your eyes and get some rest. We've a long day ahead.'

Connor could tell from the tremor in her voice that

Amber was just barely holding it together, trying not to show weakness in front of her brother. Connor admired her for that. Prodding a stick into the fire, he watched the sparks spiral up into the night. He too needed to appear strong for their benefit, but he felt the weight of responsibility on his shoulders and a knot of deep anxiety gripping his stomach at the fear of failure. If it hadn't been for Amber's brave actions, Henri would be dead or dying by now, poisoned by the black mamba. And it would have been *his* fault. Even now the very thought of that snake sent a shiver down his spine. His phobia had rendered him powerless to protect either of them. He'd not been much of a bodyguard. More a liability. What if he froze again and failed to react? Maybe not against a snake, but a lion or a leopard or some other deadly animal. The incident had sown the seeds of doubt and he seriously questioned if he was up to the task ahead.

Amber appeared quietly at his side, her eyes glistening with tears.

'Are you OK?' he asked.

She nodded and pulled her knees into her chest. They lapsed into silence, listening to the snap and crackle of the fire while staring into the flames.

After a while, she asked, 'Do you honestly think anyone else escaped?'

Connor thought back to the chaos of the ambush. 'Gunner and Buju, perhaps. Also, I'm certain Minister Feruzi and Minister Rawasa and the others in their vehicle did. They're probably raising the alarm as we speak, bringing in reinforcements. With any luck, Buju will be following our tracks and we'll be picked up by a government patrol tomorrow.'

Amber rested her head on his shoulder; whether through tiredness or for comfort he couldn't tell. 'Thank you, Connor,' she said.

'For what?'

'For saving our lives.'

Connor went back to prodding the fire. 'I'm the one who should be thanking *you*. I was useless against that snake.'

'Snake combat isn't part of bodyguard training then?'

'No, of course not,' he replied, before realizing she was teasing him.

'Don't beat yourself up about it. We all have our fears to face. And you've eaten yours!' she said with an impish grin.

Connor laughed. 'I suppose that's what you call true revenge.'

Amber sat up. 'Can I ask you a question?'

Connor nodded. 'Sure.'

'How did the gunmen know where to ambush us?'

Connor turned to face her. 'That's something that's been bothering me too,' he admitted. 'The attack had to be carefully planned; they'd even dug a trench. So they must have known the route in advance.'

Amber's eyes widened in comprehension. 'You mean someone told them. But who?'

'Your guess is as good as mine. One of the soldiers? Perhaps a park ranger?'

'Or even one of the ministers,' suggested Amber darkly.

CHAPTER 38

No Mercy had seen the white boy look straight at him just before the general gave the command to open fire. That second or so of advance warning had undoubtedly saved the boy from a bullet to the head. And, despite the number of rounds he'd drilled into the Land Rover, the boy's lightning-fast reactions had also saved the other two passengers from being killed. Much as he hated to, No Mercy had to admire the boy's warrior spirit.

The fact that there'd been three white kids travelling with the president's convoy in the first place had surprised No Mercy. But their unexpected presence ultimately made no difference to ANL's mission objective: to ambush and kill the president and all his entourage. It was just irritating that the kids had got away.

But they wouldn't be free for much longer.

'Which way did they go?' Blaze demanded of the tracker.

Buju studied the ground surrounding the crashed Land Rover. His eyes read the confusion of footprints in the dirt, identifying three different sets before his attention was caught by a line of broken fern stems. He pointed west.

'Then let's go,' said Blaze impatiently. 'They've got a night's head start on us.'

With Buju and Blaze leading the way, No Mercy followed with Dredd and two other soldiers from the jeep. The jungle was barely awake, dawn filtering through the canopy in shafts of spectral light, and birds only just beginning to sing their morning chorus. As the unit of ANL soldiers trekked through the undergrowth, the tracker paused every so often to look for another sign – a footprint, a damaged piece of vegetation, an unusual displacement of soil, a few strands of red hair caught on a vine. The going was slow but steady, despite Blaze's urgings to move faster.

Occasionally Buju would have to cast ahead, sending the soldiers in two different directions until they found the next clue. Then they would pick up the trail again and move forwards, closing in on their prey with every step. But at times the trail disappeared and Buju would be forced to make an educated guess, assessing the terrain and vegetation for the most likely direction of travel.

'Are you sure we're going the right way?' said Blaze as Buju stopped beside a fallen tree.

In answer to his question, the tracker picked up a blood-soaked wipe from the ground.

'One of them's injured!' exclaimed Dredd with glee.

No Mercy smiled to himself. Perhaps he had shot the boy after all.

'That'll slow them down,' smirked Blaze.

Buju knelt and examined a print in the earth. 'Leopard. Big one. Passed this way an hour ago.'

The soldiers exchanged uneasy looks at the thought of a man-eater in their vicinity.

'We're not hunting leopard,' Blaze snapped. 'Just tell me where they headed next.'

Buju scanned the undergrowth and noted a sharp change in direction. He pointed south.

The trail zigzagged through the jungle until the soldiers hit an animal track. Here, even No Mercy could spot the sign – a clear print of a boy's trainer heading upslope. Sensing they were drawing close to their quarry, the soldiers chambered their assault rifles. Unless the kids had walked through the night, they couldn't have made much more progress.

Cresting a small ridge, they stopped again. Buju studied the ground and surveyed the landscape.

'The trail's gone cold,' he announced.

'What do you mean *gone cold*?' snarled Blaze. 'You claim to be the best tracker in Burundi. Find them!'

'It's harder to track someone on rocky terrain,' Buju replied evenly.

Even through his mirrored sunglasses, Blaze's glare was searing. His right hand began to twitch and No Mercy took a cautious step back, recognizing the telltale signs of the man's legendary short fuse. Unless the tracker produced the goods very soon, there was little doubt that he'd be introduced to Blaze's machete and meet a gruesome end.

Further down the hillside a wisp of smoke drifted above the canopy, catching one of the soldier's eyes.

'Look! There! A fire!'

CHAPTER 39

Connor yawned, stretched and rubbed his eyes. After a night lying on the hard rock floor of the cave, his body felt stiff and sore. Amber was curled next to him, still asleep, her expression so peaceful that Connor had no desire to wake her, not with the sort of day that was ahead of them. He scratched his chest and sat up. Dawn had broken, the warming rays of the sun fingering their way into the cave. Birds warbled in the nearby treetops and Connor heard the distinctive whooping of hyenas and the gruff roars of lions rising up from the savannah below.

Africa was coming to life.

The fire had burnt out overnight, its ashes smouldering and leaving a smoky haze at the cave entrance. Connor gave himself another good scratch. His skin was feeling itchy, not surprising given the layers of grime, sweat and insect repellent. Then a painful nip on his leg caused him to wince. Glancing down, he discovered a massive ant with hooked jaws biting into his skin. He knocked it off with the back of his hand, but instantly it was replaced by three more equally monstrous ants. Then another six. As

Connor went to dislodge these, he was met by a terrifying sight – a seething column of black driver ants swarming across the floor and crawling over him.

Connor jumped to his feet and brushed them away in a frenzy. But he was fighting a losing battle as the teeming mass surged into the cave and up his body.

Amber woke with a start. 'What's wrong?' she asked as he slapped himself repeatedly.

'Ants!' cried Connor.

Seeing him prance around the cave like a mad hatter, Amber began to giggle.

'It's *not* funny!' he said, ripping off his top to get at the ones now crawling under his shirt.

But Amber couldn't help herself. After all the horrors of the previous day, her laughter was a much-needed release and she giggled uncontrollably – until she too saw the floor alive and rippling with the army of black ants.

'They're all over *me*!' she yelped, leaping up and shaking her arms and legs.

Connor had no idea if the ants were poisonous or not, but their bites hurt like crazy, leaving nasty red puncture wounds. Overrun by the horde, he realized they had to act fast.

'The pool!' he cried as she too pulled off her T-shirt.

Running out of the cave, they both jumped into the water.

The coolness was an immediate relief and the ants were soon washed off, floating away like leaves with the current. Connor helped Amber remove the stubborn ones trapped in her long hair.

'All gone,' he said, flicking the last into the water.

Amber turned back to him. As she did so, their arms became entwined and they ended up in an unexpected embrace. For a full second they simply stared at one another. Then she kissed him on the lips.

It was an impassioned, almost desperate kiss. And Connor abandoned himself to it, forgetting their situation, ignoring the danger they were in and simply relishing the moment of sweet delirium.

But his head quickly overruled his heart. He knew it was wrong, even as he continued to kiss her. Amber was vulnerable. Heartbroken from the split with her boyfriend. Distraught at her parents' unknown fate. He guessed she was seeking comfort and security, confusing it with intimacy. And he couldn't blame her – the kiss was an escape for him too. But he knew from past experience that life-or-death situations intensified feelings, leading to developments that might not have occurred under ordinary circumstances. He reminded himself that he was her bodyguard. And, as such, he couldn't cross that line into a personal relationship. Connor had made that mistake before, Charley having burst in on him and the US president's daughter at just such a moment. A second violation of the strict 'no involvement with clients' rule would undoubtedly lead to his dismissal from Buddyguard.

Connor gently pulled away.

Amber looked up at him, confusion in her eyes.

'I shouldn't . . . I can't as your bodyguard.' He glanced towards the cave, hoping that Henri hadn't witnessed their brief kiss. Then he was struck by the horrific realization that he was still in there with the ants. 'Henri?' he called.

Amber spun round, their intimacy forgotten in an instant. '*Henri!*' she shouted, Connor having got no reply.

They scrambled out of the pool, both picturing Henri covered head to foot, the ants swarming into his nose and mouth, suffocating him. Reaching the cave entrance, they found the ferocious ants still on their relentless march across the cave floor but no Henri.

'He can't have gone far,' said Connor, guessing her brother had also fled the tidal wave of insects. His eyes scanned the undergrowth, looking for any indication which direction he might have run.

'What if he's got lost? Or he's been taken by a wild animal?' Amber said in a frantic panic.

'Then we'll find him,' Connor replied, grabbing his Go-bag before it also fell prey to the ants.

'What *have* you two been up to?'

Startled, Connor and Amber spun to see Henri step from behind a bush. He stared at them, dripping wet and shirtless, with a knowing smirk on his lips.

Amber's face flushed red and she snatched up her T-shirt. Then, hiding her embarrassment behind anger, she demanded, 'Where have *you* been? You worried the hell out of me!'

Henri held up his hands, filled with fresh berries. 'Breakfast,' he said.

Relieved just to see the boy safe, Connor said, 'Next time don't wander off on your own.'

'Sorry – but I thought you'd be hungry,' he replied, offering Connor a handful.

Shaking out the last of the ants from his shirt, Connor inspected the berries. 'These could be poisonous.'

'Don't worry, I saw a bunch of monkeys eating them,' Henri explained, confidently popping one into his mouth.

Connor slipped on his shirt and, overruling his caution, ate his share of the berries. Then he spread out the remains of the fire with his foot. As he covered it with earth to ensure it was completely out, a final waft of smoke rose into the air.

'Fresh,' said Buju, examining the remains of the berries drying on the rock. 'But it could just be monkeys.'

Blaze's stony expression suggested he wasn't convinced. He nodded a silent order to the others to check the cave and its surroundings. They quickly fanned out, their eyes to the ground.

No Mercy spotted a patch of displaced earth. He kicked away the dirt to reveal the ashes of a recent fire.

'It must be them,' he called to Blaze.

One of the soldiers then found the charred skin of a snake. He held it up for the others to see.

'They killed and ate a black mamba!' he exclaimed with more than a little admiration.

Dredd wandered into the cave. His bare feet crunched on the ground. It took a moment for his eyes to adjust to the dimness before he spied the pile of leaves near the back wall.

'They slept in here,' he informed Blaze.

Feeling a crawling sensation, he looked down to see a black mass swarming up his legs. His eyes widening in horror, Dredd bolted out of the cave.

'*Siafu! Siafu!*' he screamed, stamping his feet manically to dislodge the vicious driver ants as No Mercy and the other soldiers laughed.

'Dance, Dredd, dance!' taunted one of the men.

'Silence!' barked Blaze, indifferent to the boy's suffering. Turning his back on Dredd, he demanded of the tracker: 'How long since the kids were here?'

Buju found a half-eaten berry, its skin dried out but its flesh still moist. 'Ten minutes, maybe less.'

'And which way did they go?'

The tracker's eyes surveyed the undergrowth. No stems were broken or leaves bruised. No foliage flattened. No footprints in the earth. That left only one obvious route.

'They're following the stream,' he said.

Blaze unsheathed his machete, a grin on his lips. 'Now the hunt really begins.'

CHAPTER 41

At first ankle-deep, the water was soon at knee-height and on occasions Connor, Amber and Henri found themselves wading up to their waists. The rocky bed made walking difficult and, as they followed the stream downhill, the current strengthened, threatening to sweep them away. However, without any clear paths through the dense under-growth, Connor had determined that the stream was the quickest and most direct route out of the jungle.

The three of them trekked in silence, Connor taking the lead, Henri behind and Amber at the rear. She hadn't brought up the subject of their kiss and neither had he, but whenever he glanced back to check on them she'd hold his gaze a moment before resolutely looking away. Connor couldn't tell whether this was through shyness, flirting or regret on her part. But there were far greater things to worry about than the consequences of a kiss.

Once they had navigated the stream down to the edge of the jungle, they'd have to cross the open savannah, avoid-ing elephants, buffalos and lions, while trying not to be spotted by rebel militia. To make matters worse, Connor had no map and only a vague idea of where the lodge was located. If by some miracle they did manage to reach it safely, they still had to hope the facility was in government hands and that the comms were functional.

The sheer scale of the task ahead seemed impossible. But a phrase he'd once read in a book came to mind: *Don't try to eat an elephant for lunch*. The bizarre saying had confused him at first. Then his gran had explained that it meant any task the size of an elephant should be broken down into smaller, more manageable chunks. That way it wasn't such a daunting prospect. Applying the same principle to their current situation, Connor needed to focus on leading them safely through the jungle. That would be his first goal. Anything after that could wait.

The stream widened and Henri came up by his side.

'I never thought a safari would be like this,' he said, attempting a smile that only revealed how scared he really was.

'Nor did I,' admitted Connor. 'But you'll have some story to tell your friends back home.'

'Are we going to make it back home?' he asked, the simple question striking at the heart of their predicament.

Connor looked him squarely in the eye and, with as much confidence as he could muster, replied, 'It's my job to protect you and your sister. I promise to get you both home safely.'

Henri became thoughtful for a moment. 'So, will you ask my sister out when we get back?'

Connor almost stumbled and fell into the water.

'Ermm . . . I think you've got the wrong idea. We were just washing off the ants.'

Henri gave him a sideways look that said *whatever*, then continued: 'She likes you. I can tell.'

Connor glanced over his shoulder. Amber was a few metres back, concentrating on keeping her balance over the rocky streambed.

'It would be great if you were her boyfriend,' enthused Henri. 'Then we could hang out more. We could go to football matches together –'

Connor ruffled Henri's hair. 'Enough of your matchmaking. Let's escape this jungle first, eh?'

As they were negotiating round a small waterfall, they heard a distant voice cry out, '*Siafu! Siafu!*'

'Did you hear that?' said Amber, exchanging a fearful look with Connor.

Connor nodded. He recalled Gunner's words: *It doesn't matter whether you're a lion or a gazelle in this life; when the sun comes up, you'd better be running.*

They started running.

Clambering over the rocks and splashing through the shallows, they fled downstream. While it was entirely possible the voice didn't belong to a rebel militia, Connor wasn't willing to take that gamble.

'Go! Go!' he urged, knowing they had to put significant distance between themselves and their pursuers if they were to have any chance of escaping capture.

But the water was slowing their progress. And tiring them too. Henri tripped and fell face first into the stream. Connor dragged him to standing, pushing him ahead and alongside his sister. As the jungle thinned out and the waterway broadened, they took to the bank and headed across firm ground. Despite the spiny bushes clawing at their clothes, they were able to quicken their pace. But Connor realized they'd now be leaving clear tracks for the gunmen to follow.

Behind, they heard another shout. Closer this time.

Henri's breathing was tight and ragged and he was struggling to keep up. When they finally reached the edge of the jungle, he was wheezing so badly that Connor thought he might collapse. Henri fumbled for his inhaler and took two desperate puffs.

'He can't keep this up much longer,' panted Amber, leaning her brother against a tree to rest.

Looking out across the broad expanse of the savannah, Connor knew they had no hope of outrunning the gunmen. Certainly not with Henri's asthma. Ahead of them were miles of rolling hills and high grasses, interspersed with clumps of acacia trees, tangles of thorn bushes and solitary baobabs rising up like sentinels from the red earth. In this terrain they'd be easy prey for any predator – particularly a group of well-armed militia.

'Perhaps we should just surrender?' Amber suggested. 'I mean, why would they want to hurt us? Three kids. We're not a threat to anyone.'

'The ambush we witnessed made us a threat,' replied Connor. He glanced down at his father's knife and instantly dismissed any notion of making a stand against the gunmen.

Yet while they couldn't run, they could hide.

'The baobab,' said Connor, pointing to one of the immense trees that dominated the savannah.

'What about it?' asked Amber.

'People rarely look up,' explained Connor.

Immediately comprehending his plan, Amber urged Henri to his feet. Rushing over to the nearest baobab, a ten-metre-tall gnarled specimen, Amber volunteered to climb the trunk first. The bark was knotty and offered lots of handholds, and her bouldering skills enabled her to pick out the fastest route. She ascended the trunk with the ease of a monkey. Once in the refuge of the lower boughs, several metres above the ground, she hung herself over the edge.

'Your turn, Henri,' she said, beckoning him to join her.

Her brother took one look and shook his head. 'I . . . can't . . . do it,' he gasped. 'I'm too . . . tired.'

'Of course you can. With our help,' said Connor, cupping his hands to give him a boost. 'Now hurry, they can't be far off.'

Snatching a last puff from his inhaler, Henri took hold of a groove in the bark and, with immense effort, began to haul himself up. While Amber guided her brother with the climb, Connor encouraged him from below. Exhausted and wheezing, Henri slowly inched his way up the trunk. Connor willed him to go faster, fully expecting to see the gunmen bearing down on them at any moment. But the treeline remained clear . . . for the time being at least. What he did spot, however, caused him to turn and sprint back to the jungle.

'Where are you going?' Amber cried after him as she pulled her brother up the last metre.

Connor didn't have time to explain. At the jungle edge, he used his knife to cut a leafy branch from a low-hanging tree. Then, retracing his steps to the baobab, he swept the dirt behind, obliterating all trace of their tracks. When he reached the base of the baobab, he flung the branch as far as he could, before launching himself at the tree trunk. Clawing his way up, he was almost to the top when his foot slipped off a knot in the bark. He felt himself falling.

'I've got you!' said Amber, her hand clamping on to his wrist.

With gritted teeth and her muscles straining, she dragged him into the refuge of the boughs just as the gunmen burst from the jungle.

Peering from their hiding-place, Connor was stunned to see the small lithe figure of Buju guiding the rebel soldiers on to the savannah. The tracker had seemed such a gentle and kind-hearted man. Now it was evident that his quiet nature had been serving a duplicitous purpose. It also explained why the tracker had stopped the convoy in the middle of the riverbed. And why he had suddenly disappeared when the attack commenced. Buju was the one who'd betrayed the president, his entourage and the Barbier family.

The tracker was the traitor.

Connor watched as Buju quickly spotted the hewn branch on the tree, then knelt to examine the freshly swept earth – its colour ever so slightly different from the surrounding soil. With a sinking feeling in his gut, Connor realized they never had a chance in hell of eluding such a skilled tracker. His only surprise was they'd not been found sooner.

Five soldiers – three men and two boys, all armed with rifles – stood beside Buju as he studied the ground. Connor recognized one of the boy soldiers by the black bandana on his head. He'd been the one firing with wild abandon into their Land Rover when they'd been forced to turn back at the trench. The other boy, in an oversized camo-jacket and red beret, toted a brand-new AK47 – and by the way he carried the weapon it looked like he knew how to use it.

'Which way now?' asked a tall soldier in mirrored shades, his voice travelling clearly in the still, hot air of the savannah.

Buju began walking slowly towards the baobab, following the traces of the swept track. Connor's heart was in his mouth, and his hand went to his knife in readiness. Amber and Henri clung on beside him, the boy's laboured breathing whistling in his ear. As the soldiers drew ever nearer, the three of them sank further into the hollow of the boughs, in a futile last attempt to stay hidden.

Buju knelt to examine the earth once more.

'It's hard to tell,' he replied. 'They've wiped their tracks.'

The rebel in the mirrored shades swore, kicking at the dirt with a heavy black boot.

'Spread out!' he ordered his soldiers. 'They can't be far away.'

'Wait!' said Buju, holding up his hand. 'You'll disturb any signs they might have left.'

Standing, he scanned the terrain, his gaze passing over the long grasses, the baobab tree, the tangle of bushes . . . then flicking back again to the baobab. Connor felt like a mouse caught in the deadly sights of a hawk.

It was all over. There was nowhere to run. No chance of fighting. No hope of hiding.

'What is it, Buju?' asked the rebel.

Buju's gaze immediately dropped to the discarded branch, several metres from the base of the baobab.

'Have you seen something?' demanded the rebel, his mirrored glasses glinting in the sun as he looked sharply around. 'Where are they?'

'This way,' said Buju, walking purposefully on.

CHAPTER 43

Connor peered from the bough as Buju proceeded to lead the soldiers *away* from their baobab tree and into an acacia thicket. Connor was utterly baffled, until he saw the gleam of a large machete, its tip pressed against the small of the tracker's back.

'Buju looked straight at us!' exclaimed Amber under her breath. 'He *knew* we were hiding here.'

Connor nodded solemnly. 'That's why he went the other way.'

'He's on our side?' questioned Henri, no longer wheezing so badly.

'Apparently so. By the looks of it, he's being forced to track us.'

Cautiously sitting up, Connor peered in the direction the rebels had gone. Amid the tall grasses on the next rise, he spotted the distinctive red beret of the boy soldier. They were still heading away from them. But how long Buju could keep up the pretence of following a false trail was anyone's guess. And Connor didn't think the rebel with mirrored sunglasses was likely to be taken for a fool.

'Let's move while we can,' he said. In the distance he could see the ridge upon which the lodge was located. Gloriously lit by the morning sun, it offered the promise of a safe haven. But between them and the ridge stretched the open savannah populated by herds of grazing zebra, kudu and antelope, along with the unseen threat of lion, leopard and cheetah lurking in the undergrowth.

This assignment should be a walk in the park for you, Charley had said.

Some walk this is turning out to be, thought Connor as he took a bearing on the ridge with his compass watch.

Swinging his legs off the bough and on to the trunk, he clambered down from the baobab, followed by Henri and Amber. Once on the ground they lost sight of their destination, but, relying on the compass, they set off due south.

'How long do you think it will take us now?' asked Amber with an anxious glance at her asthmatic brother.

'Depends how fast we can walk,' Connor replied as they headed up a rise, winding between clumps of bushes and trees. 'Four, maybe five hours.'

Above their heads yellow weaver birds swooped, catching tiny insects disturbed from the grass by their feet. The bush hummed with life and the sun, blazing in the powder-blue sky, was already sending ripples of heat up from the ground. Connor wiped the sweat from his brow as they continued to climb.

'Do we have any water?' asked Henri, his voice tight and hoarse.

'Sure,' said Connor, having filled the bottle back at the

cave. Stopping, he unscrewed the cap, inserted the Lifestraw and passed the bottle to Henri. 'Only take a few sips,' he advised. 'It might be some time before we reach the river and can refill.'

Henri grimaced at the taste of the warm chemically treated water. 'What I'd do for an ice-cold can of Coke,' he sighed.

As he sucked on the straw, Amber said quietly, 'It's good that Buju's still alive.'

Connor nodded, his eyes scanning the scrub for any sign of predators. The knowledge Gunner had imparted about the African wildlife made him more aware than ever of the constant danger surrounding them.

'Probably means our parents are OK too,' continued Amber, phrasing it more as a question than a statement.

'Yes, it seems likely,' agreed Connor, taking the water bottle back from Henri. As long as Laurent and Cerise served a purpose for the rebels, then Connor reasoned they might still be alive – if only as hostages to demand a ransom from the French government. It was a slender hope but a credible one.

As they approached the top of the rise, a gunshot echoed across the plain.

'Down!' cried Connor, pushing both Henri and Amber to the ground.

There was more gunfire – but at a distance. Retrieving the binoculars from his pack, Connor knelt up and searched for the source of the shots. But he didn't need binoculars to realize what was happening.

Buju fled through the bush, crouching down low as bullets tore up the undergrowth around him. The threat of his own torture and death had impelled him to track the children. But he hadn't been able to betray them. Not when he knew the horrendous fate that awaited them.

Of course he'd spotted the three youngsters in the baobab tree. To a tracker, it was the most obvious place to hide. And the red hair of the French brother and sister was like a beacon in the bush. But, when he'd seen them tucked in the hollow of the lower boughs, it wasn't their faces he saw but the faces of his own children. He realized that whatever the risks to his own life he couldn't be responsible for their capture. No parent on earth would wish their offspring to suffer at the hands of these cruel rebel soldiers.

After leading the gunmen away from their quarry, he'd kept up the pretence of following a live trail. But it wasn't long before Blaze began to suspect something. That's when he'd made the stupid mistake of fabricating a sign – to convince the rebel they were still on the right track. Asking some of the soldiers to cast ahead, he'd snapped a plant stem when he thought no one was looking. Then a minute later announced its discovery and the direction in which the children were supposedly fleeing.

But the boy soldier No Mercy had spotted his deception and declared him a liar.

That was the moment he ran for his life.

'Don't let that snake get away!' Blaze snarled over the ferocious blasts of AK47s.

Like a bolting rabbit, Buju zigzagged through bushes. If he could reach the cover of the jungle, he might have a chance of losing them among the trees. But blood flowed freely from the gash across his back where Blaze had slashed at him when he'd fled. He could feel it dripping off him, leaving a bright red trail in his wake.

The soldiers raced after him, their guns blazing.

A bullet clipped his shoulder, knocking him to the ground. Buju got up, staggering, before another shot pierced his thigh. He stumbled on, the treeline almost within reach, until he felt a rock-hard strike to his back as a round punctured his right lung. He was crawling now, the jungle only metres from him . . .

Suddenly all was calm, the heavy thunder of gunfire fading and the sounds of the savannah returning. He could hear the saw-like buzz of cicadas in the grass. The warbling of weaver birds in the trees. The braying of zebra and somewhere in the distance the mighty roar of a lion. Buju saw his lifeblood seeping into the red earth and grasped the rich soil between his fingers for one last time, savouring its warmth and comfort.

Then the tracker was wrenched from his dying peace as Blaze planted a foot on his back, seized the curls of his hair and jerked his head back.

Pressing the edge of his machete against Buju's throat, he demanded, 'Which way did the children *really* go?'

Buju gasped in pain. 'They're miles . . . away . . . by now.'

'You lie. I know we were on the right track.'

'You'll never find them . . . without me,' wheezed Buju.

'We'll see about that,' said Blaze and drew the blade sharply across Buju's throat.

Blood sprayed into the red earth and the tracker fell still. Flicking the gore off his machete, then wiping it on the dead tracker's shirt, Blaze stood and surveyed the savannah.

'Double-back to the baobab tree,' he told his gang of misfit soldiers. 'That's where we lost their trail.'

As No Mercy obeyed Blaze's order, he thought he caught a gleam of reflected sunlight on the rise. A second glint convinced him that he hadn't been mistaken.

Sickened at the sight of Buju's slaughter, Connor lowered his binoculars. He'd seen the boy soldier with the red beret point in their direction and wondered how on earth they'd been spotted so quickly. Buju no longer knew where they were so he couldn't have betrayed them. Then, as he stuffed the binoculars back in his Go-bag, Connor cursed his stupidity – he'd been looking due east so the sunlight would have reflected off the lenses.

'What's going on?' asked Amber, still lying prone in the dirt beside her brother.

'Buju's just been killed,' he explained.

'My God, no!' The blood visibly drained from her face as the hope she'd held for her parents' survival died along with Buju.

Connor dragged the two of them to their feet. 'The gunmen are coming this way. We need to move fast!'

Staying low, they kept to the cover of the bushes as much as they could. Without Buju to guide the rebels, Connor hoped the soldiers would be slower to track them. So long as the three of them stayed out of sight, they might still have a slim chance of evading their pursuers.

Cresting the rise, the savannah once again opened out before them, mounds of granite boulders breaking up the terrain between strips of dense undergrowth and islands of flat-top trees. In the distance the land flattened out into a grassy plain where the Ruvubu River wound like a glistening python, dividing the valley in two. Until now Connor hadn't given any consideration as to how they'd cross that wide stretch of waterway . . . *if* they even got that far.

He risked a quick glance back and spotted the red beret racing through the long grass and bushes towards them.

'Keep going,' Connor urged, directing Amber and Henri downslope.

Running as fast as Henri's asthma would allow, they followed an animal trail across the savannah and into a dense thicket. Emerging at the other side, Amber came to an abrupt halt, Henri and Connor almost running into the back of her before they also froze.

A few metres ahead of them a zebra was being ripped apart in a feeding frenzy by a pack of spotted hyenas. Their powerful jaws snapping, their fur stained with blood, they squabbled over the kill, cackling and giggling like lunatics from an asylum.

The lower-ranked hyenas, pushed out by the dominant females, instantly turned their attention to the human intruders. Staring at their newfound prey with dark hungry eyes, they bared their teeth, drool dripping from their ravenous mouths. One by one, the other hyenas fell silent as they became aware of the presence of Connor, Amber and Henri.

Faced by such a fearsome pack of wild animals, it took all Connor's willpower not to simply turn and flee. But he knew from Gunner's advice to do such a thing would trigger the hunting instinct.

'*Back away,*' he whispered, trying to keep the panic out of his voice. '*Slowly.*'

Amber managed the slightest of nods in acknowledgement. They retreated a step at a time, drawing back into the cover of the thicket. The hyenas advanced in slow deliberate paces, determined to keep their quarry in sight. Henri glanced behind to see where he was walking and a large hyena with a ripped ear stealthily closed the gap.

'*Don't* take your eyes off them,' Connor warned. 'As soon as you do, they'll attack.'

They were almost concealed within the thicket when the matriarch of the clan let out a haunting *whoop* and all of a sudden the hyenas launched themselves. Survival instinct overruling any ranger's advice, Amber, Henri and Connor ran for their lives. They fled through the bush, not caring as the thorns of a wait-a-while tore at their clothes and ripped their skin. Maniacal giggles and growls pursued them on all sides and Connor caught flashes of sandy-brown hair, black snouts and muscular forelegs closing in.

The three of them broke from the thicket and into the long grass. The hyenas matched them pace for pace, boxing them in but not yet attacking. For a brief second

Connor wondered why – then realized the pack was simply tiring them out to make the kill easier.

'The trees!' cried Amber, pointing to a copse of acacia further up the slope.

Connor saw them too and, recalling Gunner saying that hyenas couldn't climb, shepherded his two Principals towards the promised sanctuary of the trees. But they were forced to change direction when a huge snarling hyena blocked their path. They ran across a slope, skirting round a huge pile of boulders as they looked for another way through. Henri was wheezing heavily by now, his face pale with the exertion.

'Up there,' Connor shouted, spotting a narrow gully between the massive boulders.

Taking advantage of a gap in the pack, he led the way to the opening. But the moment they reached it the hyena with the ripped ear lunged at Henri. Panicking, Henri fled in the opposite direction and was soon lost from sight in the tall grass. Connor could hear the pack whooping and howling as they hunted down the youngest and weakest of their chosen prey.

'We have to save him!' Amber cried.

But the hunt wasn't over for them either. Two hyenas were pursuing them up the gully. Then another appeared at the top. Trapped, Connor searched frantically for a different escape route.

'In there,' he said, spotting a narrow gap between two gigantic boulders.

'It's too small,' cried Amber.

Faced with no alternative and the hyenas bearing down on them, Connor shoved her towards the hole. Slender as she was, Amber still struggled to wiggle through. He tossed in his Go-bag, then sucked in his chest as he scrambled after her. But he got stuck halfway, the rocks seeming to press down on him, crushing the breath from his body. He could hear the hyenas bounding towards his exposed flailing legs. Amber, who'd managed to crawl into a little hollow beneath the boulders, tugged frantically on his arms. With a final desperate squirm, Connor scraped through the suffocating gap, just as the hyenas' jaws snapped at his disappearing feet.

Connor and Amber lay pressed against one another in the cramped confines of the hollow. The three hyenas snarled and scratched at the entrance, frustrated at being so close yet unable to sink their teeth into their prey.

'*What now?*' shrieked Amber as she desperately tried to avoid their probing forepaws.

'Don't worry – they can't get to us,' said Connor, glad the hyenas' heavily built shoulders barred them entering any further.

'But we have to get out! We need to rescue Henri!'

A wave of guilt consumed Connor. He dared not think about the poor boy's fate. But how could he be expected to protect *two* individuals at once? Especially against a pack of hunting hyenas. He and Amber had barely escaped with their own lives – and they weren't out of trouble yet.

'We'll find him,' said Connor, hearing the hollowness in his own promise.

'Not before those hyenas have finished with him!'

Amber began to sob – fear, shock and grief all welling up at once. 'Why did we ever come to Burundi? *Why?* This is a living hell! My parents murdered . . . my brother eaten alive . . . I – I . . .'

Connor drew Amber close, letting her cry herself out. The horrors of the past twenty-four hours were enough to break anyone. In fact, he was surprised that she'd held it together for so long. Despite all his hostile environment training, even he was on the point of snapping. Connor had thought his previous two missions would have prepared him for any eventuality. But it dawned on him that *nothing* could have prepared him for Africa. Violent ambushes, murdering gunmen, deadly snakes and man-eating hyenas – Operation Lionheart had been woefully underestimated in terms of threat level and required security support. His only comfort was that he'd failed to call in at two consecutive report times. Alarm bells would be ringing back at HQ and Charley would be investigating the problem, establishing the reason for the communication breakdown and implementing a search-and-rescue operation.

They just had to stay alive until rescue arrived.

Amber's sobbing faded and Connor became aware that the hyenas had gone quiet too.

'Do you think they've given up?' whispered Amber, her head still resting against his chest.

Shifting closer to the entrance, Connor peered out. The sun glared down on an empty patch of scrub and bare rock, a flurry of paw marks in the dirt the only evidence that hyenas had been there at all.

'Maybe,' he replied, edging further out for a better look.

Suddenly he was nose-to-nose with a snarling hyena. Connor jerked back into the hollow. The hyena *whooped* and began to dig more furiously than before.

'I guess that answers your question,' said Connor, shocked at the calculating nature of the animals. He'd spotted the other two hyenas patiently waiting on a boulder, ready to pounce as soon as they emerged.

Connor searched frantically for another way out of their tiny refuge, but they were well and truly stuck between a rock and a hard place. The hollow backed up against another immovable boulder and any openings were barely large enough for a rabbit to fit through. Desperation had driven him to think this gap offered some sort of escape. Now it was destined to be their grave.

The hyena's claws continued to rip at the ground, the entrance hole growing by the minute. Soon the opening would be large enough for its shoulders to pass through and its jaws to enter the hollow and rip them limb from limb.

Amber began her own frantic attempt at digging, using a stone to gouge out a hole behind her. As dirt rained in on them, Connor realized she had entered into a race that they were guaranteed to lose. He drew his father's knife. He'd have to kill the beast before it dug its way in first. But the broad bony skull looked impenetrable, even with a survival knife, and the sharp-pointed teeth appeared fearsome weapons to overcome. It would be a bloody and fraught fight to the death for one of them.

As Connor steeled himself for an attack, a gunshot rang

out, startling the hyena, and it stopped digging. More heavy gunfire caused it to turn tail and flee. Connor and Amber exchanged a glance, at once relieved yet fearful of what was to come next.

They heard the sound of heavy boots crunching in the dirt.

'I saw them enter the gully, Blaze,' said a boy's voice.

'Then where are they?' growled a deeper voice that Connor recognized as belonging to the rebel with mirrored sunglasses.

A shadow passed across the hollow's entrance and Connor spotted a pair of black boots and the bare feet of a boy, no more than a couple of metres from their hiding-place.

'Maybe they escaped.'

Suddenly Amber's body went rigid. Disturbed by her earlier digging, a small oil-black spider with a bulbous abdomen had emerged and was crawling across her arm. Realizing Amber was about to scream and give away their location, Connor clamped a hand over her mouth. Her eyes grew wide with sheer terror as the eight-legged arachnid crept up her arm and towards her neck.

'Did you *see* them escape?' Blaze questioned.

'No,' replied the boy.

As the spider reached her shoulder, Connor noticed a distinctive red hourglass marking on its underbelly. At once he felt Amber's paralysing fear seep into his own bones.

'Then search the gully, top to bottom,' ordered Blaze. 'Leave no stone unturned.'

The black widow continued its slow yet deliberate journey up Amber's neck. Neither Connor nor Amber could move, both held captive by the venomous spider as it probed her cheek with its forelegs, its multiple eyes glistening in the hollow's dim light.

Amber closed her own eyes as her worst nightmare stared directly at her. Connor could feel a cold sweat break out on her skin as the spider crawled across her face. Its legs brushed against his fingers, which were still clamped over Amber's mouth. But he dared not knock the black widow off. They had nowhere to go and a single bite from such a spider could inject a lethal neurotoxin, resulting in burning pain, vomiting, swelling and even death.

In the gully, the soldiers were working their way down, searching every nook and crevice. Connor could hear them getting closer with each passing second. Amber was now as pale as death, the spider passing across her right eyelid. She twitched in panic and the black widow stopped, probing her soft skin with its two front legs.

Footsteps approached their hollow, the entrance darkening as a soldier bent down to look inside. Then a second gunshot went off, swiftly followed by several more blasts.

'Over here!' came a distant cry.

The shadow disappeared from their entrance, the crunch of feet on earth rapidly receding. But neither Connor nor Amber could risk moving. The black widow was now painstakingly making its way through her tangle of red hair. Connor prayed the creature wouldn't decide to make a nest there. Amber had her eyes fixed on his, utter desperation filling them as she heard the whisper of the eight-legged creature pass her ear.

After what seemed an eternity, the spider crawled out on to the rock and disappeared into a dark fissure.

'It's gone,' whispered Connor.

As if woken from a trance, Amber bolted for the entrance.

'No!' hissed Connor. 'They might still be out there.'

But Amber was paying him no heed. She scrambled out of the hollow and into the sunlight. Left with no other choice, Connor shoved his Go-bag through the opening and followed close behind. He found Amber sitting on a rock, panting rapidly, her hands trembling. Connor quickly scanned the gully. Thankfully there were no soldiers or hyenas in sight. He knelt before Amber.

'Are you OK?' he asked.

Still in post-phobic shock, her eyes glassy and unfocused, she didn't reply. But the colour in her cheeks seemed to be slowly returning. Connor touched her arm and she almost leapt out of her skin.

'It's all right,' soothed Connor. 'You're safe now.'

'Safe?' said Amber, staring at him incredulously, then waving her hand at the surrounding savannah. 'You call *this* safe?'

She stood and began striding down the gully. Connor grabbed her arm.

'Let me go,' she demanded with a fierce glare at him.

'But that's the direction the gunmen went,' argued Connor.

'It's also the way my brother went,' she replied, shaking herself free from his grip and dashing out of the gully.

Shouldering his Go-bag, Connor raced after her, expecting at any moment to run straight into the rebel soldiers . . . or the open jaws of a bloodthirsty hyena. He almost lost sight of Amber among the tall grasses but finally caught up with her kneeling at the base of a small acacia tree. Henri's inhaler was lying discarded in the dirt beside a pool of sticky blood, a cloud of flies buzzing over its surface. Connor felt his heart sink. They were too late.

'Have you . . . found him?' he asked, fearing the hyenas had torn the boy apart.

'It isn't his blood,' said Amber quietly as she retrieved the inhaler. She indicated a dead hyena sprawled on the ground behind the tree, its belly exploded open by a high-calibre round. 'My brother must have reached this tree. He was safe. He escaped the hyenas, but –' she looked up at him, her eyes rimmed red with tears – 'not the gunmen.'

They'd both heard the repeated blasts of gunfire and the rebel soldier shout out. However, that didn't necessarily mean Henri had been shot. The evidence suggested the rebel had saved her brother from being eaten by the hyenas. That was surely a good sign. But what had happened to Henri afterwards? That was the question.

Was he injured? Had he escaped? Or had the soldier captured him?

From a nearby bush came a pained high-pitched cry.

'Henri?' called Amber in desperate hope.

They rushed over only to discover a wounded hyena. It lifted its head at their approach, revealing a torn ear, and snarled at them. Bullets had reduced the animal's hindquarters to a bloody, furry mess, yet the beast still clung on to life. It lunged at them with its forepaws, its jaws snapping in agonized torment. Even as it was dying, the hyena seemed determined to kill them.

Connor and Amber backed cautiously away.

'We *have* to find Henri,' insisted Amber.

'Our best hope is to reach the lodge and call for back-up.'

'No,' said Amber firmly. 'I won't leave my brother alone in this hellhole. I need to find out what's happened to him.'

It was a catch-22 situation. Connor couldn't abandon Henri to his fate. Yet he couldn't lead Amber into further danger. She was the one Principal left under his protection. That made her his priority. *Or did it?* They were both equally important. But should he risk one to save the other? It was a gamble that could result in him losing *both* Principals, as well as his own life.

Hearing a rustle in the grass behind him, Connor spun to confront a rebel soldier emerging from the bushes. Before the man could level his AK47, Connor hip-shoved

Amber to one side, sending her flying into the cover of the tree. Then he launched himself at the soldier, taking three running steps to add power to his flying side-kick. The soldier, completely unprepared for the speed and suddenness of the attack, was struck in the chest. The technique, a speciality of Connor's in kickboxing matches, impacted so hard that Connor heard a rib crack as the soldier was knocked off his feet. The man tumbled backwards into the heart of a wait-a-while bush and was instantly ensnared. Scrambling to seize hold of his AK47, he only entangled himself further until the bush had wrapped round him like a ball of barbed wire. Helpless in its clutches, bleeding from multiple cuts and wheezing from a broken rib, the soldier cried out for help.

Connor turned to Amber to make their escape but, before they could, the barrel of a gun was pressed into the small of his back.

'Don't m–'

Not waiting for the rebel to finish his sentence, Connor pivoted on the spot, knocking the barrel aside with his elbow, and struck full force with a one-inch-push to the chest. The modified palm strike not only smashed the solar plexus, winding his attacker, but sent him flying several metres back. A burst of rapid gunfire filled the air, bullets shooting off in all directions as the rebel crashed down hard on to the ground. Connor dropped to one knee while Amber cowered behind the protection of the tree trunk, splinters of bark flying.

For the first time Connor got a good look at his

attacker. It was the boy soldier with the black bandana, the letters DREDD etched in white across the front. He wore the same dead-eyed gaze as when he'd shot at their Land Rover, and his right ear was missing, as if it had been hacked off by a machete. The boy was slightly smaller than Connor but, hardened from a life of warfare in the jungle, he was already rising to his feet. Connor couldn't let that happen. He rushed over and kicked the assault rifle from his grasp.

Trained only in fist brawls, Dredd bulldozed head-first into Connor's stomach. The tactic, inelegant but effective, knocked the wind out of Connor and they both tumbled to the ground. Dredd knelt up first, pinning Connor's arms with his knees, then pummelling him with his fists. Connor's head rang as he was pounded with knuckles hard as iron. Somewhere far off he heard Amber cry out his name and the howl of the wounded hyena. Connor bucked and arched his back, trying to dislodge Dredd from his dominant position as a particularly vicious strike split his left eyebrow. Blood pouring into his eye, Connor's vision became blurred. If he didn't do something soon, he'd be beaten to death.

He tried to reach for his knife, but the handle was caught beneath him and his arms were still pinned.

Come on, hotshot. The round's not over yet.

Ling's ringside taunts filled his head. Their matches had not only toughened him up but also taught him a trick or two. One of her favoured techniques was to attack nerve points – *kyusho-jitsu* – enabling her to disable limbs, inflict extreme pain and break down the body's ability to fight, nerve by nerve.

Dredd stopped battering him with his fists but only to grab a large stone. Through the red filter of his vision, Connor saw the boy lift it high above his head. Realizing with horror that a single strike would be the end of him, Connor reached for the *yako* point – halfway up the boy's inner thigh. He pinched and twisted the nerve near the skin's surface.

Dredd leapt off him with a high-pitched yelp of pain, then a moment later began screaming. Dazed and blood-ied, Connor crawled away. Even he was amazed the nerve point was so effective. Then he saw that the boy had rolled into the wounded hyena's reach. Its jaws had clamped round Dredd's upper arm, which it was now ravaging between its teeth. In agonized panic, Dredd battered at the hyena's head with the rock. But he was having little effect on the enraged animal.

Connor staggered to his feet, seizing their opportunity to escape.

'*Aidez-moi!*' cried the boy soldier, his attack on the hyena weakening as the animal gnawed on his arm. '*Help! Please!*'

Despite Amber being his number-one priority, Connor couldn't leave the boy to be ripped to shreds. It was too horrific a death, even for someone who'd just tried to kill him. The boy's AK47 lay in the dirt beside Connor. Snatch-ing up the assault rifle, its weight even heavier than he'd anticipated, he lined up the sights and pulled the trigger.

The AK47 roared, its butt hammering into his shoulder, the recoil of automatic fire almost knocking him over. Bullets ripped up the ground as he battled to keep control of the powerful weapon. The hyena, its jaws still clenched round the mauled arm, let out a pained whimper then went limp. Dredd collapsed back on to the earth, groaning in pain but alive.

'Let's go,' said Connor, running over to Amber. He could hear the other rebels, alerted by the gunfire, crashing through the bush towards them.

'But what about Henri?' she asked as he dragged her into the long grass.

'We'll never find him if we're dead.'

CHAPTER 49

Barely knowing in which direction they were headed, Connor's only goal was to evade the gunmen. Keeping a firm grasp of Amber's hand, he weaved a path through the disorientating clumps of bushes and trees. As he ran, the AK47 thumped painfully against his hip. Cumbersome and heavy, the weapon was slowing him down. But he rejected the idea of discarding it. The rifle was their only serious means of defence.

The shouts of the rebel soldiers continued to pursue them through the bush, drawing ever closer. Connor stopped, shouldered the rifle and fired several warning shots into the trees.

Clamping her hands over her ears to muffle the gun's thunderous blasts, Amber cried, 'You've just given our position away!'

Connor nodded. 'But now they know we have a weapon too. That should make them more cautious about following us. And hopefully slow them down.'

Avoiding the obvious trail that lay before them, Connor

checked his compass watch and altered direction, heading at right angles through the bush. The sun was glaringly hot and his throat felt parched and clogged with dust. Amber was also panting hard, but he dared not stop again, however much a drink might revive them. As they negotiated a steep rocky slope, Amber stumbled and Connor had to drag her upright. The constant running was beginning to take its toll on both of them. Their meagre breakfast of berries had been barely enough to satisfy their hunger, let alone sustain them. Now they were running on empty, only adrenalin and fear fuelling their flight.

They burst through a copse of trees and disturbed a group of dik-diks feeding on the brush. The tiny fawn-coloured antelopes bounded away, whistling a high-pitched *zick-zick* in alarm. Connor knew the soldiers would be on to them again. To make matters worse, the ridge had flattened out into a grassy plateau, leaving them dangerously exposed. As they raced across the open ground, Connor heard the sound of rushing water. It grew louder with every step until it became a mighty roar. All of a sudden they found themselves teetering on the brink of a barren rock ledge. A billowing curtain of white water cascaded some thirty metres straight down to form one of the primary tributaries that fed the Ruvubu River. A fine mist hung in the air, catching rainbows of glistening sunlight.

Connor cursed their bad luck. The overhang was little more than a picturesque dead end for them. They'd have to double back and find an alternative route to the plain.

'We could climb down,' suggested Amber, peering over the ledge at the sheer rock face. Connor took one glance at the dizzying drop and the slick, treacherous stone and felt his stomach lurch.

'Not if I were you,' said a rough voice. 'This is Dead Woman's Fall.'

The two of them spun round to find Blaze standing behind them, his shaven head glistening with sweat from the chase. A moment later the boy soldier with the red beret appeared, breathing hard, gun in hand. Connor immediately levelled his own AK47 at Blaze.

'The Batwa tribe used to throw women suspected of witchcraft from this ledge,' the rebel explained, unperturbed by the gun pointing at his chest. 'Any woman who survived the fall was declared a witch and put to death.' He thumbed the handle of his machete on his hip as he slowly advanced on them. 'But most didn't survive, and the few who did were almost always eaten alive by the crocodiles waiting at the bottom.'

Blaze smirked at their horrified expressions as they were forced to retreat to the very lip of the precipitous drop. Connor thrust the AK47's barrel at the rebel. 'Stay back!'

Blaze held up his hands in mock surrender. 'Whatever you say, chief.'

'What have you done with Henri?' demanded Amber.

Blaze's eyes raked over her. 'That little red-headed kid? I'm afraid a hyena got its teeth into him. He was screaming like a stuck pig so I put the boy out of his misery.' The rebel patted the machete, its metal blade smeared with fresh blood.

'NO!' gasped Amber, her legs giving way beneath her.

'I'm so sorry,' said Blaze with false sincerity as he edged closer. 'I can understand how upsetting this m–'

'This is your last warning,' cut in Connor. 'One more step and you're a dead man.'

Blaze cocked his head to one side and studied Connor's face intently. 'Unlike No Mercy here –' his eyes flicked to the boy soldier – 'you're no killer.'

'You want to test that theory?' said Connor, his finger primed on the trigger. But deep down he too questioned his ability to shoot a man at point-blank range.

Blaze shrugged indifferently. 'Well, if you had the killer instinct, you'd have let Dredd die. I certainly would have.'

The rebel took another brazen step forward.

Connor pulled the trigger.

There was just a dry *click*. He squeezed again. Nothing. The AK47 had jammed.

Laughing, Blaze unsheathed his machete and pointed its tip at Connor. 'Nowhere to run now, chief!'

Connor hurled the useless rifle at the rebel. Then, grabbing hold of Amber, he jumped off the ledge.

CHAPTER 50

'Connor is probably enjoying himself too much to reply,' said Jason, his feet propped up on the desk in Alpha team's operations room as Charley attempted to call Connor's mobile for the third time that morning. 'If I were him, I'd be relaxing in a private plunge pool with that French girl.'

Charley bristled at the suggestion and Ling flung a pen at Jason's head.

'I was only joking!' cried Jason, ducking just in time. 'I wouldn't cheat on you, Ling.'

Ling shot him a furious glare, then turned to Charley. 'Remember, communication's pretty non-existent within the park. He possibly doesn't have a signal.'

'I know, but it's not like Connor to miss an evening *and* a morning report-in. I can't contact him on his phone or get through to the lodge. I can't even locate his mobile using the GPS app,' she explained, pointing to the digital map of Burundi displayed on her computer screen. 'That's over twelve hours without official contact. It's time we raised the alert.'

'Aren't you being a little hasty?' said Richie, munching on a bowl of cornflakes. 'He'll have been asleep most of that time. And it's not as if they're in the middle of a war zone. He's on a safari holiday, for heaven's sake!'

Jason nodded in agreement. 'Connor would use the SOS app if he was in real trouble.'

'If he's in *real* trouble, he might not be able to use the SOS app,' Charley argued.

'Try the lodge one more time,' suggested Ling. 'Then we'll go to the colonel.'

Charley picked up the phone and dialled. The connection failed as before. She tried again. There was a distant echoing ring. Her hand clasped the receiver tighter. After eight rings, the call was picked up.

'*Bonjour, Ruvubu Safari Lodge. C'est Yasmina qui parle. Comment puis-je vous aider?*'

The line was poor, but the voice clear enough to make out.

'*Parlez-vous anglais?*' asked Charley, switching to speakerphone so the others could hear.

After a slight delay, the voice answered, 'Of course. How can I help?'

'I'm wanting to speak to one of your guests. Connor Reeves? He's staying with the Barbier family.'

There was a longer pause. 'I'm sorry. They're currently on a bush safari. Would you like to leave a message?'

'Yes, please tell him his sister Charley called and to get in touch as soon as possible.'

'Certainly. Have a good day.' The line went dead.

'See!' said Jason, leaning back in his chair, his hands behind his head. 'Told you there was nothing to worry about.'

CHAPTER 51

The lodge receptionist put down the telephone with a trembling hand.

'Well done, Yasmina,' said General Pascal, stroking the young lady's cheek with the barrel of his Glock 17. She shuddered as he then traced a line down her slender neck. 'Now get me a drink,' he ordered, waving the pistol towards the lounge area. 'Whisky. The finest.'

The receptionist hurried to the bar as the general strolled in after her.

'My apologies for keeping you waiting,' he said. 'But we need to keep up appearances to the outside world. At least for the time being.'

Mr Grey turned from studying the leopard-skin shield and spears on the wall to face the general. 'By all accounts you're ahead of schedule. I must confess even I was surprised at the swiftness of your coup.'

'You have to seize life before it seizes you!' General Pascal told him, laughing. 'But there's more work to be done. The head may have been cut off the chicken, but the body still runs around.'

'Is that why you need the heavy artillery so quickly?'

The general nodded as the receptionist gingerly stepped over the dead body of the barman, the victim's blood still pooling on the parquet floor, and brought over his whisky. 'Would you like a drink, Mr Grey?' asked the general.

'Sparkling water. No ice.'

General Pascal frowned. 'I'd have thought a man in your line of work would drink something stronger.'

'And I'd have thought a man of your strength wouldn't need to drink anything stronger,' Mr Grey replied coolly.

Their eyes locked and the receptionist took a nervous step back, sensing a change in atmosphere, as if two prowling lions were in the room. Then the general broke into an affable grin at his guest's sharp retort. He waved the receptionist away.

'Unfortunately, we still have the army to fight before we can take control of this country. But I'm confident of victory. An army of sheep –' he glanced in the direction of a boy soldier standing guard on the open-air veranda – 'led by a lion can defeat an army of lions led by a sheep. And, I can assure you, the commander-in-chief of the Burundian army is but a lamb compared to me.'

The receptionist served the sparkling water and Mr Grey took a measured sip. 'Equilibrium can supply the weapons you require at short notice,' he said. 'But we'll need payment upfront.'

'No problem,' replied the general, downing his whisky in one swift gulp. 'Come with me to the mine and take your pick of the diamonds. But first I must introduce you to the man who helped arrange President Bagaza's sudden demise.'

CHAPTER 52

Whistling past the rock face, Connor and Amber barely had time to contemplate the drop before they plunged into the bottom of Dead Woman's Fall three seconds later. Hitting the river's surface at over fifty miles an hour, Amber was torn from Connor's grip and lost amid the churning waters.

The swirling current pinned Connor beneath its surface, where he was spun, twisted and battered against submerged rocks, knocking the wind out of him. He kicked wildly with his legs, desperate for air, but the white water blinded him and he was deafened by its thunderous roar. Totally disorientated, Connor soon gave up all hope of escaping the watery clutches of Dead Woman's Fall. Blaze hadn't been lying when he'd said that few people survived the Batwa tribe's ordeal.

With his lungs burning for oxygen, Connor felt his body involuntarily start to suck in water. As he fought the overwhelming urge, his feet briefly touched down on the riverbed. Calling on the last of his strength, he thrust himself upwards. A moment later he broke the surface and snatched a lungful of glorious air . . . before being swamped by another rush of water and forced under again.

The torrent roiled and seethed around him, but glimmers of sunlight guided him back to the surface now. Coughing and spluttering, Connor swam with the current, struggling to get his breath back and control his panic. The river's rapids blasted him like fire hoses from all directions, mere seconds before another wall of white water engulfed him. Then he was spat out again, bounced off a rock and borne relentlessly through the next series of rapids.

Weakening with every wave and collision, Connor was on the point of drowning when the torrent suddenly eased and the rumble of Dead Woman's Fall began to recede into the distance. He floated limply on his back, slowly recovering his breath and strength. His body felt battered, bone-tired and bruised, but he was alive. *I must be a witch*, he thought, managing a weak laugh at his miraculous survival. Then his thoughts immediately turned to Amber.

He spun round in the murky water, looking for her. The torrent had by now calmed into a wide river bounded by steep banks of red earth, green bushes and tall trees. But there was no sign of her in the water or along the banks. Connor began to despair. He'd failed to protect Henri and now Amber. He knew his snap decision to jump off the ledge had been risky. However, faced with certain death at the hands of the rebels or a slim chance of survival in the waterfall, he'd chosen the latter.

And now he was paying for that decision – with Amber's life.

Wearily, he began to swim for the bank, then out of the corner of his eye caught a glimpse of red hair trailing in the water and spotted an inert body floating downstream from him.

'Amber!' he shouted, paddling frantically in her direction.

There was no response. He kept going, despite the gnawing exhaustion in his limbs. Seeing a log drifting along with the current, several metres ahead of him, he thought about using it for a float. Then the log swished its long scaly tail, propelling itself towards Amber's body. With primal horror Connor realized it was a crocodile.

'*Amber!*' he screamed as another croc slid from the bank into the river's murky waters.

She weakly lifted her head, smiling when she saw Connor waving at her.

'*Crocodile!*' he cried in warning.

Her smile evaporated as soon as she spotted the ominous snout and pair of slit-eyes gliding towards her. With furious strokes, she made for the bank. But the crocodile was closing in fast.

Connor swam for all he was worth. His daily pool training with Charley, which he'd begun in preparation for his previous assignment, was once again paying off as he cut through the water like a fish. He dug deep, calling upon hidden reserves of energy.

Amber was only a few metres from the bank when the crocodile shot forward with a final burst of speed. Connor plunged on, determined to protect her however impossible the odds.

Focused on its immediate prey, the crocodile didn't notice Connor's approach from upstream. As it opened its jaws to sink its teeth into Amber's trailing legs, Connor dived forward and wrapped his arms round the crocodile's snout. Praying Gunner was right about the weakness of their opening jaw muscles, Connor clung on with all his might, his legs wrapped round its body.

Unfamiliar with being the victim of an attack itself, the crocodile momentarily froze and Connor found himself eye-to-eye with the prehistoric beast. It studied him with cold carnivorous intent. Then the crocodile wrenched its head away, its unimaginable brute strength trawling Connor through the water as it attempted to shake him off. But Connor refused to let go – he had to give Amber enough time to escape the river.

Besides, once he released the crocodile, *he* would become the prey.

Enraged, the crocodile dived beneath the surface. Connor barely managed to snatch a breath before he was dragged under with it. The crocodile rolled him, its tail whipping, its body writhing. Connor lost all sense of orientation. His arms became numb as he clung on for dear life. But it was no use. He was weakening with every passing second and his lungs screamed for air. Forced to let go, Connor kicked himself away from the crocodile's jaws and came up gasping.

The crocodile vanished.

'Where's it gone?' he yelled, looking wildly around him.

Amber, who'd managed to crawl up on to the safety of

the bank, scanned the river. Then she spotted a ripple on the surface moving towards him at high speed. 'There!' she cried.

The water being shallow enough for him to touch the muddy riverbed, Connor half-swam, half-ran for the bank. He was waist-deep when the crocodile burst out of the water, its ferocious jaws open wide. It clamped down hard on Connor's back.

'NO! Connor!' Amber screamed as he was dragged back into the river and disappeared beneath the surface.

Water engulfed him once more and Connor felt himself being tugged deeper and deeper. The sunlight faded to a murky twilight and all sounds became a dull wash in his ears. Having seized its prey, the crocodile intended to drown him before devouring him. But its teeth had failed to sink into Connor's flesh. Instead all it had managed to gain was a mouthful of his Go-bag.

Connor fought to free himself, but the straps were being pulled taut around his shoulders. He was entangled like a fish in a net. The crocodile settled on the riverbed and waited it out.

With every passing second, the urge to open his mouth and take a breath increased for Connor. The compulsion built like a wave until it threatened to overpower him. Connor judged he had less than a minute before his will-power gave out and his body's natural yet fatal reflexes took over.

At least his sacrifice meant something. He'd protected his Principal with his life. No bodyguard could be asked to do more. He could only hope that Amber would reach the safety of the lodge on her own before any rebels caught up with her.

Connor continued to struggle, but his actions were becoming weaker and weaker. After all the ordeals he'd faced since the ambush, he had nothing left to give. His limbs were growing heavier, darkness was starting to encroach on his vision and he began to feel light-headed . . .

Out of the gloomy waters floated a ghostly apparition of his gran's face, stern but loving. *I want you to quit. Before something terrible happens to you.*

Sorry, Gran, he thought wistfully, *too late.*

Her face faded, even as it mouthed the words in reply: *At what cost?*

Then a brighter vision appeared. Charley's angelic features, her long blonde hair shimmering like a mermaid's. He heard himself say, *Yeah, but I'll survive.*

We're counting on it, Charley's vision replied. *Listen, I have to go. Stay safe.*

Connor didn't want her to go; he felt at peace with her. But he had no strength to call her back. All around him was now dark and cold. His mother's face swam into view. Not the lined, pained face he'd said farewell to after his birthday visit but the younger, happier one of his youth. The one he remembered before his mother was diagnosed with MS. She smiled at him. A sad smile of goodbye. Connor's heart ached as she too faded and another took its place.

His father.

Clearer than ever before, the rugged handsome features

were like a well-worn map, his green-blue eyes shining with warmth in the darkness.

Connor grinned, his heart overwhelmed with joy at seeing him again.

But his father's expression remained firm as he whispered a familiar piece of fatherly advice: *Never give in. Never give up.*

But I want to be with you, thought Connor.

Don't you dare *give up, son. It's not in our nature.*

As his body's reflexes forced his mouth open and water entered, Connor's hand brushed against his father's knife on his hip. Like an electric spark, it revived him – a sliver of hope that spurred one final bid for survival.

Drawing the knife from its sheath with a hand tingling from numbness, Connor twisted his arm round and jabbed the blade's tip deep into the open eye of the crocodile. A dark red cloud of blood burst forth and the animal immediately released its vice-like grip on his back. Half-blind and in agonizing pain, the crocodile jerked away and vanished into the murky depths of the river.

Fighting against his body's lead-like heaviness, Connor kicked for the surface. His head emerged and he gulped at the air, coughing and spluttering up the mouthful of water he'd swallowed. The hit of fresh oxygen to his lungs brought him round and with wild desperate strokes he swam for the bank.

Bedraggled and half-dead, he crawled through the muddy shallows. Amber rushed over and helped him to stagger up the steep bank, away from the reach of any crocodiles. But they managed little more than twenty steps before they collapsed together beneath the protective shade of an acacia tree.

Yellow-breasted weaver birds chirped merrily above the two prone bodies as they flitted in and out of their intricately woven nests, which adorned the tree's branches like dried fruit. A herd of tawny-coloured impala, the males proudly displaying their long lyre-shaped horns, leisurely strolled past, heading towards the grassy plain to graze. And hippos wallowed in the cool calm waters of the river, occasionally snorting or calling out in a series of deep lazy laughs. With the bright sunshine gilding the savannah, the scene couldn't appear more idyllic. Yet for the two broken individuals at the base of the tree, the paradise surrounding them was as dangerous and lethal as it was beautiful.

Connor had no idea how long had passed since Amber had dragged him from the river's edge, but he had neither the strength nor will to move again. He felt as if he'd gone ten rounds with a heavyweight boxer and been knocked out at every ring of the bell. His clothes were caked in mud and torn in several places. He was covered in abrasions and there wasn't a single part of his body that didn't either ache or cry out in pain.

'I thought . . . I'd lost you for good,' said Amber weakly.

Connor managed a weary shake of the head. 'You can't get rid of me that easily.'

Amber pushed herself up from the ground and winced, clenching her teeth against the pain.

'Are you OK?' Connor croaked.

'I think I lost most of my skin escaping that waterfall,' she replied, lifting her T-shirt to examine the extent of her injuries. 'More to the point, how are *you*?'

'I'm alive. Does that count?'

Amber managed the thinnest of laughs. 'You're crazy, do you know that? Fighting crocodiles and leaping off waterfalls. Next time we climb down!'

'Fine by me,' he replied, closing his eyes as a soft warm breeze blew over them from the open savannah. At least they'd managed to cross the river. He listened to the gentle swishing of the long grasses, content not to move ever again.

Amber finished inspecting her wounds – the whole of her left side had been scraped red raw on the rocks but nothing appeared to be broken – then she gasped as she caught sight of blood seeping into the earth.

'Connor, you're bleeding,' she said, fighting to keep her voice steady.

Connor opened his eyes, the pain suddenly intensifying as he became conscious of his own injuries. Helping him to sit up, Amber removed the tattered Go-bag from his back and gingerly raised his shirt. Her sea-green eyes widened and her mouth dropped open in shock.

'How bad is it?' asked Connor, terrified of what damage the crocodile had inflicted.

'There's barely a scratch on your back!' she remarked in astonishment. 'A few nasty bruises. The bandage round your waist has come loose and the bullet wound's opened up again. But that's about it.'

Connor breathed a painful sigh of relief. It was a miracle his spine hadn't been ripped out.

'I can't believe that crocodile didn't do more damage,' Amber continued, tenderly touching his bare skin with her fingers. 'I *saw* it bite into your back!'

A grin spread across Connor's face when he realized what had saved him from the animal's fearsome jaws. 'The Go-bag has a bulletproof body-armour panel built in,' he explained. Then, with a laugh, he added, 'I can't wait to see the look on Amir's face when I tell him the bag's croc-proof too!'

'Amir?' asked Amber.

'Yeah, one of my best friends at Buddyguard.' Connor looked thoughtfully off towards the horizon. 'I just hope he's faring better on his mission than I am.'

'That wouldn't be hard,' said Amber.

Connor's gaze dropped to the ground as a sharp stab of guilt and grief pierced his heart. 'I'm sorry,' he mumbled, unable to meet her eyes. 'I'm so sorry. I promised to protect you and your brother and I've failed.'

Amber stared at him. 'What are you talking about? You've done *everything* in your power to protect us. Who could have foreseen *any* of this happening? I only meant your friend couldn't be suffering as badly as you. It's not your fault that gunman killed my little brother . . . and my parents . . . It's *his*!'

Trembling with fury and deep loss, Amber lapsed into mournful silence. Connor reached over and took her hand, trying to offer her some comfort, conscious that words would have little impact. He knew from bitter experience the emotional devastation of losing a parent. But to have one's whole family torn from you was something beyond grief. No words could ever describe the desolation experienced after such a loss.

Amber held his hand tight, almost squeezing the life from it. Then, eventually, her grip eased and she glanced down at his weeping wound.

'We need to take care of that,' she said in a voice drained of all emotion.

Amber picked up the ravaged Go-bag, but they didn't need to open it to see that most of the contents were missing. A huge hole had been ripped in the side. The binoculars were gone. So too was the water bottle, Lifestraw, sun lotion and Maglite. Yet, by some small grace of good fortune, the first-aid kit was still in its pouch. The case had been mauled to pieces but Amber managed to cobble together enough to re-dress the wound and clean up his multitude of cuts. Then Connor tended to her injuries, Amber wincing as he gently pressed the last of the antiseptic wipes against her grazed skin. The cut on her lip was already healing, but the one on her cheek needed a fresh plaster. As he applied it, their eyes met and he saw that hers were brimming over with tears.

'I loved my brother . . . you know,' she confessed, choking back a sob. 'He could be annoying at times . . . but what brother isn't? I just never told him . . . and now . . . I'll never get the chance.'

CHAPTER 55

Connor and Amber trudged through the brush in silence, heading south once more. Flies buzzed incessantly around them and the sun beat down, its punishing heat unrelenting. They heard gunshots somewhere in the distance, impelling them onward. As they dragged their feet through the long grass, hunger sapping at their strength with every step, their thirst intensified. But without the Lifestraw they didn't dare drink untreated water from the river, afraid not just of crocodiles but of making themselves ill.

The only items Connor now possessed were his Rangeman watch – still unblemished; his night-vision sunglasses – a little bent and scratched but serviceable; and his father's knife. He'd cut away the excess fabric of the Go-bag, leaving the body-armour panel with its straps as a wearable shield in case they encountered the gunmen again.

Everything else had been lost – even hope.

But, spurred on by his father's words, Connor had eventually willed his battered body to rise and begin the long trek across the burning-hot savannah. As he put one weary foot in front of the other, his father's advice became a mantra in his head – *never give in, never give up, never give in, never give up . . .*

If they could only reach the lodge, their ordeal would be over. *For me at least*, thought Connor as he glanced back at Amber.

Her head bowed and her hair hanging like a veil across her tear-stained face, Amber's spirit was all but broken. Only Connor's dogged insistence that they keep going, that they didn't let the gunmen catch them or become carrion for the vultures, impelled her to move. But she was like a zombie, her eyes unfocused, back stooped and arms hanging loose, just shuffling along near the point of collapse.

Connor knew he looked in an equally bad way. Their fraught escape through jungle, bush and river had taken its toll. With his tattered muddy clothes, innumerable cuts and scrapes, and his half-loping gait due to the painful gash in his side, he would be barely recognizable to his friends in Alpha team. However, the promise of water, food and medical assistance at the lodge kept his spirits up.

Emerging from the brush into a clearing, Connor checked the bearing on his compass watch to ensure they were still on track. As he looked up to gauge their next landmark, he found himself face-to-face with a buffalo.

The solitary bull glared at them from the other side of the clearing. The size of a small car and built like a tank, the buffalo was terrifying in its sheer barrel-shaped bulk, the massive curved horns almost a metre across. Flies scattered in a buzzing black cloud as the bull snorted angrily and shook its colossal head.

Drawing Amber closer to him, Connor took a cautious step back. Confronted by one of the most unpredictable and dangerous animals in Africa, they couldn't afford to provoke it in any way.

The old bull stamped a hoof, kicking up dust. Then before they could retreat any further, it released another explosive snort, lowered its head and charged.

Connor stood his ground, shielding Amber behind him. He simply didn't have the energy to run. And there were no trees close enough for them to climb out of danger anyway. His only defence was to show no fear in the face of the oncoming bull and pray it was a mock charge.

But the buffalo continued to thunder towards them like a runaway truck, its nostrils flaring, its battering ram of hardened bone targeted on Connor. They'd done nothing to antagonize the animal. But the beast seemed incensed.

Amber clung to him, too afraid to flee and too trauma-tized to cry out.

Connor squeezed his eyes shut as the bull bore down on them. He could hear the pounding hooves churning up the dirt and tensed in expectation of the bone-crushing impact. He tried not to imagine the crippling pain of being tossed high in the air, a bag of broken bones, or being gored by one of its horns and trampled to death.

His last act as bodyguard was to shove Amber aside.

Then a gunshot rang out, followed by two more in quick succession.

The buffalo was stopped in its tracks and Connor heard a heavy *whomp* as its mighty body hit the earth. On opening his eyes he was enveloped in a cloud of red dust. As the dust settled, the bull's head appeared no more than a metre from Connor's feet, blood streaming from several bullet holes on its neck, shoulder and flank. Its tongue lolled out and its eyes glazed over as the beast let out one final snort and succumbed to death.

Connor barely had time to register this when a voice with a slight Germanic accent barked, 'What the hell are you two kids doing out here alone?'

From a dense thicket strode a white man in an olive-green shirt and knee-length shorts. Stocky, with a severe crewcut and grey-tinged beard, he was reloading a high-calibre bolt-action rifle fitted with a telescopic sight. In his wake trailed a thin black man wearing an earth-brown T-shirt and army surplus trousers, shouldering a canvas pack.

Connor helped Amber to her feet. 'Are you all right?' he asked.

Amber nodded.

'You could have been killed!' snapped the white man, inspecting the floored buffalo. Satisfied it was dead, he looked them up and down in wonder and horror. 'My God, what's happened to you?'

Judging by the man's attitude and appearance, he wasn't one of the rebels and Connor felt safe enough to lower his guard and explain: 'Our safari convoy –' he coughed, his throat dry and hoarse with dust – 'was ambushed by gunmen yesterday.'

'What gunmen are these?' asked the white man, offering Connor a hip flask of water.

Connor gulped down several mouthfuls before passing the flask to Amber to have the lion's share. The water revived him and he felt some of his strength return. 'Rebel soldiers. Boys too. Possibly they're the ANL, led by a man known as the Black Mamba.'

Both men's faces darkened at the mention of the rebel leader's name.

'We've been on the run ever since,' Connor continued. 'My friend here is the daughter of the French ambassador on an official goodwill visit to the park. We believe her parents, along with President Bagaza, have been murdered. So too has her little brother. We need to contact the authorities immediately.'

With a pitying look at Amber, the white man nodded gravely. 'This is serious.'

He said some words to his companion in a language Connor didn't understand but presumed was the local dialect Kurundi. The black man nodded and hurried off into the bush.

'You're lucky you ran into us,' said the white man, turning back to them. 'Listen, our camp isn't far from here. Come with me. We'll get you fed, watered and patched up. Then we'll sort this out.'

Both Connor and Amber almost collapsed with relief.

Against all the odds, they'd been saved.

'My name is Jonas Wolff,' said the white man as he escorted them through the bush. 'But my friends call me the Wolf.'

'Thank you for rescuing us, Wolf,' said Amber.

'It was either that or watching you get trampled to death by a buffalo,' he replied, his tone matter-of-fact and devoid of humour. 'Those animals show no pity. They kill more people in Africa than any other large game.'

'I was told hippos were the most dangerous.'

The Wolf snorted dismissively. 'The locals don't call a bull buffalo the Black Death for nothing. And such beasts don't go down easily. You're extremely fortunate that I'm a skilled marksman.'

As they walked, the Wolf's eyes constantly scanned the savannah and he kept his rifle primed at all times. Connor was impressed by the man's vigilance. He was taking the threat of the rebels seriously.

At the foot of a hill they entered a large copse of trees, pushing through the dense undergrowth until at its heart they came across a small rudimentary camp. Three green tarpaulins were strung between the tree trunks, the makeshift shelters pitched round a fire in the centre of a patch of cleared ground. To one side was a large pile of supplies, partly covered by a tarpaulin, plus several jerry-cans of water. Four men, including the one the Wolf had sent on ahead, eyed their arrival with curiosity as they squatted beside the fire where a pot sat amid the glowing embers, its contents steaming.

'First, food and water,' said the Wolf, gesturing for Amber and Connor to take a seat on a felled log next to the fire. 'Abel, serve our guests.'

As Connor and Amber settled down, grateful to rest their weary feet at last, the man in the army surplus trousers lifted the pot's lid and gave the contents a stir, sending up a mouthwatering waft of braised meat. Abel passed them two tin plates piled high with a thick brown stew. Too hungry to mutter anything more than a quick thanks, Connor and Amber greedily tucked in.

'What is this?' asked Connor after polishing off his plate and receiving another helping. 'It's delicious.'

'Oryx,' replied the Wolf, offering them both a brimming mug of water each.

Connor hadn't heard of the animal but, after eating snake, anything was a treat. He downed the water, ignoring its chlorinated taste, and the Wolf refilled his cup. As Connor drained that too, the Wolf noticed the bloodstain on his left side.

'Let me have a look at that,' he said.

Connor took off his shirt, grimacing as pain flared through him.

The Wolf peeled back the bandage. 'Nasty,' he commented. 'That'll need a few stitches.'

Connor managed a wry smile. 'I'm afraid I haven't come across any hospitals in this park yet.'

'Not to worry. I can patch you up.' The Wolf went over to the pile of supplies and returned with a medical kit. He took out an emergency suture pack. Removing Connor's bandage, he cleaned up the wound with a sterile saline solution, then laid out a scalpel, needle and thread.

'You've done this before?' asked Connor, growing more and more anxious as he watched the Wolf insert the thin nylon thread through the eye of the needle.

The Wolf nodded. 'A few times. I trust you're not squeamish?'

Biting down on his lip, Connor winced as the Wolf cut away a small piece of loose flesh with the scalpel. Once satisfied the gash was even enough, he pinched the skin together to seal the wound. Then Connor felt the harsh sting of the needle's tip piercing his flesh, followed by a sharp tug as the Wolf tied off the first stitch. The process was repeated three more times, each stitch more agonizing than the last.

'All done,' said the Wolf, cleaning away the blood with an antiseptic wipe.

A sheen of pained sweat on his brow, Connor glanced hesitantly down. The gash was as neatly sewn together as a woven shoelace.

'He's done a great job,' said Amber encouragingly. She turned to the Wolf, who was packing away his suture kit. 'Are you a doctor?'

'No. But I've had enough practice on myself,' he explained, lifting his shirt to reveal a massive outline of scar tissue running across his chest and belly.

'What happened?' gasped Amber.

'A lion is what happened,' he replied, but said no more. Re-dressing the stitched wound, the Wolf handed Connor two small foil packs. 'Take these.'

'What are they?' Connor asked.

'The white tablets are painkillers.'

Connor stared at him. 'Couldn't you have given me these *before* you stitched me up?'

The Wolf shrugged indifferently. 'They wouldn't have taken effect in time. The red-and-white ones are antibiotics. You'll need those to stop any infection. Take one a day for a week.'

'Thanks,' said Connor, immediately popping an antibiotic and chasing it with a couple of painkillers. He slipped the remaining tablets into his pocket.

'I don't know how we can ever repay you for your kindness,' said Amber, setting aside her plate.

'In the bush, strangers are welcomed as family. You simply never know when *you* might need help.' The Wolf stood and returned the medical kit to its place in the supply pile.

'So what are you and your men doing in the park?' asked Connor, putting his shirt back on. Revitalized by the meal, his senses were returning and he noted none of the group wore park ranger uniforms.

'We're conservationists,' replied the Wolf. 'Now, if you'll excuse me, I have to go back and examine that buffalo.'

'But what about contacting the authorities?'

'That's all in hand,' assured the Wolf, picking up his rifle. 'Abel has put a call in on the radio. The best thing you two can do now is get some rest.'

CHAPTER 57

With food in their bellies, Connor and Amber were soon overcome by tiredness and it didn't take much to persuade them to lie down beneath one of the tarpaulins. Abel had laid out two bedrolls for them and before their heads even hit the padded blankets they were asleep.

Connor entered such a deep slumber that he struggled to rouse himself when he heard Amber arguing with someone.

'But I need the toilet,' insisted Amber.

'Stay!' the man was saying.

Connor rose up on his elbows and saw Amber at the edge of the camp, attempting to get past one of the Wolf's men, a loose-limbed individual with tight-knit hair and bulging muscles that told of a hard life rather than days in the gym.

'Toilet,' she repeated. 'I have to go.'

Immovable as stone, the man stared blankly at her.

'*Les toilettes*,' Amber repeated in French.

Comprehension lit up on the man's face and he grunted, pointing to a tree a few metres from the camp. Amber hurried towards it, disappearing into the undergrowth. But the man followed part-way, keeping a close eye on her.

'*Arrêtez!*' he called after. '*Pas plus loin.*'

Connor sat up and rubbed his eyes. The sleep had done him the world of good and his strength had somewhat returned. His side still ached, though the tablets had dulled some of the pain. Glancing at his watch, he saw it was past five o'clock in the afternoon. They'd been asleep for more than four hours. Connor took another dose of painkillers, then looked round the camp for the Wolf but couldn't see him. *Surely a rescue party from the lodge should have reached them by now?*

Stepping out from under the tarpaulin, Connor felt the call of nature himself and headed into the bush. But Abel appeared in front of him, blocking his path.

'Where you go?' he asked.

'Toilet,' replied Connor, then added for clarity, '*Les toilettes.*'

Abel moved aside. 'Don't go far. Lions.'

Connor nodded and walked a few metres from the camp. As he relieved himself against a tree, he glanced back over his shoulder. Abel was watching him closely and an uneasy feeling crept over Connor. Something was wrong here. While he was only too aware of the dangers of the African bush and wouldn't be surprised if there *were* lions nearby, he was beginning to feel more like a prisoner than a guest.

When he returned to the camp, Amber was sitting by the fire, her expression unreadable.

Connor sat down next to her. 'Are you OK?' he asked.

She nodded and smiled. But the smile seemed forced, more for the benefit of Abel and the muscleman still guarding the camp. Connor wondered where the Wolf and the other two men were. *Perhaps they'd gone to meet the rescue party?* It seemed logical. After all, the Wolf had been nothing but hospitable towards them.

So why was his sixth sense for danger twitching?

Abel poured them some tea from a beaten-up kettle and handed them a packet of dry biscuits each. Then he strolled over to his musclebound friend and the two chatted in hushed tones to each other, every so often glancing in Connor and Amber's direction. The two men seemed on edge. But Connor reasoned that perhaps he was overreacting. Now he'd told them about the Black Mamba and the rebel soldiers they were probably concerned for their own lives.

Amber rested her head affectionately on his shoulder. Connor didn't mind but found it strange that she was being so familiar with him considering their circumstances. Then she whispered in his ear, 'I need to tell you something.'

Connor nodded his head imperceptibly so as not to attract the attention of Abel or the other man.

'I spotted some camouflage netting when I went to the toilet. There were *six* elephant tusks hidden beneath it.'

Connor immediately grasped the dangerous situation that put them in.

'The Wolf's no conservationist. He's a poacher,' said Amber under her breath.

It all made perfect sense now. The hidden camp. The pile

of supplies. The high-powered telescopic rifle. Even the enraged buffalo. Connor recalled seeing quite a few bullet holes in the slain animal. At the time of the attack he'd heard only three shots, but there had been some gunfire earlier in the distance. That suggested the bull was already injured and hurting when they came across it. Shot no doubt by the Wolf.

Before making any rash decisions, Connor needed to confirm his suspicions about their predicament. Leaving Amber by the fire, he strolled over to Abel and his friend where they squatted at the boundary of the camp. They stood at his approach, Abel's eyes narrowing and the muscleman crossing his arms.

'Where's the Wolf?' asked Connor nonchalantly.

'On a bushwalk,' Abel replied.

'When will he be back?'

'Later.'

'What about the authorities? When will they be arriving?'

'Soon.'

Gathering he'd get little more than one-word answers from Abel, Connor tried a different tack.

'Can I use your radio, please?' he asked.

Abel shook his head.

'But I need to contact the lodge to –'

'No radio,' he cut in.

'But Wolf said you –'

'He has the only radio.'

Connor realized he was being stonewalled. He wouldn't find out anything further from Abel or his tight-lipped companion. However, he had all the answers he needed. The Wolf had said Abel had put a call in to the authorities. But how could he if the Wolf had the *only* radio?

He returned to sit beside Amber. Finishing his biscuits, he said under his breath, 'We need to leave.'

'Surely we're safer here with the Wolf and his men, than we'll be out there alone?' Amber questioned, glancing nervously towards the savannah beyond the trees.

'Possibly,' Connor replied. 'However, I believe we're being held against our will. And I don't think they've called anyone for help.'

'But the Wolf said –'

'I know what he said, but I'm certain he's lying. Which means no one knows where we are, or even that we're still alive.'

Amber shook her head in disbelief. 'Why would he lie to us?'

Connor looked at Amber. 'He's an *illegal* poacher. He has no interest in contacting the authorities. So we have to leave while we can.'

'Shouldn't we wait until morning at least?'

'Who knows what they've got planned for us? Besides, every hour that passes reduces our chances of getting out of here alive. The rebels will soon have control of the park and, with the president likely dead, they'll try to take over the country. That means civil war.'

Amber nodded in reluctant agreement to his plan. Connor squeezed her hand reassuringly, then stood up to attract Abel's attention.

'We're going for a rest,' he said, yawning and putting his hands together in a mime of sleep. By now the sun was low on the horizon, sending golden shafts of light through the copse's canopy. In less than an hour it would be dark.

Abel nodded, but kept his eye on them as they made their way over to the tarpaulin shelter. Settling down on the bedrolls, Connor and Amber feigned sleep. Convinced by their act, Abel and muscleman returned to their conversation. A short while later Connor heard them engrossed in a game of *igisoro*, having dug pits in the earth to make a temporary playing board. Connor nudged Amber and, as quietly as they could, they slid out of the back of the shelter and into the undergrowth. Ideally he'd have liked to take some supplies from the camp – at the very least a bottle of water – but he didn't want to risk arousing the men's suspicions. As soon as they were hidden from view, Connor crept with Amber between the trees towards the open savannah.

'Where do you think you're going?' growled a voice.

Connor and Amber stopped in their tracks as the Wolf materialized in front of them, his rifle unslung. The two other men from the camp stood behind him, menacing in their silence.

'To the safari lodge,' said Connor, his tone defiant.

The Wolf glanced at the horizon, where the sun was beginning to settle. 'Too dangerous. Dusk is prime hunting time for lions and hyenas.'

'We're going anyway,' Connor insisted, despite a frisson of fear running through his veins at the mention of hyenas.

'Not a wise decision. We spotted your rebels patrolling the plain.'

'Better the devil we know,' replied Amber.

The Wolf frowned. 'What do you mean by that?'

'You haven't contacted the authorities, have you?' she accused.

The Wolf's face remained impassive, but there was a flicker of hesitation in his slate-grey eyes. 'We've tried to get through, but no one's answering.'

'We don't believe you,' said Amber, her temper rising. 'You're no conservationist! I've seen your stash of ivory. Now let us through.'

She started to stride past, Connor keeping close by her side, but one of the men blocked their path, a bloodied machete hanging loose in his hand, the message chillingly clear.

The Wolf let out a heavy sigh and shook his head regretfully. 'If you've seen the ivory, then I'm afraid I *definitely* can't let you go.'

'We won't tell anyone about it,' Connor assured him. 'Or about you.'

'I can't take that risk,' he replied with an apologetic yet cold smile. 'That ivory's worth over two million dollars on the black market. If the authorities are brought in, I stand to lose it all, including my freedom. So I'm sure you'll understand why you must stay in the camp. At least until the ivory's been transported out of the park.'

Amber glared at the Wolf. 'I thought you were a good man,' she said bitterly. 'But you're no better than those rebels out there. Killing innocent animals merely to line your own pockets. You're just a low-life *poacher*!'

The Wolf stared down his broad nose at her, offended to the core. '*I'm* one of the last great game hunters,' he corrected her, his chest puffing up self-importantly. 'Here in Africa to face down the Big Five.'

With a grand sweep of his arm, he stepped aside to reveal the severed head of the bull buffalo lying in the grass. Its dead eyes stared blankly up at them, all its majestic might extinguished.

Proudly patting the buffalo's highly prized bossed horns, the Wolf declared, 'Once I've completed my Big Five collection, I promise to deliver you to the authorities, safe and sound.'

'And when might that be?' asked Connor.

'I've one more trophy to hunt down,' grinned the Wolf. 'The elusive leopard.'

CHAPTER 59

Connor and Amber were forced to sit by the fire as their hands and feet were bound.

'I regret having to do this,' said the Wolf, watching Abel and the muscleman secure the wrist ties behind their backs, 'but it's for your own good. The African bush is dangerous at night and I can't have you wandering off.'

'*Please* let us go,' begged Amber.

'It's your own fault for prying, young lady,' the Wolf snapped.

'But it could be days before you even find a leopard,' Connor protested. 'And rebel soldiers are swarming all over the park, you said so yourself. What if they find us first?'

The Wolf dismissed the suggestion with a snort of laughter. 'The bush is my hunting ground. I can easily avoid those gung-ho rebels.'

'But don't you understand what's happening here? They've killed or, at the very least, captured the president. There's been a coup! This country is plunging into civil war. No one will be safe.'

A smirk creasing his thin lips, the Wolf was apparently

unfazed. 'That all plays to my advantage. War brings chaos. There'll be no pesky rangers to protect the park, which makes it easier to smuggle out the ivory, along with my glorious collection.'

Pulling back a tarpaulin behind the pile of supplies, the Wolf unveiled a macabre row of animal heads and skins: a once-mighty lion with a full mane; a horned black rhino, its dark eyes weeping as if shedding tears; even a gargantuan elephant head with magnificent tusks; and to this sad line his men added the disembodied buffalo.

'You're a sick, sick man,' said Amber, having to look away in sorrow and disgust.

The Wolf's eyes flashed with anger. 'You know nothing, young lady. I'm preserving these animals forever. That's *true* conservation. We'll be able to admire these great beasts for years to come –'

'Can't you simply shoot them with a camera instead?' retorted Amber.

The Wolf's brow knitted in bewilderment. 'Where's the thrill in that? I'm hunting these animals on foot. My life is on the line just as much as theirs. That's what makes it –' The Wolf stopped talking as a repeated growl, like wood being sawed, was heard amid the early-evening chorus of the savannah.

His eyes lit up. '*Leopard!*' he gasped.

Snatching up his rifle, he barked orders to his men, grabbed a handful of spare cartridges and refilled his hip flask from a jerrycan. Abel shouldered the kitbag and they prepared to leave. At the edge of the camp, the Wolf glanced back over his shoulder at Connor and Amber on the ground, almost seeming to have forgotten them in his excitement.

'Don't try to escape!' he warned, his eyes narrowing. 'Otherwise I'll hunt *you* down for my collection too.'

Accompanied by Abel, he trekked off into the darkening twilight.

Amber glared at his receding shadow. 'I wish that lion had eaten him!'

Connor nodded his agreement.

Muscleman and the two others remained behind at the camp, ostensibly to guard them. But, bound as they were, they were paid little attention by the men, who soon became involved in another game of *igisoro*. As dusk fell, the poachers rebuilt the fire and reheated the kudu stew. They didn't share their meal this time, although one of them, the youngest, made sure their captives each drank a mugful of water. Then, squatting on the opposite side of the fire, the three men chatted to one another in hushed tones, occasionally glancing over at Connor and Amber propped up against the log in the darkness.

'Can you understand anything they're saying?' Connor whispered, wishing he had his smartphone to translate.

Shifting closer, Amber replied softly, 'They're talking about what to do with us.'

The look of horror and dismay in her eyes didn't fill Connor with optimism.

'Muscleman wants to feed us to the lions,' she explained. 'The one with the moustache wants to hand us over to the rebels in return for safe passage. And the younger poacher thinks they should just leave us here when they go.'

'None of those options sound particularly promising,' Connor remarked, 'or what the Wolf threatened us with.'

Firelight flickering across her face, Amber offered him a resigned smile. 'They're also talking about the return of the Black Mamba. They sound pretty scared, even Musclema—'

'*Tais-toi!*' snapped Muscleman, ordering them to be quiet.

As they sat in enforced silence, the ache in their wrists and ankles growing steadily worse due to the tight bindings, Connor considered the implications of what Amber had just told him. It seemed as if they'd jumped out of the frying pan and into the fire – fleeing the rebels only to become prisoners of the poachers, a death sentence almost certainly hanging over their heads.

It was late when the poachers finally settled down beneath their makeshift tents, leaving the younger one beside the fire to watch over their prisoners. Amber lay contorted on the hard earth, her body twisted awkwardly by the bindings as she tried to sleep. Connor, however, was in no state of mind to rest. Through half-closed eyes, he observed their guard absently chipping away at the log with his father's knife and tried to figure out how to free them both and get his heirloom back.

The Wolf and Abel had yet to return. With the other two asleep, Connor reckoned this was their best opportunity to attempt an escape. For, despite the Wolf's initial care of them, Connor couldn't trust the man to stay true to his word. Even if it was the hunter's intention to release them to the authorities, his gang of poachers could well persuade him otherwise.

Their only chance of survival lay in running.

The sound of chipping wood ceased and Connor cautiously looked up. Their guard was beginning to doze, his head lolling, the knife left protruding out of the hacked piece of log. Connor waited another ten minutes, then, as quietly as he could, he shifted into a kneeling position. It took some time, his limbs being stiff and his muscles cramped, but eventually he got himself upright. Although his hands were numb, the blood supply half cut off, Connor was glad his bindings were tight. It would make them easier to break.

Bending over, he raised his arms up behind himself and, just as he'd been shown at his surprise birthday party, he brought them down hard on to his backside. But the impact failed to snap the plastic tie. Instead he lost his balance, toppled forward and landed face first in the dirt.

Spitting out bits of earth, Connor twisted his head round towards the guard. Thankfully the young poacher was still asleep. Convinced the technique had been easier in the company of his friends, Connor checked the tie's locking mechanism was dead-centre between his wrists and tried again. It took two more attempts before the binding actually split.

After shaking the blood back into his hands, he edged his way over to the sleeping guard and reached for his knife. The young man stirred and Connor's fingers clasped the hilt of the knife, ready to fight back. But the poacher didn't wake and Connor relaxed his grip. Tugging the blade free, he sliced through the plastic binding securing his ankles. Then he crept back to Amber and placed a finger on her lips.

Her eyes flickered open and she flinched away, but immediately calmed on seeing Connor's face in the firelight.

Connor cut her ties, then signed for her to follow him. They passed the supply pile, where he grabbed a full water bottle and found his discarded Go-bag. Leaving the muted glow of the campfire behind, the night closed in around them until they could barely see in front of their faces. From the pocket of his cargo trousers Connor retrieved his night-vision sunglasses. Flicking the tiny switch on the frame's edge, the world burst back into a ghostly light. Almost immediately he was confronted by a pair of huge round eyes and Connor almost cried out – but it was just a harmless bush baby hanging from a nearby branch.

With the copse now illuminated as if there was a full moon, Connor saw a track they could follow through the undergrowth without making a sound. But they'd only gone a few metres when Muscleman stepped out from behind a tree. Having just finished relieving himself, the poacher looked as surprised as they were. Before he could react, Connor drove a fist into the man's gut with a stepping lunge punch; it was like hitting a solid brick wall. For all his martial arts expertise, his fist crumpled against the granite-hard stomach.

Muscleman grinned in amusement, his teeth gleaming like a half-moon in the darkness.

'*Encore!*' He laughed, opening up his arms to welcome another shot.

In the second that Connor took to consider his next best target, Amber stepped up and kicked Muscleman straight between the legs. The poacher's eyes bulged and he bent double, expelling a pained gasp. Then she hammer-fisted him in the temple. Muscleman went down like a felled buffalo.

Connor stared at Amber in stunned admiration.

She replied with a shrug, 'That's what they taught me to do in self-defence class at school.'

'Then remind me never to pick a fight with you!'

Connor and Amber crept through a night alive with noise and unseen movement. The warm air pulsated with the ceaseless chirp of crickets and cicadas, the plaintive cries of bush babies and the soft flutter of bats flying overhead. Accompanying this nightly chorus of the African savannah were the rumbling vocalizations of elephants and the deep drawn-out roars of lions prowling the plain.

Connor's eyes darted to every snap of twig or rustle of leaf in the darkness. But, even with the aid of his night-vision glasses, he rarely saw the culprit – the creature disappearing into the bushes or up into the branches before he could identify it.

Amber kept a firm grip of his hand, anxious not to lose him in the unnerving dark as he guided her through the trees bordering the plain. Every so often he'd check the compass on his watch and adjust their direction. Connor had made the conscious decision not to take the most direct route to the lodge, fearing that if they broke the cover of the trees, they'd be more easily spotted by rebel soldiers, or the Wolf, or else become prey to the lions they could hear hunting.

Neither of them spoke as they hurried away from the camp. Connor presumed that Muscleman must have come to and woken the others by now. But would they come after them in the dark and without the Wolf?

Connor heard another crack of a twig close by.

He stopped still and Amber became motionless by his side. Her laboured breathing was loud in his ear as he strained to listen for what animal or person was approaching. But the night noises gave nothing away.

Continuing on, they kept to a well-used animal trail. This made the going easier and quicker, as well as hiding any potential tracks they made among the spoor of antelope and other creatures. If the Wolf really did mean to hunt them down, Connor wanted to ensure he left as little evidence of their progress as possible.

Out of the corner of his eye, he caught a flash of movement.

Connor spun in its direction.

'What is it?' Amber whispered, her eyes wide as a bush baby's.

Connor shushed for her to be silent. He scanned the bushes, their edges glowing softly in his night vision. A branch was swaying ever so slightly but there was nothing there.

'Just my imagination,' he replied, keeping his voice low as he led Amber further along the trail. But they hadn't gone far when they both heard a distinct rustling.

Was the Wolf on their trail already? Or had they run into a rebel patrol?

Connor slowly pivoted on the spot, searching the under-growth once more. But it was just a shadowy wall of bushes and grass.

Then he happened to glance up.

Peering menacingly from the bough of a tree were two glassy green orbs.

Without his night vision the leopard would have been entirely invisible to him, a ghost in the night. But Connor could just about discern the sleek outline of the big cat, the white tip of its tail twitching . . . then a flash of its fear-some pointed canines as it opened its jaws and pounced from the tree.

CHAPTER 62

'I'm getting nowhere,' explained an infuriated Charley to Colonel Black in his office. 'Connor's phone isn't responding. The safari lodge is no longer answering. The Burundian French Embassy's closed for the weekend and their emergency number goes straight to answerphone. When I did eventually manage to reach President Bagaza's office in Bujumbura, the secretary said that she'd get back to me right away, but that was four hours ago and I still haven't heard anything from her. What's more, that office is about to close too.'

'That's Africa for you, Charley,' said Colonel Black, his expression both sympathetic and grim. 'Have you tried the hospitals?'

Charley nodded. 'There's only one that answered and I spoke to some poor overworked doctor, Dr Emmanuel Ndayi . . . Ndayikunda, or at least I think that's how you pronounce it. He said he'd check the records for me now. I'm still waiting for his call back.'

'Don't hold out too much hope,' replied the colonel, leaning forward and resting his elbows on the desk. 'From my experience of Africa, "now" means some time in the next few days.'

'So what *can* we do?' Charley implored, her hands gripping the armrests of her chair in frustration. 'Connor's missed all his report-ins for the past twenty-four hours. Something's gone drastically wrong. I feel it in my heart.'

'I agree. A communication black-out of this length warrants emergency action.' The colonel picked up the phone. 'Let's contact the Burundian commander-in-chief and establish if he has any news of the situation.'

Colonel Black dialled a number that took him straight through to the military headquarters in Burundi. After speaking with several subordinates, he eventually worked his way up the ranks and was put through to the man himself.

'Major-General Tabu Baratuza here,' barked the commander-in-chief over the speakerphone. 'How can I be of assistance, Colonel? But please be quick. I was due at a formal dinner an hour ago.'

'My apologies for disturbing you this evening, General. However, we've a legitimate cause for concern regarding the well-being of your president and the visiting French ambassador and his family.'

'Go on,' said the major-general, the softening of his tone indicating that the colonel had captured his full attention.

'We have a security operative protecting the French ambassador's children,' Colonel Black explained. 'For the past twenty-four hours we've had no contact from him and we can't reach the party by any other means. This is highly irregular. Have you had any recent communication with the president or his guard at the Ruvubu safari lodge?'

The major-general paused a moment before replying, clearly evaluating his own answer. 'Yes. I received a request from the president the other day to send some soldiers into sector eight of Ruvubu National Park.'

'For what reason?'

'I'm not at liberty to divulge such information. But this morning that request was cancelled.'

Colonel Black frowned. 'Isn't that rather unusual?'

'Not really. The president is known for changing his mind.'

The colonel leant back in his leather chair, a deeply pensive expression on his face. 'Before we lost contact, our operative mentioned rumours of the Black Mamba. I am wondering if this is somehow connected to our operative's lack of comms.'

The major-general cleared his throat. 'I've heard those rumours too. But I can assure you that they're just rumours. However, Colonel, I'll look into your concerns *now now* and ensure someone gets back to you. Have a good evening.'

As the Burundian commander-in-chief cut the connection, Colonel Black raised a surprised eyebrow at Charley. 'He'll look into it *now now*! If we're lucky, that means we might hear back within an hour. Don't hold your breath, though.'

But they only had to wait half that time before the major-general himself called them back.

'Colonel, we're getting zero response from the presidential guard or any of our soldiers stationed there,' he informed them. 'Hopefully it's just a comms issue, but to be sure I'm dispatching a unit of troops to the park immediately. They'll be there at first light.'

CHAPTER 63

A spine-chilling growl. A slash of razor-sharp claws. A dead weight landing on his shoulders, knocking him to the ground. Amber pinned beneath him, screaming. Claws raking into his back. Snarling jaws ripping apart his Go-bag. His vision filling with a blinding fire. Then blackness . . .

Connor parted his eyes. The early glow of dawn was visible on the horizon. Birds sang softly from the trees and insects hummed in the long grass. The embers of a campfire smouldered gently, sending up a plume of hazy grey smoke. In the middle was a flat rock upon which three plump white sausages sizzled, browning as they cooked.

Lying prone on the ground, Connor felt as if his back was on fire, cooking like those sausages. Then someone pressed a smooth paste into his wounds, soothing the burning sensation. As the pain subsided, Connor sighed and closed his eyes. But the relief was short-lived. All of a sudden he felt a sharp pinch on his shoulder as if he'd been bitten.

Looking for the source of the attack, he saw a young black girl with rounded cheeks and bright eyes kneeling beside him. He also spotted four raw bloody lines across his left shoulder, scored by the claws of the leopard, one gouge particularly deep. The girl applied more red-brown paste to this cut, then held a wriggling driver ant between her fingertips and brought the insect near to the wound.

'No!' he croaked, but was too late to stop her.

The driver ant's pincers bit either side of his cut, closing the wound. As soon as its jaws had clamped on to his skin, the girl ripped the ant's body off, leaving the head behind. Too stunned and too weak to protest, Connor watched as she methodically stitched together his injury with live driver ants. Soon he had a neat row of ant heads, like black sequins, across his shoulder.

'Who are you?' he groaned when she'd finished.

'Her name's Zuzu,' replied Amber on the girl's behalf. 'She's from a nearby Batwa tribe.'

Connor turned his aching head the other way. Amber was sitting on a rock, picking at the dry white flesh of a baobab fruit and chewing contentedly. 'You saved my life yet again,' she said.

'Did I?'

Amber smiled. 'Don't you remember?'

Connor shook his head. For him the whole experience of the leopard attack was a fragmented series of flashing nightmares.

'All I heard was this terrifying roar,' she explained. 'I couldn't see a thing. But you wrapped yourself round me, shielding me from the leopard. You wouldn't let go, even though the leopard was ripping *you* to shreds.' Amber shook her head in disbelief at his courageous act. 'Now I know what you mean by body cover!'

She winked at him and took a sip from the water bottle stolen from the poacher's camp.

Connor tried to sit up, but pain flared across his back.

'Is it bad?' he asked, imagining his skin flayed and the flesh stripped to the bone.

Amber glanced at his wounds and grimaced. Then she asked Zuzu, '*Est-ce qu'il va s'en sortir?*'

The girl replied in French and Amber translated, 'Zuzu says they have a saying in their tribe: *From every wound there is a scar. And every scar tells a story. A story that says, "I survived."* So I think that means you'll live.'

Amber held up the tattered remains of his Go-bag. 'But I'm afraid your backpack isn't leopard proof.'

She then showed him his bloodstained shirt. Four claw marks were ripped across one shoulder, but the rest of the fabric was undamaged. 'What saved you was your shirt! I've no idea how, but it's a miracle your back wasn't torn apart.'

'The shirt's stab-proof,' Connor explained, groaning as Zuzu helped him into a sitting position. 'Unfortunately, it doesn't stop you from being beaten to a pulp. But how on earth did we escape the leopard?'

Amber directed her gaze to Zuzu. 'That's thanks to our new friend here. Zuzu was camped nearby. She heard my screaming and came running. She chased off the leopard with a flaming branch from her fire.'

Zuzu rattled off some more words as she lightly rubbed

the oil from a split aloe-vera stem on to Connor's bruises and scrapes, delivering instant relief. Connor looked to Amber for a translation.

'She says we're extremely lucky to have survived the attack. That particular leopard's known among her tribe as the Spotted Devil. It's a man-eater!'

As Amber told him this, there was an incongruous smile on her face.

'What are you looking so happy about?' asked Connor, perplexed by her upbeat mood. 'We could have been killed!'

Her smile widened. 'Henri's alive!'

CHAPTER 64

Any pain Connor had been feeling was washed aside by a wave of elation. He couldn't believe what he was hearing. He'd given Henri up for dead.

'How do you know this? Where is he?' Connor asked hurriedly.

'Zuzu saw a group of rebel soldiers taking a white boy with red hair towards Dead Man's Hill,' Amber explained as she passed him the water bottle. 'It can only be my brother.'

'We should have known that rebel was lying to us!' muttered Connor, shaking his head bitterly at the man's callous deceit. Taking a swig from the water bottle, he knocked back another antibiotic and a couple more painkillers. 'We have to reach the lodge as soon as possible and –'

'No,' cut in Amber. 'We're going to Dead Man's Hill.'

Connor blinked, stunned at her unexpected announcement. 'But we don't even know where that is from here.'

'Zuzu does. She says it's that way,' responded Amber, pointing north across the plain. 'And she'll guide us there.'

The bush girl nodded emphatically as she finished tending to his back.

'But that's the opposite direction to the lodge,' said Connor. 'Besides, what are you planning to do when we get there?'

'Rescue my brother, of course.'

Connor stared open-mouthed at Amber, wondering if she'd lost her grip on reality. 'Look, we're tired, hungry and hurting. We're in no state to launch a rescue mission. More to the point, those rebels won't let us simply stroll into their camp and take your brother from under their noses. Not without a fight.'

'I know that,' snapped Amber, glaring at him for even suggesting she was so naive. 'But if we don't try to rescue him now, we might never find him again . . . alive, at least.'

Connor rubbed his dirt-stained face between his hands and sighed wearily. 'I realize you want to do everything you can to save your brother. I'm as desperate as you to get him back safe and sound. But I can't have you risking your life in a suicide mission. I honestly think our best plan is to return to the lodge and call for back-up.'

'And how long will that take? A day? Two days? Maybe more in this godforsaken country. We don't have that time to waste. Every minute counts. Who knows what they're doing to my brother? Henri's life could be in the balance.'

'And so is yours,' stated Connor, feeling himself torn between rescuing Henri and keeping Amber out of danger. His head told him one thing; his heart, the other. In the end, reason won out. 'I'm sorry, but I can't let you go. It's too much of a risk.'

Amber looked at him, her eyes blazing. 'I lost Henri

once. I won't lose him again. He's the only family I have left. I *have* to save my brother.' She stabbed a finger at him. '*You* have to save my brother. You're supposed to be his bodyguard, aren't you?'

'I'm your bodyguard too,' he reminded her. 'I have a duty to keep you *both* safe from harm.'

Amber stood and crossed her arms defiantly. 'Well then, you'll have to protect me rescuing my brother. Because I'm going, with or without you!'

'Your parents are dead!' Blaze shouted as he struck Henri with a long, thin bamboo cane. *Whack!*

Henri fell to the rocky ground, crying out in agonized shock as a large red welt flared across his upper arm.

'Your parents were weak. They failed to protect you.' *Whack!*

Tears burst from Henri's eyes as the cane whipped across his back, the pain so intense that he couldn't even cry out.

'Your sister ran away.' *Whack!*

Henri instinctively curled into the foetal position, his hands over his head, as more blows rained down.

'Did you hear me? She failed to protect you too.' *Whack! Whack!*

'Now she's dead. So is her boyfriend. And you're all alone.'

No Mercy watched impassively as Blaze beat the white boy. He recalled his own initiation ritual beginning in a similar way. Having been abducted from his village, he was beaten day and night until his body and spirit were broken down to nothing. Poisonous words were whispered in his ear to convince him of his family's treachery and abandonment before their deaths at the hands of a rival rebel group. Then the Black Mamba had come to him, offering salvation and relief from the constant physical and mental abuse. At that point, lost in a world of pain and grief, he'd been willing to do anything to make the unbearable suffering stop. *Anything.* Even kill a man with his bare hands. That's when he was reborn, piece by piece, killing by killing. The Black Mamba rebuilt him into a warrior, a soldier of God. Gave him a new name. His past no longer relevant. He existed purely to fight and die as if there were no tomorrow.

Blaze ceased his brutal punishment of the boy.

Wheezing and sobbing, Henri lay trembling on the rocks, a splatter of his blood smeared across their surface. Kneeling down, Blaze ran a hand gently through the boy's red hair.

'But we can protect you,' he said softly in the boy's ear. 'We can make you strong. But first you must prove yourself. Earn our respect. Become worthy of the name Red Devil.'

The sound of an approaching jeep caused Blaze and No Mercy to look up.

General Pascal had returned from the lodge, bringing with him the Grey Man, as they now all called him.

'Put the boy to work with the others,' ordered Blaze, handing No Mercy the bamboo cane. 'And beat him if he slows or stops.'

Nodding, No Mercy dragged Henri to his feet and

half-carried him over to where the enslaved workers were digging up and panning the riverbed. Blaze strode across the river to greet the general, saluting him as he stepped out of the jeep with the Grey Man.

'Welcome, Mr Grey, to Diamond Valley,' declared General Pascal with a majestic sweep of his arm at the hidden gorge being stripped back and plundered. 'That's what I call it anyway. This place is so rich with minerals that at night the ground sparkles as if the stars had fallen from the sky.'

'Very poetic,' replied Mr Grey flatly, without any real sign of appreciation. His almost colourless eyes were trained on No Mercy, handing a battered bucket to a bleeding and sobbing child. 'Who's the white boy?' he asked.

'Some foreign ambassador's son.' The general laughed as he waved his hand dismissively. 'White men are always taking from our country. It's time for them to pay the price.'

'You could ransom him,' suggested Mr Grey. 'He'd have value.'

'Why? I've all the riches I need here,' retorted the general.

Ordering Blaze to bring over the lock-box from his tent, he opened the lid and spread out a collection of rough diamonds on the bonnet of the jeep. 'Now let's do business, Mr Grey. Take your pick. I want to have the best-equipped army in Africa.'

CHAPTER 66

Striking camp, Connor, Amber and Zuzu set forth across the plain. Zuzu walked ahead, her bare feet noiseless on the red earth. Her body small and slender like a gazelle's, she wore a mottled-brown wrap-around sarong, with a simple shawl slung over her left shoulder. In her right hand she carried a wooden bow and several black-tipped arrows. Aside from a gourd containing water, a fire-lighting stick and a small knife, she possessed little else.

Connor was amazed that she could survive in such a wild place with no supplies. When he'd asked her about this through Amber, she'd replied that the land provided all she needed to live. And, as if to prove her point, she'd plucked some small orange berries from a nearby bush and popped them in her mouth before offering some to them. The fruits were bitter-sweet, but a great deal more palatable than the 'sausage' Connor had consumed for their bush breakfast.

Earlier that morning, as he'd wrestled over the dilemma of whether to let Amber attempt to rescue her brother or not, Zuzu had handed him one of the plump white blobs cooking on the open fire and he'd bitten into it with barely a second thought. He soon discovered that the 'sausage' had a strange fluid consistency and tasted a bit like a nutty mushroom, but rather less pleasant. Zuzu had looked on encouragingly as he chewed. Then Amber had taken great pleasure in informing him that he was eating fried rhino-beetle larva! He'd almost gagged but managed to keep the smile on his face for Zuzu's benefit, reminding himself that the larva was a bush delicacy. But, rather than subject himself to a second helping, he'd hurriedly agreed to Amber's change of plan. Besides, he'd realized that he couldn't carry his Principal kicking and screaming all the way back to the lodge. Nor could he leave her to walk alone and unprotected into a kill zone. And, the most persuasive reason of all, how could he live with himself if, as his bodyguard, he abandoned Henri to his fate?

Yet as they followed Zuzu through the stiflingly hot bush, Connor began to question the wisdom of his decision. Lacking Zuzu's intimate knowledge of bushcraft and now possessing only his father's knife – the night-vision sunglasses having been crushed beyond repair during the leopard attack – he felt woefully under-prepared for the ordeal ahead. It seemed as if they were about to enter the lion's den with little more than a toothpick for protection. Moreover, he couldn't believe they were putting their lives into the hands of a complete stranger again. They'd done that once with the Wolf and almost paid the price.

Connor quietly drew up beside Amber. 'Are you sure we can trust our guide?' he whispered, avoiding using Zuzu's name in case she realized he was talking about her.

'Why not?' said Amber, surprised by the question.

'For all we know, she could be leading us into a trap. Maybe hoping for payment from the rebels for finding us.'

Amber frowned at Connor. 'I can't believe *everyone* in this country is corrupt. She saved our lives, remember? In fact, she tried to dissuade me from going to Dead Man's Hill in the first place, saying it's cursed by evil spirits and is where that leopard lives.'

'Now you tell me!' said Connor, feeling somewhat duped into agreeing to their crazy rescue mission.

Amber kept talking as if she hadn't heard him. 'But I told her how much my brother meant to me and she understood, having lost a brother herself.'

'Even so, we know nothing about her,' Connor argued, keeping his voice low.

'I do,' replied Amber. 'While you were out cold, we talked a lot.'

Zuzu glanced over her shoulder to check they were still keeping up. Her smile was bright and innocent and Connor couldn't detect any trace of deception in her eyes. He felt a touch guilty at talking behind her back, but it was a bodyguard's job to be suspicious – at least until the person in question proved worthy of trust.

'It's a really sad story,' Amber explained. 'Remember I told you that Zuzu's from one of the local Batwa tribes. Well, the government forced them out of their ancestral lands to create this national park. Minister Feruzi was lying when he said that the Batwa had been given lovely new homes, schools and freshwater wells. The tribes were lucky to get a well, let alone housing. Most were given no land and left to fend for themselves. Zuzu tells me only a few Batwa men were offered work in the park, despite their knowledge of the bush, so many have had to resort to begging or manual labour just to survive. Zuzu and her family are essentially conservation refugees!'

'So how come she's in the park if it's a restricted area?' questioned Connor.

'Hunting for food,' replied Amber. 'The Batwa are traditionally hunter-gatherers. Since her father died, his heart broken by the loss of both his son and homeland, it's fallen to Zuzu to provide for the entire family. But the government's outlawed all forms of game-hunting. So, if she's caught, she'll be arrested as a poacher and then she doesn't know how they'll survi–'

Up ahead Zuzu suddenly became still as a rock, her hand held up in warning for them to be silent. Connor's eyes immediately scanned their surroundings, searching for the threat. With infinite care Zuzu nocked an arrow and took aim at something hidden among the brush. Connor's hand went to his knife. The savannah around them grew deadly quiet, as if sensing the danger in their vicinity. Connor felt his pulse quicken and drew Amber closer, ready to protect her from whatever predator appeared.

All of a sudden Zuzu let loose her arrow and disappeared into the long grass. Connor only caught a glimpse of her lithe body as she silently dashed through the brush. Grabbing Amber's hand, he pursued their guide, not wanting to let her out of his sight. They caught up with her in a small clearing, kneeling beside a dying dik-dik.

It dawned on Connor that *Zuzu* had been the predator the savannah had gone silent for.

Plucking her arrow from the tiny antelope's chest and putting it aside, she laid her hands on the animal and softly uttered what sounded to Connor like a blessing. Then Zuzu glanced up and spoke to Amber.

'The Batwa take what they can, but only what they need,' Amber translated for Connor.

As Zuzu bound the little antelope's hooves together, Connor went to help by picking up the discarded arrow. But Zuzu quickly said, '*Ne touchez pas! C'est toxique!*'

'Stop!' Amber warned. 'The tip's poisonous.'

Connor nodded, leaving the deadly arrow where it lay. 'Yeah, I got the gist.'

Zuzu slung the dead antelope over her shoulder. '*A manger*,' she said with a smile before picking up her bow and arrows and continuing along their previous trail.

Astounded at her expert hunting skills, Connor and Amber followed speechless in her wake. Zuzu's pace was steady yet relentless. She seemed neither to need rest nor to drink water, and, despite the disorientating nature of the landscape, always appeared to know exactly where she was headed, following trails and tracks invisible to their eyes.

Having heard Zuzu's story, Connor felt a little reassured about their guide but still questioned her motive for helping them. If her family was that desperate, surely she'd be tempted to sell Amber and him to the rebels at the first opportunity. He resolved to keep a careful eye on her.

After two hours' solid trekking beneath the sweltering sun, he and Amber were beginning to flag. Just as he was about to ask Zuzu to stop, she pointed to a craggy peak in the distance, atop which perched a lone acacia tree: Dead Man's Hill.

CHAPTER 67

Too late to turn back now, thought Connor, steeling himself for the climb ahead.

At the base of the hill, Zuzu halted for a water break and took a measured sip from her gourd. Severely dehydrated from their long trek, Connor and Amber sat down on a rock and drained their remaining supply in one hit. Connor held out the upturned bottle to Zuzu to indicate it was empty. She smiled, said something to him and pointed up the slope.

'There's a freshwater spring halfway,' interpreted Amber.

Guessing they might be hungry too, their guide strolled over to a clump of palm trees. With the accuracy of a sharpshooter, she slung a rock up into its branches and knocked down three round red fruit. The shiny outer skin was as hard as a nut, but Zuzu showed them how to crack it open with a stick. Connor was taken aback at the flavour: the light brown flesh inside tasted just like dried ginger cake.

'It's as if she's walking round her very own supermarket!' remarked Amber, tucking into the unexpected treat.

Re-energized, Connor got back to his feet, ready to tackle the hill. However, Zuzu remained squatting on her haunches, picking at her fruit. 'Aren't you coming?' he asked.

Zuzu shook her head, her eyes glancing fearfully up at the peak as she replied in French.

Amber translated, 'She says she'll wait here until we return with Henri, then guide us back to the lodge.'

Connor stared at Amber. 'We can't go on without her,' he said firmly. 'We've no idea what's on the other side or where your brother might be.' And, although he didn't say it, he had no intention of letting their guide out of his sight.

'But she's adamant she won't go,' replied Amber.

'Then we're not going either. If we have to make a quick getaway, we'll need Zuzu's local knowledge.'

'But . . .' Amber stopped. Connor's stern expression told her there'd be no negotiation on the point.

Kneeling down beside Zuzu, she spoke rapidly in French, her tone shifting from gentle cajoling to obvious pleading. Zuzu was distinctly reluctant, repeatedly mentioning *les spectres* and *le léopard*. The conviction of her objections was making Connor ever more uneasy at the prospect of scaling Dead Man's Hill. Eventually, though, Zuzu caved in to Amber's pleas and nodded. As she rose to her feet and picked up her bow and arrow, Amber glanced over her shoulder at Connor with a triumphant yet strained smile.

'How did you persuade her?' he asked.

'I told her that you're a mighty warrior in your land and have the power to protect us from all evil.'

'No pressure then,' said Connor.

'I also offered her the pick of my clothes and jewellery when we return to the lodge,' Amber admitted.

Connor did a double-take. 'She's taking us up the hill for a *dress*?'

Amber nodded. 'That sarong and shawl are the only clothes she owns. Zuzu thought it more than a fair trade.'

Zuzu led them through the scrub and up a winding animal trail. She climbed the rocky slope as surefooted as a mountain goat, making Connor feel distinctly unfit and ungainly by comparison. Even Amber was struggling despite her climbing skills. Zuzu kept looking furtively around, but nothing hostile materialized. The ascent was hot, tiring work and Connor was glad for the spring halfway up, where they could replenish their water bottle and cool down.

By the time they neared the peak, the sun had passed its zenith. The ancient acacia tree cast a dark shadow that looked like a twisted and tortured man upon the bare sun-bleached rock. As they approached, Zuzu slowed and became even more guarded in her tread. Clearly nervous, she indicated for them both to keep low and stay silent. Hiding behind a boulder, the three of them cautiously peered over the edge.

Connor was astounded at what he saw.

They had a bird's-eye view over the hidden valley. Protected by its steep sides and fed by a number of springs, a thick blanket of trees and plants had flourished in the natural haven. The lush foliage cascaded down like a green curtain to a broad glistening river below, which snaked its way towards a drop-off to feed the Ruvubu River in the distance. It was as if they were staring into a lost world, except for the fact that the landscape was being torn apart and the river had been dammed. At the bottom of the valley, bare-chested workers toiled with picks and shovels, ripping up the soil and clearing away the vegetation. Others were sifting through piles of dirt or panning the muddied waters with rusting metal sieves. Dotted around this scene of devastation like an army of soldier ants were boys toting AK47s.

Zuzu sorrowfully shook her head at the sight. '*On dirait qu'ils mangent de la terre.*'

Connor looked to Amber.

'She says, it looks like they're eating the earth.'

'What are they digging for?' he asked.

'*Des diamants,*' Zuzu replied under her breath.

Amber sighed in dismay. 'All that destruction for a diamond ring!'

'*C'est le Black Mamba!*' hissed Zuzu, ducking down.

Connor followed her line of sight and spotted a large man in army fatigues. Even from a distance, the infamous warlord struck an imposing figure. Barrel-chested and with bulging muscles, General Pascal towered over his fellow rebel soldiers, even Blaze who Connor easily recognized from the flash of his mirrored sunglasses. So his hunch had been right: the Armée Nationale de la Liberté had ambushed the president and his entourage.

By the look of deep-set fear on Zuzu's face, Connor's

suspicions about her trustworthiness were allayed. She seemed only too aware of the rebel leader's reputation as a cold-blooded murderer of women and children.

'*C'est trop dangereux ici!*' she was saying, pulling at Amber's arm to leave.

Amber shook her head. '*Non! D'abord nous devons trouver Henri.*'

Scanning the rebel camp, Connor began to search for her brother among the groups of bone-tired, mud-smeared workers. If Blaze was here, there was a strong chance Henri would be too.

'There he is!' he gasped, pointing past a sad collection of tarpaulin shelters to a waif-like boy staggering across the rocky riverbed. Henri's red hair and pale skin made him easily identifiable among the other enslaved workers as he struggled to carry a heavy bucket of earth. After stumbling a few more metres, he dropped the bucket, hunching over, clearly fighting for breath.

'He needs his inhaler,' cried Amber, her fingers clutching at the medicine in her pocket.

Then they watched in horror as the boy soldier with the red beret – No Mercy, as Blaze had called him – strode over and raised a bamboo cane high above Henri's head. Henri cowered at the threat, picking up the bucket and tottering a few more paces before collapsing again.

'He could *die* if they force him to go on,' said Amber, her face paling in shock at the state of her brother.

As No Mercy began to beat Henri with the cane, she let out a stifled cry and rose from behind their hiding-place.

'No!' hissed Connor, grabbing her arm and pulling her back down. He pointed to a rebel soldier standing guard on an outcrop of rock further down the slope. 'We wait until dark.'

CHAPTER 68

Connor peered through the undergrowth at the rebels' camp. In the pale light of a waning moon, he spotted several guards patrolling the perimeter, their weapons slung lazily over their shoulders. The rest of General Pascal's soldiers were gathered round glaringly bright kerosene lamps, drinking, smoking and playing cards. A row of canvas tents formed the centre of the camp from which hardcore rap music blared out of a ghetto-blaster, the heavy beat pulsating through the valley. Further downstream, fires dotted the ravaged banks of the river where clusters of enslaved workers lay exhausted beneath ragged tarpaulin shelters.

That was where Henri would most likely be. If he was still alive.

The hours to dusk had been the longest Connor had ever experienced in his lifetime. The image of Henri being beaten and forced to work while fighting for breath had played over and over in his mind. But he knew that striding into the rebels' camp in broad daylight would have been tantamount to signing their own death warrants. So they'd descended part-way back down the hillside to bide their time, Zuzu cooking the dik-dik straight on the embers of an open fire for an early dinner while Amber sat silent, her knees clasped to her chest.

As soon as the sun had dropped below the horizon, the three of them returned to the hilltop, then worked their way down into the hidden valley. Zuzu had been careful to avoid any rebel lookouts, a task made easier as the light rapidly faded. But this also meant the jungle trails were now pitch-black, making the route treacherous under foot, and Connor doubted they'd have reached the bottom of the valley without Zuzu to guide them.

'Can you see Henri?' whispered Amber, who crouched next to Connor in the darkness, Zuzu on his other side.

Connor shook his head. 'Stay here. I'll find him.'

'Don't forget this,' said Amber, passing him the inhaler. As he took it from her, she gave his hand an anxious squeeze.

'Don't worry,' he assured her. 'I'll get him back, I promise.'

As he was rising, Zuzu tapped him on the shoulder and signed for him to wait. Scooping up some mud, she smeared his face and arms until his skin was all but blackened. '*Camouflage*,' she whispered.

'Good thinking,' he replied.

Connor waited for a guard to go by, then crept from the cover of the bushes and into the rebels' camp. His heart raced as he clambered down the riverbank. With nothing to hide him but the moonlit darkness and his improvised camouflage, Connor felt very exposed and prayed he wouldn't be spotted. The riverbed was a patchwork of puddles and pits, loose gravel and thick mud. His boots sank into the soft ground, slowing his progress, and he was still negotiating his way across when a boy soldier suddenly appeared on the opposite bank. Connor dropped into a shallow pit, flattening himself in the dirt as the boy approached. The rebel stopped only a couple of metres from where Connor was hiding.

Had the boy seen him?

Connor pressed himself further into the earth, his heart in his mouth as he waited for the alarm to be raised or a gun to be put to his head. A still-glowing cigarette butt landed by Connor's face, ashes spurting into his eyes. Connor tried not to cough as acrid smoke wafted up his nostrils. Blinking away the ash, he glanced up, half-expecting to see the boy's face leering down at him, but all he could hear was the splash of water as the soldier relieved himself before heading back along the bank to rejoin his companions.

Breathing a sigh of relief, Connor crawled out of the pit. Crouching low, he darted up the bank and over to a pile of earth near the workers' encampment. It was truly a hell on earth. The flickering fires illuminated the haggard faces of men and children, half-dead from exhaustion and hunger, their eyes sunken and their cheeks hollow. The smell of stale sweat from days of hard labour was thick in the air, along with the stench of urine and faeces from the nearby bushes.

Connor ducked down as another guard strolled past.

For no apparent reason, the soldier kicked one of the sleeping workers in the gut. As his victim groaned in shock and pain, the soldier walked off chuckling to himself. Connor realized more than ever that he had to get Henri out. The boy wouldn't last another day under such treatment.

He finally spotted Henri, slightly apart from the other men at the back of one of the shelters. He was curled up in the foetal position, his body trembling like a leaf, his strained wheezing for breath cutting through the ragged snores of the other workers.

Silently Connor crept round, keeping to the shadows and away from the light of the fires. Kneeling beside Henri, he placed a gentle hand on the boy's shoulder and a finger to his lips. Henri flinched and his eyes widened in horror.

'It's me, Connor,' he whispered, realizing his blackened face must look nightmarish to the poor traumatized boy.

'They said . . . you were dead,' he rasped.

'Well, I'm not. And neither is your sister.'

It took a moment for this to sink in, then Henri managed a weak smile. Connor produced the inhaler and helped Henri with it. After a minute or so, his breathing hadn't eased, so he administered two more doses until gradually the wheezing subsided. Although Henri needed more time to recover, Connor couldn't risk delaying much longer. A guard could pass by at any second.

'Can you walk?' he whispered.

Henri nodded. As Connor pulled him into a sitting position, one of the workers opened his eyes and looked directly at them. Connor froze, waiting to see what the man's reaction would be.

'*C'est mon ami*,' Henri explained.

The man winked, as if to say their secret was safe with him, and closed his eyes again.

Henri winced as Connor dragged him to his feet.

'I'm OK,' he whispered, putting on a brave face.

Connor could feel the criss-cross of raised welts that the bamboo cane had inflicted upon his body and realized that Henri must be in excruciating pain. Admiring the boy's courage, he gently placed Henri's arm over his shoulder and helped him towards the river. As they stumbled through the dug-out pits and waterlogged ditches, Connor glanced back to check there were no guards in sight. Thankfully the rebels still appeared to be absorbed in their card games. Helping Henri up the opposite bank, Connor knew they were going to make it.

They were almost within reach of the cover of the bushes when there was a shout. All of a sudden torchbeams cut through the darkness like swords. More shouts broke out and for a moment Connor believed they'd been spotted.

But the alarm hadn't been raised for them.

Further upstream Amber was being frogmarched into the rebel camp at gunpoint.

Connor bundled Henri into the bushes. They charged along a trail, foliage slapping at their faces in the pitch-darkness. Gunfire roared and the jungle erupted around them, tracer bullets shredding leaves and pulverizing tree trunks. As they ducked the gunfire, Henri's foot snagged on a root and they both tumbled to the ground. The shouts of the rebels closed in on them. Winded, Connor hauled Henri back to his feet and they stumbled on blindly.

Connor cursed his luck. He was back to square one, his only achievement being to swap one Principal for the other. *But how had Amber been caught?* Zuzu must have betrayed them. He realized her superstition of the hill and fearful reaction to the Black Mamba had merely been an act. He *should* have trusted his gut instinct and overruled Amber, making sure they returned to the lodge.

But it was too late for hindsight and regret. The jungle was swarming with rebels and survival was all that counted.

Soldiers crashed through the bushes to the right and left of them, bursts of gunfire lighting up the darkness like firecrackers. Connor, however, sensed some chaos in the rebels' movements. Their search seemed too widespread and too random for them to be hunting him and Henri specifically. Connor guessed that they didn't yet know Henri was missing and so the mobilization of soldiers was just a knee-jerk reaction to an unexpected intruder. This might play to their advantage if they could find a place to hide and wait out the haphazard search.

As they scrambled up a slope, they passed an old tree with a hollowed-out trunk.

'In there,' Connor instructed, hoping no poisonous insects or snakes had made it their home.

Henri knelt down and looked inside. 'But it's not big enough for us both.'

'It doesn't need to be. I'm going to rescue your sister.'

Henri's eyes widened. 'How?'

'I've yet to figure that out. But I need you hidden from the rebels to do so.'

Henri reluctantly crawled inside the hollow. Connor covered the entrance with fallen branches and leaves. It wouldn't fool a tracker, but at night it disguised the hole well enough to pass a cursory inspection.

Henri peered out. 'You won't leave me here, will you?'

Connor shook his head. 'No – but, if for any reason I'm not back by dawn, head south to the lodge.'

Connor could see this prospect terrified him. Removing his Rangeman watch, he reached in and attached it to Henri's wrist. 'Press here for the compass,' he explained. 'It was a special birthday present, so take good care of it until I return.'

Henri nodded, the responsibility of the watch appearing to give him some comfort, or at least a sense of purpose.

With a final check that the hole was completely hidden, Connor doubled back down the trail, being careful to avoid detection by the soldiers still scouring the jungle around him. His aim was to infiltrate their line and find a concealed spot on the riverbank from which to locate Amber. After that –

The barrel of an AK47 materialized from the darkness and was thrust into Connor's face.

'Don't shoot!' he cried, holding up his hands as the boy in the red beret began to squeeze the trigger.

CHAPTER 70

His eyes flickering open, Connor found himself staring into the face of death for a second time that night. He'd seen it first when the boy soldier had pressed the cold steel barrel of the AK47 against his forehead. Believing his life to be over, a nightmarish vision had flashed before him until, at the very last second, No Mercy had released the pressure on the rifle's trigger. Instead Connor had received a brutal blow to the jaw with the gun's stock. When he came to, Connor was confronted by death again. But this time the face was real. Black as coal, with pockmarked skin and fathomless eyes as inhuman as a snake's, it glared at him with cruel hard intent.

'*Où est le garçon?*' it asked him.

In his dazed state, Connor didn't answer. His lack of response resulted in a savage slap across his cheek, the blow so hard his head rang like a bell. Blinking back tears of pain, he tried to focus on his tormentor's face. He was almost blinded by the harsh light from a kerosene lamp, then the Black Mamba himself swam into his vision.

'*Où est le garçon?*' General Pascal repeated.

'I . . . don't understand,' Connor murmured.

'*Anglais!*' he remarked, raising an eyebrow in surprise. He switched to a heavily accented English. 'Where's the boy?'

'What boy?' Connor replied.

The general struck him again. Stars flared before his eyes and Connor tasted blood as his lip split. But he'd been knocked around enough in kickboxing class to be able to take a few blows.

'The ambassador's son. Or do you need another reminder?' The general raised his hand again to strike.

Bracing himself for the inevitable pain, Connor didn't even flinch at the threat. But, rather than hit him, General Pascal broke into a broad grin. 'I like this one. He's got spirit,' he announced to the soldiers encircling them. The general turned back to Connor, propped up against a rock in the heart of the rebel camp. 'It's no matter. We'll find the boy in the morning. I hear from Blaze you're quite some fighter. Defeating *two* of my soldiers.'

Connor glanced over and spotted the rebel he'd kicked into the wait-a-while bush. The man's face, arms and legs were lacerated with small weeping cuts. Beside him stood Dredd, his mauled arm hanging useless in a bloody bandage at his side, but at least he was alive.

'Let's have some sport, boys,' declared General Pascal. 'I want to see this White Warrior in action for myself. Hornet!'

He beckoned over a boy soldier wearing a blue New Orleans Hornets T-shirt. Thickset with a heavy brow and a permanent scowl, the boy matched Connor for height but easily out-gunned him in the muscle department. He looked like he'd been raised on a diet of buffalo and pure brutality.

'Let's see how you fare against my champion.'

'I've no desire to fight him,' said Connor tiredly, aware he probably didn't have much choice in the matter.

The general jutted his chin in the direction of Blaze, who stepped into the circle of light, dragging Amber with him. She appeared shaken but unhurt.

'Connor!' she gasped, rushing forward.

But Blaze yanked her back, unsheathed his machete and held the blade to her throat.

General Pascal grinned at Connor. 'Is that enough incentive for you?'

A ring of kerosene lamps marked the boundary of the dugout pit, casting a bright stadium-like glow over the waterlogged ground. Rebel soldiers jostled for position on the edge, eager for a good view of the impending death match between Hornet and the White Warrior.

Connor glanced up at the hostile crowd. He'd experienced some tough bouts in his rise to becoming UK Junior Kickboxing Champion, but this made each and every one of them seem like a playground fight by comparison.

On the opposite side of the pit, Hornet pulled off his T-shirt to reveal a rippling six-pack and a multitude of scars, clear evidence that he was a hardened fighter. In his injured and exhausted state, Connor realized his chances of defeating the boy were close to zero. But he refused to let himself think like that. His kickboxing trainer, Dan, had instilled in him an indomitable fighting spirit: *The will to win is the way to win.*

Connor went through his pre-match rituals, shaking his limbs loose, stretching and bringing his mind into sharp focus. He knew he couldn't conquer his opponent through strength, so he'd have to be quicker, more agile and more cunning in his fight strategy. He needed to end it fast and hard.

'This isn't a dance!' shouted one of the boy soldiers as Connor limbered up his legs. The crowd burst into mocking laughter.

Connor ignored the heckle and called up to General Pascal, reclined in a deckchair at the edge of the ring as if he was some Roman emperor. 'What if I beat your champion?'

Glugging from a bottle of beer, General Pascal snorted in amusement. '*If* you win, I'll let the girl go. If you don't, then –' the general shrugged – 'you won't be in any state to care what happens to her.'

Amber stared down at Connor in mute terror as Blaze ran the back edge of his machete across her cheek, goading Connor to react. But this threat to Amber's life only strengthened Connor's resolve to fight to his dying breath to save her.

'Let battle begin!' General Pascal announced, raising his beer bottle in a salute.

Like a pack of ravenous hyenas, the crowd whooped and whistled their approval.

Hornet roared straight in, charging across the pit like a bull elephant. Connor stood his ground, poised on the balls of his feet, waiting for the exact moment to make his move. Hornet lowered his head, turning it into a battering ram that would flatten a tank. At the last second Connor sidestepped the boy and simultaneously directed a hammer-fist strike to the base of his skull, targeting a knock-out pressure point just below the right ear.

Hornet went down as hard and heavy as the buffalo that the Wolf had shot. He slumped face first in the mud. The whooping crowd fell silent, shocked at the impossibly swift defeat of their champion. Then they began to jeer.

'I win,' declared Connor.

General Pascal smiled knowingly. 'I don't think so,' he replied, tilting his beer bottle in the direction of his fallen soldier. 'All you've done is make him angry.'

Connor turned to see Hornet up on his feet, shaking his head clear, and back on the attack. Yelling a battle cry, he swung a sledgehammer of a fist at Connor's head. With barely time to duck, Connor stepped forward and drove a vertical punch into the boy's solar plexus. Grunting from the force of the blow, Hornet grew more furious and elbowed Connor in the jaw. Already weakened from No Mercy's assault with his AK47, Connor was momentarily stunned and reeled away as Hornet pressed his advantage and launched a blistering attack. He hook-punched Connor in the gut, then pummelled him in the lower ribs. Connor gasped as a fist struck home and opened up his stitched wound. Hornet saw the increased flare of pain in Connor's eyes and struck again.

As the boy pounded him with relentless fury, the soldiers surrounding the pit began to chant, '*Hornet! Hornet! Hornet!*'

Forced to retreat from the onslaught, Connor soon found himself up against the wall of rebels. They pushed him back into the pit. Hornet was waiting for him. He grabbed Connor, lifted him high in the air, then brought him crashing down into a large pool of muddy water. Connor crumpled like a rag doll. Hornet dropped on top of him and shoved his head beneath the surface.

Cut off from air, Connor struggled in the boy's merciless grip. The shouts of the crowd became distorted and his mouth flooded with marshy water. Briefly his head came up and, as he snatched a desperate breath, he heard Amber screaming his name above the baying of the crowd. Then Hornet forced him back under.

Spluttering and blinded, Connor tried to buck his attacker off. But Hornet was simply too heavy and too strong. Feeling his own strength fading fast, Connor knew he was in a fight to the death. In a last-ditch attempt to free himself, he reached behind for Hornet's inner thigh and pinched the *yako* nerve point.

Nothing happened.

Connor squeezed harder. But Hornet kept him pinned under the water. Perhaps the boy was tougher than Dredd, but Connor had seen Ling use the exact same nerve point on a two-hundred-pound hitman and that guy had leapt away as if electrocuted. For some unexplained reason, Hornet was immune to the technique.

Connor clawed at the mud around him, trying to pull himself free. His hand came across a stone. He grabbed it and, in a final act of survival, smashed the rock down on to his attacker's bare foot. Hornet let out a grunt of pain. Connor struck again. This time he heard a sickening crack of bones and Hornet released his grip, rolling away in agony.

The crowd booed as Connor clambered back to his feet.

However, by the time he turned round to confront his opponent, Hornet had limped over to the edge of the pit and picked up a shovel.

Wielding the shovel like a weapon, he snarled, 'Time to dig your grave!'

Connor instinctively reached for his father's knife on his hip, but discovered it missing. From the sidelines, No Mercy waved the knife teasingly at him.

Hornet swung the shovel. Connor leapt back as the metal edge almost sliced him in half, then ducked as the shovel came back at him. Hornet roared in frustrated anger and brought the shovel arcing down on to Connor's head. With nowhere left to retreat, Connor had to dive to one side. As he rolled back to his feet, Hornet took another swing and the shovel hit him square in the back. Connor went down as if he'd been hit by a bus.

Winded and in pain, he crawled away through the mud. Hornet bore down on him, raising the shovel to land the killing blow. In that moment, Connor realized it was all over.

Then he heard Amber scream, '*Behind you!*'

Connor glanced over his shoulder. A metal panning sieve lay discarded at the edge of the pit. It would have been out of his reach, except that the boy soldier Dredd had casually kicked it down the slope to him. A small gesture for the life debt he owed Connor.

Connor seized it and held it over himself as a shield. Hornet's shovel clashed loudly against the metal pan. Infuriated, he struck again. Connor deflected the blow, then kicked out with all his might at Hornet's knee. There was an excruciating crunch and the boy staggered backwards, screaming in pain.

Leaping up, Connor smashed the shovel from Hornet's grip with the pan, then caught him across the jaw with it. Discarding the pan, he locked his hands round the dazed boy's neck and yanked him down hard on to his driving knee. Blood spurted from Hornet's flattened nose. Connor repeated the knee strike over and over, knocking the boy senseless. When his opponent's legs went from under him, he released his grip and let Hornet collapse in the mud. Fuelled by rage and the instinct to survive at all costs, Connor now picked up the shovel and lifted it high above his head to strike a final blow. Crippled and half-unconscious, Hornet held up a hand in a pitiful attempt to defend himself.

'*Kill! Kill! Kill!*' chanted the soldiers, caught up in the bloodlust.

Connor hesitated only briefly, then brought the shovel down with all his strength, striking a rock beside Hornet's head.

There was a groan of disappointment from the crowd.

'How could he miss?' cried one of the soldiers.

Weary and battleworn, Connor tossed the shovel aside. 'I don't kill,' he said, more to himself than the rebel crowd. 'I protect.'

Connor stood defiant before General Pascal. 'You promised to let Amber go.'

The general drained his beer bottle and discarded it in the pit. 'Only if you won.'

Gloating at Connor's indignant and crestfallen expression, Blaze kept holding the machete to Amber's throat.

'But I defeated your champion!' Connor protested, pointing to the groaning Hornet being borne away by his fellow soldiers.

'No, you lost,' declared the general. He stabbed a finger in Connor's chest. 'Showing mercy makes you weak. Only the death of your enemy makes you a true victor. But you will learn that – in time.'

'What do you mean?'

General Pascal's eyes twinkled. 'You're *my* White Warrior now.'

Connor stared at him in disbelief. 'I'll never fight for you.'

The general laughed. 'But you just did!'

'No, I fought for Amber's freedom.'

General Pascal laughed. 'How romantic. For that gesture, I'll let her live. But only for as long as you remain my champion.'

He turned his attention to Amber. Stroking a lock of her fine hair between his fingers, he mused, 'Maybe I could take this flame-haired beauty for my wife?'

Connor felt his blood start to boil.

'Oh, don't worry, my White Warrior. I'll take *good* care of her.'

The general looked to Blaze. 'Tie them both up. We don't want them running away. And in the morning hunt down her baby brother. I want that little rat back in its trap.'

Blaze sheathed his machete with a growl of disappointment and ordered No Mercy over. 'Help me secure these two,' he muttered.

With a gun to his back, Connor realized any further resistance was futile. As the two of them were roughly manhandled over to a stand of trees, Connor caught a faint whiff of expensive aftershave. The scent was out of place among these unwashed rebels and he looked sharply round. Just beyond the light of the kerosene lamps, a man stood in the shadows. It was too dark to make him out, but General Pascal had walked over to talk with the mysterious stranger.

As Blaze and No Mercy bound them, Connor strained to hear their conversation.

'. . . keeping these children captive could draw unwanted international attention,' the man was saying.

'Why? They'll be presumed dead in the ambush,' replied the general. 'Besides, the boy has great potential.'

'I don't care what you do with them,' said the man. 'Just make sure they never leave this valley alive.'

CHAPTER 73

Broken, beaten and bleeding, Connor bowed his head in defeat. Bound to the trunk of a tree, the prisoner of a crazed rebel tyrant and lost to the outside world, their fate was all but sealed. He knew that by now Buddyguard would be going into overdrive to locate him and his Principals. But what hope did they have of finding them in a hidden valley in a country soon to be torn apart by civil war? General Pascal could spirit them away into the jungle at a moment's notice. Or kill and bury them at the first sign of a rescue attempt.

No Mercy stood guard a short distance away, playfully flipping Connor's knife in his hand. Connor watched bitterly as the blade twirled and glinted in the light of a kerosene lamp. He could hear his father's voice ordering him to *never give in, never give up*. However, confronted with the harsh reality of their situation, he couldn't even hold on to the slightest shred of hope. His spirits were at their lowest ebb, lost in a pit of despair. He'd given his all to protect Amber and Henri, but in the end it hadn't been enough.

'Are you OK?' whispered Amber. She was slumped in the dirt beside him, her arms lashed behind her back to the opposite tree.

Connor raised his lolling head. 'I've been better,' he replied, attempting a smile, but even that hurt.

Amber looked his battered body over with sad guilt-ridden eyes. 'I'm . . . so sorry,' she wept.

'For what?' he murmured.

'For getting us into this mess. For the pain you've gone through trying to protect me.' The tears now flowed freely down her dirt-stained cheeks. 'You were right. We should have gone back to the lodge. Contacted help. I don't know what I was thinking. I was just so desperate to get Henri back. This is *all* my fault –'

'No, it's not,' Connor cut in. 'I made the decision to come here. It was my duty to protect *both* of you.'

Amber gazed at him with deep affection. 'And you did rescue my brother. For that, I'll be grateful for the rest of my life . . . however long that might be,' she added with a weak smile.

Connor's thoughts went to Henri hiding alone in the dark hollow of the tree, waiting for their return. A return that would never happen. He prayed the boy would leave at first light, before the rebels began their search. Otherwise their sacrifice would have been for nothing.

'How did you get caught by the way?' Connor asked Amber.

'A guard sneaked up on me from behind.'

'What happened to Zuzu?'

Amber shrugged. 'When the soldier grabbed me, I looked round, but she was gone.'

'So, do you think she betrayed us?' said Connor, the girl's deception leaving a sour taste in his mouth.

'I guess she must have,' sighed Amber. 'How else would the guard have known where I was?'

In the distance, a flash of forked lightning lit up the pitch-black sky. The lone acacia tree atop the peak was starkly visible for a brief second, appearing like a warped gallows, before plunging back into darkness. As the bleak image faded, and Connor and Amber resigned themselves to their inevitable fate, a long, low ominous rumble thundered overhead.

Alpha team fell silent as Colonel Black marched into the operations room. The stiff measured stride and grim expression on his face told them he wasn't delivering good news.

'Take a seat, everyone,' he instructed, his voice rough from a night of no sleep.

Exchanging anxious looks, they hurried to their places. Charley rolled to the front, braced for the worst.

'This is the situation,' said the colonel. 'The Burundian president has been assassinated in an ambush. The army found the remnants of his safari convoy in sector four of the park, some twenty miles from the lodge.'

Colonel Black tapped a command on his tablet computer. Wirelessly linked to the widescreen wall monitors, a satellite image of a dried-out riverbed appeared on the display. The resolution was low but the scene was clear enough. Four immobilized vehicles, one of which was overturned and burnt out, another no more than a smoking charred shell. A bomb crater from an RPG was also visible.

'What are the dark blobs?' asked Jason, squinting at the screen.

'Bodies,' replied the colonel.

The mood of the room dropped another notch.

'Are there . . . *any* survivors?' asked Charley.

The colonel nodded. 'The major-general reports that two ministers and their wives were rescued from the lodge, where they were being held prisoner by members of the Armée Nationale de la Liberté led by General Pascal, aka the Black Mamba.'

'But what about Connor and the Barbier family?' pressed Ling.

'That we don't know,' the colonel admitted with a heavy sigh. 'The ambush site is still being investigated by the army. If they were in one of the burnt-out vehicles, it'll take some time to identify the bodies.'

Choking back her rising emotion, Charley asked, 'Don't the survivors know what happened to them?'

'Not according to the major-general. The ministers fled during the initial phase of the ambush only to be caught later. There is some hope, though. One of the Land Rovers from the safari convoy is missing.'

'So you think Connor may have got away?' questioned Richie.

'That's the scenario I'd like to believe. And the one we're going to work to. However, forty-eight hours have passed since the ambush with no communication from Connor. From that, we can presume four possibilities: one, he's in hiding; two, he has since been captured; three, he is lying injured somewhere; or worst-case scenario, he's . . .' The colonel didn't need to finish the sentence for Alpha team to guess the fourth and final possibility.

'So what's the plan?' asked Ling.

'The Burundian army have taken back the lodge from the rebels,' Colonel Black explained. 'The major-general is sending in reinforcements, and his army have begun a sector-by-sector search of the park. If Connor or any of the Barbiers are still alive, they'll find them.'

Charley raised her hand. 'I think one of the team needs to fly out there and help with the search.'

'I agree,' said the colonel.

'Then I volunteer.'

Colonel Black emphatically shook his head.

Charley frowned at him. 'Is it because I'm in a wheel-chair you won't send me?'

The colonel shot her an affronted look. 'I appreciate you're upset, Charley, but you know me better than that. The fact is I wouldn't send *any* of you to a country that's on the verge of a civil war.'

'But we *need* somebody on the ground, in situ,' Charley insisted.

'You're not going and that's an order.'

'So who is going?' asked Jason.

'I am.'

The colonel handed out folders as he headed for the door. 'Here are your individual tasks. I depart in one hour for Burundi and want updates from all of you by the time I leave.'

335

As Alpha team digested their assignments, Charley stared at the satellite image of the burnt-out vehicles surrounded by countless dark blobs. She wiped away a tear with the back of her hand.

'Don't worry,' said Ling, putting an arm round her. 'Connor's a survivor.'

CHAPTER 75

Some time during the night, the first drops of rain fell on Connor's face. Cool and refreshing, he let the drops roll down his cheeks. As the rain intensified, he opened his mouth, relishing the life-giving water. Then the shower became a torrential downpour, drumming on the tree canopy overhead and drowning out all other noise. The layers of dirt and blood were washed from his skin and clothes, his wounds cleansed and his body partly revived.

The rebels hurried to the shelter of their tents, while the enslaved workers shivered and shook out in the open, their tarpaulin roofs having collapsed under the sheer weight of the water. The stand of trees Connor and Amber were tied under offered scant protection from the storm and, exposed to its full might, they too began shuddering from the rain-drenched cold.

With the guards huddling in their tents and the kerosene lamps guttering in the deluge, Connor realized that this was their best, and possibly only, opportunity to escape. But, try as he might, he couldn't free his hands. He thought the rain might help him slip out of his bindings, but the wet rope had swelled up and was now even tighter round his wrists. Connor struggled until exhaustion overwhelmed him.

He must have drifted off because the next thing he heard was a massive explosion and the distinctive *crack* of gunfire. The rain still fell in sheets, but a pale pre-dawn light was now battling to push through the tail end of the storm. Throughout the camp, rebels were snatching up weapons and firing indiscriminately into the surrounding jungle. Another explosion ripped through the valley as a mortar detonated in the riverbed, sending up a shower of dirt and debris. The enslaved workers ran for cover, but many were cut down by gunfire from the bushes.

'*What's happening?*' cried Amber, her wet hair matted to her face.

'It must be the army,' Connor replied. 'Somehow they've found us!'

'Then we're saved?' She seemed not to know whether to laugh or cry with joy at the news.

But Connor realized this was no time to rejoice. They were stuck in the heart of the kill zone, at risk from both rebel *and* friendly fire. Whether rescue was coming or not, Connor knew they had to A-C-E it out of the camp as fast as possible. *Assess the threat. Counter the danger. Escape the kill zone.* Otherwise they'd be slaughtered like the rest of the workers.

He renewed his effort to free his hands, the skin around his wrists scraped raw as he twisted and pulled. Amid the chaos of the surprise attack, General Pascal barked orders to his rebel army of men and boy soldiers. Despite despising the rebel leader to his very core, Connor couldn't deny the man's military expertise. Honed through years of guerrilla warfare in the jungle, the general quickly rallied his troops into several cohesive fighting units, then launched a counter-offensive against the enemy hidden in the forested slopes of the valley.

As he commanded his forces, the general shouted at No Mercy to keep guard over Connor and Amber, his remit to kill them if any government soldiers entered the rebel camp.

Connor yanked harder on his bindings, but still they wouldn't give. Amber was struggling too.

No Mercy sneered at their pathetic attempts and, after checking the knots were still secure, turned his attention to the firefight raging all around them. Tracer bullets zipped overhead and another mortar exploded nearby, destroying a rebel tent. Screams of wounded men filled the air. As debris and shrapnel rained down on them, No Mercy unleashed the full force of his AK47 at the first of the government troops advancing from the bushes.

With the boy distracted, Connor drew on all his strength and tugged at his bindings with every fibre of his body. The rope didn't give an inch. Infuriated, he yanked again and again.

Then, when he'd given up all hope, the rope unexpectedly snapped.

Connor jumped up and seized No Mercy in a rear chokehold, a classic jujitsu technique used to subdue an opponent. Unable to breathe and with the blood flow cut off to his brain, No Mercy struggled violently to free himself. But in less than ten seconds he fell limp in Connor's grip. Despite the boy's merciless nature, Connor had no desire to kill him or leave him brain damaged. So he immediately released the choke and let the boy collapse, unconscious, to the muddy ground.

Recovering his father's knife, Connor raced over to Amber and cut her bonds. It took several slices and Connor was amazed that he'd managed to snap his own bindings. As soon as she was free, Amber grabbed hold of him in relief, her body trembling like a sparrow's. Then she suddenly stiffened and Connor turned his head to see General Pascal standing over them, his Glock 17 handgun aimed squarely at his back.

'You certainly live up to your name, White Warrior,' declared the general, glancing down at the inert body of the boy soldier. 'And you will die by it too.'

CHAPTER 76

An arrow flew out of nowhere, piercing General Pascal's forearm and knocking his aim. He screamed in agony and fury as the round missed its target and obliterated the bark beside Connor's head. His gun slipping from his grip, the general clasped his injured arm, blood spurting from the wound as he yelled to his soldiers for assistance.

Before reinforcements could come to the general's aid, Connor pulled Amber to her feet and they both fled. Only now did Connor catch a glimpse of what had actually broken his own bindings. A second arrow was embedded in the trunk of his tree, the sharpened tip having severed the rope in two.

On the other side of the riverbed, concealed among the bushes, Zuzu urgently beckoned Connor and Amber across. As she loosed another arrow at a rebel trying to stop them, Connor rebuked himself for having thought the girl had betrayed them. He vowed to buy her a whole wardrobe of clothes if they ever got out of this valley alive!

Behind them, the Black Mamba was bellowing his rage

above the noise of the firefight and relentless rain. '*Stop them!*'

Glancing back over his shoulder, Connor spotted several soldiers sprinting after them with the machete-wielding Blaze, his murderous intent clear in the bloodlust set of his eyes. Pushing Amber ahead, Connor followed her down the slippery bank. The storm had turned the riverbed into a quagmire and they found themselves knee-deep in mud and water. As they waded across the boggy terrain, the rebels rapidly closed in.

After taking two more of the soldiers down, Zuzu had run out of arrows and could only urge them on from the bushes. Then she started to shout and point manically upstream. Hearing an ominous rumble, Connor turned to see a wall of brown foaming water thundering down the riverbed. The makeshift dam had burst and a flash flood was sweeping through the valley.

'Go! Go!' Connor screamed at Amber.

They tried to increase their pace, but the ground sucked at their feet, seemingly intent on holding them in the path of the oncoming flood. Confronted by such a terrifying force of nature, their pursuers gave up the chase and turned back.

Flinging themselves forward, Connor and Amber reached the opposite bank and desperately clawed their way up. But the slick mud made the slope treacherous and they slipped back down. The flood was almost on top of them when Zuzu raced over and pulled Amber to safety.

Connor felt the ground washed from under his feet. Then his legs were whipped away. Zuzu and Amber grabbed for his outstretched arms. The bushgirl missed, but Amber managed to clasp his trailing hand. She dug her heels into the mud as the current threatened to drag Connor away and her back in.

'*Stay with me!*' Amber cried as she felt his fingers slipping from her grasp.

Connor strained with all his might to hold on, but the flood seemed determined to claim him. Zuzu now wrapped her arms round Amber's waist in a frantic tug-of-war for Connor's life. With a final desperate pull, they hauled him clear from the torrent of debris, water and rock hurtling past.

'Thanks,' Connor gasped as the two girls helped him to his feet. 'That was rather *too* close for comfort!'

On the other side of the churning river, Blaze was also dragging himself out, plunging his machete deep into the mud as an anchor. But the other soldiers weren't so fortunate and were borne away, screaming, on the tide of foaming water.

Zuzu tugged on Connor's elbow, urging him and Amber to leave, but Connor was rooted to the spot.

'Let's go!' implored Amber, then she saw the pale, wide-eyed expression on his face. 'What's the matter? You look like you've seen a ghost.'

'*I have*,' he said, his reply barely more than a whisper.

Through the haze of falling rain, Connor saw an

ashen-faced man with eyes of death and a stillness that was perturbing amid the chaos and destruction of the battle and the flood. A deep shudder ran through Connor at the ghostly vision. He'd met this man once before – upon a burning tanker off the coast of Somalia. He'd been presumed dead, no trace of him having ever been found. Now that very same man stood on the opposite bank, staring directly at Connor.

The man raised his semi-automatic pistol and took careful aim. Connor instinctively ducked. A bullet shot past his ear. There was a scream of pain. Connor spun, expecting to see Amber or Zuzu lying dead in the mud. But it was a rebel soldier who'd been killed.

Not waiting for the ghost from his past to take another shot, Connor fled with the two girls into the jungle.

CHAPTER 77

Connor ripped aside the clump of foliage but found nothing. It was the wrong tree. He went from one trunk to the other, searching for the hollow he'd hidden Henri in. But the jungle had looked completely different during the night and he was now totally disorientated. 'I'm certain it's around here somewhere,' he assured Amber.

The sound of gunfire was drawing ever closer. Zuzu pleaded with them to keep moving.

Torn between locating her brother and taking Zuzu's advice, Amber questioned, 'Will he still even be there? You told him to leave at first light.'

'I know,' Connor replied, their search becoming more and more desperate. 'But we *have* to check in case he hasn't.'

'Maybe the army has found him,' said Amber hopefully.

A hand grenade detonated close by and they all dropped to the ground, burning leaves and scorched earth raining down on them.

'You go with Zuzu,' Connor ordered Amber, their ears ringing from the blast. 'I'll find your brother.'

Amber shook her head. 'No, we stick together.'

'You don't have a choice,' said Connor, dragging her to her feet. 'I'm not risking you getting caught again. Now go with Zu–'

'*Connor! Amber!*' a voice hissed.

They both spun round. Further up the slope, a pair of scared eyes peeked out from behind a thick layer of leaves and branches. Connor had concealed the hollow's entrance far better than he'd ever imagined.

'Henri!' Amber cried, scrambling up the slope and pulling away the branches. Henri crawled out and Amber embraced him so hard Connor thought she'd never let go.

'Sorry, Connor,' Henri mumbled, his face pressed against his sister's chest. 'I was too scared to leave with all the fighting.'

Connor smiled kindly. 'It's a good thing you didn't, otherwise –'

'*Allons-y!*' called Zuzu, frantically beckoning them to follow her.

'But the lodge is that way,' Connor argued, pointing upslope.

Zuzu vehemently shook her head and rattled off some French at him.

'When two elephants fight, it's the grass that gets trampled,' Amber interpreted, finally relinquishing her grip on her brother. 'She says it's safer to go the long way round. Avoid the fighting.'

As another grenade exploded off to their left, Connor didn't need any further convincing. They dashed along an animal trail, following the course of the river. With every step they took further down the valley, the sounds of battle gradually receded and the rain began to ease. Zuzu slowed their pace a little, allowing Henri to grab a couple of puffs from his inhaler. By the time they reached the drop-off at the end of the valley, the storm had passed and dawn's light had broken through the clouds in golden rays.

They stopped at the edge of the waterfall, its glistening curtain cascading some forty metres down to a large plunge pool below. From their viewpoint looking out across the park, Connor was once again astounded at the majestic beauty of Africa. The rolling savannah, fresh with rain, appeared to be reborn. The trees and bushland had taken on a lusher shade of green and seemingly blossomed over-night. Birds sang a mellifluous chorus as they fluttered and swooped in the crystal-clear air. On the plain, herds of zebra, antelope and wildebeest grazed in countless num-bers, braying and snorting, while a parade of mighty ele-phants strode towards the Ruvubu River, grown pregnant with floodwaters and now sparkling like a jewelled ribbon in the early morning light.

The storm had brought more than rain – it had brought life.

Amber peered over the lip of the waterfall, then glanced at Connor. 'No jumping this time,' she said, the corner of her lips turning up into a teasing smile. 'We climb down.'

'Fine by me,' he replied.

Being careful on the slippery rock, Amber picked the easiest route down the face, following a natural fault line.

It was slow going, but the handholds were positive and plentiful and they all reached the bottom safely. From the plunge pool, Zuzu guided them along the line of the tributary river through the trees towards the plain. Connor took up the rear, ensuring they weren't being followed. No one talked, all of them shattered and shell-shocked from their harrowing night and fraught escape.

Up ahead, Zuzu came to a sudden halt. Amber asked in a whisper what was wrong. Zuzu put a finger to her lips and unsheathed her knife.

The birds had stopped singing in their part of the jungle.

Connor sensed the danger too. He felt eyes upon them. Watchful and waiting. Drawing his father's knife, he scanned the thick undergrowth but saw nothing. Zuzu was as still as a startled deer, using all her senses to pinpoint the threat. Amber held her brother close, fearful of what new peril they faced.

A whisper of movement in the bush caused them to turn. From behind a tree emerged the Wolf.

The hunter had his bolt-action rifle shouldered and aimed at them.

'Are you lost, children?' he said quietly. 'You're a long way from the lodge and heading in the wrong direction.'

Connor felt deeply uneasy at the hunter's tone. He gripped his knife tighter, sensing he might have need of it. 'No, we have a guide, thank you,' he replied.

'That I see.' The Wolf glanced at Zuzu, then his pale eyes flicked to Amber and Henri. 'I thought you said your brother was dead.'

'We rescued him,' replied Amber curtly.

'Ah! Like I rescued you,' said the Wolf, a pencil-thin

smile on his lips. 'And how did you repay me?' His expression hardened, the smile vanishing. 'By sticking your nose into my business and injuring one of my men.'

He swung the barrel of his rifle, aiming at Amber.

'You do realize there's a full-on battle raging up in that valley?' said Connor, hoping to divert his attention away from her.

The Wolf nodded. 'Your concern for my well-being is touching,' he replied in a sarcastic tone. 'But I have little problem avoiding the government troops and Abel is smuggling the ivory out as we speak. You need to be more concerned about *your* future.'

The Wolf kept his weapon trained on Amber.

'What are you going to do then? Shoot us all?' she challenged, her patience wearing thin.

A snarl of a grin spread across the Wolf's bearded face. 'When a hunter has his prey in his sights, there's only *one* thing to do.'

He curled his finger round the trigger. 'Which of you wants to join my collection first?'

Connor instinctively stepped in front of Amber, shielding her with his body.

'Ahh! We have a volunteer,' said the Wolf, closing one eye and lining up his sights.

Connor judged the distance too great for him to tackle the hunter before the gun went off. But he thought he might be able to distract or even injure the man, by throwing his father's knife.

350

As he went to sling the blade, a dark shadow dropped silently from the bough above them.

The leopard landed full on the shoulders of the Wolf, knocking him to the ground. The rifle went off, tearing a hole in a nearby tree trunk. But the ambushing leopard wasn't frightened off by the blast. Instead the creature gave a ferocious growl and sank its fangs into the hunter's neck. The Wolf let out a strangled scream. He tried to fight off the beast, but the animal was too powerful for him.

As the leopard slowly suffocated the hunter, its green eyes glared at Connor and the others, daring them to approach. Connor, knife in hand, was tempted to attack it but the leopard, pinning its victim beneath its razor claws, hissed a warning at his first tentative step. Then the animal bit down hard again and the Wolf fell still. As Connor cautiously backed away, the leopard dragged the limp, lifeless body of the hunter up into the tree.

The dishevelled group of sister, brother, bodyguard and Batwa girl trekked slowly across the blisteringly hot savannah, keeping a clear distance from Dead Man's Hill as they negotiated their roundabout route to the lodge. Unnerved by the sheer brutality and savage swiftness of the leopard attack, their eyes constantly darted from bush to tree to scrub, alert for the slightest sign of danger.

'I think it's poetic justice,' Amber declared as they passed safely through a thicket. 'The hunter killed by the hunted.'

Connor was inclined to agree. He held his father's knife close, having no intention to fall prey to the next predator they encountered – whether that be lion, hippo, hyena, snake or rebel soldier. 'The Wolf deserved what was coming, that's for sure,' he said. 'But we must remember, he did help us in our time of need.'

'I suppose so,' said Amber reluctantly. 'Of course, he then tried to kill us.'

'Seems like everything in this country is trying to kill us!' remarked Henri with a weary laugh.

He limped ahead of Connor, the welts from his beating still causing him serious discomfort. Although Henri didn't complain, the sight of his suffering stirred up a tight knot of anger in Connor's belly. The cruelty inflicted by Blaze on a defenceless boy deserved retribution. And Connor hoped that the rebel had got his come-uppance at the hands of the government troops.

He wondered if the battle was over by now, with General Pascal either captured or dead. At the time the fighting had been too chaotic to see who had the upper hand, but the government soldiers had secured the advantage of surprise and it seemed highly unlikely the rebels would survive the attack.

Zuzu suddenly signed with the flat of her hand to get down. The four of them crouched behind a bush as an open-topped jeep crested the rise ahead. The vehicle drove hard and fast in their direction.

'Should we run?' suggested Henri, his voice tight with fear.

Connor shook his head. 'They'll see us if we do.'

The guttural roar of the diesel engine drew closer. Connor peered through a gap in the bush as the 4x4 skidded to a halt a stone's throw away from where they were hiding.

The driver stood up in his seat and scanned the terrain with his binoculars. 'Damn it!' he swore.

'It's *Gunner*,' hissed Amber in shocked delight.

Connor put a hand on her shoulder, preventing her from rising. She frowned in confusion. Connor shook his head and put a finger to his lips. After all they'd been through, he was wary of anyone they encountered in the park – especially an unexplained survivor of the ambush.

'Connor! Amber!' shouted the ranger, his tone urgent.

When no one appeared, Gunner shook his head in frustration and put the jeep into gear. At the very last second, Connor decided that answering the ranger was worth the risk. They were tired, hungry and hurting, and far from the lodge. They couldn't afford to miss a genuine chance of rescue. As Gunner was about to drive off, he stepped out from behind the bush and called to him.

Gunner's craggy face broke into a relieved smile. 'Connor! Thank God you're alive. I've been looking for you everywhere. Where's Amber and Henri?'

'How did you escape the ambush?' Connor questioned, his knife behind his back.

'By the skin of my teeth,' Gunner replied, grinning. 'I hid in an aardvark burrow. But it was a close call. Are Amber and Henri with you?'

Connor ignored the question and asked his own. 'Why did you and Buju stop the safari convoy?'

Gunner's eyes narrowed at the surprise line of questioning. 'Buju spotted a landmine. We were trying to establish if it was from the war or recently laid when the attack happened. Now tell me, are the Barbier children alive or not? Their parents are sick with worry.'

Amber stood up with Henri in astonished disbelief. 'They're *alive*?'

'Yes!' Gunner replied, hurriedly clambering out of the

jeep to greet them, his glee turning to a mild look of surprise as Zuzu also emerged from behind the bush.

'But we saw their Land Rover crash and burn,' said Connor, still cautious.

'I did too. So, while the rebels were slaughtering the presidential guard, I left my burrow and pulled them free.' Gunner stared gravely at Amber and Henri, the siblings clasping hands. 'I'll be honest; your parents weren't in a good state. But they could just about walk. It took us all night and most of the next day to reach the nearest medical centre. The good news is they're recovering fast. But their major concern was for you two. So I promised on my life to find you. And here you are!'

Turning to Connor, Gunner half-raised his hands in surrender and smiled. 'Now, Connor, are you going to put that knife of yours away or not? I've no wish to get stabbed trying to rescue you.'

After a moment's deliberation, Connor decided to give Gunner the benefit of the doubt, at least for now. He produced his father's knife from behind his back and sheathed it.

'I don't blame you for not trusting me,' said Gunner, patting Connor on the shoulder. 'Given the situation I don't trust anyone either. That's why I admitted the Barbiers to the medical centre under a false name. Now let's get back to the lodge. Your friend too. This park is swarming with soldiers and we don't want her mistaken for a rebel.'

Amber explained the danger to Zuzu and, after some

uncertainty on her part, Amber managed to convince her to climb into the jeep with them. The ranger gunned the engine and they shot off at high speed.

'Time is of the essence,' said Gunner as he drove straight over some bushes. 'I've a plane on standby to take us to the capital. There you'll be reunited with your parents.'

Gunner drove up to the safari lodge's rarely used rear entrance, unlocked the gate, closed it behind them, then parked beside one of the guest suites.

'Why all the secrecy?' asked Connor as the ranger checked the grounds were clear for them to proceed. 'Surely the Burundian army is in control of the lodge?'

Gunner responded with a sceptical raise of an eyebrow. 'Don't take anything for granted, Connor, especially in Africa. The Black Mamba has defeated forces five times his rebel group's size in the past. Besides no one knows where you are or even that you're alive. I want to keep it that way until you're safely back with your respective parents. Now grab your essentials only: passport, travel documents, a change of clothes, and leave the rest.'

They moved from room to room, quickly gathering their most important belongings – except Amber, who stuffed a bag full of her best clothes and jewellery for Zuzu, fulfilling her promise. 'I don't suppose we've time for a quick shower?' she asked, tugging at her dirty matted hair.

Gunner shook his head regretfully. 'Sorry, can't risk it. That'll have to wait until later.'

Next they entered the lodge's kitchen through the staff entrance. Some dislodged pans, a crumpled white hat and a pool of dried blood were the only remaining evidence of the chef's presence. Connor's alert level shot up and he looked uneasily at the ranger.

'As I said, you can't take anything for granted,' whispered Gunner as he raided the pantry. Then, peering through a small window in the kitchen's service door, he led them into the lounge.

The lavish room was deserted but appeared to have been the scene of some riotous celebration. The mirror behind the bar had been shattered. A spray of bullet holes peppered the main wall, several of the rounds having gone through the tribal shield, knocking the display askew. Connor also noticed the zebra-skin rug on the parquet floor was stained red – whether from blood or red wine it was impossible to tell, but there was an ominous dark trail leading from the bar out into the reception area.

'Do you think there's anyone still here?' asked Amber nervously.

'By the looks of it, we've missed the party,' replied Gunner, plundering the bar for bottles of Coke and fresh water.

But Connor couldn't shake the feeling that they'd been led into a trap, one just waiting to be sprung. 'So where's the army?'

Gunner shrugged. 'Killing rebels in the park, I suppose. Now you all look like you need refuelling, and I don't want you dropping dead on me before we reach our final destination,' he said, popping the tops of the drinks and handing them out. 'Wait here while I call in the plane.'

The ranger disappeared into the lodge's back office.

As the four of them glugged on sugary Coke and greedily tucked into the chocolate bars, bananas and the other snacks Gunner had gathered, Connor strode over to the bay windows overlooking the veranda and the plain beyond. Despite his fatigue, it was clear they weren't out of the danger zone yet and he needed to maintain a Code Orange level of alertness. Peering through the glass, he surveyed the lodge's grounds, keeping his eyes peeled for any sign of approaching rebels. There was no movement in the bush. In fact it looked almost too still. Then he spotted the body of a government soldier lying by the electric fence, half-obscured in the grass. 'Amber, we need to g–'

'My word, it's a miracle!' exclaimed a voice in accented English.

Connor spun to see the bulging figure of Minister Feruzi standing in the doorway.

'I'd heard you'd escaped the ambush,' said the Minister for Trade and Tourism, smiling profusely and waddling over to the bar like a hippo heading for its watering-hole. 'But I would never have believed it until I saw you with my own eyes.'

'Did you know one of your soldiers is lying dead out there?' said Connor, pointing to the electric fence at the lodge's boundary.

'Oh yes! Minister Rawasa has returned to the capital

and I've been left here to pick up the pieces,' he replied with a what-can-you-do shrug. 'But, joy of joys, we have good news at last! You're all safe and sound.'

His gaze fell upon Zuzu standing with them at the bar, his nose turning up slightly at her presence. 'And who's this?'

'Our guide,' replied Amber with enthusiasm. 'She's been a lifeline to us.'

'I'm sure she has. Burundians are a most hospitable people,' said the minister assuredly. 'But now it's *my* responsibility to look after you.'

He wrapped his chubby arms round their shoulders, Amber looking distinctly uncomfortable and Henri wincing beneath the man's sweaty touch. Only now did the minister notice the red welts covering Henri's body and he let go. 'Oh, my poor boy, what have they done to you?'

The ranger strode back in. 'Plane's on its way. Let's make a –' He stopped and stared at the minister.

'Gunner?' exclaimed Minister Feruzi, staring back in equal amazement. 'My God, another risen from the ashes! Are there any more of you?'

With a solemn stern shake of his head, the ranger replied, 'I found Buju, or what was left of him.'

'That's tragic to hear,' said the minister. 'But have you any news of Laurent or Cerise? We've reason to believe they may have escaped the ambush too.'

'I wouldn't know,' replied Gunner as he beckoned Connor and the others to join him. 'Time to go, kids.'

'What's the rush, Gunner?' Minister Feruzi demanded,

his pudgy eyes narrowing in suspicion. 'This lodge is now secure.'

'Are you sure about that, Minister?' questioned the ranger with a sharp jerk of his head at Connor, Amber, Henri and Zuzu, urging them to hurry.

'Children, you *mustn't* go with him,' insisted Minister Feruzi. 'This man's a prime suspect in the ambush.'

Connor and the others froze halfway between the two men. *So he had been right to be suspicious of the ranger?*

'Don't believe him,' said Gunner. 'He's the one behind all this. *He* dictated the viewpoint and the route for the sunset safari, even though there's a far better place closer to the lodge.'

Minister Feruzi laughed. 'That's ridiculous! Think about it, children: who stopped the convoy in the middle of that riverbed?'

'That's only because Buju spotted a mine!' argued Gunner. 'Otherwise we'd have all been blown to pieces. Connor, why do you think Minister Feruzi was so far back in the convoy? His vehicle escaped unharmed because he *knew* the ambush was going to happen.'

Caught between the ranger and the minister, Connor wondered who to believe. One of them was lying. Amber and the others looked to him to make the decision.

'We have to go *now*!' insisted Gunner, his eyes darting from the door to the veranda.

'Given the situation I don't trust anyone,' said Connor, repeating the ranger's words back at him.

For Connor, Gunner's story of his escape had always

seemed too good to be true. He also thought it unlikely that a government minister would be in league with a rebel military group. He made a move towards Minister Feruzi, the man opening his arms to receive them. Then Connor remembered the dead body of the soldier by the wire. The minister had said the lodge was secure, but how could that be if the guards were dead?

At the last moment Connor changed his mind, nodding to Amber and the others to go with Gunner instead.

'I can't save you now, children,' said Minister Feruzi as General Pascal strode into the lounge, accompanied by Blaze, No Mercy and half a dozen rebel soldiers.

'I see you found my strays,' remarked General Pascal, heading straight for the bar as if he owned it. His eyes bloodshot, his skin oily with sweat and his injured arm wrapped in a bandage, the rebel leader looked the worse for wear following his battle against the government troops. But the infamous military skill of the man had evidently secured him another victory.

'Whisky!' he barked to one of his soldiers. Scurrying behind the bar, the boy grabbed a bottle and filled an empty glass. The general drained it in one hit and the boy replenished it immediately.

'I understood that the army had been diverted to sector *four* of the park!' growled General Pascal, glaring at the minister. 'So how come soldiers attacked our camp this morning in sector *eight*?'

Minister Feruzi blanched at the news. 'Th-the major-general must have changed his plans without informing me.'

General Pascal stabbed a finger at the minister. 'You realize I've lost good warriors,' he snapped. 'What's worse, the army's probably blown half the diamonds to dust!'

Tugging a handkerchief from his shirt pocket, the minister mopped his brow in panic. 'I assure you, the major-general was instructed to search the south of the park. But what about the diamonds? Do you still have control? Are there *any* left?'

'Don't worry your fat face about it! My forces still command the valley and there'll be plenty enough for everyone,' replied the general, grimacing as he inspected his swollen arm. 'First let's deal with this little problem of my strays. Then we can discuss the future of this country, and your place in it.'

Stepping forward, Gunner spat at the minister's feet. 'You treacherous piece of scum, you traded our lives for diamonds!'

Minister Feruzi glanced down at the spit smearing his shoe. 'You shouldn't have done that, Gunner.'

General Pascal nodded a silent order to No Mercy. A deafening *bang* rang in all their ears as the boy soldier shot Gunner in the chest.

'Consider yourself fired,' said Minister Feruzi with a gloating smirk as the ranger writhed and groaned in pain on the floor.

'No, Gunner, no!' cried Amber, dropping down beside the ranger and pressing her hands to his wound, blood oozing from between her fingers. Connor kept Henri close as Zuzu stared in wide-eyed shock at the boy soldier standing over the ranger.

'Finish him off,' said the general, his tone bored. 'I can't stand the groaning.'

On a do-or-die impulse, Connor snatched one of the tribal spears from the wall. 'Stay back!' he warned.

General Pascal eyed the old weapon with amusement as he leant against the bar, swilling his whisky. 'Now what are you going to do with that, my White Warrior?' he enquired. 'Spear a lion?'

'No,' Connor replied, pointing the iron tip at him. 'Skewer a snake!'

The Black Mamba laughed. 'You have fighting spirit, I grant you that. But playtime's over. Drop the spear or Blaze kills your girl.'

Blaze drew a handgun and aimed it at Amber's head. Connor turned the spear on the rebel. If he was quick, he could perhaps drive it through the man's chest before he pulled the trigger. But No Mercy would have more than enough time to shoot Gunner again. And then what? Connor glanced towards the bay doors. He wondered if they could flee via the veranda. Then a rebel soldier appeared on the other side of the bay windows, cutting off their escape route. Left with no option, Connor discarded the spear, the weapon clattering on to the wooden floor.

'You disappoint me,' said General Pascal, knocking back the last of his drink and coughing into his fist. 'I'd hoped you would die fighting like a warrior.'

The general headed for the main door, beckoning Minister Feruzi and the half-dozen rebel soldiers to accompany him.

'Blaze, kill the strays,' he ordered. 'Any way you wish. Just make sure the Batwa girl, who put the arrow through my arm, suffers most.'

Forced at gunpoint to kneel, Connor, Henri and Zuzu joined Amber on the parquet floor slick with Gunner's blood. The ranger's breathing was now laboured and rasping. He'd fallen unconscious with the pain but was clinging to life. Connor's mind was racing, trying desperately to think of some way out of their predicament. But No Mercy kept his AK47 trained on them and Connor knew at the first sign of resistance he'd simply shoot them dead.

Blaze unsheathed his machete and caressed the razor-edged blade with a finger. 'This is my weapon of choice,' he said with a sadistic grin. 'I can cut, cleave, slice, hack, chop or behead you with one stroke of this beauty.'

The rebel paced slowly in front of them, drawing out the tension as he casually swung the blade.

He jutted his chin at Zuzu. 'I'll leave you to last, Batwa,' he spat with contempt. 'Then you can know of the suffering that awaits you.'

Understanding the threat but not the words, Zuzu shrank away but her eyes remained fixated on No Mercy.

Blaze prodded the tip of his machete into Henri's chest.

'You, I'll skin like a rabbit. Hang your hide out to dry in the hot sun.'

Confronted by his tormentor once more, Henri began to sob and tremble uncontrollably. Blaze laughed. 'Pathetic!'

Leaving the boy quivering at the thought of his impending gruesome demise, Blaze crouched before Amber. He pushed aside a lock of her hair with his machete, then rattled his macabre necklace in front of her face.

'Perhaps I'll add one of your teeth to my necklace,' he said, leering at her.

'I hope you burn in hell,' she said, her eyes fierce and defiant.

Blaze blew her a mocking kiss. 'And I hope I meet you there.'

Connor was driven to the point of madness. Powerless to do anything, he could only watch as Blaze tormented each of them in turn. Grimly aware that it was now a stark matter of life and death, Connor resolved to die trying to save Amber and Henri. He still had his father's knife tucked on his hip. He wondered if Zuzu was thinking the same thing. She hadn't taken her eyes off the boy soldier and his gun. Perhaps if he made a move to tackle Blaze, she'd go for No Mercy and try to wrestle the weapon from him.

The rebel regarded Connor. 'I know what you're thinking, but if I see you even twitch I promise to make your girl *truly* suffer.'

Connor glared up at Blaze. 'I'll tear you limb from limb if you dare lay a finger on Amber or Henri.'

Blaze smirked. 'It's me who's going to enjoy taking *you*

apart, piece by piece. But who should go first? Eeny, meeny, miny, moe,' he said in a sing-song voice, the tip of the blade swinging from Connor to Amber to Henri and back again. 'Catch a lion by the nose. If he roars, let him go. Eeny, meeny, miny, *moe.*'

The machete came to a stop in front of Connor. Blaze grinned. With a violent sweep of the blade, he cleared one of the lounge's coffee tables, the candles and place mats scattering on to the floor. Then he grabbed Connor by the hair and held the blade to his throat.

'So, what will it be – long or short sleeves?'

Connor stared up at him, at once baffled and petrified by the question.

'No Mercy, hold out his arm,' Blaze ordered.

Suddenly it dawned on Connor what the rebel had in mind. He struggled wildly but Blaze pressed the machete harder into his neck, drawing a thin line of blood.

'Don't fret. It only hurts *after* I cut your arm off,' explained Blaze as No Mercy slung his AK47 over his shoulder and seized Connor's wrist. With surprising strength, he pinned Connor's arm down on the coffee table.

'*Deo?*' uttered Zuzu, staring at No Mercy.

The boy soldier didn't react.

'*Deo! C'est ta sœur!*'

No Mercy looked at her uncomprehendingly.

Zuzu became more frantic. '*Deo! Mon frère! S'il te plaît, ne lui fais pas de mal! Je t'en prie.*'

'*Tais-toi!*' barked Blaze, striking her with the back of his hand.

The blow was so violent that Zuzu was flung against the bar, her head cracking against the mahogany panel.

No Mercy frowned, still holding Connor's arm, but his attention now on Zuzu. Her lip bleeding, tears rolling down her cheeks, she continued to beg the boy soldier to listen to her. Connor couldn't understand a word. His heart thudded in his chest as the blood rushed through his ears. A paralysing wave of panic overwhelmed him and his limbs refused to respond as Blaze took up position to hack off his right arm.

'Don't close your eyes. You need to see this,' said Blaze, licking his lips in anticipation. 'I promise you'll remember this for the rest of your life.'

The machete came down. Amber screamed and Henri covered his eyes. Zuzu's shouting grew louder. Connor fought to break his paralysis, scrabbling for his knife. At the last second No Mercy let go of his wrist and Connor snatched back his arm, the blade embedding itself deep into the wooden table.

Blaze glared in furious outrage at No Mercy. 'You idiot! Why the hell did you let go?' he roared.

As he tried to yank the machete out of the table, No Mercy picked up the discarded spear. Before Blaze knew what was happening the boy soldier had buried the iron tip deep into his back. Blaze let out an agonized howl as the spear pierced his heart and burst out through his ribcage.

No Mercy twisted the shaft one last time and Blaze slumped to the floor. 'That's for making me believe my family were all dead!'

Still trembling from shock, his arm clutched protectively to him, Connor watched in stunned amazement as Zuzu rushed over and embraced her long-lost brother. No Mercy stood rigid and emotionless, unsure how to handle such affection, his first in years. Then he surrendered himself to his sister, resting his head against hers.

Amber, clasping her own brother, smiled with joy at the heaven-sent reunion. His eyes red and puffy, Henri stared at the contorted body of Blaze, the spear tip protruding from his chest. 'Is he dead?'

No Mercy nodded.

'Good,' said Henri, free at last of his tormentor.

Connor snapped back to his senses. Blaze might be dead, but there were at least half a dozen more rebels led by the Black Mamba that weren't. Getting to his feet, Connor rushed over to Gunner. The ranger was still breathing.

Judging that the boy soldier was now on their side, Connor said, 'No Mercy, help me.'

'My name is Deo,' said the boy soldier softly. 'That's my *real* name.'

'Well, Deo, I'm Connor, and I need your help to carry the man you shot.'

Zuzu let her brother go and between them they lifted the ranger off the floor. Gunner came round with a gasp of pain. Manhandling him out of the lounge, they staggered into the kitchen. Halfway across, straining under his dead weight, they were forced to put him down and rest a moment.

'Leave . . . me,' moaned Gunner.

'No,' said Connor, putting the ranger's arm over his shoulder to try again. 'You came back for us. We're taking you with us.'

Gunner grimaced. 'I . . . won't . . . make it.'

'Yes, you will,' said Amber firmly, grabbing a first-aid kit from a shelf. Rifling through the box, she pulled out a dressing and bandage and worked fast to staunch the bleeding.

'Hurry,' urged Henri, peering back into the lounge. 'I can hear someone coming.'

Amber wrapped the bandage several times round Gunner's chest, then tied it off. Connor and Deo picked up the ranger and lurched towards the staff exit. Zuzu opened the door, first checking the way was clear before giving them the thumbs up and hurrying out into the bright sunshine. Using as much natural cover as they could to stay out of sight, they stumbled from building to building. Deo warned them that the main gate was guarded by rebel soldiers. More were congregated beside a bunch of jeeps parked outside the lodge. Henri even spotted two boy soldiers smoking cigarettes, their feet dangling in the private plunge pool of one of the guest suites.

Panting heavily from the exertion of carrying the ranger, Connor and Deo eventually reached Gunner's jeep. Between them, they lifted him into the rear passenger seat. Amber clambered in beside him, keeping the ranger upright. The others crammed themselves into any remaining space. Connor jumped into the driver's seat and turned the key in the ignition. The engine kicked into life, sounding ferociously loud amid the silence.

'Here goes nothing,' he said, engaging first gear and shooting off with a spin of the tyres.

As he headed for the lodge's rear entrance, there was a shout. One of the rebels in the plunge pool had heard the jeep start and raised the alarm. Gunfire raked the ground on either side, some of the bullets ricocheting off the jeep's metalwork. Ducking down, Connor floored the accelerator and drove straight at the closed gates. With a tremendous crash, the metal gates flew apart as the jeep careered on through. Hurtling on at high speed, the vehicle thumped and bumped along the dirt track as Connor zigzagged their way down the ridge towards the savannah plain.

'They're following us!' cried Amber, who was desperately trying to keep pressure on Gunner's chest wound.

Connor glanced in the rear-view mirror and saw a convoy of rebel jeeps racing after them.

'There's the plane!' shouted Henri, pointing to a private jet making its approach towards the airstrip in the distance.

As they reached the base of the ridge, Connor checked

his mirror again. The rebels were close on their tail and gaining fast. If they made it to the plane at all, Connor knew they'd be cutting it fine. He tried to recall the route their driver had taken on their arrival but there was no obvious road in sight. So he decided to head directly for the airstrip.

'Hang on!' he warned. 'This could get a little hairy.'

His passengers clinging on for dear life, Connor drove even harder, weaving between rocks and bushes. The rutted terrain punished the jeep's suspension, threatening to shake the vehicle to pieces. Behind, the sound of gunfire pursued them, several bullets finding their mark in the rear panel, but Connor didn't dare look again for fear of colliding with a half-buried rock or dropping into a hidden gully.

Less than a mile away now, the jet plane had landed and was turning round at the end of the runway in preparation for take-off. More bullets whizzed past. The jeep's windscreen shattered and glass showered down on Connor and the others. Deo knelt up in his seat, shouldered his AK47 and returned fire, trying to slow their pursuers down.

They hit the runway at speed, Connor almost rolling their vehicle as he spun the wheel and headed towards salvation. He skidded to a halt beside the jet, its engines still turning over. The pilot lowered the automatic air-stairs, urging them from his cockpit to hurry.

Scrambling out of the jeep, Connor yanked open the passenger door and helped drag Gunner out. They had almost reached the steps when four rebel jeeps surrounded them.

CHAPTER 84

As the dust settled, the Black Mamba stepped from his vehicle.

'I gravely underestimated you, my White Warrior,' he declared, his tone bitter yet admiring. 'I don't know what training you've had but you're certainly no ordinary boy.'

With the barrels of a dozen AK47s pointed at their heads, Connor and the others lowered the ranger to the ground. They'd been so close to making it out alive. In a final act of protection, Connor shielded Amber and Henri behind him and waited for the rebel leader to give the order to open fire.

General Pascal turned his bloodshot eyes upon Deo. 'Of all my boy warriors, you were the *last* I expected to betray me. After all I've done for you. I made you into a man. A great warrior!' The general shook his head in dark disappointment. 'But I am a forgiving commander. Return to your rightful family and I'll let you live.'

Like a benevolent father, the general opened his arms wide to welcome him back to the fold. Deo glanced at

Zuzu, his sister looking up at him with eyes pleading for him to stay.

'Make your decision,' said General Pascal impatiently. 'On which side do you stand, No Mercy? Life or Death.'

Drawing his sister close, Deo removed his red beret and tossed it at the general's feet. 'Zuzu's my *real* family,' he replied. 'I'd rather die in love than live in hate.'

'Oh well,' said the general, raising his Glock 17 and taking aim. 'It saddens me to have to execute you but –'

General Pascal spluttered and choked, his hand going to his heart. Suddenly he collapsed to the dirt, his eyes bulging and his body contorting. Connor glimpsed the general's swollen-veined arm and recalled what Zuzu had said about her arrow tips. *Toxique*. The lethal poison had worked its way round the general's system and was now attacking his heart.

In the resulting confusion as his soldiers rushed to his aid, Connor and the others dragged Gunner up the steps and into the plane. Before any rebel had even noticed, the pilot was raising the air-stairs and rolling for take-off. The blast from the jet engines sent up billowing clouds of red dust, blinding the rebels. By the time the air cleared and they started to fire off rounds, the plane was already half-way down the runway and gathering speed to take-off velocity.

Connor and the others buckled themselves into their seats as the jet lifted off the ground and soared into the air. And with it soared everyone's hearts. Against all the odds, they had escaped. No one could stop them now.

As the pilot banked the plane towards the country's capital, Connor caught a glimpse through the window of the Burundian army, a full contingent of reinforcements closing in from all directions of the park. Faced by an overwhelming force, the rebels were either fleeing in panic or laying down their weapons in surrender.

Lying back in the impossibly plush leather seat of the private jet, Zuzu muttered something to her brother and he nodded in agreement.

'What did she say?' asked Connor.

Amber looked over, a relieved smile on her face as she held Henri tight, having just told him that she loved him.

'Cut the head off the snake and the body dies.'

CHAPTER 85

'The Black Mamba poisoned! How apt,' remarked Major-General Tabu Baratuza with a deep rumbling laugh, his French translated a second later in Connor's new earpiece. 'Let it not be said that justice isn't served in Africa.'

There was a ripple of appreciative laughter among the guests assembled by the champagne bar in the Burundian presidential palace's ornate ballroom. The expansive hall was brimming with politicians, foreign dignitaries, well-to-do businessmen and their accompanying wives, all gathered to celebrate the inauguration of Adrien Rawasa, the former Minister for Energy and Mines, as the new president of Burundi.

'So what's Michel Feruzi's punishment going to be?' asked Gaspard Sibomana, the newly appointed Minister for Trade and Tourism. 'Death by eating?'

The guests laughed heartily.

Ambassador Laurent Barbier and his family did not. Less than a week since their escape, the ambush and its fallout was still too raw for them.

'How can they joke about such things?' said Cerise

bitterly. While her husband appeared relatively unscathed as a result of the car crash, Cerise now bore a slight limp and still wore dressings on her arms where she'd been badly burnt in the vehicle fire.

'Death is all too familiar in Africa,' explained Colonel Black. 'If they don't laugh about it, then the only other option is to cry. And that's not in the nature of these people.'

'But who'd have believed Feruzi was a traitor?' said Laurent with a sorrowful shake of his head. 'After the wonderful work we'd accomplished together on the park, I considered him one of my friends. All I can say is that I'm very glad I hired your services, Colonel. If it wasn't for Connor here, we'd be mourning today, not celebrating.'

'I'd have expected nothing less of him,' declared Colonel Black, glancing at Connor. 'After all, he's his father's son to the core.'

For Connor that was high commendation indeed and he felt a swell of pride at being compared to his father. Colonel Black didn't need to say any more to express his deep regard for Connor's accomplishments. The colonel was a man of action not words. He'd been first to board the plane when they'd landed in Bujumbura to check on Connor, before organizing the group's swift transfer to a private health clinic for immediate medical treatment. And, while Connor was treated for his wounds and spent the following days recuperating, the colonel had been a constant presence on the ward.

Cerise leant forward and kissed Connor lightly on both

cheeks. '*Merci, merci,*' she said. 'You kept our children safe. You'll always be welcome at our home in Paris, Connor.'

'Thank you, Mrs Barbier, that's very kind of you,' he replied. 'After all we've been through together, Henri, Amber and I have certainly become close friends.'

Henri stood by his mother's side, the red welts across his arms and body all but faded, only the memory of his beating leaving a scar on him. He smiled shyly up at Connor, then hugged him hard round the waist. 'Can't you protect us forever?'

Connor ruffled his hair. 'You're going home, Henri. No one's going to hurt you there.'

'But I'm still scared,' he admitted quietly. Then he rummaged in his pocket. 'I almost forgot. Your watch.'

He passed Connor the Rangeman, still barely a scratch on its face.

'No, it's yours,' said Connor, pushing it back into his hand, realizing the boy needed his birthday gift more than he did. 'Any time you feel scared, just put it on.'

Henri gratefully clasped his gift. 'I will,' he said.

Amber stepped forward and took Connor's hand. She stared at him a moment, her green eyes as striking as ever but now more wary and worldly-wise since her ordeal with the rebels. Her lustrous red hair brushed against his face as she kissed him warmly on both cheeks, lingering a little longer than necessary. She clearly wanted to express her true feelings for him but felt restricted by the presence of her parents. 'You'll always have a place in my heart,' she whispered, squeezing his hand one last time before letting go.

As Laurent and his family were called away to meet with a contingent of reporters, Connor and Colonel Black hung back, keeping a low profile. Then a wheelchair rolled unexpectedly into the ballroom and Connor stared in astonishment.

'Gunner!' he exclaimed, hurrying over. 'I didn't think we'd see you out of hospital so soon.'

'In Africa only the strong survive,' replied the ranger, his chest heavily bandaged and his voice even more gravelly than before. 'And *you* are definitely a lion.'

Connor was honoured by such a comparison. 'What does that make you then?'

'At the moment, a sloth!' He winked at the young nurse pushing his wheelchair. 'But I'll soon be back on my feet.'

'Joseph Gunner, I assume?' said Colonel Black, striding over to introduce himself. 'Colonel Black, Connor's . . . guardian. You were unconscious when we first met but I want to thank you for helping rescue him and the Barbier family.'

Gunner laughed, then winced in pain. 'It was Connor who saved *me* in the end! You've a remarkable boy there.'

'Yes, I know,' replied the colonel. 'In fact I want to talk to you about that. Connor's spoken well of you and I've a proposition you may be interested in.'

'Well, I'm all ears, Colonel,' replied Gunner. 'In my current state I'm not exactly inundated with work.'

'If you'll excuse us, Connor,' said the colonel, inviting the ranger to join him in a side chamber off the ballroom.

'Gunner, I'm looking for a man I can trust to teach survival skills to some other . . .'

As Colonel Black pushed the ranger's wheelchair towards the room to discuss his proposal in private, Gunner looked back over his shoulder and called to Connor. 'Just remember: it doesn't matter whether you are a lion or a gazelle; when the sun comes up, you'd better be running.'

Connor laughed. He'd had quite enough of running for a while and was looking forward to the relatively quiet life of overseeing an operation from the safety of Buddyguard HQ. He helped himself to a fancy chicken skewer from a passing waiter and was wondering where Amber had got to when a finger gently tapped him on the shoulder. He turned round to find himself face-to-face with the new president.

'I just wished to personally express my appreciation for ensuring the safe return of the Barbier children,' said President Rawasa, his tone surprisingly soft and delicate for a man now in charge of a whole country. 'It would have been a tragic outcome with serious international repercussions for our nation if they had not survived. In fact I don't know how you made it out of that valley alive.'

'We were very fortunate,' replied Connor, 'and were helped by Zuzu, the girl from a local Batwa tribe.'

'Yes,' he said thoughtfully. 'I must not forget her either.'

As President Rawasa lightly shook his hand, Connor caught a strong scent of fine French musk cologne emanating from him. The distinctive smell instantly transported Connor back to the hidden valley and the mysterious stranger who'd stood just beyond the light of the kerosene lamps. Connor had assumed it had been the white man from the burning tanker. But he'd smelt the exact same aroma the first time he'd been introduced to Adrien Rawasa at the safari lodge. And how many other men in this third-world country wore such an expensive and particular cologne?

'Anything wrong?' asked President Rawasa with an enquiring smile.

Connor shook his head. 'No, not at all. I just remembered I have to tell the colonel something.'

CHAPTER 86

Forcing himself to walk slowly so as not to arouse the president's suspicion, Connor headed for the side chamber that the colonel and Gunner had disappeared into. Finding the room empty, he passed through a set of double doors leading to a long hallway. The corridor was deserted but Connor could hear voices in a room further down. Quickly and quietly, he hurried along the polished wooden floor, the sounds of revelry fading behind him with every step.

As he approached the door to the room, he noticed it was slightly ajar and through the gap saw Laurent Barbier. Connor judged the ambassador needed to know about his suspicions just as much as the colonel. He was about to knock on the door and go in when he spied the man Laurent was talking to and froze in his tracks.

The ghost from his past had materialized once more.

The ashen-faced stranger stood opposite the ambassador. Unremarkable in height or appearance, he nonetheless exuded a sinister and baleful presence that seemed to contaminate the room like a virus. Just looking at him made Connor's skin crawl as if he was covered with driver ants all over again. Connor flattened himself against the wall and, with a growing disquiet, eavesdropped on their conversation.

'You never told me my children would be in danger!' snapped Laurent.

'Such risks go with the territory,' replied the man, indifferent to the ambassador's fury.

'But why wasn't I informed about the ambush in advance? We could all have been killed!'

The man replied with a barely perceptible shrug of the shoulders. 'Sometimes, the less you know, the better. You hired protection – of an unorthodox sort, granted – so your children are alive. Besides, you're going to be one very rich man.'

'Mr Grey, when it comes to life, there's *nothing* more important than family.'

'Ah, yes,' he replied with a scornful smirk. 'So that's why you had an affair?'

The ambassador was embarrassed into silence.

Mr Grey evidently enjoyed putting the man to shame as he pressed the point. 'Now you don't want Mrs Barbier knowing about your other little liaisons, do you?' His eyes flicked towards the door and Connor sharply pulled back.

His breath catching in his throat, Connor prayed the ghost hadn't spotted him.

'So let's proceed with our business,' continued Mr Grey, returning his attention to the ambassador. 'Tell me, is the new president fully on board?'

'Yes,' replied Laurent tersely. 'The Ruvubu National Park will only be a park in name. We'll keep up the appearance of a functioning safari destination but there'll be no tourists. The park's to be closed off for diamond mining.'

'Excellent. And Equilibrium has the sole mining concession?'

'In return for keeping President Rawasa in office . . . by whatever means necessary.'

Mr Grey nodded. 'And you, Ambassador, will smuggle the diamonds out, using your diplomatic immunity from customs clearance, and ensure they're properly certified.'

'Yes,' replied Laurent. 'That is the agreement.'

Mr Grey produced a small suede bag full to the brim with stones and handed it to the ambassador. Laurent went over to a table upon which lay a black leather diplomatic briefcase. He unlocked it and deposited the bag inside a hidden compartment.

'Now our business is concluded, Ambassador,' said Mr Grey, heading out of a side door, 'you can enjoy the party. After all, you've just become a multimillionaire.'

CHAPTER 87

Connor darted across the hallway and into the opposite room just as Laurent Barbier emerged, carrying his brief-case. Reeling from the shock of the ambassador's corrupt dealings, it dawned on Connor that he was amid a nest of vipers. With their lives in potentially grave danger, the colonel was the *only* man he could trust. Connor had to find him, and fast.

'You crop up in all the wrong places and at all the wrong times, Connor Reeves.'

Connor spun to find Mr Grey directly behind him.

'Yes, I know who you are,' he said, relishing the wide-eyed look of horrified surprise on Connor's face.

As desperate as Connor was to escape the room his feet were rooted to the spot. Up close Mr Grey was an unnerving sight. His lean face was plain and ordinary – but it was that dull ordinariness that made him terrifying, like a waxwork come to life. His skin was dry and anaemic, his ice-grey eyes devoid of all human warmth. And his breath, as he moved closer to Connor, possessed the dank smell of a tomb.

'So, Connor, what do *you* know?' he asked, almost as

casually as if he was enquiring about the weather. But the underlying menace was still there.

'I know your name, but not who you are,' replied Connor, his mouth going dry with fear.

'I'm afraid that's *more* than enough.' Mr Grey let out a sigh, then went silent as if contemplating Connor's fate.

'I saw you on that tanker in Somalia,' said Connor, finding his tongue again. 'What were you doing there? Why did you shoot that pirate? Are you an assassin?'

Mr Grey narrowed his eyes at him. 'Young boys have such enquiring minds. So many questions. But you know what they say?' He paused for effect. 'Curiosity killed the cat.'

Connor wanted to run for his life. But his legs failed to respond. A good thing perhaps, since he sensed that the merest attempt to flee would prompt Mr Grey to eliminate him in the blink of an eye. Now, instead of surrendering to his fear, Connor became defiant.

'Well, if you intend to kill me you'd better not miss this time,' he said.

'I *never* miss,' snapped Mr Grey, evidently offended at such a slur on his marksmanship.

'You did at the mine.'

Mr Grey answered with a thin dour smile. 'I shot exactly who I meant to.'

Connor frowned. 'The rebel soldier?'

Mr Grey nodded once.

'You were *helping* me to escape?' said Connor, incredulous at such a notion.

'I wouldn't call it help exactly. Just balancing the odds. Equilibrium, one might call it.'

'What is this Equilibrium?' demanded Connor. 'You mentioned it before.'

Mr Grey tutted. 'Remember the cat! On that point, neutralizing you here and now would raise too many awkward questions.' He leant forward, ensuring he had Connor's full attention. 'This is our second encounter, Connor Reeves. Pray that we don't have a third.'

Connor swallowed uneasily. 'So what are you going to do to me?'

Mr Grey leant in even closer, his pale face filling Connor's vision. Connor found himself mesmerized by the man's fathomless eyes. He seemed to be plunging into their icy depths, drawn down deeper and deeper like a drowning man. At the same time, Mr Grey whispered words like drops of poison in his ear, his hushed almost breathless voice worming its way deep into Connor's subconscious. '*Forget my face . . . I never existed . . . You never heard my name . . . Equilibrium means nothing . . . I am just a ghost to you . . .*'

'There you are! I was beginning to think you'd gone without saying a proper goodbye.'

Connor blinked, shaking his head as if he'd been woken from a trance.

'What are you doing in here all alone?' asked Amber as she entered the room.

Connor looked around, somewhat bewildered. He found himself in a little-used office with an old wooden chair, a desk and an out-of-date calendar on the wall. The last thing he could recall was helping himself to a chicken skewer from a passing waiter in the ballroom. Wondering how on earth he'd ended up here, a vague recollection surfaced in his foggy mind. 'Erm, looking for Colonel Black, I think.'

Connor knew there was something very important he had to tell the colonel. It was on the tip of his tongue but for the life of him he couldn't remember.

'Well, he's in the main ballroom,' said Amber. 'And did you know Gunner's turned up? That man must be as strong as a lion to recover so fast.' Noticing the dazed look on Connor's face, she asked, 'Are you all right?'

Connor nodded. 'Yes, fine. A little tired, that's all.'

'I'm not surprised,' said Amber kindly as she stepped closer to him, a joyful smile on her lips. 'By the way, I've some great news.'

'What is it?'

'My father's just come out of a meeting.' Again something stirred in Connor's memory like an itch he couldn't scratch. 'He's organized for a French aid fund to sponsor Zuzu and Deo. They're going to be given a proper home, an education, an income. A chance to live a normal life.'

'That's wonderful,' said Connor, the good news clearing his sluggish mind. 'We should go and congratulate them.'

'Hold on a minute,' said Amber, grabbing his hand and pulling him back. She gently closed the door to the room. 'Before we return to the party we've some unfinished business.'

'We have?' said Connor, trying to jog his memory again.

'This time there are no snakes, ants, crocodiles or leopards to disturb us . . .' She pinned him to the wall, kissing him full on the lips. A true French kiss.

Connor's breath was taken away. He wrapped his arms round her and kissed her back. The horrors of their recent ordeal seemed to shrink to nothing in their passionate embrace. In the back of his mind, though, a voice was telling him to stop. The Buddyguard organization had laid down specific rules.

But, hey, if he hadn't taken a few risks in his life, he probably wouldn't be around to enjoy this one . . .

Yet in his heart of hearts he knew what was *really* wrong

about kissing Amber. The revelation caused Connor to pull away.

'Don't stop,' she murmured, her eyes half-closed and dreamy.

'I'm sorry. But I must. I'm supposed to be your bodyguard.'

'And you're making me feel safe. Very safe.' She leant in for another kiss.

Connor gently held her at bay. 'I can't be your boyfriend. I made an oath not to get involved with clients. When I commit to something, I don't break that commitment.'

Amber studied him intently with a mixture of longing and bitter-sweet admiration. 'You're the first boy I've met who actually does what he says and stands by his word.' She seemed about to cry. 'I respect you for that.'

Stepping away, she straightened her hair and regained her composure. Her green eyes glistened, but her expression remained strong and self-assured.

'When you're ready for another commitment, Connor, give me a call. But I won't wait forever.'

Amber kissed him briefly on both cheeks, then opened the door and headed out of the room. Connor's last glimpse of her was a flash of flame-red hair disappearing down the hallway.

CHAPTER 89

'How's Operation Hawk-Eye going?' asked Connor, happy to be back in the comms seat in Alpha team's briefing room.

'Well, there've been no more eggs!' Amir replied, the monitor revealing a more confident expression on his friend's face compared to the last time they'd spoken. 'But there was a bomb.'

'A bomb!' Connor exclaimed. 'Are you all right? What happened?'

Amir nodded. 'Thanks to your advice I spotted it early.' He waved a pair of sunglasses in front of the camera. 'You reminded me that the mind is the best weapon. So, using my IT skills, I upgraded the lenses to detect sudden movements. My early-warning system helped me to save my Principal by leaping in front of him as the bomb was thrown.'

'How on earth did you survive?'

'It was a *water* bomb,' explained Amir, laughing at Connor's wide-eyed look of shock. 'I got soaked!'

Connor laughed too. 'Well, I'm pleased you're in such

high spirits. I'm just sorry I wasn't around the last couple of weeks, but I've been a little tied up.'

'Don't worry about it,' said Amir. 'Charley's been my support and I know you were gunning for me too.' He moved closer to the screen and squinted. 'I see you lost your watch. That thing was indestructible! Is there nothing you can't lose or break on an assignment?'

Connor felt his face flush at being found out. He'd replaced the watch he'd given Henri with a brand-new Rangeman at airport duty-free on the way home. 'How do you know?' he asked.

Amir rolled his eyes. 'That's the series 3 edition. Only just come on the market. You can tell by the red accents on the dial. Yours was a series 2.'

'Well, whatever series, your gift was a godsend,' said Connor with a rueful smile. 'I'd have literally been lost without it.'

'So how was Africa?' asked Amir.

Connor hesitated before replying. 'It's the most beautiful, awe-inspiring and . . . lethal place on Earth. Africa just gets under your skin. Despite everything that's happened, I'd go back in a heartbeat. Although I might not take a safari any time soon!'

'Sounds to me like you need a *proper* holiday,' said Amir.

Connor nodded in agreement. 'When you're back, let's ask the colonel for some time off.'

'Great idea! A buddyguard break!' There was a voice in the background and Amir glanced off-screen. 'Sorry, Connor, I've got to go. Duty calls.'

'I understand. Stay safe, Amir. Alpha Control, signing off.'

As Connor closed down the video app, a clawed hand suddenly grabbed his left shoulder and he half-jumped, half-winced.

'Hey, pussycat!' said Ling, baring her teeth in a mock snarl. 'When are you up for our final deciding match?'

'Not for a good few weeks,' he replied, loosening up his stiff shoulder. 'The doctor says I need to rest, otherwise I'll rip my stitches again.'

Ling tutted in disappointment. 'Excuses, excuses,' she said. 'I suppose we could play noughts and crosses with your scars while we wait!'

'You need to let him rest, Ling,' said Charley, glancing over as she typed up the team's daily occurrence log. 'He's still in recovery.'

'Why does Connor get all your sympathy?' Marc questioned, raising his own shirt to reveal a small scar across his belly. 'I had my appendix taken out in an emergency operation!'

'Shame they didn't take your voice box out at the same time,' said Jason. 'Then we wouldn't have to listen to all your whinging.'

'It's nothing to joke about,' protested Marc. 'I almost *died*.'

Connor said nothing, but he thought he'd prefer acute appendicitis to fighting rebel soldiers and wrestling crocodiles any day of the week. His lack of communication home would also have been far easier to explain to his gran. Instead he'd received a tongue-lashing over the phone from her that would've put even the fearsome Black Mamba in his place. Yet, while he was in the doghouse with his gran, Connor received the good news that his mum's MS was in remission, for the time being at least.

Richie shut down his laptop and headed for the door. 'Hey, it's pizza night in the dining hall. Who's coming?'

Everyone started packing up, apart from Charley.

'I'll be along shortly,' she said, then sighed. 'Just finishing off the log.'

'We'll save you a slice,' yelled Ling, disappearing down the hallway with Jason.

As Marc hurried after them, Connor hung back. 'I'll catch you up,' he said in answer to his friend's enquiring glance.

Alone in the briefing room with Charley, Connor wondered how to broach the subject that had been on his mind since his return from Burundi. As he tried to pluck up the courage, Charley looked over and said, 'You don't have to wait for me.'

'No, it's OK,' he replied, feeling even more nervous than he did prior to an assignment. 'I've been wanting to ask you . . . do you fancy going out? Catch a movie or something together?'

Charley stopped typing. 'Are you . . . actually asking me for a *date*?'

She suddenly sounded as nervous as he was.

Connor nodded.

Charley's sky-blue eyes studied his face as if trying to judge whether he was joking. 'Are you sure about this?'

'I've never been more sure,' he replied, remembering his kiss with Amber and what had really been wrong about it. The simple fact was that it hadn't been Charley.

She spun her wheelchair towards him. 'Because if you're serious you need to understand how I ended up in this chair and how that's changed me.'

'I want to know,' said Connor, sitting down next to her. 'I want to know everything about you.'

Taking a deep breath, Charley steeled herself to revisit her past. 'Well . . . This is the first time that I've ever told anyone the full story . . .'

ACKNOWLEDGEMENTS

This is my eleventh full-length novel. My twenty-first published book! When I wrote that first line in *Young Samurai: The Way of the Warrior* back in 2006, I never dreamt that it would take me on such a long and incredibly rewarding journey. And there is much more to come with six books (including three in the Bodyguard series) under contract to be written. With so much action and adventure ahead, I need to thank those who have helped get me this far and hopefully will continue to carry me into the future . . .

First and foremost, my wife Sarah – yes, this was perhaps the least stressful of all the books I have written. Who knows, one day I might actually be 'normal' when I'm writing a book! My two awesome sons – Zach and Leo – my reward is getting to play and have fun with you at the end of each day. My mum and dad – my first readers, I value all you do for me. Sue and Simon for your constant support. Steve and Sam for just being lovely and a rocking uncle and aunt to our boys! And Karen, Rob, Thomas and Benjamin for being there for us at all times.

It goes without saying that none of this would have been possible without my dear friend and agent, Charlie Viney. Pippa Le Quesne, thank you as ever for your guidance on the crafting of each book. And Clemmie Gaisman and Nicky Kennedy at ILA for conquering the world, territory by territory.

I have a new Puffin editor for this book – Amy Alward. Change is always difficult but thank you, Amy, for making the transition so smooth and for your insightful comments. A big bow must go to Sara for overseeing the awesome design of the Bodyguard book covers – this is perhaps my favourite of the series so far. Helen Gray for the final polish of the diamond! And, of course, a huge hug and thanks to my constant star since being at Puffin, Wendy Shakespeare.

Authors Abroad are a crucial linchpin of the team organizing all my tours – so a big thank you to Trevor Wilson and Shelley Lee (especially!) whose attention to detail and brilliant logistical skills make my touring life very easy.

My constant friends (young and old) Geoff, Lucy, Matt, Charlie, Russell, Hayley, Mark Dyson and my goddaughter Lulu, plus the members of the HGC to whom this book is dedicated: Dan, Siggy, Larry, Kul, Andy, Dax, David, Giles, Riz and any other poor unfortunate souls who might join our clan . . .

But the most important people to thank are you, my readers, for following both the Young Samurai and Bodyguard series, telling your friends and family about the books and posting reviews online. Without you, there would be no point in writing. So thank you for reading!

Stay safe.
Chris

Any fans can keep in touch with me and the progress of the BODYGUARD series on my Facebook page, or via the website at *www.bodyguard-books.com*

AN INTERVIEW WITH CHRIS BRADFORD

What inspired you to set *Ambush* in Africa?

I lived for a short while in Africa and have done some charity work out there and it's a fantastically rich place in which to set an adventure. I wanted to give Connor and the bodyguards a new challenge, which involved protecting them not only from a legitimate threat, like gunmen in this instance, but also from the wilds of Africa. From my experience of being in Africa, it's a fantastic continent, but it's also a very dangerous one and I wanted to bring out those survival skills in Connor.

How did you go about researching *Ambush* and the dangers Connor faces?

I had the personal experience of encountering lions, scorpions and snakes so I've used those experiences, but I've also researched these animals too. I looked at the most dangerous creatures – for example, crocodiles, hippos and mosquitos – and the ways to overcome them from a survival point of view, if you've got nothing around you.

Connor has to combat his fear of snakes in *Ambush*. What would you be most afraid of encountering?

My worst nightmare is sharks. I get a shiver of fear even if I just see a picture of one! You do see them in Africa but only on the coast. In the chapters where Amber encounters the spider, I used my own phobia of sharks to describe her paralysing fear.

What are your top three tips for surviving in the African bush?

The three basics of survival are water, food and shelter. Without these, your chances of staying alive for any period of time are seriously reduced.

1. FIND WATER

In the savannah, it might not rain for weeks or even months. This makes finding water a difficult task, but there are ways:

- Search for animal tracks and follow them to see if they lead to water.
- If you find a fast-moving river, you're in luck. Beware stagnant streams and rivers as these can harbour parasites and bacteria.
- If possible, boil any water you find to make it safe to drink.
- If you don't find water, dig at the lowest part of a river. Often water lies beneath the surface of a dried-up riverbed.
- If you do find water, use a piece of clothing to act as a sponge and trickle the water into your mouth.

2. FIND FOOD

Food can also be difficult to source, but if you find water then you'll likely find food nearby too. Berries and fruit might be your easiest and most abundant source of nutrition, but, before eating any, it's crucial to check if they're poisonous or not:

- First, cut open the fruit and smell it. If it smells like peaches or almonds, it's poisonous.
- Rub the fleshy part of the fruit on your skin and wait at least a minute to see if it produces a rash or reaction. If so, it's poisonous. Discard it.
- Next, touch the fruit to your lips. If you feel a burning sensation, the fruit is not safe to eat.
- Otherwise, move the fruit to your tongue but don't swallow. If the fruit doesn't aggravate your tongue, take a bite of the fruit and wait several hours to see if you become sick. If not, the fruit is edible.

In addition, good sources of protein are termites or larvae!

3. FIND SHELTER

To sleep safely at night:

- Make a *boma* – a circular enclosure of acacia branches. The thorns will keep nocturnal predators away.
- Climb a tree and tie yourself securely to the bough.
- Find a hollowed-out baobab tree to take refuge inside.
- Or climb up to a wide rock ledge and secure yourself so you don't roll off in the night.

The key factor is to keep out of reach of any potential predators while sleeping at night.

AFRICA'S DEADLIEST PREDATORS – AND HOW TO SURVIVE THEM

1. LIONS

- Lions are the second largest big-cat species in the world, after tigers.
- Adult males can eat up to forty-four kilograms of meat in one sitting! How much do you weigh?
- A lion's roar can be heard from eight kilometres away.
- Equipped with teeth that tear effortlessly through bone and tendon, lions can take down an animal as large as a bull giraffe. Once grabbed, the prey is subdued and suffocated with a quick neck bite or a sustained bite over the muzzle.

How to Survive a Lion Attack: If you encounter a lion, never turn your back and try to run. That is a death warrant. Your best chance is to stand still, stretch out your arms to look as large as possible, and try to outface the lion!

2. NILE CROCODILES

- A crocodile can snap its jaws shut, trapping prey within fifty milliseconds.
- Crocodiles have the strongest bite of any animal in the world. The muscles that open the jaws, however, aren't so powerful. A reasonably strong person could hold a crocodile's jaws closed with their bare hands!
- Each crocodile jaw has twenty-four teeth that are meant to grasp and crush, not chew. They swallow stones to grind food inside their stomachs.
- 'Crying crocodile tears' – displaying fake sadness – comes from the myth that the reptiles weep when eating humans. They do wipe their eyes when feeding, but only because their eyes bubble and froth when eating.

How to Survive a Crocodile Attack: Most victims never see the crocodile coming. If caught in its jaws, trying to pull free is usually futile and may induce the crocodile to go into an underwater death roll. The only hope of survival is to fight back: hit or poke the eyes, the most vulnerable part of a crocodile's body. If that fails, strike the nostrils or ears. As a last-ditch attempt, go for the palatal valve – a flap of tissue behind the tongue that covers the crocodile's throat and prevents the animal from drowning. If your arm is stuck in a crocodile's mouth, you may be able to prise this valve down; water will then flow into the crocodile's throat, and hopefully it will let you go.

3. BLACK MAMBAS

- The fastest snake in the world, the black mamba is capable of moving at speeds of up to nineteen kilometres per hour for short distances.
- Its venom is highly toxic. Two drops of venom can kill a person, and a mamba can have up to twenty drops in its fangs.
- The black mamba gets its name because of the black colour inside its mouth (its body is usually olive brown).
- It is easily identified by its length (2.4 metres, average), slenderness, speed of movement and its coffin-shaped head.
- The black mamba has a reputation for being very aggressive.

How to Survive a Black Mamba Attack: Untreated bites are fatal. Put a tourniquet above the puncture wound to slow the spread of poison and seek medical attention immediately. The sooner a person is treated after the bite with antidote, the better the chances of survival.

4. HIPPOS

- Extremely aggressive if threatened, the hippo is responsible for more human fatalities in Africa than any other large animal.
- Hippos can easily outrun a human, reaching up to fifty kilometres per hour.
- Hippos can kill crocodiles.

- The most common threat display is the yawn, which is telling you to back off!
- An overheated hippo looks as if it is sweating blood; glands in its skin secrete a sticky red fluid that acts as a natural sunscreen.

How to Survive a Hippo Attack: Never get between a hippo and water. It panics them and they charge. Most human deaths happen because people surprise hippos accidentally.

5. LEOPARDS

- Built for hunting, leopards have sleek, powerful bodies and can run at speeds of up to fifty-seven kilometres per hour.
- Leopards are also excellent swimmers and climbers, and they can jump long distances.
- Mostly nocturnal, leopards hunt prey at night. A common tactic is to leap out of trees on to their victim.
- Leopards protect their food from other animals by dragging it up into a tree. A male leopard can drag a carcass three times its own weight – including small giraffes – sixteen metres up a tree!
- A leopard's characteristic call is a deep, rough cough, repeated ten to fifteen times, sounding like a saw cutting wood. An aggressive charge is heralded by two or three short coughs.

How to Survive a Leopard Attack: You probably won't!

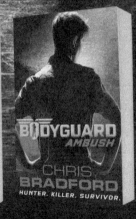